Soldiers, Witches and Taverns

The Story of Two Families in

Colonial America

D1437843

A Historical Novel by

William O. Dwyer

Copyright © 2023

By William O. Dwyer

All rights reserved.

ISBN: 978-1-916964-91-4

All rights reserved. No part of this publication may be
reproduced, distributed, or transmitted in any form or by
any means, including photocopying, recording, or other
electronic or mechanical methods, without the author's
prior written permission, except in the case of brief
quotations embodied in critical reviews and certain other
non-commercial uses permitted by copyright law. For
permission requests, please get in touch with the author.

Contents

Dedication

I wish to dedicate this work to my mother, Norval Kramer Dwyer (1915-2004) who, throughout her life, was an avid reader, writer, and lover of prose and poetry, a contributor to magazines and journals, and a college English instructor. From the age of fifteen, until she was eighty-nine, she kept her own journals, which were replete with her thoughts about the works of other writers, philosophers, historians, and great thinkers. She consistently encouraged us children to read the works of great authors and to express our own thoughts and opinions in writing. Through her own mother, she was also my genetic link to the Hughson Family. She gave us an appreciation for our own family heritage, for the promise of America, and for the men and women who helped make it all a reality.

In her later years, she encouraged me to write this book, reading early manuscripts and making insightful comments during our long phone conversations, which often lasted late into the night. She wanted me to work on it diligently so she could read the finished version while she still lived. Unfortunately, I didn't make her timeline, which gives me a certain amount of remorse. Then again, who knows what technology exists in those celestial libraries, reading rooms, and coffee shops?

Thank you for everything, Mom…

Preface

During my long adventure into family history research, I discovered that the progenitor of my mother's Hughson family in America was a twenty-year-old Scotsman named Thomas Hughson (1670-1741) who immigrated to New York by himself in 1691. I met my wife, Judy Meyers, in southern Illinois, where she had been raised on a farm. I discovered that Judy's Griggs ancestors arrived from England in 1635 and settled in Salem, Massachusetts. One of progenitor George Griggs' sons, John, moved to Gravesend in what is now south Brooklyn around 1665. It turned out that John Griggs lived three miles from Walter Dobbs, a farmer on Barrent's Island, to which a person could wade from Gravesend at low tide. Because of their proximity, Griggs and Dobbs must have been acquainted with each other. Walter had a daughter, Maria, and in 1694, this same Maria became Tom Hughson's wife. As we genealogists say, "Small World!"

Through some tedious research, I eventually discovered that another one of George Griggs sons, William, remained in Salem, became the village doctor, and was the one who, in 1691, had diagnosed the two young girls, Abigail Williams and Elizabeth Parris, as victims of satanic influence, launching the famous Salem Witch Trials episode. It turned out that Judy's 11th g-uncle, Dr. William Griggs, was also the 11th g-grandfather of her close friend and Maine native, Amy Bryant. "Small World!"

Thomas and Maria Hughson farmed a land lease in Westchester County, 27 miles north of New York City, and had several children (I descend from William). Another son, John, left the farm in the late 1730s, moved to New York City with his wife, Sarah Lockstead, purchased a tavern on the West Side, and were both eventually hanged in the aftermath of the famous New York "Negro Revolt of 1741". They made the mistake of allowing "off-duty" black slaves to frequent their establishment, one of whom, a man named Caesar, was the leader of the failed revolt.

It turned out that Caesar had an Irish mistress named Peggy Kerry, and he paid Hughson rent so she could live upstairs in the tavern. In the spring of 1741, Peggy gave birth to Caesar's baby boy, and after she, too, was hanged, John Hughson's daughters took the infant back to the Hughson compound (by this time now in Dutchess County, NY), where the family raised him as their own.

Adding to the saga, I also learned that Hughson men served in a New York militia during the American Revolution and that a Hughson wife, Penelope Codwise was the daughter of 1st Lieutenant Christopher Codwise, 2nd New York Infantry, Continental Line during the War. As a result, I am a proud member of the Sons of the American Revolution, the New York Society of the Cincinnati, and the

3

Descendants of Washington's Army at Valley Forge. My sister is in the DAR.

All this family history was too much for me to ignore, so I decided to write a historical novel to tie it all together. I love historical novels, especially the ones for which the authors took the time and energy to incorporate as much accurate historical detail as possible and then lace it together with some fiction that is engaging yet plausible. *Soldiers, Witches and Taverns* is a product of my multi-year attempt to follow this model.

I took advantage of my 40 years of family history research on the Hughson, Griggs, and Codwise families to make much of this story factual. Most of the people, places, dates, place names, major events, births, and deaths are real. I tried to create the fiction woven among them as plausible as possible. If you have the time, please let me know if it worked.

How could I possibly give appropriate thanks to all the people who contributed to my knowledge of these characters and the historical settings in which they lived? Books, articles, visitations, tours, teachers, parents and grandparents, internet, movies, the History Channel, presentations, meetings, pictures, encyclopedias, newspapers, friends who read and critiqued drafts, and Wading River, my colonial-era hometown on eastern Long Island, all of it contributed to my endeavor.

4

I attended a two-room wooden schoolhouse with two teachers and five grades. Before recess, some of us boys would have to go out and chase the cows off the playground so the girls could get to the swings. My mother was good friends with an elderly widow in the village, Emily Bruen, whose husband, Norman, was a direct descendant of John Jay, the first Chief Justice. She had inherited a lot of his China dishware, and she gave my mother some of it. I held John Jay's birding gun in my very own hands! Emily's home had been built by her ancestors in the 1740s; it had its original cedar shingled roof, still tight, still keeping out the rain. There was a huge fireplace in the main living area. During the Revolutionary War, her Miller ancestors hid their calf in it (behind the summertime wooden cover) so a British foraging party wouldn't find her. Luckily, the calf kept her mouth shut, and it worked! Emily's home made it into my story.

I would like to give special mention to one person, my eighth-grade American History teacher, Karl Mendel. He taught at Port Jefferson Elementary School on Long Island, sixty miles east of New York City. It's where we went after fifth grade. Karl was a confirmed bachelor, an immaculate dresser, demanding, strict disciplinarian, yet a caring and warm-hearted teacher and mentor. Mr. Mendel treated us like scholars; he lectured, and we took notes. He inspired me, and I was motivated to read *The Secret Road* by Bruce

Lancaster (1940), the story of George Washington's Culper Spy Ring. In fact, our school was only three miles from the ring's headquarters in Setauket. It marked the beginning of my life-long interest in the Revolutionary War. Thanks to Mr. Mendel, that year, I got a 100 on the American History State Regents Exam.

One way or another, all of these threads found their way into *Soldiers, Witches and Taverns*, and I am extremely appreciative of how they have enriched the fabric of my life.

Thank you, everybody!

Finally, thank you so much to my dear Judy…it was a wonderful 54 years…

Bill Dwyer

Somerville, Tennessee

November 2023

dwyer245@gmail.com

Chapter 1

Memphis, Tennessee

November 1998

Although it seems like a thing out of the past, some guys still end up marrying the girl next door. Jeff Hughson worked a slight variation on that theme; he married Lori, the girl across the street. When he was courting her, he said that the arrangement saved gas and mileage on his Nissan pickup, which was, at the time, the other great love of his life.

One advantage of marrying the girl across the street is that you get to drop in on your own parents on a regular basis, borrow tools, wrestle with your kid brother, commune with the two aging dachshunds, Shelby and Ginger, that were a central part of your childhood, and see what's in the refrigerator. Jeff did all of that. He was 28, blue-eyed, tall, athletic, and a lieutenant in a suburban police department just outside of Memphis, Tennessee.

Jeff wasn't one of those police officers who brought the job home with them. He didn't go drinking with the boys after the shift, and he hadn't shut himself off from his non-police friends. Furthermore, he rarely carried his Glock off duty. Of course, his life was made easier because Lori was the daughter of a retired sheriff's deputy, and she didn't engage in all those spousal ruminations that many police officer husbands must contend with, worrying that their men would be killed or run off with their female partners. Lori was close to her parents, a relationship that brought Jeff into the neighborhood on a regular basis.

Whenever he dropped in to borrow a wrench or surf the refrigerator, his daily experiences on the job generally served as the conversation opener, especially with his father, Bill, who had, himself, once worked in law enforcement. On these occasions, Bill's salutation typically began with, "Well, Jeff, how was crime last night?" Usually, the question was followed with a "Nothing out of the ordinary; same ole stuff. Well...except for a stray cat that got killed on Poplar Avenue."

After all, it was a suburban police department; no inner city, no housing projects, no drug-related shootouts in the streets, no major gang wars, no bodies dumped in the city parks. Burglaries, break-ins, drugs, domestics, and an infrequent convenience store robbery or a suicide were the normal fare.

Occasionally, however, the news was more exciting, like the day last August when two angry teenagers carjacked an elderly woman at a fast-food restaurant and killed her. Violent crime had dropped off seventeen percent in this country, but not for Barbara Ann Hill. The police managed to catch the pair; Jeff was in on that one.

Then there was the time a truck driver robbed a local bank and tried to escape in his semi. The police cornered him, and the SWAT team was summoned, whereupon they dispatched the truck's engine with their .50 caliber motor snuffer. Jeff took it from there and spent two hours talking the armed and desperate trucker out of his cab and onto the ground in return for a pack of cigarettes, which Jeff delivered to the man's pocket after he was safely subdued and cuffed.

It was already November, however, and people had forgotten about the trucker and Mrs. Hill. November 13th, to be exact. Jeff's mother was about to celebrate her 49th birthday. Judy had grown up on a farm in southern Illinois, worked her way through college, and obtained an MBA but, once Jeff came along, she chose to stay home to raise him. Bill would tell friends that he made the living, and Judy made the living worthwhile. It was clear to all that she had done a very good job with her three children. Judy was a very attractive woman in an aristocratic sort of way; she gave her blue eyes and fine features to Jeff, and she loved reading, going to the country, and gardening.

That particular afternoon was sunny and unseasonably warm, and she and Bill were in the backyard planting what would become a wash of yellow and violet pansies to brighten the gray Memphis winter days. Jeff dropped in to get briefed on the party plans. He made a pass through the kitchen—a turkey and cheese sandwich on marble rye bread—and then out the back door.

"Well, what do ya think?" his father asked, standing up and brushing the soil off his knees. Dozens of freshly-planted alternating yellow and violet pansies lined the edge of a large oval bed where the roots and bulbs of daffodils, hyacinths, and irises were patiently waiting for spring to arrive. Judy was around the corner of the house, working in a rose bed.

"They'll be gorgeous if you can just keep Shelby and Ginger from digging 'em up. Put some of their doggie do-do in the bed. They say it'll keep 'em from digging." Free gardening advice from a cop!

"Sounds like a bunch of crap to me, but I'll take it under advisement! I'm still mad at them for drinking the beer out of the pie pans your mother put out to catch the slugs in the tomatoes last summer! Oh, well, I guess they are German after all. And it was only Bud Lite anyway and not fit for human consumption, at least not by a Celt like myself, don't ya know. I wasn't about to waste any Guinness on 'em," in an oblique reference to his Scots-Irish ancestry. "Maybe I'll make those dogs watch *Victory Garden* this winter!"

Jeff managed a chuckle.

"Speaking of do-do, how was crime last night?"

"We had some real excitement for a change. At about 8:30 in the pouring rain, two punks attempted to rob Flanagan's Quik Stop. They pistol-whipped one of the female clerks and were trying to get the other clerk to open

10

the cash drawer when some Good Samaritan passing through on his way back to Ohio came out of the restroom, saw the commotion, and decided to join the party. Apparently, he took a flying leap over a candy rack and plowed into the two bad guys. One of 'em hit his head on the counter and passed out cold on the floor. The other turned and shot the Samaritan in his thigh, but then he grabbed the thug's pistol and, in the ensuing scuffle, shot him once in the stomach."

"Wow! Is he O.K....the Samaritan, I mean?"

"Yeah, he'll be fine; he's recuperating in a private room at St. Francis. His wife is providing comfort. I imagine he'll be on his way back to Ohio in a couple of days."

Jeff paused and then picked up the story.

"The guy dialed 911, and when the call went out from dispatch, I was only a minute away. When I got there, one clerk and one bad guy were still out cold on the floor, the second clerk was screaming, and the Samaritan was trying to stop the bleeding from the shootee's second belly button. Did a good job, too. When I followed up at the hospital, they told me that the little thug was going to live to rob another day. During the excitement, the Samaritan's wife was in their Cadillac talking on her Nokia cell phone. I guess the thunderstorm kept her from hearing any of the racket inside the store."

Bill dropped back to his knees and tapped another yellow pansy out of its black plastic container. "So, now you're

11

getting citizens to do your dirty work for you and visitors to your fair city at that!" he commented with a grin.

"And you'll never guess what, Dad; the Samaritan is a black guy, and his name is Hughson…Sean Hughson!" You reckon he's a cousin?" Jeff asked with a smile.

"Sean Hughson?" There was a pause. Bill set the pansy down and leaned back on his heels. "About how old is this guy, Jeff?" he queried.

"As a matter of fact, he's your age, 53. In pretty good shape, too, I'd say. Can you imagine that, a black guy with our Scottish last name and an Irish first name, taking on the criminal element with gunplay, at that!"

It was Bill's turn to chuckle. "Sounds like a true Scotsman to me."

He paused for a few seconds and then added, "You know, Jeff, I knew a black guy named Sean Hughson back at college in Carbondale, Illinois, in the late '60s. In fact, he was there the night I met your mother. Wouldn't that be interesting if he's the same guy? You didn't charge him, did you?"

"CID is looking into it, but what's to charge? You might say he was merely taking out the garbage for us. I don't think the State Attorney's office will be interested in it."

"Where did you say they've got him?"

"At St. Francis."

"He just might be the same Sean Hughson," Bill mused, his curiosity growing. "Do you think it would be O.K. if I went over to visit him?"

"Don't see why not. After all, you guys are cousins, aren't you?" Jeff added with a grin.

Forty-five minutes later, Bill Hughson was standing at the main reception desk at St. Francis Hospital. Like his son, Bill was tall; he appeared younger than his 53 years, and he had the bearing of someone in charge. Twenty-five years ago, he had come from New York. He still talked like a Yankee, a fact that provided fodder for occasional good-natured ribbing from his children. Bill's grandfather told him that the Hughson line went way back in New York, even before the French and Indian War. His mother, on the other hand, was born in England.

"He's in room 436," the middle-aged and still-attractive nurse told him. "You'll have 45 minutes before visiting hours are over."

"Thanks, Ma'am. I'll be quick."

A knock on the almost-closed door of room 436 elicited a soft "Come in" from a very pleasant-sounding female voice. Bill opened the door and stepped into the room. The TV on the wall was broadcasting a mute "Jeopardy" game, the Samaritan was propped up in his bed, his wife sitting in a chair beside him, holding his hand. They both looked at

13

Bill as if to ask, "May we help you?" but Bill spoke first, flashing a friendly smile.

"I apologize for barging in on you like this," he began, "but I'm Bill Hughson, and yesterday my son, Jeff, was the lieutenant at the Quik Stop robbery. He told me all about your heroic effort, Mr. Hughson." Bill moved toward the bed and shook the hand that the Samaritan's wife released.

"Well, come in and sit down. I'm Sean Hughson, but you probably already know that. And do call me Sean. This is my wife, Catherine." An aristocratic-looking black woman with very short hair and hoop earrings extended her hand to Bill.

"There really wasn't much to it," Sean Hughson explained in a rich baritone voice, the kind of voice you might hear on an all-night radio station playing easy-listening music. "I guess I was just there at the right time, and I acted without really thinking."

"You're very lucky you weren't killed, Honey!" his wife reminded him. "Promise me you won't do anything like that ever again!"

"I promise, Baby, I promise." Then the Samaritan changed the subject.

"It was nice of you to come by, Bill…and I must say I'm impressed with Tennessee hospitality. I'm no expert, but I bet it's not often that a policeman's father comes by the hospital to do a follow-up on a shooting victim, or did you drop in to see if we might be cousins?" he inquired with a chuckle. "Draw up a chair and sit a spell."

Bill added his own chuckle. "Well, Cousin, ya never know." He pulled up a chair by the bed and dropped into it. Then he got down to business.

"Back in the '60s, did you attend Southern Illinois University at Carbondale by any chance?"

"As a matter of fact, I did between '65 and '69. How did you"—a pause—"Wait a minute. You're not the same Bill Hughson who helped me pull that girl to safety during the big campus riot?"

"Yep, I'm the very same guy."

Well, I'll be…what do ya know!"

There was immediate warmth in the room, and Bill continued. "It's a small world, isn't it, Cousin? How's your hip?"

"I guess I'm gonna live, but they tell me I may not be able to get all the lead out of my ass." Catherine rolled her eyes and groaned. Sean looked over at his wife. "I found Catherine in a graduate class in business law at Ohio State University."

Catherine entered the conversation, "That's a fine son you have. He did a good job there yesterday. You must be very proud of him."

"I am, indeed!" He got back to the story. "Well, Sean, it turns out that you've already met my wife, Judy Griggs, the very same girl we pulled to safety that evening during the campus riot. So, I guess Jeff was merely returning a favor, Mrs. Hughson."

"What's he talking about, Sean?" Catherine demanded. "You two actually know each other?" She was having a hard time following the growing animism in the room.

"It was in 1969, Kate," Sean began. "You must have been a freshman at the time at Ohio State. Vietnam was in full swing, and the university's president, a man named Harris, had managed to get a very large grant from the federal government to set up a Vietnam Cultural Studies Center on campus. At other campuses, the Students for a Democratic Society were causing all kinds of havoc. Remember when the Weathermen blew up the mathematics center at the University of Wisconsin? There was no official SDS at Carbondale. Southern Illinois was down in the sticks, and the students didn't get too politically involved. There were 20,000 of us, mostly kids who were not smart enough or wealthy enough to get into the University of Illinois. The place was wild. Drugs, sex, and rock 'n roll were everywhere. Wednesday night was known as Mid-Week, and half the campus went out to nearby roadhouses and got plastered to neutralize the stress created by their draft status and the first two days of classes since the weekend."

16

"The poor town only had 14,000 people in it, and the students basically overwhelmed it," Bill interjected.

"There may have been no SDS chapter," Sean continued, "but there was plenty of excitement about joining some of the other big campuses and staging a demonstration, or sit-in, or walk-out over anything; it didn't really matter what, as long as drugs, sex, and confrontation were involved. The Vietnam Center provided the perfect excuse. One evening all hell broke loose, and that's when Bill, here, and I met, the night we rescued his Judy."

Chapter 2

Carbondale, Illinois

Friday, May 30, 1969

Unlike many other universities in the late 1960s, you couldn't really describe the Southern Illinois University campus as a powder keg; it was more like a plain ole' keg than a powder keg. It's located in Carbondale, Illinois, ninety miles southeast of St. Louis and not that far from Paducah, Kentucky. During the Civil War, the area was full of southern sympathizers, Knights of the Golden Circle they called themselves. People can still visit the Old Slave House in nearby Pope County, where northerners bred and sold slaves before the war. Violence was in its history. The town was near a coal mining area that endured bloody confrontations between mine owners and a burgeoning union movement in the 1920s. In the 1960s, there were still hamlets around Carbondale where blacks dared not set foot after dark. Thanks to the presence of the university, Carbondale itself was a little more cosmopolitan than much of the surrounding area. But in many ways, it was more southern than northern.

In 1963, *Playboy* magazine dubbed the university the "number two playboy school in the nation." And the students tried to live up to that distinction. It seemed like most of them were immersed in the classic carnal pleasures: sex, drugs, and booze, in no particular order, and in keeping their II-S student draft deferments current. Nonetheless, someone had recently burned down the "Old Main" building, the centerpiece of the campus. No group came forward to take credit for it, although the building was the home of the Air Force ROTC program on campus, a burr under the saddle of many of the radicals who found America's involvement in the Vietnam War offensive to their sensibilities. A month before, someone had opened all the gas jets in the laboratories of the chemistry building. An explosion was narrowly avoided, however, by an alert graduate student from Pakistan who, at great risk to himself, ran through the building, turning off the gas jets and throwing open the windows.

For a week, word spread on campus that there would be a demonstration against President Harris's Vietnam Culture Center, along with the Air Force ROTC program, both symbols of the university's complicity in an immoral war. The demonstration was to be held Friday evening in front of the library. Professional agitators from Chicago would be there, armed with bullhorns, to help get the crowd going. The goal was to force the university to close the center. Some instructors, mainly the social science graduate student teachers, the hippies who wore sandals, used profanity in the classroom, had sex with students, and smoked copious amounts of dope, encouraged their classes to attend. One guy even offered his students extra credit for attending. The university would not issue a permit for the demonstration in a vain attempt to maintain control that only spurred the promoters to greater action.

The evening of the big event finally arrived; it could not have been more perfect for such a gathering. A clear spring southern Illinois evening, lower 70s, with a gentle breeze blowing out of the south. Just the kind of evening to attract a large crowd. Tee shirts would be the appropriate attire for the evening; that is, tee shirts, signs, booze, and drugs. It was before the days when gas masks were considered a necessary part of one's ensemble for a riot event, and cell phones hadn't even been invented. Of course, the police were equally unprepared. They lacked the training, skill, and technology to engage in effective crowd control.

The word was out. Show up at 7:00 PM in front of the library ready to wave signs (they'd be provided), scream slogans, and follow the orders issued by the guys from Chicago with the bullhorns. Like 4,000 sheep, the students were led, not to the library, but over to the center of campus, in front of the president's stately old home. Surprise, campus security; there was another agenda afoot.

Unfortunately for Dr. Harris and his wife, they had not gone out that evening, against the wishes of the director of campus security; they didn't want to appear intimidated by the students. Before Dr. Harris and his wife detected the change in plans and could make their last-minute exodus, the students had their lovely old Georgian home surrounded. Campus security and local police were at a loss. There were no police horses, no dogs, no fire hoses, no liquid banana peel, no rubber bullets or bean bags, no crowd control training, no flexi-cuffs, just the old standbys: riot batons, and CN tear gas. They stood around in groups of two and three, staring at the students and talking excitedly on their radios.

As the jubilant crowds poured in, the bullhorns began their chants, "HELL, NO—THE CENTER MUST GO! WE WON'T TAKE IT ANYMORE! HELL, NO—THE CENTER MUST GO! WE WON'T TAKE IT ANYMORE!" There were some short bullhorn speeches with much profanity, more chanting, more speeches. Someone threw a wine bottle at the front door of the president's home. It smashed to pieces and was greeted by a loud roar of approval from the crowd. Two revelers climbed onto the roof of a parked Volkswagen bus, complete with flower and peace stickers, and burned what they said were their draft cards. The crowd roared again. A coed emerged from the bedlam and attempted to join the two card burners on the vehicle. She had trouble getting on its roof, a couple too many beers, and the card burners gave her a hand up. On wobbly feet, she pulled off her sweatshirt and, to the delight of the crowd, removed her bra. She swung it around her finger, and once more, the crowd roared. Someone yelled.

"Burn the bra!" Taking the cue, one of the now draft-cardless resistors produced his lighter and set it afire. The liberated coed held it as long as she could, the flame illuminating a large tattoo of a snake that crawled from her left armpit, over her left breast, and down to her belly button. When the flames got too hot, she flung it out into the crowd, where it landed on a fire hydrant, quickly morphing into a smoldering ember and adding its own odor to the pungent-sweet aroma of marijuana that wafted about in the evening air.

Repeated bullhorn demands for President Harris to come out and explain himself. Again, the crowd roared its approval. No president appeared. The town police and campus security standing around the fringes of the crowd didn't really know what to do next. An Illinois State Police car pulled up, red lights ablaze, and a smartly attired trooper got out with his baton in hand. He spied a huddle of local officers and proceeded at a quick pace to join them for a briefing. His big mistake! He should have left his expensive beaver campaign hat in the car. In a matter of seconds, it was jerked off his head by a skinny girl who immediately jack-rabbited back into the crowd. In a few more seconds, the hat-turned-Frisbee was sailing back and forth among the revelers to the hoots and hollers of the crowd. Three or four more bottles smashed on the front porch. Still no president.

All the noise and commotion began to create a general awareness throughout the campus and in the numerous off-campus housing units that ringed the university. Students, hundreds of them who were not politically incensed, men and women who actually wanted to get an education, took a break from their studies and began filing over to the center of campus to watch the excitement. Most didn't join the main crowd; rather, they formed little clumps on the fringe, close to the action but at a great enough distance to avoid being confused with the demonstrators. These observers watched with growing anticipation as the bullhorns continued doing their work.

Two young men were part of this crowd of onlookers. Both were Hughsons. Strangers to each other, one white, one black, living out their college lives in very different campus subcultures. One was majoring in accounting, the other in mechanical engineering. One from New York and the other from Ohio. Both were serious students, both striving to live up to the high expectations their parents had placed on them.

Several more bottles and cheers, the Frisbee was still aloft. And then the main bullhorn, operated by a guy with dreadlocks and a Black Power Fist tee shirt, issued a terse directive to the crowd. "LET'S GO GET HIM...LET'S GO GET HIM...LET'S GO GET HIM!" In obedience to the order, the forward elements of the crowd surged toward the president's home and onto its porch. Three or four swift kicks provided by an obese long-haired low-life in biker duds, and the front door flew open. The first contingent of enraged, socially aware students funneled through the opening. Immediately, one member of the entry party returned to the porch, carrying a large, framed portrait of some past university president he had jerked off a wall. He hurled it toward the screaming crowd, and it was immediately trampled to pieces.

This assault on the president's home had finally energized the police officers into action. As if on cue, they launched teargas canisters into the crowd from three different directions. Panic ensued. A few enterprising demonstrators attempted to pick up the teargas canisters to hurl them back at the police, but they were the "burner" type, too hot to touch. Being new to the riot game, no one had thought to bring insulated oven gloves for that purpose. The slight southern breeze had abated, and there was a stillness in the air, allowing the tear gas to linger in misty clouds among the increasingly panicky demonstrators. There was no good place to run, no exit strategy; the gas and patrol vehicles had them boxed in and prevented an easy escape route.

In the confusion, the students afforded avenues for the now gas-masked officers to rush the house. About a dozen police and the hatless state trooper quickly gained access to the porch and treated the male and female students caught on it to their riot batons. They entered the house, using the same behavior-management strategy on the students inside. They found the president and his wife in the upstairs master bedroom. She had a pain in her chest.

Eventually, a breathable escape route opened through the tear gas, and hundreds of students and non-students took off at a run between the classroom buildings and toward the refuge of fresh air and open space under the gigantic elms that awaited at the east end of campus. Not knowing what else to do, the police let them run, concentrating their efforts on the few unlucky students they caught in the president's home. Oh, yes; somehow, they had also managed to capture and handcuff the still bare-chested coed who had volunteered her bra, her snake, and her dignity, to the cause.

Oblivious to the whole happening, Judy Griggs was spending the evening in the basement of the chemistry building working on a project a Chinese professor got funded to develop a harder rubber for the treads on military tanks. Ironic, a Chinese professor working on tank treads for the American military. Oh, well; it was a job, and Judy had to pay her own way through college. She was a hard worker and very focused. She was also very pretty, five-foot-seven, with blue eyes and light brown hair that fell around her shoulders. She was slender but had an athletic carriage, the kind of frame you might encounter on a girl walking the Appalachian Trail or riding a barrel horse at a show somewhere in Oklahoma or Colorado on a Friday night in the summer. The highest grade in an introductory chemistry

25

class had landed her this part-time opportunity. The work had little to do with her marketing major, but it paid $3.00 an hour, and she took it.

More like the catacombs than a basement, the sounds of the evening had not penetrated the chemistry laboratory where Judy and three graduate students had been recording thermocouple measurements in vats of liquid rubber. Her recordings finally completed, she picked up an armload of textbooks—this was before the age of campus backpacks—grabbed her purse, and headed up the stairs and out the door for her off-campus apartment that she shared with two other girls. What greeted her on the sidewalk, however, was the pungent odor of tear gas and the onrush of the advanced contingent of retreating demonstrators. They had just turned the corner and were swarming into the street, separating the chemistry and biology buildings.

At first, stunned into inaction, Judy stared at the throng as it approached. Then she turned and tried in vain to make her way back into the chemistry building. The herd of demonstrators immediately engulfed her. She was pushed back against a bicycle parking rack; she lost her balance and fell over it, landing on her back, still clutching her books and purse. Two black men in the crowd, visitors from Chicago, saw her fall. One of them leapt over the bike rack and grabbed for her purse. Its strap was over her shoulder. She screamed and tried to kick at him, but he quickly produced a knife and cut the strap.

Bill Hughson, one of the curious onlookers, had been caught up in the retreating crowd. As he turned the corner to the chemistry building, he became a witness to Judy's predicament. At first, he thought the guy was going to help her up. Then he saw the struggle over the purse. It must have been the running and all the adrenaline it produced in him. Also, he didn't see the knife. Leaping to the rescue over the same bike rack, he crashed into the assailant with such force that it knocked both of them down. Seeing that his friend was in trouble, the other Chicagoan ran to his aid. For an instant, fists and feet flew, but it was only for an instant.

It was as though the fourth man had been jettisoned from the crowd of escaping demonstrators. He also had witnessed Judy's situation. He sprinted across the street, vaulted over the hood of a parked car, and by the time he reached Bill and the two thugs, he had picked up a bicycle that was leaning against an elm tree. Using the bike as a pugil stick, he slammed it against first one assailant and then the other in rapid succession, like something a person might see in a martial arts movie. The two would-be muggers crashed to the ground; one had the wind knocked out of him, but the other regained his footing, and cradling a broken wrist, he dropped the pocketbook and made a very rapid exit into the throng of retreating demonstrators.

For the first time, Bill had a chance to look at the fourth man, the Good Samaritan. He was a college student type, like himself, and he was black.

"Come on, let's get her inside the building!" the Good Samaritan shouted.

"It's locked," Judy gasped, "but I have the key!"

Bill got to his feet, and the three of them pushed and shoved their way back to the front door of the chemistry building. Once inside, Bill asked Judy in a heavily panting voice, "You O.K.?"

"Yeah, I think so. What in the world is going on out there?" Judy asked through her pounding heart and heavy breathing.

The other student answered, "That Vietnam Center rally got out of hand. They even broke into Harris's house. I came over to watch the excitement, but when the police had enough and gassed everyone, I got caught up in the rout."

"That's basically my story, too," added Bill. "Thanks for your help out there. I think I was in over my head."

"Don't mention it, man. They weren't my type of people."

By this time, Judy had caught some of her breath. "Thanks, guys. I thought I was a goner, especially when he flashed that knife."

"Knife?" queried Bill. "I didn't see any knife."

"He had one, alright," added the other rescuer. "It's a common move among street muggers. Instead of fighting over the woman's pocketbook, they just cut the strap."

"Well, that's the first time I've ever been mugged, and I hope it's the last!" A pause. Then she said, "My name's Judy. . . Judy Griggs. Who are you guys?"

"I'm Bill Hughson."

"You're who?" the black student demanded.

"Bill. . . Bill Hughson."

"This can't be for real! I'm Sean Hughson. Are you Hughson as in H-U-G-H-S-O-N?"

"That's right," Bill confirmed, "an old Scottish name. Maybe we're cousins!"

"Yeah, sure. And I'm wearing kilts under these jeans."

Judy chuckled and flashed a smile at both Hughson men.

There were a few seconds of silence during which the three sat there on the floor, looking at each other and listening to the commotion out in the street. Finally, Judy broke the silence. "I was rescued by the Hughson boys! This is really weird!"

Later that evening, when it was finally safe to venture forth, Sean headed for what he hoped would be a beer with his friends at the Village Inn, and Bill walked Judy to her off-campus dorm on Washington Street. Along the way, they chatted about the evening's adventure; she said she'd write

29

an extensive diary entry about how two Scotsmen rescued her when she was a fair damsel in distress. During the walk, Bill experienced a warm fuzzy feeling, and not seeing any fraternity pin or engagement ring, he took a shot.

"By any chance, would you be available for a hamburger and a cup of coffee at the Hub Sunday evening?"

"I think I could arrange that. What time?"

"How about 8:00? I'll have you back home by 9:30. Let's exchange phone numbers in case you land a better deal between now and then."

Judy laughed. "Sounds good."

"I'll pick you up in my sexy 1957 Chevrolet two-door Nomad station wagon. You'll be able to recognize it because it is robin's egg blue with a smattering of rust here and there."

Chapter 3

Back at St. Francis Hospital

"Wow! That's some story! And, Bill, you ended up marrying Judy?" Catherine queried.

"About two years later, just before we moved down here to Memphis." I walked her back to her off-campus dorm that night. Two days later, we had a hamburger date; the next weekend, we went to see a movie, and the rest is history. Every once in a while, Sean and I would run into each other on campus. We'd make some crack about being cousins, and we'd be on our way again. When we graduated, Judy and I got married, and here we are 30 years later, and you show up in a shootout. Small world."

Sean chuckled and then groaned as he shifted his weight in the hospital bed. Once again, Catherine grabbed hold of his hand. "It is, indeed, a small world," he said. And then he added, "I wonder if there really is any Hughson connection."

"In the strange world of genealogy, anything's possible... what's your family story, Sean?"

"I don't know a whole lot. When I was a little boy, my grandfather, Michael Hughson, told me that we go way back in New York and that our Hughsons were never slaves. My father told me that Sean was an old family name, but he wasn't any more specific than that."

"My Hughsons came from Westchester County, forty miles north of New York on the east side of the Hudson...right in the Legend of Sleepy Hollow country. Maybe we are connected somehow."

Sean smiled. He took a sip of water that Catherine offered him. "Well, anything's possible, Cuz...or should I say 'Ichabod'?" Then he added, "Well, Kate, what do you think? Two Hughson lines, both from New York. Do Bill and I look related?"

"Yeah," she smirked, "You both look something like a Southern Illinois Saluki!"

"That skinny dog? Kate!" he replied, feigning hurt feelings. "Come on, now; surely we're both more buff than that ole' hound!"

"I was thinking more about your brown eyes, dear," she added in a quick retort. The two men laughed.

Returning the conversation to the Hughson connection, Sean said, "I don't have any records of our Hughsons that I know of. When I get home, I think I'll look into my family history and see what I can find."

"Give me a ring if you discover anything, Sean. Who knows what interesting tidbits could be hiding in the murky world of genealogy?"

"Will do, Cousin. As they used to say on T.V. in the old days, 'News at 9:00; film at 11:00'."

Catherine became increasingly energized as she listened to the two Hughsons devote the next few minutes to swapping notes on their respective ancestries.

"You realize, you two guys probably really are related! Wouldn't it be interesting to know how?"

Then she reached into the bedside table drawer, extracted her husband's wallet, and removed two business cards. This is for your genealogy records," she said, handing Bill a card. "And would you be kind enough to put your address and phone number on the back of the other one? I want to add you to our Christmas card list."

At this point, a rather rotund nurse entered the room and cryptically announced that visiting hours were over. Bill got up.

"Is there anything I can do for you folks?" he asked.

"Well, if it's not too much trouble, and if you're in the neighborhood tomorrow around noon, could you sneak me in a Big Mac with a large order of fries and a Dr. Pepper...and maybe another one for Catherine here? I'd send her out for one, but I am afraid she'd get lost or, worse yet, bring me back a vegetable plate!"

Catherine groaned again.

"What's the matter? The hospital food not that tasty?" Bill asked.

"You guessed it. I'm in need of a backup plan!"

"I'll do it. And be sure you call me when you get released. Judy and I will want to introduce you to some Memphis hospitality, maybe barbecue ribs, at our home before you return to Yankee land."

Sean flashed a big grin. "We'll take you up on that. As they say back in New York, 'Such a deal!'"

Chapter 4
The Griggs Family
Salem, Massachusetts 1635

It was the first ship of the new year to enter the harbor at Salem, the *Hopewell* from London, loaded with tools, glass, nails, farm implements, cloth, horses, cattle, sheep, and people. It was the people who were especially valuable. The town was only eight years old. Founded by Puritans, it was growing, but it still skated on the thin ice of survival, never all that far from extinction, especially since John Winthrop had taken 1,000 of its settlers with him down to Boston four years before to take advantage of its natural harbor by the Shawmut Peninsula. Boston had potential; someday, it may even be bigger than Salem. What thickened the ice for Salem was more people, people to build and farm, create and repair, preach and teach, heal and lead, buy and sell, and mostly, procreate. If Massachusetts was to survive, it must have people.

Forty-one-year-old George Griggs (Judy Griggs' 9th g-grandfather) had been a shipwright in England. He was born in Boxted, Suffolk, on the east coast of England, and since he was nine years old, he had been working with boats. He knew how to design boats and build boats, boats of any size. At 28 and thinking that his future as a shipwright was secure, he married Alice Winthrope, beautiful, ten years his junior and more than a match for her hard-working husband. Two years after they were married, however, the shipbuilder for whom George worked went bankrupt; his demise stemming from the centuries-old error to which countless businessmen over the ages had fallen prey, overzealous expansion.

Responding to what they thought was an opportunity, George and Alice moved inland to Laden in Buckinghamshire, where George applied his carpentry skills to erecting edifices on *terra firma*. It was in Laden where Alice gave birth to their first six children, two girls, Elizabeth and Mary, and four boys, Thomas, William, James, and little John, this latest arrival named after his paternal grandfather.

Although building taverns, barns, and country estates provided a living for the Griggs family, George was not satisfied. He missed the ocean, the tides, the cry of the gulls, and the fog that rolled in from the North Sea, enveloping the coves, inlets, and harbors. Most of all, he missed building boats and taking them out for sea trials; they were in his blood. Alice was sympathetic and supportive when he shared his discontentment with her.

These conversations inevitably led to talk of the New World, of New England. He heard about the pine trees, endless forests of huge, straight pines, many of them tall enough for main masts on the largest ships. Those trees and the New England in which they grew became an increasingly frequent topic of conversation around the Griggs supper table. He told Alice that his skills as a shipwright could provide a future for them in the new world, a future, perhaps, of wealth and prosperity.

"George, if we go to America, will you promise to build me a cottage as nice as this one?" Alice asked.

"Of course I will, Alice, even better. It would be the first thing I'd do."

"Will it have a porch and a fireplace with a bread oven?"

"Maybe two bread ovens, one on each side."

"Will we have our own bedroom?" she asked, squeezing his arm.

"Aye, our own bedroom, complete with a leaded window for letting in the moonlight," he said, applying a pat on her derriere for emphasis.

"Will we go to Virginia or New England?" she asked, those being the only two places she knew about.

"Probably to Salem or Boston in New England. The harbor in Plymouth is not very deep. We just completed a stable for a man whose cousin is a merchant in Salem. I was talking about shipbuilding in America, and he suggested that I write the gentleman. Do you remember Richard Lumpkin from Parsonage Farm in Boxted?"

"I do. His wife, Sarah, was very nice to me when we first got married. She taught me to make that mutton stew you like so much."

"Aye, that's him. He came by our shop last week and said a group of folks from Boxted are going to America in the spring. They've heard from Rev. Phillips that his settlement in Massachusetts is well-established, and they are looking for people. Lumpkin said the Warners and Bakers are going…and the Stones, too, so we would have many Boxted friends around us. Richard said they'd be taking a ship called the *Hopewell* that will be leaving from London in April. We could go with them. The ship is headed for Salem and Boston."

After four letters and six months, George and the Salem cousin, Ephriam Tuttle, agreed to a business arrangement, and the decision was finally made. George would build boats in Salem, where the lumber was plentiful, the harbor protected, and the prospects enticing. Ephriam Tuttle would help develop the business and underwrite the start-up costs for a percent of the profits.

George had engaged an apprentice, Thomas Doubleday, to help with the business. The young man was hard-working and skilled beyond his 19 years. Furthermore, young Tom had the eye of an artist; he could stencil the curves without a template, and he had carved some figureheads that brought George a handsome profit from other shipbuilders. Tom would help ensure the success of the New England venture. Taking Tom, Alice, their six little children, and a seventh, Sarah, still under construction, George put the tools of his trade and the family's worldly possessions in a rented dray and set out for the port of London and the waiting *Hopewell*.

In addition to his family, during the voyage, George made the acquaintance of two other men on the *Hopewell*, Isaac and William Drummond, cousins who were looking for an opportunity in the new colony and who would be willing to work for him building boats at first and then, as the business grew, ships.

Isaac and William Drummond were both 50, one a widower, the other a bachelor. This voyage on the *Hopewell* was their second to New England. Twenty-seven years before, in August 1607, they had been part of the founding of Popham, a colony of 100 British men and boys established by the Virginia Company on a bluff at the mouth of the Kennebec River, where it meets Atkins Bay and the Gulf of Maine. It had been founded with a royal charter one month after its sister colony, Jamestown, down in Virginia. Unlike Jamestown, the colony of Popham was not destined for permanence. Its demise, however, was not brought about by disease, starvation, or Indian raids. Rather, upon the death of its aging aristocrat leader, George Popham, command fell upon another aristocrat, Sir Raleigh Gilbert, a young man who came to the New World because his birth order stripped him of his right to the Gilbert lands and fortune back in England. As fate would have it, his older brother died. When this news reached Sir Raleigh at Popham, he returned to England to inherit what was now rightfully his, and the rest of the colony returned with him. Thus, Popham was to last only 13 months; it would never make it into the children's history books or the folklore of colonial New England.

During the summer of 1608, however, some of the Popham men built a 50-foot sailboat, they called the *Virginia*; it would become the first sailing vessel constructed in New England. The *Virginia* was seaworthy and, in fact, became the conveyance that carried the colonists back to England. Sixteen-year-old Isaac and his cousin William helped construct the *Virginia* out of the pine and oak forests that surrounded Popham, and it was then that shipbuilding became central to who they were. They were both certain that meeting George Griggs 27 years later aboard the *Hopewell* was ordained by God.

Three weeks into the voyage, the *Hopewell*, an 80-ton square-rigged barque, encountered a storm, which caused some barrel frames in the hold to break loose. While attempting to secure the barrels and repair the damage, the ship's carpenter, Bruce Ferguson, broke his right arm when a beam supporting the frame fell on him. The captain, a man named William Bundocke, was familiar with George and his three associates, and the day after the incident, he summoned them to his cabin. After pouring five glasses of port, Captain Bundocke got right down to business.

"Gentlemen, you undoubtedly heard about Ferguson's accident yesterday, and I am told you are experienced in the trade of shipbuilding and repair and that you plan to practice the same in Massachusetts. Is that correct?"

George answered for the men. "Aye, Sir. We have already made arrangements to build a yard in Salem. Our tools are crated in your hold."

"What sorts of craft have you built?"

"Everything from fishing, long boats, and shallops to fifty-ton traders."

"Well, I have a problem with Ferguson unable to work, and I may need your help. Can I count on you gentlemen to assist me for the duration of the voyage?"

"Of course, we will help wherever we're needed, Captain. Is Mr. Ferguson able to acquaint us with the ship and show us his tools?"

"Aye, he can do that. I think he would be glad to talk with you. Remember, he's still my ship's carpenter, so please follow his directions."

"We will, Captain; you can be certain of that, Sir."

Bundocke pushed back from the table and stood up, indicating that the meeting was over.

"Thank you, gentlemen. I'm much obliged to you for your help."

Tom Doubleday had one final question for the captain.

"Sir, I noticed that the *Hopewell* is dragging two long lines from the starboard and port rails. I don't understand what purpose they serve."

"That's a good question, Tom, and I'll tell you the story behind it. In 1620 a ship called the *Mayflower* brought the first settlers to New England. You probably already know that. About halfway through the voyage, they encountered a huge Atlantic storm during which one of the passengers, a young man name John Howland, was washed overboard. By some miracle, he managed to grab onto a halyard that had broken loose from the topsail and was trailing in the water. The sailors were able to pull him back aboard with the help of a boat hook. When the *Mayflower* returned to England the next year, Howland's story quickly spread over the docks and through the taverns, and now he's famous."

The captain paused and then added, "Since I heard that story, I've ordered that those two lines be deployed. I suppose they produce a little drag for the ship, but angels may have need of them some day. Never doubt the existence of angels, my boy."

"No, Sir, I won't." The other men added their agreement.

Ship's carpenter, Ferguson, proved to be a very friendly, knowledgeable, and inquisitive Scotsman who welcomed the company of George and his three associates. After some initial salutations and introductions, Ferguson, sporting a big grin through his red beard and a right arm in a sling, got to the point.

"Gentlemen, in my present condition, I am surely blessed to make the acquaintance of four fellow shipwrights! I foolishly tried to do the work of two men when that barrel rack broke, and now I have this to show for it. The surgeon says my arm will be fine, but it will take six weeks."

Ferguson guided the men up and down the ship's ladders and stairs, pointing out various problem areas that needed to be addressed with some creative carpentry. He was particularly interested in Griggs' plans for his boatyard and the designs for the boats and ships he planned to build. During a break in their tour, Ferguson got down to brass tacks.

"George, what's your opinion as to the best design for ships that can run the coastal trade as well as survive the open sea?"

"We've given much thought to that question. It seems that mariners need ships that are fast, able to run close to the wind, carry large cargos, and are manned by small crews. We think what they are beginning to call a sloop may be the answer. A single mast carrying a triangular mainsail and jib, with a sleek hull designed to require less ballast, which allows more room for cargo. Perhaps forty to sixty feet stemto-stern. I plan to experiment with different variations to see what works best."

Ferguson produced a pencil and a piece of lumber.

"Could you sketch a picture for me?"

In two minutes, George passed the board back to Ferguson.

"No gaff rigging, I see."

"No. The triangles are easier to manage for a small crew, and I think the ship will be able to run closer into the wind."

"Could you add a second mast?"

"We may end up doing that, but it would require a larger crew and may not add much to the speed or maneuverability. And, of course, it would take more money and time to build."

Ferguson's enthusiastic interest energized the four passengers, and for a moment, Griggs contemplated an attempt to recruit the man to his new enterprise. He decided he would wait for Ferguson to mention it first, something he never did.

The remaining weeks of the voyage passed quickly. There were no major incidents aboard the ship that required emergency carpentry, but the four volunteers worked on a list of minor projects under Ferguson's direction that made the *Hopewell* more livable. The most appreciated was a wooden seat that Tom Doubleday carved for the "head," the rounded surfaces of which greatly increased the user's comfort. For two days, it was the talk of the ship.

On May 13th, seagulls appeared in the sky, and the next day the long-awaited announcement of "Land, Ho!" resounded from the *Hopewell*'s crow's nest. There was an immediate increase in energy, both above and below decks. Along with the twenty-eight other relieved passengers, George and Alice busied themselves, making their children and belongings ready for the first day in the New World.

As a result of George's correspondence with Ephriam, some of Salem's residents already knew that George and his family were coming. Ephriam operated the town's new water-powered sawmill, and he perceived in George an opportunity to expand his lumber business. Ephriam and his wife, Emily, were among the crowd of people on the wharf watching as the gentle onshore breeze so typical of spring afternoons in Salem brought the *Hopewell* to an easy docking.

With their six young charges in tow, George and Alice stood by the rail in great anticipation as the ship was warped to the pier and the gangplank lowered. They were among the first passengers down onto solid ground, the first solid ground in five weeks. A twinge of panic shot through George; what in the world was he doing here? What had he gotten his family into? Whatever made him pursue this crazy idea? He offered a quick prayer heavenward; "Lord, please help me and my family!" His prayer was answered immediately by a voice from the crowd.

"George? . . .George Griggs? . . ."

"Ephriam?"

"Aye, Ephriam Tuttle," the man responded. "And this must be Alice. Welcome to Salem, George!"

The plump Mrs. Tuttle caught up with her husband, and after the round of introductions, the panic that had washed over George subsided. There would be a place for his family and Tom Doubleday and the cousins to stay tonight and food to eat. The food, it turned out, was delicious. The Tuttle home was one of the larger ones in the village. It had two full stories and a spacious kitchen that easily accommodated a long trestle table on which Emily Tuttle had placed an assortment of meats, pies, bread, and vegetables. Elizabeth was amazed, and she asked George in a whisper if these Americans celebrated Christmas in May.

"It is indeed a table suitable for a Christmas dinner," he responded with a wink. George Griggs was now a pioneer in a new land. It would be good to him. His and Elizabeth's table, too, would be filled with delicious things to eat. Not only would they survive in this new land, he told himself, but they would flourish in it!

****

By the time the Griggs family arrived in Salem, the snow was gone, and the arbutus and mountain laurel were in bloom. The May skies were clear and blue. Porpoises were already playing in the ocean not far offshore, and the gulls, thousands of them it seemed, soared effortlessly on the warming air currents, called to their mates, and basked in the sunshine along the rocky shore.

Accompanied by Isaac, William, and Tom Doubleday, George reconnoitered the shoreline and coves surrounding the village, absorbing the majestic presence of the New England spring as they searched for the perfect place to build his boatyard. He soon found one on the south side of the town, where a natural deep-water cove indented the shoreline. At its head, the South River emptied into the cove. On one side of the cove, a marsh extended inland to meet the rising land to the west. On the other, the land gently rose into the forested hills and, eventually, to the growing town of Salem Village. It was the perfect site for a boatyard. One hundred and fifty years later, Salem's most noted master shipbuilder, Enos Briggs, would rediscover the site and use it to build over 50 ocean-going vessels.

After finalizing the business arrangement with Ephriam Tuttle, George set to work with his apprentice, Tom Doubleday, and the Drummond cousins. To this initial group, George added Matthew Maule, a talented young carpenter who had arrived from England the year before. The house and buildings went up fast, made with wood cut from the surrounding forest and sawn into timbers and boards to the sound of falling water at Ephriam Tuttle's mill. Alice loved her new home; on the main floor, it had four rooms with low ceilings and exposed beams and, in the main room, a big open stone and brick fireplace for cooking and providing heat in the winter. Built into each side of the chimney were the small ovens that Alice had requested for baking bread. Not all that common in the village, there was also a second floor with three more bedrooms. A cedar shingle roof kept out the elements, and thanks to a surprise gift from the Tuttles, two leaded glass windows adorned the front of the structure. Best of all, George had added a real extravagance, a covered front porch that overlooked the South River and would be the perfect spot for clay pipes on balmy evenings.

By September, George and his three artisans were already building their first watercraft: a 24-foot, single-masted fishing boat. It was broad in the beam and well suited for the heavy seas often encountered by the Salem fishermen, especially in the late fall. By November, it was finished, well-made, and seaworthy. It sold quickly, and with it, George Griggs' reputation was already on the move. Ephriam Tuthill was ecstatic; in church on Sundays, he fervently thanked his Creator for his new business partner and prayed for his continued health.

Chapter 5

Salem, Massachusetts

September 1659

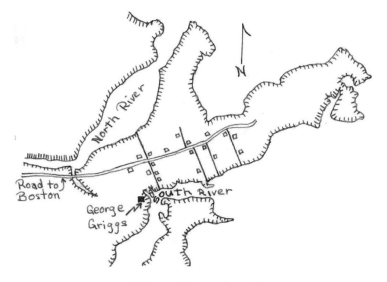

Salem, Massachusetts

The Septembers flew by, 25 of them to be exact, and George and Alice had, indeed, become prosperous. With the help of three of his sons, Thomas, James, and John, and Tom Doubleday and the Drummond cousins, George had become well known along the New England coast as a builder of fine boats and sailing ships. His youngest son, John, was now 26 years old. He had taken to the boat-building business but even more to the sailing business. He and his two brothers, often accompanied by Tom Doubleday, had been on many a voyage, delivering boats from the Maine coast to Boston, Cape Cod, and, recently, New Amsterdam.

Unlike his brothers and sisters (there were now three more of them, Elizabeth, Sarah, and Ann), however, John did not fit in with the Puritans of Salem, their strict religious beliefs, or the intolerance they exhibited toward people whose faith or behaviors didn't exactly meet with their rigid interpretation of the Gospel. In fact, many settlers with similar views to his had already left and resettled in Boston, Connecticut, Rhode Island, and Long Island.

George's second son, William, did not follow in his father's shadow. He was thirteen when his family came to America, and he and his older brother, Thomas, dutifully helped their father in his growing business. By the time he had reached his late adolescence, however, it was clear that William had no inclination toward shipbuilding. He did, on the other hand, express repeated interest in medicine, and acceding to his wishes, George arranged to have the lad apprenticed to the one physician in Salem.

Before he came to New England, Dr. Samuel Fuller had worked as a country doctor in Derbyshire, England, where he had become an ardent opponent of the Church of England. After an unfortunate incident involving a young girl and some poor medical judgment, he thought it best if he were to start afresh in the New World. He brought his contempt for the Church to America, and countering the work of the devil grew into an obsession with him, an obsession that he had passed on to his young protégé. With the help of Dr. Fuller,

William planned to establish a medical practice in Salem and Salem Village among a community of people who would share his views about Satan and the evils of Anglicanism.

Only two years into William's apprenticeship, however, Dr. Fuller fell through the ice and drowned one cold January evening while taking a shortcut across a pond on his way to deliver a baby. Although unfortunate for the doctor, the incident catapulted young William into a prominent role in the community that, much to his mother's pleasure, he filled with amazing competence and aplomb. While some of the townsfolk recovered Dr. Fuller's body that night, William delivered the baby. A week later, he moved into the doctor's house in Salem village, and three months later, he married Rachel Hubbard, a young woman who ardently embraced both his religious fervor and his growing stature in the community.

By the time he was in his late twenties, William Griggs had already established himself. Not only did his medical practice grow, but he thrived on issues of good and evil. He became one of the pillars of the church and a staunch advocate of the Puritans' passion for thwarting Satan and all those who came under his influence.

His younger brother, John, however, remained in his father's business and became quite adept at shipbuilding in his own right. When he was 23, and much to his mother's relief, John had become attracted to a young lady in the

51

village. Elizabeth Cooke and her family were recent immigrants from Shropshire, England. Elizabeth was tall, lithe, and she moved with the fluidity of a gazelle. She had light blond hair and pale blue eyes, which only served to add to her mystique. John was transfixed. Their relationship quickly developed; he became a frequent visitor at her parents' home, and it wasn't long before they discussed the prospect of marriage. John eventually garnered the courage to ask Cooke for permission to marry his daughter, and much to the young man's relief, Cooke gave his immediate and heart-felt approval.

"Can you wait until Christmas for the wedding, John? It would make her mother and me very happy."

"I'm sure that would be fine, Mr. Cooke."

"Good… John, please call me John."

"Yes, Sir."

The two men chuckled.

Elizabeth was a free spirit, lively, athletic, expressive, and carefree. Also, she had an active sense of humor that John adored. In many ways, she was a woman ahead of her time. Much to her mother's chagrin, she was occasionally in the habit of wearing her brother's old britches and shirts during the day when she did her chores around the house. She and John took frequent walks in the woods and devoted many hours to sharing their feelings and discussing their future and what it might hold for them. During one of these outings in early September, the couple followed a deer trail into the woods and discovered that it opened into a small moss-covered clearing amid a grove of fir trees.

"Isn't this a pretty spot! Let's stop here and rest a bit, John."

She sat down on the moss, and he dropped down beside her. The couple immediately entwined themselves in an embrace, and when they finally separated, John had something on his mind.

"Liza, do you like living in Salem?"

"It's certainly a beautiful place," she answered, "but my family is concerned about the Puritans and their twisted notions of religion and right and wrong. My father wants to move away from here, maybe to Connecticut or down to Long Island, and start over again. None of our family harkens to the Puritan notions of witches, demons, and evil spells or how Puritans treat their women.

"We're the same except for my brother William and his wife, Sarah, of course. She sees a witch under every stone and behind every tree. I think that the whole Hubbard family is that way. She constantly speaks of that nonsense to Will, and I believe it's beginning to have an influence on him. She calls birthmarks 'witch marks,' and she wants Will to tell her about any he may find on women he examines as a physician."

He continued. "The Puritans have driven scores away, mostly to Connecticut and Rhode Island…and, even over to Long Island."

There was a pause in the conversation; then Elizabeth broke the silence. "John, when we're married, we'll be kind to each other, won't we?"

"Yes, Eliza, very kind. No witches, no spells; just love and Christian living."

"I can even wear britches whenever I want?"

"Of course, you can. There are no rules about britches in the Bible. But please wear a dress to church, however!"

"What if I want to wear nothing sometimes?" she added with a wide grin.

"Any time, if you don't mind me staring at you, but please, not to church!"

She giggled. "John Griggs, I think I shall enjoy being married to you."

Christmas came, and the couple was married by the Reverend James Palin amidst family and friends in the little log church filled with candles and pine branch decorations, a scent-filled ambiance made even cozier by a howling blizzard. Two years later, in 1665, their first child arrived, a handsome little fellow they named John.

******

Despite his increasing stature in the community, and a comfortable living, John and Elizabeth Griggs were enduring a growing discontentment with Salem, its religious zealotry, and its intolerance. The town meetings and church services were becoming increasingly venomous. At one point, the community's religiosity even focused on the Griggs family's shipyard when a committee of village leaders tried to persuade George to not hire a skilled shipwright, Patrick Finn because he was an Irish Catholic. With increasing regularity, John and Elizabeth considered joining the many people who had left Salem to escape the town's Puritanical ways.

For the sake of his father, George's, business, however, John kept most of his feelings and beliefs to himself, but when George asked him to take Tom Doubleday, Enoch Williams, and David Redding and sail the *Pemaquid* to Sag Harbor, Long Island to deliver two fishing boats to a man named Halsey for use in its growing fishing industry, John was eager to go. Perhaps Sag Harbor would be the solution to his discontent. Of course, he had heard about Long Island. That's what it was; a long 15-mile-wide island that stretched from the Dutch port of New Amsterdam, 120 miles east into the Atlantic, paralleling the coast of Connecticut and Rhode Island. Eighty miles east of New Amsterdam, the island forked, like a lobster's open claw, creating a natural sanctuary for boats and the fishermen in them. Sag Harbor, called Wegwagonock by the Indians who lived there, was on the inside of the southern claw, a perfect location for a harbor.

The first Englishman to settle in the area had been one Isaac Halsey in 1630. It took 12 more years before one could say that there was actually a village there. In 1646 the village was incorporated, the first in what would eventually become Suffolk County, and it was home to several fishermen who cast their nets in the surrounding bays. It would be yet another half-century before the Atlantic whaling fleet would discover Sag Harbor and transform it into a major port.

The fishermen of Sag Harbor needed good boats, strongly built open crafts that were capable of bringing in a large catch and riding out the squalls that could materialize so quickly off the eastern end of Long Island. George Griggs was known for building such sturdy and dependable boats; they withstood the abuse these fishermen would give them.

As the time approached to make the delivery, John became increasingly obsessed with the idea of making a living as a mariner, moving cargo among the harbor towns of New England and New Amsterdam. What he needed was a plan.

Chapter 6

Sag Harbor, Long Island

October 1660

The tide was high at 10:00 AM; the *Pemaquid* was outfitted and ready to sail, the two new fishing boats tied to her stern, one behind the other. Elizabeth and the baby accompanied John to the dock. She kissed him good-bye.

"Godspeed, John, and be mindful of the weather and the Indians." Then she added, with a giggle, "especially the squaws! I'll be praying for you."

"I shall certainly be careful," he replied. "Perhaps I'll bring you some wampum."

"Please do, and also a pair of moccasins for little John, if you should find any," she added.

"We'll return in six or seven days. Take care, dear wife. Remember that I love you."

With that, John Griggs, Tom Doubleday, Enoch Williams, and David Redding cast off the lines, and the *Pemaquid* eased away from the dock. The voyage took two days. By the evening of the first day, they had cleared Cape Cod and were off the shore of Rhode Island. By the afternoon of the second day, they passed Gardiner's Island in the pincers of Long Island's claw-shaped eastern end, and before nightfall, they were tied up at Sag Harbor's dock. Hardly a voyage to test their metal as mariners, perfect winds, perfect seas. Surely Alice and Elizabeth Griggs must have been praying for their safe voyage, and surely God answered.

That evening, fisherman Thomas Halsey, son of the first English inhabitant of Sag Harbor, took possession of his new boats and paid John for them in silver, a bag of Dutch lion dollars, and Spanish reales (what some called "pieces of eight"). Halsey was a rough yet friendly man, his face and hands weathered by years in fishing boats and farm fields, but he had a bright and cunning eye, the eye of a man who knew the business.

What was most intriguing to John was the man who fished with Halsey. He was a lean and dark-complexioned black man, an African, whom Halsey called "Richard." Halsey did not seem to treat him as an equal or a partner, nor did he treat him as a servant, at least not to John's way of thinking. Richard spoke English well, and he was cordial yet reserved toward the four New Englanders. He took control of the new fishing boats, expertly sculling them into a natural slip formed by an outcropping of rocks. The four mariners had not seen many Africans. There were, as yet, no slaves in Salem. Of course, they knew of the African slave trade that was developing from its Dutch beginnings in Virginia and was even becoming prominent in New Amsterdam. John stared at Richard as he masterfully handled the boats. Somehow, he looked more normal, more European, than

John had expected. And he wore a cross around his neck. Could Richard be a Christian?

Dinner that night was at Halsey's house, a four-room log structure dominated by a huge fireplace at one end of the largest room, big enough for a short man to stand in. Cooking pots hung on the ends of two long iron cranes that were hinged on either side of the fireplace and swung over the fire to catch the heat. Judging from the smells, they were being put to good use by Halsey's wife, Martha, a pleasant woman who welcomed the strangers to her table.

After a dinner of fish, kidney, two types of turnips, cabbage, bread, and pumpkin pudding, there was the obligatory brandy and pipe. John thought that Halsey and his wife were surviving quite comfortably in this little frontier village of Sag Harbor. Soon after the pipe, the other three mariners returned to the *Pemaquid*, leaving John and Halsey to continue their animated discussion about fishing and business opportunities in New Amsterdam, a discussion that lasted well into the night. But before returning to that topic, John had something else on his mind.

"If I may inquire, Mr. Halsey, does Richard work for you as a slave?"

"Nay, John; he's a free man, or as free as a man can be and still be black."

"How did he get here to eastern Long Island?"

"Like many of them Africans, Richard was brought here by the Dutch as an indentured servant. He worked as a smith for a man in New Amsterdam for seven years and then bought his freedom. Most of the African indentured servants never do work off their indenture; certainly, none of the women or the children they bore. Richard was one of the lucky ones. But, he found out soon enough that a free black in New Amsterdam ain't really free. He was free to starve to death, and that was about it. Two years ago, I took a load of salted fish to New Amsterdam to trade. He was on the wharf, and I hired him to help me unload the boat. He's been with me ever since. He fishes with me and works a small blacksmith's shop I recently built here in Sag Harbor."

"Doesn't he want to go back to Africa?"

"Nay, he'd never want that. He'd probably get captured by some warriors from the Ashanti tribe and sold back into slavery again. According to Richard, they all live in terror over there. Tribal chiefs attack each other. The winner captures the other chief's people and trades them to the Arabs in exchange for a few bolts of cloth or some copper pots. The Arabs march men, women, and children to seaports and auction them off to the Portuguese and Dutch. During the march, they make 'em carry elephant tusks for the ivory trade. If any get weak or sick, they kill 'em off since they ain't worth anything at the auctions. And the damn Arabs know how to do it profitably; they've been at it for a

60

thousand years. Even the British are beginnin' to get into the slave business. A pact with the devil, in my judgment, tradin' with them heathen Arabs for slaves. Mostly they take 'em to the West Indies and Virginia, but they're beginnin' to bring 'em here to New Amsterdam. They make better workers than the Indians; they don't get sick or run away as much, and you can trust 'em a little more."

There was a pause in the conversation as Halsey poured John and himself another brandy. Then, in a tone meant to change the subject, Halsey said, "John, are you and Tom takin' your boat back to Salem?"

"Aye. We'll leave in a day or two if the weather permits."

"Perhaps you might consider coming back here with your *Pemaquid* and starting a transport and trading business. The farmers are comin' in, John. The land out here is good, but there ain't no decent roads between here and New Amsterdam harbor, just some Indian trails that a man's wagon can hardly negotiate. Between the fish, lumber, cattle, and farm produce, John, we could keep you and your boat busy. I can see she's a well-built craft; your father sure has an eye for boat-building".

Not waiting for John to say "no," Thomas Halsey continued, "With you haulin' my fish, I could double my production. Back in '48, a man named John Hand, a farmer from Kent in England, brought a group of farmers to settle just a few miles southeast of here in East Hampton. They've

61

done well; they have money, but they all need markets for their harvests. You could do well there, too, John. I'd bet old Stuyvesant's wooden leg on it."

Then Halsey added, "A man named John Cox is the town marshal over in Southampton, and he's made money farming. He's a good friend, and I know he could send some business your way, too."

As Halsey talked on into the night, John became more and more convinced that he did, indeed, have a tempting proposition. The next day aboard the *Pemaquid*, John laid out the idea to his crew. Tom and the other two men were convinced and agreed to give Sag Harbor a try.

After informing Halsey of their decision to take him up on his offer that afternoon, the mariners scouted the area for a place to build two cabins. Following a suggestion from Halsey, they decided on a spot in a clearing that overlooked the harbor. The next day, they left on the tide for the voyage back to Salem.

After tying up at the Salem dock, John went immediately to his parents' home to deliver the sack of silver to his father. Elizabeth and the child had been staying there during his absence, so general greetings ensued, followed by the promise of a celebratory dinner that evening. On the walk back to their home that evening, John told Elizabeth all about Sag Harbor and Halsey's business proposition.

"Would you like to try it, John?"

"Aye, Eliza. I think it would be an opportunity to make a good living for our family and for us to escape the religious suffocation that's growing month by month here in Salem. There are several families there already, and you would make friends quickly."

"What about your father's business?" she inquired. "Doesn't he need you?"

"I'll ask his permission, of course, but over the years, he has developed a skilled crew at the yard. I think he'll be fine."

"Well, if that's what you want to do, then little John and I are ready to go. If, for some reason, it doesn't work out, we can always come back."

"I already explained the idea to Tom, Enoch, and David, and they're eager to join in the venture. While we were there, we even located a good spot for two cabins. I'd go down ahead of time with them for a month or two to build the cabins and arrange things. Then, we'd come back for you and the baby."

"Will our cabin have a porch?" she inquired with a coy smile.

"Aye, a fine porch, Eliza, and a rocker for you and Johnny."

The next evening after dinner, George and John repaired to the front porch for a pipe. It was one of those evenings created to perfection. Down the hill from the house, the ocean was as smooth as glass; the outlines of George's three ships moored a short distance from shore were barely visible in the receding light. Behind the house, two whip-poor-wills were staking out territories with their familiar calls. Crickets and peeper frogs filled the evening air with their cadence, and the meadow just east of the house was ablaze with the yellow lights of thousands of fireflies. As was his practice, George rocked on the front porch of his now enlarged and comfortable home, smoking a long-stemmed clay pipe and doing his best to absorb the totality of the evening's splendor, an effort that he knew from many years of experience was futile. It was, indeed, impossible for anyone to capture the totality of such an evening in his consciousness.

At first, neither man said a word as George passed his pipe to John, who took it and began to draw on it. As the whip-poor-wills, crickets, and peeper frogs continued their serenade, George finally broke into their cacophony.

"So, how did you find Sag Harbor, John?"

"It's a pleasant village, and I found Mr. Halsey to be friendly and welcoming." John paused and then continued.

"In fact, he presented me with a convincing argument that there is an excellent opportunity to establish a shipping operation between eastern Long Island and New Amsterdam. Right now, they have no reliable transportation for their salted fish, lumber, and farm produce to get them to market. I could easily fill that need with the *Pemaquid*." Then he added, "Also, more farmers and fishermen are moving into the area, which means there would be an increased need for my shipping services." He paused to let the argument sink in.

"Is this something you'd like to do, John?"

Aye, Sir. I think I would like to try it. During our stay, I spoke with the other three about the idea, and they want to join me." He paused and then added, "Of course, I would want your blessing for the venture, and I would like to take the *Pemaquid*, which I would pay you for with my first profits. She's a sturdy and dependable two-master, and you know that Tom and I can handle her. They say there is a great opportunity for ships to carry cargo along the Atlantic coast. We would eventually work out of the harbor at New Amsterdam. It won't be long before it is busier than Philadelphia."

Ever the businessman, his father expressed a concern "What about the business prospects, John? Can they keep a ship and its crew busy?"

"I'm confident that it's going to work, Father. You should see Sag Harbor. It's tucked into the south fork of Long Island and very protected. There is much farming and fishing going on, and they need a way to bring their produce to market. Traders come by, but it's on a very irregular basis, so I'll have plenty of work to keep us busy.

George was an insightful man, and his son's request didn't come as a great surprise. He knew about John's feelings toward the Puritans. The young man needed to leave; his father could see that. In fact, George, too, shared his son's discomfort with Salem, and he was considering moving his operation down to Boston, 16 miles to the southwest, a move his business was eventually to make.

"Do you think the *Pemaquid* is enough ship for the job, John?" he asked, trying to enter the conversation with as little emotion as possible.

"Aye, Sir, I do. She's 52 feet long, she can carry ten tons, and we would stay near the coast, anyway. I know she would do, at least for a start. If, for any reason, the venture is not successful, we'd come back here and build ships with you. But, if our venture on Long Island is successful and grows like I think it will, I'll pay you for the *Pemaquid* and purchase more and bigger vessels from you."

"Where will you and your young family stay?" George asked, thinking about Elizabeth and the baby.

"Tom, Enoch, David, and I would go down ahead of time for a month or two and build two cabins; then, we'd come back for Elizabeth and little John."

"And Elizabeth…what does she think about your plan?"

"She assured me that she's eager to give it a try."

"Are there other families and women to befriend her?"

"Aye, there are several and more families are moving there every month."

"Well, let me think about it, John, and we'll talk tomorrow. I would certainly hate to see you go, but I also understand your dream."

"I'm sure I would see you and Mother often," John added. "The trade between Salem, Boston, Gloucester, and New Amsterdam is growing every day. You've said so yourself!"

"Aye, John; I'm sure you would." He paused for a moment. "John, I believe that when you visit us, you will have to come to Boston to do it."

"What do you mean, Father?"

"I've been giving some thought to moving my shipyard to Boston. Your mother and I are growing more uncomfortable with the Puritans here in Salem. They talk too much of Hell and witches and evil spells. We no longer fit in, John. I believe no good will come of it. These people have forgotten why they came to America. Besides, Boston is growing, and business should be good there."

"When will you move?"

"Soon, but we will do it in steps, and it'll take about a year."

"Will you need my help?"

"I don't think so. Thomas would oversee the move. He has developed a love for the business, and he's good at organizing. Anyway, we'll talk in the morning."

John and Elizabeth walked through the darkness back to their house. He carried the sleeping little boy and talked so animatedly about their future that Elizabeth cautioned him not to wake his son. He was confident of his father's answer. He would give the move his blessing, and John renewed his resolve to make the venture a success. He picked up his step. After all, he was Griggs, wasn't he?

****

A week later, the four mariners were back in Sag Harbor, beginning construction on the two log houses. Thanks to periodic assistance from Halsey and Richard, the cabins were finished in four weeks, complete with six-foot porches that ran the length of the structures. They would be especially useful for smoking a pipe in the evening and rocking babies while watching the moon rise over the bay. The house for the young Griggs family wasn't spacious, but the four mariners/carpenters judged that it would do quite well. The main focal point of the structure was a beautifully-built large fireplace at the back of the main room. Its design and construction were the handiwork of Richard, who was placed in charge of the task.

"You won't be sorry," Halsey told John. He wasn't. The stones were artfully placed and fitted into each other. And there was a three-inch thick oak mantel, into the front of which Richard had carved "Peace to All Who Enter This Home."

John was especially impressed. "It's a beautiful piece of work, Richard. You certainly are talented. Where did you learn to work with stone like that?"

"I jus' watched other men do it, and I learned from them."

"I want to pay you something for it, Richard."

"No need, Sir, I jus' get pleasure from doing it."

"Richard, I insist. It says in the Bible that an ox is worth its hire. Well, if an ox is, a man certainly is, especially one with your talent. Here, take these fifteen shillings."

Richard glanced over at Halsey, who nodded in assent.

"Well then, alright. You're very kind to me, Sir."

"And, Richard, stop calling me Sir. My name is John. Or if you prefer, you may call me 'Captain' due to that ship moored out there," he added with a chuckle.

The rest of the crew began to laugh. Tom Doubleday, always ready with the quip, bellowed out, "Yes, Sir, Captain Sir. What's your pleasure for us swabbies, Sir? Should we swab the deck, or is it time to eat some dinner, Captain Sir? Should I ascend to the crow's nest and be on the lookout for

Spanish galleons, Sir? Wait a minute…the *Pemaquid* doesn't have a crow's nest. Should we go to dinner instead, Captain Sir?"

"Enough, Tom. Enough. Richard, I guess you shouldn't call me Captain after all, at least not until I get around to building a crow's nest in the *Pemaquid*. When I do, Tom, you'll be going up during the first lightning storm to be on the lookout for the Spanish! Now, let's eat, Gentlemen!"

Two days later, the men sailed the *Pemaquid* back to Salem, where they devoted the next three days to stowing aboard various stores, tools, provisions, and other household items. On the fourth morning, John retrieved his wife and child, and after hugs and goodbyes on the dock, the group of six Pilgrims were on their way to a new life.

George was happy for his son. "Maybe we'll move there in our old age," he told Alice that evening. "You can help with the grandchildren, and I can keep John's ships in repair."

Alice sighed. "I'm afraid most of our other grandchildren will be in Boston, George…except for William's, that is. He and Rachel seem to be well-suited to these Puritans and their rigid beliefs. It will be a difficult choice for us."

There was a pause. And then, "I know…I know. However, he is a good doctor, and the town folk all seem to admire him."

George would never see his son, John, again. That next June, George, his eldest son, Thomas, and two men from his boatyard sailed to Boston to look at a location to move his shipbuilding enterprise. While they were tied up at the Boston dock that first evening, a fire broke out in a nearby galleon. The four men rushed to help the vessel's owner fight the blaze and save some of the cargo of molasses and tobacco. George's aging heart was not up to the task, however, and he died carrying two buckets of water up the gangplank to the stricken ship. It was June 23rd.

The next morning Thomas and his two shipmates bore George home to Salem in a canvas bag, and he was buried the next day in the church cemetery. Over sixty people were present at the graveside, as the minister assured them that George was, indeed, in the glorious presence of his beloved Savior.

It began to rain; Alice knelt down to brush the drops of water off the top of George's coffin as it was lowered into the grave. Thomas and William retrieved their mother and slowly walked her back down the hill, one hesitating step at a time, to the company of consoling neighbors and to their home, where her neighbors had collected an abundance of food that had been gathered in her parlor. George had done well; he provided for his family, raised his children, held his grandchildren, and established the Griggs family in America, one of whom, John William Griggs, even became

President McKinley's Attorney General. General Griggs also happened to be Jeff Hughson's fourth cousin, six times removed. Enough for any man, George...

Chapter 7
Western Long Island

Summer 1664

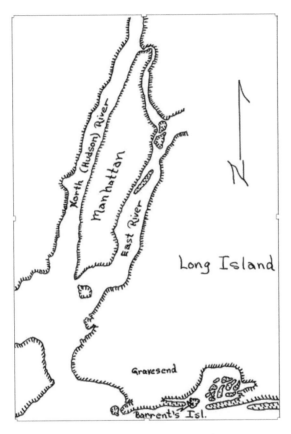

1664 Map of the New York area

John's business continued to grow, and in 1661 he paid for the *Pemaquid* and ordered another ship from his brother Thomas's yard. As the trade opportunities expanded, John could see that he needed to be closer to New York, the new name for that harbor, since Peter Stuyvesant had surrendered it to the British. The city now boasted over 1500 residents

73

and an additional 300 slaves, and it looked like mercantilism would certainly command its destiny. As much as he loved Sag Harbor and eastern Long Island, John knew that he had to be nearer New York, where commerce was growing and deals were being struck. After unloading a cargo of fish and wheat onto New York's bustling dock, he made arrangements to purchase some property in Gravesend, on the southwestern tip of Long Island (now south Brooklyn), where his father-in-law, John Cooke, had already settled.

The first settler in Gravesend was Anthony Jackson van Vaes in 1635. Although he was black, van Vaes arrived in the colony as a free man and became known as a merchant and a litigator in court against his foes. He and his Dutch wife lived on their 200-acre grant in Gravesend until business interests eventually drew him back to New Amsterdam.

After van Vaes' exodus, Gravesend was settled again in 1643 by a head-strong woman named Lady Deborah Moody, who wanted to live with her followers in absolute religious freedom. They were soon driven out by hostile Indians, but in 1645 they returned to make Gravesend permanent. Perhaps as a reaction to his early feelings about the rigid and intolerant Puritans, Lady Moody's aspirations for Gravesend resonated well with John. Gravesend, Saxon for "end of the grove," was very suitable to his needs.

The village was designed around four common areas, each one being about four acres, with ten house lots around its perimeter. John bought one of these, along with one of the 100-acre fields outside the village that were assigned to each lot. He was to become a pillar of the community and one of the major landowners in the village, also owning much of what was eventually to become Coney Island in another era.

Soon after his move to Gravesend, John developed a business relationship with his father-in-law. Like George Griggs, Cooke had immigrated from England to Salem with his wife, Sarah, in 1635. Their daughter, Elizabeth, was born soon after. Like George's son, John, Cooke ended up in Gravesend, where he had moved with his family to improve his business prospects.

After their move to Gravesend, Elizabeth Griggs gave birth to four more sons: Thomas, Benjamin, Daniel, and Samuel. One winter evening, while she was nursing little Samuel in a new rocking chair John had made for her, she said,

"John, I love every one of our boys more than I can even express, but wouldn't it be fun to have a little girl? There must be something in me that just makes boys. I guess it's God's providence that I am this way."

John looked up from his account book. "I wonder how God decides whether a baby will be a boy or a girl. I don't think there's anything in the Bible about it. But we do have some fine sons." Then, he returned to his ledgers.

Three days later, however, he consulted with a fisherman, Ian MacGrath, who happened to have four daughters and one son. Affecting a light-hearted manner, he asked Ian, "So, what's your secret to having all those beautiful daughters, anyway?"

Well, John, me boy, I'll tell ye my secret, and when I discovered it, I changed my ways, and then little Ian was born to carry on me name." He chuckled and then offered his advice.

"It's you, John, it's not Elizabeth. I believe you're the cause. For eleven years, I carried a pink ribbon in the pocket of my jerkin. It belonged to my mother before she died. I lost it when I fell overboard during a chop one day. Ten months later, young Ian was born. I think the ribbon was the cause of my beautiful girls. You might consider carrying a pink ribbon in your pocket." He winked at John and chuckled.

On his way home, John was certain that he had been the object of another one of Ian's Scottish jokes. Pink ribbon— ridiculous! Just in case, however, and unknown to Elizabeth, he procured a small piece of pink ribbon and put it in his coat pocket. Sure enough, eleven months later, and much to Elizabeth's surprise, little Martha arrived. John never did mention the ribbon, and he was still skeptical. Nonetheless…

Over the years, John exposed his sons to the life of a mariner, as well as to the life of a farmer. Supplemented with hired hands, the boys helped run the family farm at Gravesend. At an early age, Benjamin (Judy Griggs' 7th g-grandfather), the third son in line, exhibited a mechanical talent that later, as a young man, he put to good use by constructing and operating a flour mill on the outskirts of the village.

As John Griggs, Sr. got older, he spent less time on the water and more time buying and selling, arranging the voyages and the cargo, and overseeing the work on his farm. Soon after his long-term employee, Tom Doubleday, died in 1676, he made the acquaintance of a mariner named Walter Dobbs. Dobbs was older than Griggs, but he was a hard worker, and he knew the sea. It wasn't long before he trusted Dobbs as a junior partner, and Dobbs began skippering some of his ships as they carried cargo back and forth among the increasingly busy ports of New England, New York, and Charleston.

Dobbs lived on Barrent's Island in Jamaica Bay, four miles east of Gravesend village. He was married to Mary Merritt Dobbs, an English woman motivated by a desire to achieve entrance into the social order that was developing in New York. In fact, her brother, William, would be elected mayor of New York for three terms between 1695 and 1698.

In 1697 he would also become a vestryman in Trinity Church, for some an even greater honor.

Although Walter worked hard and was prosperous by Long Island standards, thanks in part to his relationship with Griggs, he never reached the social heights the Merritts set for themselves. Like John Griggs, Walter Dobbs also worked a small farm. Unlike the Griggs, however, he and Mary had only two children old enough to help with the chores, Maria, born on Barrent's Island in 1670, and John, born a year later. If anything, Walter worked too hard, and by 1687 his health was failing.

His daughter, Maria, grew into a very pretty and strong-willed young woman. At one time or another during their adolescence, both Samuel and Benjamin Griggs developed a romantic interest in her, but she rebuffed their advances, somewhat to the displeasure of both John Griggs and Walter Dobbs. Maria, however, was sixteen at the time and had definite notions of a life with more adventure.

One evening, Walter brought up the subject of the Griggs boys at the dinner table.

"Maria, I am told by John that the Griggs family thinks very highly of you."

"Father, are you referring to Samuel and Benjamin?" she asked with a small giggle.

Well, I…"

Maria interrupted and got right to the point. "They are both very polite, and they pay attention to me when I see them. They're my friends, but, Father, you must know that if I were to choose one over the other, it would make things difficult for me to be in that family. Besides, the last time Samuel was here, he told me I shouldn't wear britches when I worked with the crops. He was already trying to boss me."

Walter admitted to himself that his daughter had a point, and he attempted to lift the conversation to a higher level.

"Maria, have you thought about your future or what sort of man you'd like to be married to someday?"

"Someone just like you, Father…someone who will love me, let me wear britches, and encourage me if I want to become a mariner or a soldier, or even a mother of ten children."

She flashed her father a big smile and placed her hand on his.

Walter sighed and returned the smile.

"I can see we've raised quite a hard-headed and wonderful young woman, Maria. I'm sure God will send you a man who will love you and accommodate you at the same time. We will pray for our Lord's help."

Maria stood up, leaned over, and kissed him on the cheek. "Yes, Father, we shall pray."

Maria Dobbs aspired to something more, something different, although exactly what, she wasn't certain. However, she would soon find out.

Chapter 8

The Hughson Family

Scotland 1691

Thomas Hughson was an old Scottish warrior. He came from the Isle of Skye off the western coast of the Scottish Highlands. As his name implied, he was born into a sept that was part of Clan MacDonald, an infamous clan that many an English monarch and warlord found hard to pacify. Despite his age, Thomas was still a powerful man, barrel-chested, with massive shoulders and arms, still capable of wielding a Claymore long sword to great effect. He had a beard and a full head of hair, both of which were finally beginning to turn gray, and he walked with a slight limp in his gait, the result of some battle in the distant past. He had spent a lifetime fighting the English. With the help of his wife, Elspeth, and his 20-year-old son, Tom, he worked a small farm near Portree on the eastern shore of the island.

In recent years, however, during the reign of King James II, he had found some peace, largely because the king was sympathetic toward Catholicism, common among the Highlanders. Although Thomas was not a particularly religious man, he counted himself among the Catholics, and when King James decreed that the Presbyterians of the Lowlands would be executed if they attended any

Covenantings (secret Presbyterian meetings), Thomas was not particularly concerned.

In 1688, William of Orange changed all that. He convinced Parliament to bring the House of Stewart to an end by deposing King James II. The Lowlander Presbyterians were ecstatic over William of Orange, the Dutchman who would save England for Protestantism. The Highlanders, however, were a good deal less enthusiastic. Many became Jacobites, supporters of the deposed and exiled King James. They had fought the combined forces of British and Lowlander Scots before, and Thomas knew that it would happen again. He had seen too many battles, too much blood, too many hacked bodies, and too many young boys die before they even had beards to shave. He could feel the carnage coming again. He had already lost one son to it, and he did not want that destiny for his other son, Tom. He became convinced that the solution lay in America.

After dinner one evening, Thomas and his son, Tom, walked out to the barn through a thick fog to check on the pony, which was about to foal. Tom was a handsome young man, powerfully built and possessing a square jaw, like his father. He also had thick, dark brown hair, just like his father in his younger years. His blue eyes, though, were from his mother, a major contribution that was plain to all who knew the family. He had grown to just over six feet, undoubtedly genes from some ancient Viking, and now could look his father straight in the eye.

"She won't come tonight," the older man muttered, almost to himself. He stood by the pony, gently resting a hand on her still-firm rump.

"Perhaps tomorrow, Da?" young Tom conjectured.

"Ooh, aye, I think tomorrow. See how her udder is filling."

"Good luck, lass; tomorrow then." Tom grabbed Madeline by her ears and kissed her forehead, bringing a smile to the old warrior's face.

Then Thomas changed the subject.

"Tom," he began, "I want to speak with you about your future."

"Aye, Da?" the young man answered with an inquisitive tone in his voice.

"I have concerns about this recent turn of political events. Down in London, that Dutchman, William of Orange, got Parliament to remove our Catholic King James because he doesn't favor the Catholics. That doesn't bode well for us Highlanders."

"What do you mean, Da?" Tom queried.

"I'm fearful the Lowlanders will join the British and try to turn us from our Papist ways."

"But, what does that have to do with me?"

"There will be fighting, Tom, lots of it, and it will go hard on us. I've seen too many battles in my years, and I don't want you to follow in my path. You are the only son I have left."

"I am my father's son," he declared defiantly. "I am not afraid to fight; not British, not Lowlanders, not the Campbells, not anyone on earth!"

"I know, me boy; you can shoot a gun with a keen eye and handle a Claymore as well as anyone of your young age. Your father has, indeed, taught you well." The older man chuckled. "But if you succeed in battle and slaughter many of the enemy, it merely means that you'll live to be slaughtered yourself another day. I am not a good example of what happens to warriors, Tom; I've been very lucky. But, look what happened to your brother, Ian. I want more for you, Tom; you're the only one left to carry on the Hughson name."

Thomas paused for a few seconds and then continued. "I've been thinking about America, Tom. I believe there is a great opportunity over there. You can already speak and write English, thanks to your mother and the time she spent working in the household of that baron before I met her. I ken that you would survive very well in America." He continued before Tom could respond.

"I know a man named Robert MacFie, a gunsmith, who has been to the city of New York. He came back home to sell his family property so he could get the money to establish his gunsmith trade in New York. He's an honest man from a good family, and he's looking for a young man to serve as an apprentice for three years. I spoke with him about you. I told him you were intelligent, honest, and hard-working and that you would learn the skills quickly. He said he was willing to take you with him. He'll provide your passage, board, and room, look to your needs, and even pay you a small wage. And he will instruct you in a very valuable trade. At the end of three years, you can work with him or go to work for yourself and perhaps even become prosperous."

"But Da, all I know is farming and what you taught me about fighting," the young man protested. "And what about you and Ma and the farm? Who will help you if I go to America? Why can't you and Ma come with me? We can go together!"

"Tom, we haven't the money. Our farm is too small, and I am past the age where I could make a new start in America. You go on, son. And after you're established, I ken we will come to New York and live in the back room of your big house and rock our grandchildren. You'll see that those three years will pass quickly. As for our farm, your uncle and I can work out some arrangement. We will be alright here, Tom."

"But there are English in New York, too," the young man continued to protest.

"Ooh, aye, but it's different over there. There's more freedom, more opportunity. It's a long way from William of Orange and his Campbell conspirators. Your mother and I have discussed this opportunity, Tom. Of course, she will miss you terribly, but she wants me to encourage you to take Mr. MacFie up on his offer. You're the only son we have left. Go with MacFie and make a place for us. You can do it, Tom; you're a Hughson, aren't you?"

The older man hugged his son, and he had to blink the tears from his eyes as the two turned down the damp path back to the house. That evening around the dinner table, the tension subsided as Thomas gave encouraging words to his son and then began joking about Tom finding a wife in America in one of the Indian tribes. "I've heard that their women are hard workers and have a quiet way about them that's pleasing to men folk!"

"Just make sure she's not a Campbell, Tom," Elspeth chimed in. "That's my only requirement. I wouldn't know what I'd do if Campbell blood flowed in my grandchildren's veins."

"I'll remember, Ma, no Campbell Indians! Perhaps I'll find some Irish lass with red hair, green eyes, and wide hips for giving me many wee bairns! Or, perhaps one of those flat-chested English girls with stringy blond hair and yellow teeth!"

"Enough of that, Tom!" his mother ordered, suppressing a chuckle.

"Let the boy dream, Elspeth. Do ya' want grandchildren or not? As for me, I'd prefer you to find a Scottish lass, maybe from the clan MacGregor. With Hughson and McGregor blood mixed, your sons would surely be feared wherever they go."

Tom's heart began to lighten. After all, if this adventure didn't work out, he could always come back home.

****

Three weeks later, Robert MacFie, young Tom, and a cartload of tools and other provisions were making their way through the Scottish Lowlands and down through England to the Port of Plymouth, where MacFie had booked passage on the *Victory* for the voyage to New York. MacFie made a pleasant traveling companion. He was a portly man, a full head shorter than Tom and bald on top, a condition about which he was quite sensitive, causing him to wear a leather cap everywhere except to bed. He had been a gunsmith for over 20 years, a trade he learned from his father. He was good-natured, and he talked incessantly about the wonderful opportunities that awaited them in New York.

MacPhie did not treat Tom at all like an indentured apprentice but rather as a young colleague with whom he was ready to share the new life he had discovered. He had been married once and fathered two children. After he lost his whole family to the fever back in 1683, he decided he would conquer his misery by going to America. His original destination had been Virginia, but a chance storm had caused the captain to veer north, eventually placing them in Long Island Sound (known then as the "North Sea") and into New York harbor. The ship went on to Virginia, but MacFie stayed in New York, made new friends, and planned his business venture. The *Victory* would take over six weeks to reach New York because it was scheduled to stop in Jamaica to unload cargo and take on more cargo for that quickly growing seaport on the southwestern tip of New England.

"Once you get used to it, you're gonna like New York, Tom. It has a bit of everything. Forts, buildings, warehouses, taverns, women, churches, and people, all kinds of people of all colors. A man can hear more than twenty languages on the wharves. And vessels, all types of 'em; even the pirates come in to trade their booty and refit their ships. New York is growing, Tom, and they're gonna need guns, plenty of 'em. We should make a good life of it."

While the two traveled southward in MacFie's cart along the rutted and muddy roads, the gunsmith took the opportunity to begin Tom's education in the art of crafting fine weaponry.

"When we get to New York, Tom, we'll be making rifles and pistols with the new flintlocks. They're an improvement over the snaphaunce locks, Tom; more reliable. We'll file spiral grooves in all our barrels, too. The rifling makes the ball rotate and fly true." He demonstrated by extending his right arm toward Tom and twisting his hand through the air.

"I've experimented with different types of rifling. . .more turns, less turns, straight, progressive. I've also studied the accuracy of different barrel lengths, and I believe I've landed on the right combination, Tom. My weapons shoot as true as any you'll find. You'll see for yourself soon enough after you make your first one."

"How long do you judge it will take me to build my first rifle?" Tom inquired.

"I'd say about a year. Maybe less if you're quick to learn and half as talented as your father claims." MacFie chuckled and winked at Tom.

"I will not disappoint you, Sir." Tom declared.

"Tom, please call me 'Robert.' 'Sir' and 'Mr. MacFie' sound a wee too much like I'm getting old."

MacFie smiled as he drew a pipe and tobacco from his leather jerkin and commenced to light it with a flint and steel he retrieved from his coat pocket. He liked the young man; he'd make a fine protégé…maybe even a partner someday. He'd need someone eventually; indeed, he wasn't getting any younger.

When they reached Plymouth, MacFie sold the pony and cart and saw to the stowing of his chests aboard the *Victory*. The ship, a 250-ton Dutch fluyt, was not due to depart for three days, and MacFie and Tom passed much of the time scouring the local merchants and blacksmith shops for anything they could use in their upcoming enterprise in New York. For their short stay in Plymouth, the two travelers found accommodations at the Rose & Crown Inn on Market Street. The establishment was almost full and very rowdy, and they had to share a bed, but Tom allowed that it was better than sleeping in a field, even with MacFie's ferocious snoring. Before retiring on the first evening, MacFie introduced Tom to his first taste of rum. There would be more rum on the *Victory* over the next six weeks, the gunsmith promised.

Chapter 9

In the Atlantic

September 1691

The three days of waiting passed quickly, mostly filled with tutoring on various aspects of gunsmithing, and at 8:00 AM, the *Victory* cast off her lines and let the outgoing tide take her to the outer harbor and into a breath of wind to carry the canvas. Responding to the barked commands of the first mate, the sailors set the sails and adjusted them until the tell-tales streamed aft from the gaff canvas. Soon the hills of Manor Bourne, Cawsand, and Penlee had slipped past the stern, and the *Victory* was in the Channel and on her way to Jamaica and thence to New York. The ship was not new, but she was well maintained. Like most Dutch-built fluyts of her time, she was not big, 80 feet long, with three masts, two square-rigged, one gaff-rigged, and a bowsprit. The passenger quarters below decks were cramped, with only about 5½ feet of headroom and no privacy. The sleeping accommodations consisted of hammocks strung from the bulkhead and very close to each other. They were taken down each morning to make room for the various activities the passengers engaged in to pass the time. The passenger list for this voyage consisted of 27 men, women, and children, some headed for Jamaica, but most, like Tom and

MacFie, continuing on to the city of New York to start their new lives in the New World.

The passenger in the hammock next to MacFie was a middle-aged Presbyterian minister named Uriah MacArthur, who was going to pastor a flock in some place called Hempstead on Long Island. MacArthur was suffering from a terrible cough. Fearing that he might infect the crew and other passengers, the captain was at first unwilling to let him on board, but some guineas changed hands, and an accommodation was reached.

At first, the Reverend MacArthur appeared to improve; the sea air seemed to be doing him some good. About three weeks into the voyage, however, his cough worsened, he developed a high fever, and two nights later, he was gone. The next morning, he was buried at sea, stitched into the canvas hammock that had been his sickbed, and weighted down with three cobblestones from the ship's ballast. The sailor deftly placed one last stitch through the reverend's nose, a tradition meant to assure that he was, indeed, dead. As expected, the corpse didn't flinch. MacFie helped bury the poor man. It was pouring down rain, and he ordered Tom to stay below and keep dry.

"No sense in you gettin' wet and catchin' the fever yourself, Tom, me boy. You ain't no use to me, sick or dead."

Tom gladly did what he was told and carved on a piece of walnut that would become the stock for a MacFie flintlock rifle, while on the deck above, the Reverend MacArthur slipped into the sea to the cadence of "May God have mercy on his soul!" All those who attended the burial did, indeed, get wet and cold.

The minister had a wife and a teenage son on board, and Tom felt much pity for them. Too poor to return to England, headed for a strange land, their livelihood jerked out from under them by the cruel machinations of fate. Perhaps, Tom thought, the boy would grow up quickly so he could support himself and his mother. Or perhaps the widow will find a new husband. She was getting on in years, though, and this latter option would not be easy.

Four days after Parson MacArthur's burial, MacFie developed a cough himself. At first, he discounted it. "Only a slight tickle in me throat, Tom," he would answer to his young protégé's expressions of concern. A few days later, however, his condition seriously worsened. He began running a fever that, at times, was so high as to make him delirious. There was little in 1691 that could be done for pneumonia, especially onboard a ship with no trained doctor among the crew or passengers. Vacuum bottles were applied to his chest but to no avail. MacFie knew he was dying, and in a lucid moment, he prepared his young apprentice for the worst.

"Tom, I believe I'm not gonna make it to New York, me boy."

"Yes, you will, Robert. You'll see as soon as. . ."

"Don't interrupt me, boy. I'm near the end, and you're a lucky fellow since you'll be free of your indenture. I'm going to will everything to you, Tom. You can claim my chests in New York and try to sell the tools to give yourself a start. . ." He had to stop for a coughing spell that lasted over a minute. Then he began again in a very weak voice.

"Perchance, you can locate another gunsmith to work for. You'll find all my calculations about the rifling in my notebook in one of the chests. . ." There was a long pause. "And don't forget what I told you about the flintlocks, Tom. They're the best way to touch off the powder."

"I won't forget, Robert," Tom replied, fighting back tears.

"Now, go fetch me some paper and a quill and ink. I'll make out a proper will for you to present to the authorities."

Ten minutes later, the brief document was completed. In an amazingly steady hand, it read,

"On this 23rd day of September in the year of our Lord 1691, I, Robert MacFie, of Glen Carron in the Highlands of Scotland, being of sound mind but failing body, do bequeath all of my worldly possessions to Mr. Thomas Hughson, late of the Isle of Skye."

He signed it, with the widow MacArthur and the first mate also signing as witnesses. Then he handed it to his never-to-be apprentice.

"You're a good lad, Tom. . ." Another long pause. "I ken you'll do fine. As you told me before, you're a Hughson, aren't you?"

"Aye, Sir; I'm indeed a Hughson."

Those were the last words exchanged by the two men. At 3:00 that morning, Robert MacFie died. At 8:00 the same morning, he, too, was buried at sea, his body and leather cap stitched into his own hammock and laden with three cobblestones for a quick descent.

For Tom Hughson, the ensuing days were filled with sadness, anxiety, and feelings of total helplessness. At first, he resolved to go home to Scotland; perhaps a ship would be leaving Jamaica for England. As the days and nights passed, however, he found himself thinking more and more about what New York must be like. He devoted his evenings on deck to smoking MacFie's pipe and thinking. Perhaps there would be a gunsmith in New York who would take him, and his tools, in and teach him the trade. Or, perhaps, there was fighting to do; the Spaniards or even the Indians. Perhaps someone needed a soldier who could shoot straight and wield a Claymore. Tom wondered if they even used Claymore long swords in America. They weren't very effective against muskets.

On an impulse, Tom descended into the *Victory*'s cargo hold and found MacFie's chest of tools. He extracted the gunsmith's notebook with all its drawings, figures, and calculations and took it back up on deck. Perhaps he could teach himself something about the trade before landing in New York, so he could be of more value to some future employer. Finding a coil of rope, he took a seat, opened the book, and began reading. In ten minutes, he fell fast asleep.

Chapter 10
Kingston Harbor

October 1691

By the time the *Victory* tied up at the wharf in Kingston harbor, Tom no longer considered returning to Scotland. He was ready for New York, and the two-day stopover in Jamaica made him impatient. He managed to pass the time and earn a little money by helping to unload the *Victory* of some of its cargo, which consisted largely of manufactured goods, tools, glass, and even two carriages. Thus cleared, the *Victory*'s hold was replenished with lumber and barrels of molasses.

Just before the *Victory's* departure on the afternoon tide, its cargo manifest was completed with the arrival on the wharf of 24 African slaves, men, women, and children, the men chained together at the ankles, and the whole group under the watchful eyes of four traders armed with pistols and leather whips. With much yelling and cursing, the traders drove the pathetic group up the gangway, across the deck, and down into the stern end of the *Victory's* hold. Tom stood on the deck and watched the spectacle in utter amazement. He had never seen Africans before; in fact, he had hardly even thought about slavery before that moment. As the slaves approached the wharf, the chained males were the first to appear, and for a moment, Tom thought they were convicts. When the women and children came into view, however, he realized that his initial assessment had been wrong.

As he stood there leaning on the rail, one of the *Victory*'s crew, a fellow named Peter and not much older than Tom, came up beside him and watched the procession of slaves as they descended into the hold. Peter and Tom had talked before. In fact, he was one of the crew members who helped commit Robert MacFie to his watery tomb.

"A bad lot, that bunch," Peter mumbled.

"They're African slaves, aren't they?" Tom asked.

"Aye, but most of 'em, the men anyway, are real troublemakers. They're being sent to the auction in New York because they gave their owners trouble down here. Probably some tried to escape, and a few of 'em were rebellious against their masters."

"But what about the women and children? They weren't rebellious, were they?"

"Nay, but the women will bring a good price at the auction because many of 'em speak English, and they're used to domestic service. Their owners probably made a good profit on 'em, and so will the slavers when they get 'em to New York."

"I didn't know there were any slaves in New York." Tom said with disbelief in his voice.

"Hundreds of 'em, Tom. Some work in the trades, some are common laborers, and some are sent to the farms and estates north of the town. Most of the African slaves are here in the islands and in Virginia, but New York has its share."

"How do you know so much about the slave trade?" Tom asked.

Peter paused for a moment and then replied, "For 18 months, I sailed on a Dutch slave ship. I learned more than I ever wanted to know about the African slave trade. You wouldn't believe the stories I could tell you. Slavin' ain't right, Tom. I know that they ain't fully human like us, but it still ain't right. . . It's surely the work of the devil, I tell ya. The Lord won't allow it to go on forever; you'll see. Do ya see the scar on the back of that young buck at the end of the chain?"

"What is that?"

"They branded him, Tom, probably for runnin' away. It's a trick the slaveholders picked up from the Portuguese. It identifies the slave as a troublemaker and someone to watch. I've seen that done, too. It smells awful. . .like when a farrier sets a hot shoe on a draft horse's hoof. It's a smell that'll stick with you."

"Who's going to keep them from rebelling during our trip to New York?" Tom was worried.

"Those four slavers will sail with us. They're responsible for 'em. They won't take the chains off 'em anyway, and the women won't cause no trouble. If any of 'em create problems, they'll be thrown overboard in front of the others, and that'll keep the rest of 'em straight. I've witnessed it many a time; some nights, I still have dreams about it."

Peter spat over the rail, wiped the back of his hand across his mouth, and walked away, leaving Tom to stare into the water.

A few minutes after the slaves were herded onboard, the *Victory*'s bow lines, stern lines, and springers were cast off, and Tom leaned over the rail, watching the ship drift away from the wharf. He contemplated the scores of white and pink jellyfish that were bobbing up and down with the wavelets. Slavery. . .he didn't know quite to think. What did Peter mean, "They ain't fully human like us"? They seemed human enough to him; downtrodden, perhaps, like the poor people he saw when he was in Glasgow once with his father, but still human.

For over two hours, he resisted going below deck, but eventually, a developing light rain drove him down. The slaves were huddled up against the bulkhead, the men still chained together, as Peter had predicted, with the chain, in turn, secured to a ring in the bulkhead. On the deck near them, there was a bucket of water with a ladle in it for drinking and a larger bucket for urinating and defecating. They had been given mats to lie on. The slavers, who were drinking and playing cards, cast an occasional eye in their direction. It was clear the four men were not totally comfortable with the accommodations of their charges, the *Victory* not being designed for the slave trade. Everybody was too much out in the open, not adequately confined, they thought. Oh, well, it would only be a few days until they reached New York.

For the rest of the day, Tom was uneasy. When the rain stopped, he went back up on deck. He skipped the evening meal and strolled on the deck until well after dark. Eventually, he went below, strung his hammock, and attempted to sleep, but it was long and difficult in coming. Somewhere in the group of slaves, he heard a little child begin to cry, and her mother try to quiet her. She spoke to her in English. Why English? It would be easier if she spoke something else, African or Spanish or Portuguese or something. English made her seem too human, too suffering. He thought about the slaves and then about his own situation. Had it not been for MacFie's demise, he, too, would be a slave, a temporary one perhaps, and with a kind master, but still a slave. He could not wait for this voyage to be over.

As the five-day voyage to New York progressed, the men in charge of the slaves seemed to relax a little, especially with respect to the freedom they gave the women to walk about the deck. The men remained chained to each other and to the bulkhead. Twice a day, they were loosed from the bulkhead, but not from each other, and allowed to walk on deck for a few minutes.

On the evening of the third day, Tom was leaning over the starboard rail of the ship, puffing on Robert MacFie's pipe and watching the eerie green light of the phosphorescing plankton as the disturbed ocean water rolled off the vessel's bow. As he contemplated the mystery of it all, one of the young slave women walked up the deck. She stopped about six feet from him, leaned over the rail, and stared down at the same light show. She was, perhaps, 16 or 17, quite pretty, Tom thought, from what he could see in the combined light of the mast lamp and the three-quarter moon. Her hair was tied behind her head, and she was wearing an old dress, the bodice of which fit snuggly around her slender frame. For over a minute, neither she nor Tom spoke. Then she broke the silence, still staring over the rail. "Ain't that light pretty?" she said, almost to herself.

Another slave who spoke English! How are you supposed to talk to a slave? Tom's thoughts rendered him mute, and he continued to stare at the green light.

The girl broke the silence again. "Many people think it's some sort of magic," she said, this time with words definitely directed at Tom.

He felt obligated to say something. "Some of the sailors say it's escaping energy from the souls of men drowned in the sea, but I don't believe it."

102

"Did you ever see glow worms?" she asked.

"Aye."

"Well, I think they're little animals, like glowworms, only much smaller, that ride on the waves and light up when they are bothered."

Tom didn't respond. He leaned on the rail, continuing to stare into the water, not knowing what to say, what to think. The slave…no, that wasn't quite right…the young woman was articulate. She thought about things. She had answers. She was also, he noted once more, pretty, quite pretty, as a matter of fact. He didn't like the thought that someone could own her.

"My name's Elizabeth," she broke the silence again. "What's your name, Sir?"

"Tom. Tom Hughson."

"I don't really have a second name. I guess I'll go by my new master's name when I get to New York."

"Who would that be?"

"Verplanck. Karl Verplanck. He's Dutch. The people I worked for in Jamaica lost their money, and they sold me to him. I'm gonna work in his house and help take care of his three children. I can read and cipher. My master in Jamaica did business with Mr. Verplanck. That's how they knew about me and knew I could read and work in a house. I'm luckier than the other slaves on the ship; they'll be sold at the auction and no tellin' where they'll end up."

She turned and looked at Tom. "You speak funny for an Englishman," she said, changing the subject.

She was a forward young woman, especially for a slave, but somehow Tom wasn't offended; in fact, he was a bit intrigued by her.

"Well, that's because I'm not English. I come from an island off the Scottish Highlands."

"Are you going to New York by yourself?"

"I was indentured to a gunsmith, but he died of the fever during the crossing, so now I'm free."

Free. Tom immediately wished he hadn't used that word.

"I wished I was free like you," she said. "But I ain't, and there ain't no sense in worryin' about it."

"We don't have any slaves where I come from…I'm not used to the idea of someone being a slave." He paused. "How did you get to be a slave anyway?"

"Where I come from, we live in villages, and the people grow food and tend flocks. When I was six, the men from another village came to ours and killed some of our men and took the rest of us with them. They made us walk for two days without food, and then they sold us to some Sons of Allah. The Sons of Allah tied us together with chains and made us walk for over a week until we got to a harbor with big ships. The Sons of Allah sold us to some Portuguese slave traders. For several days we waited in the harbor. Then many more slaves were brought to the ship, and the Portuguese took us to Jamaica. When we got to Jamaica, Mr. Thornhill bought my mother and me at the auction, and we went to work in his house. My mother died from the fever three years later, but I was there for ten years."

"What about your father?"

"He was killed when the men attacked our village. My mother said he was a very good man. He was strong and owned many goats."

"How did you learn to read and cipher?" Tom inquired.

She sat down on a coil of rope, her back against the rail. "Mr. Thornhill's daughter, Angeline, taught me," she answered. "She also taught me about Jesus. She was my friend. I hate that I won't see her again. She went back to England with her father."

Elizabeth paused, and then she asked, "What are you going to do in New York now that you're free? Can you make guns?"

"Nay." Tom chuckled. "I don't know a thing about makin' guns. I guess I'll have to find someone I can apprentice to."

At that moment, one of the slavers, a heavy-set man with a thumb missing from his left hand, appeared on the deck.

With a curse, he yelled at Elizabeth to get down below decks. She immediately ran to the hatch and disappeared down the ladder. For a second, Tom felt an impulse to kill the man. He could have made quick work of him, too, if only he had his father's claymore in his hands. But, at the moment, he had no claymore, and the man followed Elizabeth down the ladder and was quickly out of sight. Tom could not wait for the voyage to be over.

Chapter 11

New York City

October 1691

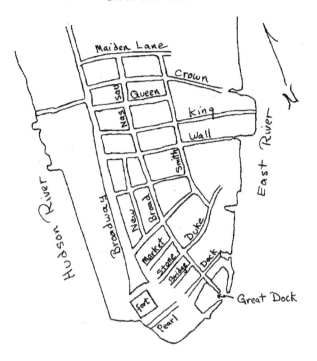

New York at the Tip of Manhattan, 1691

In five days, the voyage was over. The *Victory* sailed into New York harbor and dropped anchor in the East River to await the incoming tide. Tom occupied himself on deck with MacFie's pipe and his gunsmithing notes. From his vantage point out in the harbor, New York seemed much bigger and much busier than he expected. A bustling city of 4,000 people, where a mere 76 years before, only Indians lived. Numerous ships, mostly sloops, barks, and brigs, were tied up along the wharf, and many more were anchored in the harbor. At the foot of Whitehall on the southeastern tip of Manhattan, a large stone pier jutted out into the East River, and the waters around the pier were protected by a huge semicircular breakwater with an opening in the center for ships to pass through. He could see dozens of homes and buildings, several of them multiple stories. People, horses, and wagons were everywhere. As he contemplated the scene, Peter, the sailor who had given him his lesson in slavery, approached and leaned on the rail next to him.

"What are you goin' to do in New York, Tom?" Peter inquired.

"I don't know. I have MacFie's tools but no skills to use them. MacFie gave me the money he had, but it's not enough to get a start. I'll have to find work somewhere until I find a situation."

"Why don't you come with me, Tom? I've been thinkin' about it for the past year. There ain't no money in bein' a lowly mariner like myself. These merchants are makin' thousands of pounds with every voyage, and my share will hardly get me through the celebratin' of our successful voyage in the New York taverns. I've been thinkin' about joinin' up with a pirate ship, Tom. Five years of that, and I could be a rich man."

"A pirate ship! Peter, what are you talkin' about?"

"This harbor here in New York is filled with 'em. They're protected by the politicians. They call themselves privateers, and some of 'em have letters of marque authorizing 'em to attack French, Spanish, and Dutch merchant ships. But in truth, they often take any merchants they find. They run the trade routes between Africa and India and between Europe and Madagascar. They come back to New York to sell the booty and get their ships outfitted for the next adventure. If they don't get captured and hanged, they become very rich men. You'd like the life, Tom. From what I hear, you're treated right, and you share in the booty. We could do it for a few years and then go in business together…maybe get a ship of our own."

"I don't know anything about being a pirate…or even a mariner, for that matter."

"You could learn, Tom. And you told me yourself that you come from a fightin' family and that your father taught you how to handle a sword. Look back over our stern there. Do you see that vessel coming up behind us?"

"Aye."

"That's the *Charming Mary*. She's captained by a pirate named Richard Glover. He has friends among the powerful people here in New York. His boys will take booty from any merchant, even English ships. Around here, some folks treat him like a prime minister 'cause he spreads the booty around in the right places. We could see if Captain Glover has a spot for us if you want. If not him, some other captain. There'll be a bunch of 'em here in New York this time of year, refitting their vessels for another go at it. You're a stout lad, Tom; I think you'd make a good pirate. And you Scotsmen have no love for the English anyway. What would you care what port the merchant sailed out of? They're all money grubbers, the whole lot of 'em, and they'd just as soon see you starve in a London gutter as spit on the cobblestones."

"I don't know. I never considered bein' a mariner before, let alone a pirate. I don't take to the thought of bein' hanged neither."

Peter chuckled. "Think about it, Tom." He paused and then added, "Look at that *Charming Mary* out there. Think what it must be like to be aboard her when they run up the black flag and fire a shot over the bow of some fat merchant's pride and joy that will never make it back from Madagascar with its cargo of riches for the ladies and gentlemen of London. After we dock, come with me for a stroll up Broad Street. We'll visit a few of those taverns where the proprietors stoop low enough to serve us swabbies. We'll see what we can find out. If you decide against it, you can always leave."

Tom nodded reluctantly. "I won't get kidnapped and impressed into service, will I?"

Peter laughed. "Heavens, no. We're not talkin' 'bout the Royal Navy here. These are all proud businessmen of good character. They'll only want you if you want them. Certainly, I speak the truth, Tom. Come on, me boy; I'll buy you your first tankard of ale in the new world. New York is known for its fine breweries and fine wenches."

It was Tom's turn to laugh. "Peter, you possess a silver tongue. I'll go with you for a tankard, but I'm afraid I'm not disposed to serve the black flag."

"We'll see, lad; we'll see."

Two hours later, the *Victory* was tied up at the Great Dock, and Tom stood once again on *terra firma*. He leaned against a piling and waited for Peter to be released from his dockside chores on the ship. He studied the stevedores as they began the arduous task of unloading the ship's cargo onto the dock and into the waiting wagons and drays. He watched as the slaves were herded off the ship. For a few seconds, he caught Elizabeth's eyes as she walked with the others down the gangplank and across the wharf. She held his gaze for as long as she could until one of the slavers roughly pushed her forward into the crowd. The pathetic group was herded around the corner and up Broad Street to some warehouse that would serve as a holding cell until they could be transferred to their new masters. By 1711 the Meal Market at the foot of Wall Street would be the city's venue for such transactions, but for now, slave trading was not yet that organized. For a few moments, Tom felt a violent hatred well up inside him and an urge to kill.

In very short order, however, it subsided and was replaced by a feeling of panic, the same panic Tom felt the night MacFie died. For the first time in his life, he was thoroughly scared. He felt a sense of foreboding; he did not know how he could survive in this new land...this New York. He missed Scotland and the comfort of his parents' home. Even Elizabeth was better off; after all, she had a place to sleep and food to eat, didn't she? Damn, Mr. MacFie, anyway! Tom was glad for Peter's friendship, but their planned adventure to the mariners' taverns made him uneasy. He'd never consider going to sea...but would he? He had nothing else to do and nowhere else to go. MacFie's chests wouldn't be offloaded until tomorrow morning, anyway. Tomorrow perhaps he could look for a gunsmith.

An hour and a half later, Peter finally surfaced. Tom noticed that he had changed his blouse, and he appeared ready to introduce his young Scottish friend to the underside of New York. Tom was impressed with the way Peter seemed to know his way around. Of course, this was his sixth voyage to New York. The pair walked north on Broad Street. People seemed to be everywhere. A couple minutes later, Tom found himself at the door of his first tippling house, an establishment called Lovelace's Tavern.

The tavern consisted of one large room, dark, filled with pipe smoke, and very noisy with talk, laughter, and copious amounts of profanity. A huge fireplace blazed away in the far wall, and the patrons were gathered on benches around six long heavy trestle tables roughly hewn out of oak. On the left was a dark oak counter that ran almost the entire length of the room. Behind its protection sat the kegs of ale and, on two shelves, rows of pewter tankards and a few bottles of brandy and rum, undoubtedly imported from some distant land. What light there was came from the fireplace as well as several candles mounted in lanterns on the walls and placed in holders at irregular intervals along the tables.

It was clear from their dress and their talk that most of the 35 or 40 patrons in the establishment were sailors; some of them Tom recognized from the *Victory*. The proprietor was a huge man with arms, Tom judged, as big as his own thighs. He wore a leather apron, the pocket of which jingled with a good deal of silver. He was assisted by three young women, certainly some of the wenches Peter had been talking about. They moved expertly among the men, filling tankards, taking money, and warding off the comments and pinches from men no longer in complete control of their faculties or inhibitions. An older plump woman remained behind the counter, busying herself with various minor chores. She had an air of self-importance about her, which Tom took to mean that she was probably the proprietor's wife.

Tom found the place a little frightening, and he hesitated in the doorway. But his guide nudged him forward and toward a table where one of Peter's shipmates was entertaining five fellow drinkers with a story about a wench he had recently met in Jamaica. As the two approached the table, he stopped his story and said,

"Ah, Peter, come here, me lad, and take a seat. I see you've got the gunsmith in tow, and already you're tryin' to corrupt the poor lad's morals and assure his passage to Hell."

Everyone laughed, including Peter and Tom, and Peter added, "Boys, meet Mr. Tom Hughson. He's Scottish, and this here's his first voyage to New York."

One of the other men at the table said, "Sit down, lads. Let's see how this here Scotsman holds his liquor." Another well-intended and humorous comment was made about the convenience of kilts, and everyone laughed again. Tom was surprised at how friendly the drinkers seemed to be, and he felt his anxiety begin to subside over his present situation.

As fate would have it, the conversation around the table turned to the topic of privateering. One of the men had been on Captain Glover's ship, which had, like the *Victory*, docked that afternoon. He recounted the highlights of their last voyage and the plunder they had just brought back to New York. The final settling-up with the ship's crew would not come for two weeks, but Caleb—that was his name— reckoned his share would be substantial.

"Why does it take two weeks?" Tom inquired.

"Well," replied Caleb, "the loot has to be gone over by associates of some important Dutchman named Frederick Philipse and a price agreed upon. Philipse takes his share, re-outfits Glover's ship, and we go out and do it again. Philipse owns a manor north of the city. He's got to be the richest man twixt here and London. Right upstanding member of the community, he is, too. Everyone treats him like royalty, despite the fact he's Dutch. When the English took New York, that Dutchman managed to hold on to everything. For certain, he knew whose palms to grease, bless his greedy soul."

Caleb had the floor. He felt himself beginning to wax eloquent despite his ale-thickened tongue. He continued Tom's civics lesson. "I never did like the Dutch myself. They're an arrogant bunch. They call us Englishmen 'John Cheese,' I guess because we favor it so much on our tables. Only they can't say the words right. When it comes out, it sounds more like 'Yankee.' I'm glad the Duke of York and his buddy Nicolls finally ran the bastards out of New York."

Peter got right to the point. "You reckon Captain Glover could use a couple extra brave seamen on his next voyage?"

"Peter!" Tom interjected.

"Who you got in mind, lad?" the swashbuckler asked.

"Why me and Tom, here, of course," Peter replied in a voice that sounded as tough and manly as possible. "I've been at sea for four years already, and Tom here is new to

115

the sea, but he's stout and a good fighter, and he can hold his own with a sword against any of the lot of you!"

"Peter, stop it!" Tom demanded once again as some hissing and cursing rose from a few of those seated around the table.

In a good-natured way, Caleb put a stop to the developing situation by addressing Peter's question.

"Well, Peter, me boy, the captain would likely have a spot for you, but Tom here has to get his sea legs before he can sign on with the likes of us. The brother tars can't have anyone pukin' over the rail while there's piratin' to be done amongst the swells if you git my meaning."

Another man at the table weighed into the conversation. He was older than the rest, with gray hair, and the top of his right ear was missing. He addressed Tom.

"Scotsman, if you want to get some water under your keel, you can always talk with one of them cut-throat crimps."

"What's a crimp?" Tom inquired.

Peter interjected, "It's a mariner recruiting agent. Those scum are all over these docks. I don't recommend that you deal with 'em, Tom."

Ignoring the interruption, the older man continued. "Or, you might talk with one of these merchants who run the sloops in the coastal trade between here and New England,

116

Tom. That way, if you git green around the gills, you can always be set ashore." The other men laughed.

"Matter of fact, there was a gent in here not an hour ago lookin' for a deck hand to help him run a cargo of wheat and molasses up to Boston and then over to Salem."

"Salem is a piece north of Boston," Peter interjected. "Where can we find him, friend?" he asked the old mariner.

"I believe his name is Griggs. Said his sloop was tied up almost to the end of Great Dock, and he'll be spendin' the evening on it."

"Let's go talk with him," Peter encouraged. Tom merely stared at his tankard. "Come on, Tom. You ain't got nothin' to lose. Who knows, maybe you'll even have a place to sleep tonight." Then he added, "We'll go find Mr. Griggs. Let me do the talkin'. I feel a wee bit responsible for your future now that I got you started thinkin' these mariner thoughts."

A minute later, the two were back out on Broad Street headed for Great Dock. There was a slight chill in the October evening air. It was a short walk to the Great Dock, and just as Caleb had directed, there was a sloop, perhaps 50 feet long, tied up on the north side almost at the dock's end. A man was on the deck, sitting on a keg and smoking a clay pipe. As the two young men approached, he was the first to speak.

"Evenin', lads. You boys out for a stroll along the dock?" John Griggs was a powerfully built, handsome man beyond

117

middle age, but presenting a youthful demeanor enhanced by his still-brown hair tied neatly behind his head. He was busy splicing a rope through a brass ring.

"Aye, Sir," Peter replied. "We're looking for Captain Griggs. Are you, by chance, the same?"

"I am. And who might you lads be?"

"The name's Wilkins, Peter Wilkins, and this here's Tom Hughson. I am a mariner by trade, and I'm proud to say that I sail under Captain Hastings, master of the *Victory* you see at dockside over yonder. We sailed from England by way of Jamaica, and our holds are filled with cargo sure to satisfy the cravings for delicacies of the ladies and gentlemen of this fine city. We're here because the boys at the Lovelace's tavern said you, Sir, were lookin' for a good man to help sail this beautiful vessel to Boston and Salem." He continued.

"Tom here is lookin' for just such a situation. He doesn't know much about the sea, just what he learned being a passenger aboard the *Victory*. However, he's a stout fellow and willin' to learn, and I can vouch for his character. He's honest as any Scotsman can be." Peter was waxing eloquent; the drink had loosened his silver tongue just the right amount.

John Griggs chuckled in a good-natured way, in the process reducing the tension Tom was experiencing over the whole situation. "Well, come aboard, gentlemen, and we'll discuss this over some rum."

118

The *Prudence*, that was her name, seemed to be a sound vessel, painted, washed, and everything in its place. A single lantern hung from the boom on her mast and cast a friendly glow on the deck. The gentle evening swells in the harbor made the lantern swing back and forth ever so slightly, creating slowly undulating patterns of light and shadows on the deck and piles of canvas-covered cargo.

"So you're a Scotsman, Tom Hughson," Griggs began as he produced two more pewter cups and a bottle of rum.

"Aye, Sir. I was indentured to a gunsmith who planned to establish a business here in New York, but he died of the fever on the voyage over. He gave me his tools, but I lack the skill to use them. I need to find work, and my plan was to try to find another gunsmith, but Peter, here, suggested I come to see you about a situation as a mariner."

"A situation, huh?" Griggs chuckled again. "Well, Tom, I may have a situation for you, as you call it. This here is my vessel. She's loaded with pork, molasses, wheat, and gunpowder. She's usually skippered by a man named Willis Henry. I sent him on a run down to Charleston in another one of my boats, and he hasn't returned yet, so I'm makin' this trip myself. I planned to set sail for Boston tomorrow, but one of the crew changed his mind at the last minute. Said his wife was about ready to give birth, and he wanted to be near her. That left me one man down for the trip. Time's gettin' awfully short, and I guess the good Lord sent you to me, so you'll have to do. Are you a quick learner, Tom Hughson?"

"Aye, Sir, very quick," Tom assured him even as he was trying to assure himself that he was doing the right thing.

"Did you come down with the collywobbles on your voyage over?"

Collywobbles? Tom shot a quick inquiring glance in Peter's direction.

"No, Sir," Peter assured him. "Never once did his gills turn green that I ever saw. Isn't that right, Tom?"

"Nay, Sir," Tom confirmed. "The seasickness never visited me, not even during the big storm we passed through."

"Well, it's settled then. I'll feed you and pay you six pounds wages; three when we arrive in Boston and three more when we return to New York. You'll help me sail her and unload and load her cargo. I've got two other men in the crew. They'll be here tomorrow morning, and we'll go out with the tide at 8:00 o'clock. You'll learn a lot about the sea from them if you've got a mind to."

Griggs looked at Peter and said, "I don't reckon I could interest you in a 'situation' like I have for your friend here."

"Aye, that's correct, Captain Griggs. I appreciate the offer, Sir, but I plan to sail with Captain Glover, if he'll have me."

"Glover! You may live a short life, my boy, but if you don't swing from a yardarm or get drawn and quartered by a French marine's cutlass, you'll come back with more in your purse than I could ever pay you."

"I'm prayin' it will be the latter, Sir," Peter said with a convincing air of confidence that brought out another chuckle from Griggs.

At that moment, Tom felt a wave of relief that, unlike Peter, he was not on his way to becoming a buccaneer. Already John Griggs and the *Prudence* were providing him with a sense of comfort that he had not felt since before MacFie's death.

"Captain Griggs, I have a chest of tools Mr. MacFie gave me before he died. It'll be offloaded tomorrow from the *Victory*, and I have to see to it before I leave."

"We'll take care of that in the morning, Tom. I have a warehouse off Pearl Street. One of my agents can see that the chest is taken there for safekeeping until we return. Where are your accommodations for the evening, gentlemen?"

"I have none, Sir," Tom offered.

"Well, then, you can stay on board with me if you wish. The crew's bunks are still empty. Where are your belongings?"

"I have a duffel still on the *Victory*," Tom said. "I can go now to fetch it."

Peter bade his farewell, and the two young men hopped down to the dock and struck out for the *Victory*.

"See how easy that was?" Peter said encouragingly. "Captain Griggs seems like a good man. I believe he'll treat you fair. Do what he tells you, and learn fast. After you get your sea legs, perhaps we'll sail together someday."

"Thank you, Peter, for looking after me. I count you as a real friend."

Peter didn't answer, and the two walked in silence until they reached the *Victory*, where Tom retrieved his duffel. Peter accompanied Tom back down the *Victory's* gangplank.

"Be a good sailor, Tom, and look out for a red sky in the morning. In these waters, it means foul weather is coming." The two young men shook hands, and Tom turned and walked back down Great Dock toward his new life.

He strolled slowly along Great Dock back to the *Prudence*. Despite the late hour, the dock was very busy with people: sailors, stevedores, merchants, even women. Each of them seemed to be preoccupied with buying, selling, organizing, arranging, and talking. The number of languages they spoke amazed the young man from Scotland. How could so many different people have come to this place so quickly? Dutch, British, French, Swedes, Italians, Spaniards, Portuguese, Iberian Jews, and, of course, the black Africans.

And who knows how many others? New York...this strange city, cut out of the wilderness, and hardly 50 years old. What would it be like in another 50 years? Tom wondered if he'd be anywhere near New York in 1741 to find out or, for that matter, if he'd even be alive.

At one point, he stopped to watch three sailors, too full of rum, fishing their comrade out of the water after he fell in while trying to relieve himself. They hollered and shouted directions at each other in some foreign tongue, Portuguese, perhaps, Tom conjectured. Finally, a line offered from a nearby barque did the trick, and the dripping sailor was hauled to safety amid boisterous laughing and cursing.

Upon reaching the *Prudence*, Tom found John Griggs still on deck and still smoking his pipe. "Come aboard. Tom, my boy," he said. "Pass up that duffel."

Tom handed his bag over the vessel's rail and climbed aboard. The two men shook hands again.

"I want to thank you once more, Captain Griggs, for taking me on. I promise that I'll work hard and learn fast. I already learned much about the sea on my voyage over to New York."

"I'm sure you did, but there's lots more to learn. Please call me 'John.' This vessel, although a truly noble piece of work and out of my own brother's shipyard in Boston, is not large enough to merit a 'Captain' or a 'Mr.' for its skipper," he said with a smile. "Richard Perkins and John Dobbs make up the rest of the *Prudence* crew. They'll be here early in the morning. They're both good men and experienced mariners. There's much that you can learn from them. I'll show you where you can drop that duffel."

Tom followed Griggs into a small cabin aft on the boat. Its low ceiling forced Tom to duck considerably, more than Griggs because of the young man's six-foot frame. The cabin contained a table and four stools, a cupboard, and some shelves holding everything from candles and eating utensils to charts, gunpowder, and shot. The cabin also contained three narrow bunks; two were built into the aft end of the cabin, one above the other. The third was along the port side of the cabin. It appeared to Tom to be a bit longer than the other two.

"We share the bunks, Tom, but for tonight take that one on the port side. It's a little longer and may better accommodate those long Scottish legs of yours. I'll be down directly. You try out the bunk. I'll need you fresh come morning. By the way, we'll be taking on a passenger tomorrow, a preacher making his way to his new parish out on Long Island."

Tom dropped onto the bunk. He was in the middle of a silent prayer of thanks for God's quick delivery from his plight when he lost consciousness.

Chapter 12

Elizabeth

New York, October 1691

Elizabeth and the group of slaves from the *Victory* were herded off the dock and up Mulberry Street to a warehouse owned by Uriah Lockley. It was a large, dark structure with a loft, and it contained an array of cargo stacked against its walls. The slavers drove the men and boys to a corner, the chain connecting them secured to a beam with a lock. They shut the women and children in a room in another corner, the walls of which were solid for four feet and then made of thick wooden bars that extended to the ceiling. It was more like a large stall than a room. There was no furniture in it, but the floor was covered in several inches of straw. The slavers placed a bucket of water with a dipper and an old chamber pot in the room with the women so they could attend to their needs.

The person in charge of the warehouse was John Cruger, a big, powerfully-built man, rough-hewn, with a large purple birthmark that covered his left cheek and eyelid. In one hand, he carried a coiled whip made of braided leather.

"Give me the papers, Cunningham," he ordered one of the slavers from the ship. "Let me make sure I've got the whole lot before I sign off on 'em."

Cruger and Cunningham went, first, to the men and boys, making them identify themselves by name and comparing their names and descriptions with the bill of lading.

"Be careful of those three with the brands on their backs, Mr. Cruger," Cunningham warned. "They have been considerable trouble to their previous masters in Jamaica…runnin' away and thievin'. Whoever buys them'll have their hands full, I expect." Both men laughed.

Cruger walked closer to the group and stood directly in front of the three branded men.

"Now, listen good, you black heathen!" he began. "You're gonna be here a few days 'till we can sell you to some fine folks in this here city. Until that time, and as long as you're here with me in my place of business, you will mind your behavior and give neither me nor my men any trouble. Anyone who forgets what I just said will feel my lash upon his back, or maybe I'll just hang him from that loft over there to let it be a lesson to the rest of ya. If any of you unlucky vermin thinks I am just waggin' my jaws, try me, and I assure you'll find out. You English speakers, tell the others what I just said."

As a group, the slaves remained motionless on the floor and looked at the dirt. All that is, except for a young branded man named Bartholomew, who stared into Cruger's eyes as he talked. Cruger stared back, and when he finished his remarks, he said. "Stand up, boy. What's your name again?"

The young man hesitated just an instant.

"I said, what's your name, boy?"

"Bartholomew."

Well, Bartholomew, let me start with you. Unchain him from the others and tie him to that post."

Two of Cruger's employees did as they were told.

"Strip his shirt off him."

It was done.

"Boy, you need to learn to respect your superiors better and act more lowly. Maybe a few lashes will help."

With that, Cruger uncoiled the whip he was carrying and proceeded to apply ten lashes to the young man's back. For the first three or four lashes, the slave uttered nothing, but by the fifth lash, he was screaming. By the tenth lash, he was unconscious.

"Untie him and chain him to the rest," Cruger ordered.

"Mr. Cruger," one of the men offered, "with that back, he won't be ready to sell this Tuesday with the rest of 'em."

"We'll keep him here a couple weeks," Cruger retorted, already regretting his excessive punishment. A short temper can be a costly thing to a trader in slaves.

After dealing with the men and boys, Cruger strode over to the stall and turned his attention to the women and children, verifying each one's presence and giving them much the same warning. He was about to turn and go when he remembered.

"Which one of you is the Elizabeth who's going to Verplanck?"

"I am, Sir," Elizabeth responded softly.

"Well, get up, girl, and come with me. We're gonna deliver you to your new master today. His wife has been askin' after you for the last two weeks. My, you're a fine lookin' one, and they say you can read 'n write, too. You're a lucky girl to be bought already by them folks."

Clutching the small burlap sack that contained all her worldly possessions, Elizabeth got up from the straw and followed Cruger out of the dark building.

"Jeremiah!" he hollered at another one of his workers. "Take the cart and deliver this slave girl to Karl Verplanck over on Stone Street." He owes me £65 pounds for her, so make sure you come back with every farthing of it in your possession. Now get along!"

Elizabeth climbed onto the back of the cart and, with Jeremiah at the reins, she began the last leg of her journey to a slave's life in New York.

****

The Verplanck residence was a large, fashionable, three-story brick home of the classic Dutch stepped-gable style.

128

Like others of its type, it was on a narrow lot that extended for some distance behind the structure, providing ample space for other buildings, a stable, and gardens. Elizabeth judged that Karl Verplanck must be quite wealthy.

Holding Elizabeth by her arm, Jeremiah tapped the big brass doorknocker three times. Mrs. Verplanck opened the front door.

"This here's your new slave girl, Mum," Jeremiah said. "Mr. Cruger says I'm to bring back £65 pounds for her, or he'll tan me hide."

"Take her around back to the cabin. I'll come there presently with your money," the mistress of the house responded.

The cabin was an old wooden two-room structure, each room with its own door. One room was where the slave, William, stayed. William's duties included general maintenance at the residence and keeping the gardens, which were quite substantial. The other room provided the quarters for Mariah, an elderly slave who was responsible for cooking and sewing for the family. Mariah would now have to share this room with Elizabeth.

In three minutes, Mrs. Verplanck appeared, paid Jeremiah, and opened the door to Elizabeth's room. There was a table and two chairs on one side and two cots on the other. Clothing and some other articles hung from pegs on the walls. In addition to the door, there was one window facing out the west side of the room. A small fireplace in the rear would provide heat in the winter.

"Elizabeth," she began rather stiffly, "I want to welcome you to our house. You may address me as 'Mrs. Verplanck,' and my husband as 'Mr. Verplanck.' You will sleep here with Mariah. She's my house servant and is responsible for cooking and other household chores."

"Yes, Ma'am," the young slave girl answered.

"Because Mariah is getting on in years, you are to help her with her chores as well as tend to the needs of our three young children. I understand you can read and write. Is that true, Elizabeth?'

"Yes, Ma'am. I learned from my mistress in Jamaica. I can read the Bible real good!"

"Well…yes." There was a pause. "That's fine, Elizabeth. You will be reading to the children, then, and providing them instruction if we decide you are able."

"I will try, Ma'am," Elizabeth responded.

"You will take your meals with William and Mariah in the kitchen after the family has eaten. You do not have to work on Sundays unless there is a special occasion. You can attend Negro church services with Mariah if you wish." A pause. "You said you read the Bible. Does that mean you are a Christian, Elizabeth?"

"Yes, Ma'am, I am. I was baptized when I was eight. Thank you, Ma'am."

"Elizabeth, it is not my habit to be overly strict with our servants. You will have the freedom to come and go as long as you do your chores. I will give you four shillings a month for you to spend."

And then she added, "I expect you to be moral and well-behaved and not bring any disgrace on our family. You will keep yourself clean at all times; I'll not have you in a soiled dress. Do not become familiar with any males, Elizabeth. You will find Mr. Verplanck to be fair, but he will not tolerate insolence, laziness, rough language, or misbehavior in any form. He will whip you, Elizabeth, if you engage in any behavior not appropriate to your station. Do you understand?"

"Yes, Ma'am, I understand," the girl replied.

"Also, I want you to speak the best English you can, especially around the children. I'll have none of that slave talk from the islands in my home."

"Yes, Ma'am, I will try."

"Fine. If you have any questions, you may address them to me or ask Mariah. I have a dress here that will fit you. Put it on, and then I want you to come to the house and meet our children."

131

Having completed her welcoming remarks, Margrietje Verplanck turned and walked out the cabin door.

Chapter 13

Captain Griggs

New York Harbor, October 1691

Early the next morning, Tom Hughson was awakened by the footsteps of men on the deck of the *Prudence*. Richard Perkins and John Dobbs had arrived, and they were discussing the upcoming voyage with Captain Griggs. From the enticing aroma wafting through the air, Tom knew they were drinking coffee that someone, probably Griggs, had made on an open fireplace on the dock. Tom jumped to his feet and appeared on the deck.

"Mornin,' Tom," Griggs greeted. "Boys, this here's Tom Hughson from Scotland. He'll be takin' Matthew's place for this voyage. Tom, meet John Dobbs and Richard Perkins. Tom doesn't know much about being a mariner yet, just what he learned watching the swabbies on his recent trip over from England. But I told him you boys would teach him the ways of a seafarin' man."

Richard was the older of the two, probably in his early forties, hair already speckled with a little gray. John, on the other hand, was about Tom's age, well-built, and with a seaman's tan, despite his blue eyes and blond hair. Richard spoke up first.

"We'd be delighted, Tom, me boy. Welcome aboard." Both men extended a hand to the rookie sailor.

It was a beautiful late October morning, typical for that time of year. The sun was already up over the Brooklyn hills, and the cloudless sky signaled the makings of a great day to begin life as a mariner. Gulls seemed to be everywhere, and off in the distance, Tom spotted a V-shaped squadron of geese on their way south for the winter. This morning, however, winter seemed very far away. Already the Great Dock was awash in people, horses, wagons, carts, and cargo. The ships tied at the dock bobbed up and down in cadence with the gentle swells that managed to survive the harbor's protective seawall. Tom and the other two men got to work loading the last of the cargo, barrels of pork, from a wagon and down into the hold of the *Prudence*. The men were friendly enough, and Tom found them accepting of his newcomer status. While they worked, Richard, the more talkative of the two, began Tom's education with some basic principles of seamanship and sail handling. During a break, Tom got his first knot-tying lesson from John Dobbs, who was impressed that Tom already knew how to tie a square knot, bowline, half-hitch, clove-hitch, and sheepshank.

"Where did you learn to tie those knots, Tom?" John inquired.

"From my grandfather in Scotland. He used to sail between the Highlands and the Isles when he was a young man, and he did some fishing. He also taught me how to mend nets."

"You know how to use one of them flat wooden needles?" Richard interjected.

"I could handle one real well when I was young, and I guess I could recall it."

"Maybe you could whittle one and show me how to use it. What are they made of?"

"I guess anything would do, but my grandfather made them out of ash. Ashwood keeps sharp longer."

Their conversation was interrupted by the arrival of the Reverend Reginald Avery MacLeash, the passenger to Long Island whom John Griggs had mentioned. He came in a wagon and was accompanied by a large chest full of his worldly possessions. He was a slender man of about 40, Tom guessed. He had the look of a person who worked hard for a living and was used to the out-of-doors. His flame-red hair was beginning to recede, and he wore it long and tied it back with a blue ribbon. Tom thought that blue was an odd color for a man of the cloth, but then he'd come to learn that preachers were often an unpredictable lot.

"Gentlemen," he began, addressing the whole group in a Scottish accent. "Is this the ship owned by Master John Griggs?"

"Aye, that it is, and I am he," replied John, who was at the bow inspecting the lashings securing some cargo on the deck. "You must be the Parson Reginald Avery MacLeash bound for Long Island."

"That I am. You may call me Reginald, for I am also a lowly schoolmaster and farmer, trades that I hope will sustain me whilst I spread the gospel to the kindred spirits of Wading River. You can, I trust, take me and my trunk to Wading River in this worthy ship?"

"We'll have you there by dark if the winds blow fair, Parson MacLeash. This here's my crew. John Dobbs, Richard Perkins, and Tom Hughson."

"Tom Hughson, is it?" MacLeash inquired as he shook Tom's hand. "Aye, a highlander and probably a Catholic or Anglican, too. That means I have one day and a short ride on the sea to convert you to Presbyterianism," he said with a good-natured laugh. "It will be good practice for what awaits me in Wading River. They tell me I'll be bringin' the gospel to fallen Puritans. Oh, well, the work of the Lord is never easy."

Chuckles circulated among the crew, and then Griggs organized the group. "Men, haul the parson's trunk aboard, cast off the lines, and let's repair to Wading River with all dispatch."

Griggs gave the commands while his crew of three scurried about the ship, casting off lines, hauling in fenders, securing the skiff to the stern, and setting the sails. For all his inexperience, Tom held his own, following orders and responding positively to the corrections the three men handed out. Once the mainsail and jib were set, the *Prudence* began to make good headway, aided by a westerly breeze that had come up and for which MacLeash took credit. He had been praying to the Lord, he said, for a speedy and safe voyage. With John Griggs at the tiller, the *Prudence* moved smartly through the seawall and north up the East River, through Hell Gate, and into Long Island Sound. Tom noticed how the ship picked up speed as the men trimmed the sail, pulling the boom closer to the centerline of the vessel. He watched the tell-tales flutter aft on the canvas, and he was lectured on how to use them to set the canvas to its greatest advantage.

When they had been underway about an hour and had passed the several small islands on the western end of the Sound, Captain Griggs called Tom to the stern, gave him some brief instructions, and let him have the tiller.

"Tom, you are now a helmsman, a most important person aboard any vessel, responsible for its safety and direction. You are in command of the ship unless, of course, you are relieved of your duties by the captain."

He then gave Tom his first order. "Hold her steady a mile or two off the shore and about eighty degrees on the compass for a while. I'll tell you when to change the bearing."

"Aye, aye, Sir," is all Tom could think to say.

The other crew members shouted words of encouragement and smiled as they watched Tom, with a serious countenance, rise to the gravity of his task, eyes glued to the ship's needle, with occasional glances over the bow and the horizon beyond. According to the chart, it was about 60 miles to where Wading River should be, a good place to anchor for the evening.

In the event of inclement weather, there was a good-sized harbor twelve or so miles west of Wading River that the voyagers could slip into if the need arose. Captain Griggs learned about that harbor from a man named John Roe. He and his wife and two children had been the first to settle there in 1682 at the edge of the harbor, a place he called "Drowned Meadow." Since then, others had moved to the harbor, mostly to fish. It would take many years before the harbor, eventually known as Port Jefferson, would take its place among the great shipbuilding communities along the Atlantic coast.

Parson Reginald Avery MacLeash, it turned out, was a very interesting character. As a young man, he had been in His Majesty's army. He was severely wounded while protecting the king from an unsuccessful assassination attempt, and during his long convalescence, he became a Christian and entered into a four-year self-study of the scriptures and the writings of the great Christian thinkers of the period. During this time, he supported himself by farming a small plot of land with his family in Bannockburn in the central Lowlands. He had been married four years when he lost his wife to the fever before they had any children. His wife's death was a turning point in his life, and he made the decision to come to the new world. His original thought had been to become a missionary to the Indians, but upon arriving in New York, he was dissuaded from that plan by tales of brutal savagery committed by the Iroquois. It was then that he learned of the need in Wading River for a parson. It was nothing more than a small village, founded by eight families, mostly from Southold, less than twenty years old, but it was a place to begin. The hamlet now had over twenty families; its roots had taken hold. Perhaps someday, Parson MacLeash would become the rector in a church like Trinity in New York, but for now, he'd have to get his start, and Wading River seemed as good as any other place that would have him.

True to his word, the Reverend produced a pipe, lit it quite expertly with a flint and steel, and then sat down near Tom with his Bible in hand.

"Tom, my boy, let me tell you about how almighty God is in charge of everything. Before the foundation of the world, He ordained that you should be, even at this moment, at the tiller of this magnificent vessel."

Thus began Tom's tutorial on predestination. Tom was a good student; he was polite and respectful, but he never let his attention sway from the all-important task at hand; helmsman for the *Prudence*, piloting the good ship toward her destination. Occasionally Griggs would look up from a worn book he was reading and shoot an approving glance in Tom's direction. The parson's lesson lasted until it was time to eat lunch when John Dobbs mercifully called a halt to the discourse by asking the man of the cloth to bless the breaking of the noontime bread.

"All-powerful and most merciful Father," he began. "We praise Thee and confess before Thee all our sins, consisting of things we have done and things we have left undone. We thank Thee for this fine vessel and the sinful creatures who are guiding it safely to its proper destination, which would be Wading River. We thank Thee for this fine day, for the favorable winds, and for the bounteous meal Thou hast, in Thy Providence, set before us. Bless us as we partake of these morsels, and bless especially young Tom Hughson as your humble servant attempts to show him the true Presbyterian way. We pray these things in Jesus' name."

And all the crew said, "Amen."

After their lunch of bread and cheese, Richard asked Tom if he wanted him to spell the young sailor at the tiller. Tom, of course, graciously declined the offer and maintained his coveted station as the ship's helmsman. The warm October afternoon sun beat down on the voyagers, and before long, the parson was fast asleep on a pile of canvas on the deck, his Bible open to the Book of Psalms, the words resting on his chest. Tom uttered a short prayer of thanks.

As is typical for that time of day, the wind died down a little, and the *Prudence* slowed her pace through the two-foot swells. Two porpoises fell in behind the ship, keeping perfect pace as they leapt back and forth in front of each other, their bodies occasionally coming completely out of the water. Tom had heard the stories about porpoises, how they had been known to protect sailors from sharks and even push them ashore when they had fallen overboard. They seemed to Tom like very comical creatures, able to enjoy life to the fullest, a life, he thought, well worth imitating.

The course set by Captain Griggs kept the *Prudence* about a mile or so offshore, far enough out to avoid the possibility of encountering rocks or sandbars but close enough for Tom to take in the beauty of the shoreline as they proceeded eastward. At some points, the shore sloped gently up into hardwood forests that hadn't yet given up their leaves to the coming winter. At others, tall sandy bluffs separated the shore from the woods beyond. At one point, Tom saw the smoke from fires on the beach, which were surrounded by clusters of Indians, mostly women and children. Richard said they were probably drying fish for the winter. That distant view was Tom's first exposure to Indians, the heathen about whom so many stories had been told.

"How many of 'em are out there?" he asked Richard as the two men watched the scene on the beach.

"Nobody knows for sure, but they're less than they were, what with the whites taking over and the Mohawk raiding parties from Connecticut. They are dying off more from the white man's diseases than anything else. It won't be long before they're gone from Long Island and everywhere else," he added. "They should 'a known their number was up when that black Portuguese sea captain...what was his name...Gomez, that was it...first sailed into New York harbor 150 years ago, grabbed 50 of 'em, and took 'em back to Europe to be sold as slaves.

"How did you learn that, Richard?" Tom inquired.

"My great grandmother," he replied. "She was Portuguese, and she hated slavery with a passion. She said that when her grandfather was a young man, he was in Lisbon when Gomez brought the Indians in. He watched 'em being sold at auction. Poor bastards, those savages. They didn't have a horse; they never got to the wheel or figured out how to use metal. They're doomed."

"You sound like you feel sorry for 'em," Griggs interjected, looking up from his book. He had been listening to the conversation.

"Well, maybe I do a bit. But they're in the way, and they got to go, and I guess disease is better than shootin' them all. They ain't quite human like us, but the Good Lord must of made 'em for some purpose."

Tom's mind flashed back to Elizabeth and to Peter's comment, "Ain't quite human." If you ain't quite human, you're in trouble.

In the mid-afternoon, John Dobbs finally took over the tiller from Tom, and the young sailor found a comfortable spot near the bow. The parson was up and about, but when he approached Tom, the latter feigned sleep to avoid another Sunday school lesson. With the help of the afternoon sun, his feigned sleep was soon supplanted with the real thing, and for the next 45 minutes, *Prudence* had to get along without him.

Around 4:30 that evening, the *Prudence* passed the harbor containing John Roe and his "Drowned Meadow" that was to be a sanctuary, should the weather turn. Tom noted how pretty it was in the late afternoon sunlight, protected by two spits of shoreline and surrounded by gently rising forested land on its three remaining sides. He wondered why the people of Wading River hadn't settled there instead. Eventually, people would find it, settle there, and boats would fill its protected waters. Some day in the future, it would become Port Jefferson, but its time had not yet arrived.

Chapter 14

Wading River

October 1691

Half an hour later, anticipation was growing among the voyagers as the sun drew low on the horizon. It was especially evident in the parson. "Captain Griggs, in my letter I posted over a fortnight ago, I asked Mr. Hallack, that's the farmer I'll be staying with, to send his son to the beach to meet me. I asked him to light a fire in case we arrived later than expected. If he received that letter, perhaps we'll have a welcoming committee."

Griggs, impressed with MacLeash's foresight, relaxed a little. Of course, he had sailed these waters before and had a good idea of the landforms, but his course typically took him further offshore, so a fire would never hurt.

MacLeash continued. "From what Hallack told me, I believe you'll see the bluffs drop off and give way to some low sand dunes with a great marsh behind. A small river flows into or out of the marsh, depending on the tide. The road from the village meets the beach at the east end of the marsh. That's where Hallack's boy should be, that is if the Indians didn't get to the post rider first," he added with a faint laugh.

"Aye, I recall the location, Parson," Griggs replied, relieved to have his knowledge of the area confirmed and elaborated. Twenty minutes later, a red sun was dropping below the western horizon, and the bluffs, as if on cue, gave way to sand dunes and the great marsh behind. And the little river appeared, dumping its water into the Sound in response to the receding tide. Another 200 yards and a fire materialized on the beach about half a mile away.

"Praise the Lord, God almighty!" the Parson exploded. The captain and the rest of the crew remained silent but were, in concert, thinking the same thing. Tom was especially relieved. His first day as a mariner had gone off without a hitch.

John Dobbs took some soundings that persuaded Griggs to anchor about 100 yards offshore. On the beach, three men and an oxcart had assembled to welcome the new preacher/schoolmaster/farmer to Wading River. Tom brought the skiff around, and John and Richard expertly lowered the parson's large chest into the craft. The chest went ashore first, with John at the oars. Ten minutes later, he returned with a message to relay.

"Captain, Jacob Hallack, himself, is on the beach, and he wishes the pleasure of our company at his home for dinner this evening, and he insists that we stay the night. He says that his straw mattresses far surpass in comfort any bunk in a rocking boat. He lives in the village, which is a mile or so from the beach, just past that marsh."

"Take him up on his offer, Captain," Tom chimed in. "I'll stay here and keep an eye on the *Prudence*."

"No, Tom, I can't do that. If she slipped her anchorage, or if Indians came aboard. . ." he chuckled, "I'm afraid you'd be at a loss for what to do."

"I'll stay with her, Captain," Dobbs interjected. "You can bring me back some mutton stew in the mornin'. That's what Mrs. Hallack's cookin'. Hallack seems like a mighty fine gentleman. Should be an enjoyable time, what with good food, good ale, and good conversation. It's a beautiful evening, not a cloud in the sky. I should be able to handle it fine, I'd wager, Sir."

Despite his youth, John Dobbs sounded convincing, and the Captain of the *Prudence* made a command decision that all hands, save John, would spend the evening ashore as guests of farmer Hallack. Dobbs rowed Griggs, MacLeash, and the two seamen ashore, and in a few minutes, the men and the ox and cart, loaded with the parson's chest, were headed down the dirt path toward the village.

Thirty minutes later, at the bottom of a small hill, the village came into view in the bright moonlight. It consisted of a handful of log cabins strung out along the road, some with barns and sheds, others standing alone set back off the road. Most of the cabins had gardens beside them, and Tom could see in the waning light that a few were still laden with yet-to-be-harvested squash, turnips, pumpkins, and who knows what else. On the west side of the village, a creek had been dammed, and a good-sized millpond was in the making.

On the east side of the village, the men and the ox ended their journey at Jacob Hallack's farm. He must have been one of the more prosperous men in the hamlet. The house was of log construction, but it was large, with a chimney at either end. It had a porch on the front that extended the entire length of the structure. There was a stone well in the front yard. To the east, there were five acres of cleared land, a large barn, and several outbuildings. One of these was to be the parson's temporary living quarters until he could build his own dwelling that would be next to the church, which he also had to build. Of course, the men of the village would help. Hallack's son and the other man who had accompanied them from the beach unloaded the trunk at the parson's cabin and then saw to the ox and cart. Hallack took his guests inside, where they were greeted by his wife, Sally, and the tempting aromas wafting from the meal she had prepared.

After a dinner of mutton stew, turnip, corn, bread, and mince pie, the men adjourned to the porch, where pipes and tobacco were produced. Tom withdrew MacFie's pipe from his wool jacket and expertly lit it. The evening had a bit of a chill to it but nothing that interfered with their enjoyment of a full stomach and the prospect of some lively discussion.

Hallack set the tone for the evening's discussion. "So, Rev. MacLeash, are you ready to take charge of the lost flock of Wading River?"

"That I am, Mr. Hallack. Where is the church building to be located?"

"We passed the spot on our way from the beach. It's back a couple hundred yards west of here where the road from the south comes down the hill and intersects this one." He pointed to the road in front of his house.

"We decided that it should be north of the road," he continued, "and just east of that little pond that feeds into the millpond. We'll help you build your cabin first, and then, if the weather holds, we'll build the church building."

"Sounds like a fine plan," the parson said encouragingly. Then he asked, "How many families are here in the village?"

"We started out with eight back in '71, all Congregationalists from Connecticut. Then several Presbyterian families joined us from Massachusetts, and now there are 21 families in all. Most of 'em are farmers, but some fish and we have a cooper, a blacksmith, and a tradesman. So, you'll have to preach Congregational and Presbyterian doctrine to please everybody. I can't tell the difference between 'em anyway, and I suppose you'll manage just fine," he said with a chuckle.

"I'll do my best to spread the true gospel, Mr. Hallack. You may be assured of that, Sir. Certainly, the Lord has ordained me to the task!"

Hallack continued, "Recently, we've been joined by a few families that came from Salem, Massachusetts, through Connecticut and across the North Sea. They have some frightening stories to tell about the religious fervor of the Puritans in Salem. They believe in God but even more in the work of the Devil. They think they were placed on earth to purify the lost souls and stop the Devil and those possessed by him in their tracks. They look for witches behind every tree and under every rock. They even think that animals can be possessed. They've driven off most of the normal folk, either to Boston or down into Connecticut. That's how we got the ones who came here after a short stay in Southold. I expect your Presbyterian view of God, Heaven, and the world will come as a welcomed relief, Parson."

"I will assure them, Mr. Hallack, that I look for witches neither behind trees nor under rocks nor any other place for that matter. The Good Book makes no mention of witches." MacLeash added with a smile.

Tom noticed that John Griggs was listening intently to this conversation. Finally, Griggs remarked, "I came from England to Salem as a boy. I know what you mean about their religious fervor. In fact, it's what made me leave Salem 30 years ago. I've been back several times since, but only to

149

the docks to drop off and pick up cargo. I have an older brother there, William Griggs; he's the town doctor, but I haven't seen him in over three years. When I knew him, he was an ardent Puritan, and he believed in the evil work of the Devil. His wife, Rachel, was even worse!"

"I imagine if he's still there, he fits in very well with the fine citizens of Salem," Hallack added.

MacLeash rejoined the conversation. "The captain, here, is on his way to Boston and thence to Salem, Mr. Hallack, with provisions for the folks in those fair towns. Perhaps, Sir, you could look in on your brother, the doctor, whilst you are in Salem and report back to us on your return trip. It would be nice to know if he's discovered any remedies for demonic possession. One never knows when there might be an outbreak amongst the new Presbyterians of Wading River!"

"I will certainly look into it, Parson," Griggs promised.

Hallack blew a smoke ring, stuck his finger through it, and then announced, "I can assure you that we don't have any witches here, Parson, but we do have skunk cabbage in the spring. It grows below the millpond. I like the smell of it, myself, but I think I am alone in that attachment."

The comment brought a few chuckles from the group. Then the men fell quiet as pipes were puffed. Tom grew sleepy listening to the last frogs of autumn. Somewhere in the distance, an owl was staking out his territory in the darkness. Being a perceptive man, Jacob Hallack broke the silence. "You men must be tired from your journey. Let me show you to your beds." His offer sounded very good to Tom.

****

At 6:00 the next morning, Captain Griggs woke his crew, who had bedded down in a barn and escorted them to the breakfast table that had been laid out by Sally Hallack. After a lengthy blessing offered up by the Reverend MacLeash, the group sat down to eggs, cured bacon, more turnips, bread, and a coffee-like drink that Tom did not quite recognize. Thirty minutes later, the mariners thanked their hosts, bid their farewells, and, accompanied by Hallack's son, Joshua, and some mutton stew for John were making their way through the little village, past the pond and onto the dirt road to the beach.

Like the day before, it was a bright, crisp morning, one that seemed to portend a good day to sail. It was chilly, though, and Tom buttoned his wool jacket. As the group walked past the great marsh on the left, Tom saw a huge flock of ducks take flight, circle once, and head south. The marsh grasses, although still green, were beginning to take on a dusty brownish tinge that signaled the inevitable. Winter was on its way.

When they reached the beach, the group was welcomed by the sight of *Prudence* still on her anchor and the aroma rising from a pot of coffee brewing on a fire that John Dobbs had rekindled in a circle of rocks on the beach.

"Well, how was the evening?" he asked as tin cups were passed out to the four newcomers.

"Just as you said it would be," the captain responded. "Excellent food, good conversation, and a comfortable straw mattress. Only, there wasn't any ale," he added with a chuckle. "Wading River is a pleasant little village, and Joshua, your mother is a fine cook. Please thank her again for her kind hospitality."

He passed the covered bowl of stew over to John. "Here's your mutton. You might as well warm it up on the fire. It'll make a fine breakfast. We promised Mrs. Hallack that we'd give her bowl back to Joshua." Then he added, "Thank you, John, for minding the ship."

As the men sipped their hot coffee, Dobbs described the herd of deer that visited the beach early in the morning and how they were licking the kelp to put some salt in their diet. He also thought he spotted a gray wolf in the distance, crossing the marsh at sunrise, but he wasn't sure.

While sipping his coffee, Griggs thought of an idea. "Tom, see if you can row the skiff out to the *Prudence* and grab a sack of sugar from the crate for Mrs. Hallack. If you get in trouble, John will swim out and rescue you."

Everyone laughed while John Dobbs came to the rescue with some rowing advice.

"It's easy, Tom. Just put the oars in the locks, lower the blades into the water, and pull. Don't let the blades go too deep, and don't pull too hard because the oars will jump out of the locks. Just go easy and let the oars do the work. And, for Heaven's sake, before you climb aboard the *Prudence*, tie the skiff's rope to the rail. That way, it will still be there when you're ready to row back."

With a serious countenance, Tom got in the skiff, sat down, and set the oars. John pushed him out while the others shouted encouragement. After a minute or two of floundering around, Tom got the idea, and the skiff headed for the ship. John, who wasn't certain about the captain's swimming-out-and-rescuing comment, breathed a sigh of relief. It was late October, and the water had already cooled down considerably.

When Tom beached the skiff a few minutes later, Griggs said, "That was a good job, Tom; two days at sea and you've already become an oarsman, well...at least compared to most Scottish landlubbers."

"Aye, aye, Sir," was Tom's response as John flashed him a grin.

A half-hour later, Joshua had possession of the sugar and his mother's bowl, and the voyagers were back aboard the *Prudence*, anchor weighed and canvas set. An offshore breeze got them underway in quick order. Captain Griggs set a course that was very familiar to him from years of sailing these waters. East down the Sound, south of Fisher's Island, north of Block Island, and into the Atlantic. If the winds were right, he would take *Prudence* between Martha's Vineyard and Nantucket Island, then due northeast, staying ten miles or so off the Massachusetts shoreline, catch the currents and winds to slip around Cape Cod, north through the eastern reaches of Boston Bay, past Marble Head, and into Boston harbor. The trip would take two days. And there were any number of protective places, harbors, and the lee sides of islands, to ease into should the weather turn foul. In a repetition of yesterday morning's voyage, Tom was at the tiller and, in his youthful imagination, the fearless captain of his own privateer.

Chapter 15

The Storm

October 31, 1691

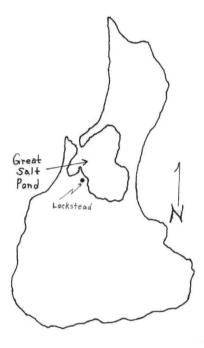

Block Island

By mid-morning, the wind had picked up and was now blowing a good breeze from the northwest. The sky in that direction had clouded over, and it appeared to Captain Griggs that a storm was on the way. Not wanting to get caught in a following sea that might overtake him, he came aft and took over the tiller from Tom. He changed course to starboard and headed for an island that lay about seven miles away. Known as Block Island, it was longer north to south than it was east to west, with high ground in the middle. The island had been settled in 1661 and was home to a score of families, most of them making a living by fishing the nearby waters. At the island's northwest end, a slip opened into a large, protected bay the settlers called Great Salt Pond. It was the perfect sanctuary to wait out a storm. The wind picked up smartly, and after the course change, it was dead on their stern. With the increasing wind came the increasing swells of the following sea. Tom was surprised by how quickly the weather could change for the worse, and the developing situation made him tense.

"If that island wasn't here, Captain," he asked John Griggs, "isn't the *Prudence* large enough to ride out a storm like this?"

"I expect we'd be alright, but there's no sense in tempting fate if you don't have to. I lasted many years on the sea by being careful. Some say I'm too careful, but I'm still here, and I have yet to lose a ship. God has been good to me, Tom. With the wind blowing like it is, it'll be a challenge getting into Great Salt Pond. We'll have to approach it just right 'cause that wind'll be square on our starboard beam."

"What do you want me to do?" the neophyte sailor asked.

"Stand by, and we'll let you know. John and Richard will soon need help with the sails, and I may need some help holding the tiller. I'll call you if I do. And whatever you do, Tom, don't fall overboard. We won't be able to stop and pick you up!"

A bolt of lightning crashed across the sky, and it began to rain. As the *Prudence* approached the northern tip of Block Island, John Griggs noticed the masts of a large ship that had already entered the Great Salt Pond. The westerly direction of the wind told him that the ship must have been there for a while. In the last couple of hours, its captain could not have sailed directly into the wind and made it through the inlet into the Pond.

In ten more minutes, the *Prudence* had reached the narrow inlet that gave way to the safety of Great Salt Pond. With a combination of the correct orders smartly obeyed at the right time and some expert maneuvering at the helm, the *Prudence* slipped through the inlet to the relief of everyone aboard, but especially Tom. By this time, the full violence of the thunderstorm was upon them, and the relatively calm waters of the Pond provided an immense amount of solace to the young mariner. With the wind square on their starboard beam and the boom of the mainsail off the port, the *Prudence* moved down the Pond as Captain Griggs looked for a place to anchor. The rain beat in sheets down on the deck and rushed in rivers through the boat's scuppers as it rolled back and forth.

On orders from Griggs, Richard and John let out the sheets, and the *Prudence* slowed. Griggs noticed a shack on the beach and a dock reaching out into the Pond, with four fishing boats tied to it. A few more boats were on moorings just off the dock; their bows pointed to the northwest as if in defiance of the storm that had assaulted them from that direction. A couple hundred yards farther out in the Pond, the ship whose masts Griggs had seen lay at anchor; it, too, facing into the storm. Griggs maneuvered the *Prudence* another fifty yards and then ordered his crew to lower the sails. Then he directed Tom to drop the anchor, which the young sailor did expeditiously, unwinding the windlass attached to the anchor chain.

"How much chain do I let out?" he yelled at Dobbs.

"Three times the depth, Tom; the scope should always be three times the depth. That way, the anchor will take a hold of the bottom. In this wind, she might drag a bit anyway, dependin' on what's down there."

Tom let out what he judged to be three times the depth and then expertly locked the windlass in place. The *Prudence*, deprived of her sails and her headway, joined the rest of the vessels and swung around to the northwest to meet the wind.

Later, as the storm began to abate, John Griggs found time to study the large three-masted galley pitching on its anchor two hundred yards off *Prudence*'s port side. It was a big ship, well-built and sporting a gun deck, the gun ports closed against the weather. Atop its main mast, it flew the English flag. Griggs took out his glass and gave the ship a visual once-over. It didn't take him long to recognize it as

158

the *Adventure*, a three-masted privateer captained by the infamous pirate, Captain William Kidd himself.

"What do you make of it, Sir?" Tom asked.

"Tom, my boy, it's none other than the ship of Captain William Kidd, a privateer, a pirate, and one of your fellow Scotsman."

He went on to tell Tom how Kidd had gained quite a reputation with letters of marque from the English crown authorizing him to prey on the merchant ships of England's enemies. At one time or another, the French, Spanish, Dutch, and Portuguese fell under that definition, and they all learned to fear the sight of the *Adventure*. The agreement was that Kidd would bring the booty back to London, and he and his crew would receive a portion as a prize, the rest going to the King.

Of course, much of the prizes taken from the unfortunate vessels plying the waters between Madagascar, east Africa, the Mediterranean, and the French harbors never made it back to the king's coffers. Rather it ended up in New York, where the good captain exchanged it for gold and silver through arrangements with some of the most prominent merchants and businessmen of that city. The most notable was Frederick Philipse, a Dutch landowner and merchant who, through cleaver machinations, managed to keep his lands and riches when the English took over that Dutch colony.

It was common knowledge that Philipse would fence the merchandise that Kidd brought to the harbor and finance Kidd's next voyage. When Kidd sailed into New York Harbor, he was wined and dined by that city's upper class as though he were English royalty, perhaps the Duke of York himself. As fate would have it, however, Kidd would eventually lose favor with His Royal Highness, and his lot would be the hangman's noose. But in 1691, he was still almost a decade away from his demise. His star was still rising, and life was still good.

A short while later, Tom and John Dobbs found themselves together on the stern deck, a canvas protecting them from the misty rain. John Dobbs had recognized the *Adventure* also, and he spoke in admiration of the famous Captain Kidd.

"The captain of that ship is one of the finest seamen around, Tom. Before my father died two years ago, he had some dealings with him. My father was also a mariner and a merchant. He owned a coastal and sailed between New York and Charleston before he sold his boat and became a skipper for Captain Griggs. When he died, Captain Griggs took me on. He pays good and, along with our small farm, it keeps us comfortable."

"Are you married, John?" Tom asked somewhat incredulously.

"Not I, Tom." John laughed as though he had never considered the prospect. "I live on Barrent's Island with my mother and sister, Maria."

"Where's Barrent's Island?" Tom inquired.

"It's in Jamaica Bay off the south shore of Long Island, about four miles east of Gravesend, where Captain Griggs lives. It's not very big, about a mile and a half long and three-quarters of a mile wide. Only about thirty acres of it are upland and useful for farming; the rest is salt marsh. A fellow could walk out to it at low tide if he didn't mind getting his knees wet."

While the two young men talked, the rain let up, and they noticed that a boat was being lowered from the *Adventure*. Five sailors climbed down into it. Two took command of the oars, and the group headed toward the beach, rowing into the wind, which by now had subsided considerably. Tom noticed that they were armed with cutlasses, which seemed strange to him. What threat could the fishermen of Block Island pose to these men, these privateers? Or...was it the other way around? Tom thought about Peter, and he wondered if he fulfilled his wish to sail for Captain Glover.

"What do you think those sailors from the *Adventure* are doing on the island, John?" Tom asked in a somewhat pensive tone.

"Ain't no tellin'. There weren't any barrels in their longboat, so they ain't takin' on water. No tellin' what they're up to, but it's probably no good. I'd wager that they intend to get into some mischief."

Tom fixed his gaze on the half dozen log cabins with outbuildings that dotted the island's most prominent hill. Except for the light from their windows and the occasional sparks from their chimneys, they were barely visible in the approaching darkness.

"You figure any of the farmers and fishermen in those cabins over there on the ridge need to fear for their women or their possessions on account of them?"

"I don't think so, Tom. Nothing more than a chicken or two, anyway. Not this close to New York. After all, Ole Captain Kidd is known as a great merchant and gentleman around here. He's a loyal Englishman and friend of the king; he'll get a duke's reception when he finally ties up in New York. And many of the city's merchants will share in the booty that's stowed in the hold of the *Adventure* over there. Look how much water she's drawing; probably got gold and silver bars for ballast."

As the evening progressed, the sky continued to clear, the wind shifted around to the north, and the fresh air became noticeably cooler. A full moon, gigantic and orange, floated up from the eastern horizon. The *Prudence* swung around on her anchor and pointed her bowsprit toward the North Star, exposing her port side to the beach seventy yards to the west. The men busied themselves with the various tasks required to put a vessel to bed. Tom was assigned the duty of preparing the evening meal, which would consist of salt cod, some of Mrs. Hallack's turnips, bread, and hot tea. With efficient expertise, he struck flint to steel and captured the sparks, thus created in a small piece of char cloth. He blew on the char cloth and wrapped it in tinder and blew some more. In a few moments, the tinder ignited, and he transferred it to the stove and the awaiting pieces of wood. The stove was a big, thick iron bowl on short legs designed to not capsize with the pitch and roll of a vessel at sea. After several breaths, the wood caught fire. Tom added bigger sticks to the little blaze, and in short order, the stove was serviceable. From the corner of his eye, John Griggs watched this activity with a certain degree of satisfaction that he had made a wise decision in hiring the young Scotsman.

Thirty minutes later, the storm clouds had completely passed, dinner was ready, and the four men gathered around to fill their plates with the cuisine Tom had prepared. While they ate, the conversation was minimal, although there were a few good-natured comments about the questionable quality of Tom's cooking. The captain, however, was quick to come to his defense.

"Leave him alone, boys. I believe Tom did quite well. After all, he is a landlubber and a Scotsman, at that!" There were snickers. "And he even lit the fire without our help. Tom, don't listen to 'em. You're doing fine!"

After their meal, the men relaxed on the deck, the bowls of their pipes glowing red. John Dobbs brewed some coffee, which he poured into tin cups and passed around to his shipmates. Being at the bottom of the seniority list, Tom was served the cup with the handle broken off. The empty cup was lying on its side between his feet, and he watched it slowly roll back and forth with the movement of the *Prudence* while he puffed on MacFie's pipe, continuing the dead man's legacy. The gunsmith may have gone to the hereafter, or at least he settled to the bottom of the sea, but his pipe was still in service. The four men sat huddled around the stove, still glowing with coals from the preparations of the evening meal. Its warmth felt good against the growing chill of the late October evening. A single lantern hung on the mast, its candlelight creating undulating shadows on the deck as the *Prudence* slowly rolled back and forth to the rhythm of the sea.

The men smoked in silence. Tom thought about his mother and father. He wondered if he would ever see them again. He thought about MacFie and then about Elizabeth and the other slaves on the *Victory*. He wondered where she was, what she was doing…what her new owner was doing to her. He wondered what Boston and Salem would be like and what he would do with his life after this voyage was over. Tears welled up in his eyes. He blinked them away.

Fifteen minutes of puffing in silence were finally broken by an order from the captain.

"Stoke the fire a bit, Tom. I'm not yet ready to give up on this beautiful evening."

Tom carefully arranged three short oak logs on top of the coals in the iron stove. He blew on them to provide some encouragement, and in a couple minutes, they flamed up. One by one, the circle of men inched their way closer to the heat and found comfortable positions for their tired frames. Pipes that had gone out were relit. No one spoke; they drew on their pipes and stared at the stove as if mesmerized by its burning logs and embers.

Finally, Richard broke the silence.

"Tell us a story, Captain. Tell these boys about the Indian raid you survived back in Sag Harbor. It would be new to them, and I'd get pleasure from hearing it again."

Griggs obliged, settled himself on some canvas, and launched into his narrative about the war party of Shinnecocks who appeared one evening, faces painted up for trouble.

The crew gave the captain their full attention as he recounted his story, but about ten minutes into his epic, he noticed that Tom appeared to be distracted. The young man took the pipe out of his mouth and seemed to be staring intently at the cup, rolling back and forth between his feet.

"Tom," he said, "please tell me I am not boring you. Your mind is somewhere else. What's attracting your attention?"

"I'm sorry, Captain." A pause. "I was thinking about the tiller and how it was hard to control during the storm. A longer tiller would make it easier, but it would take up too much space. Then, I thought about this cup rolling back and forth. It's like a wheel but without an axle. Back in Scotland, a farmer near us built a contraption over his well so his wife could draw water more easily. He took a small cartwheel and fixed an axle to it so that it would turn with the wheel. He set it in a frame and tied a rope to the axle. Then he fashioned a wooden handle and attached it to the rim of the wheel. When he wanted water, he lowered the bucket by turning the wheel with the handle, which unwound the rope. Then, he would raise the bucket by turning the wheel backwards, winding the rope back up. A metal hook kept the wheel from turning by itself when it wasn't being used. I was thinking that something like that could be used to control a ship's rudder."

Griggs leaned forward. "What do you mean, Tom?"

"I don't know how it would actually work, but is there a piece of string I can use, maybe three feet long?"

John Dobbs got up and went to the cabin and returned with a leather thong.

Leaving about a foot loose at the end, he wrapped the thong around the cup several times until there was about a foot left on the other end. He held the cup sideways.

"John, would you hold one end of the thong and Richard, the other?"

Tom held the cup in the middle.

"The cup is like an axle. If I turn the cup in one direction, John's end is shortened, and Richard's is lengthened, and if I turn the cup in the other, it's just the opposite. That's about as far as I got in my thinking."

Captain Griggs was immediately energized. "Tom, you may have something there. Let me think about it for a minute or two."

The crew sat in silence while the captain thought.

"Richard, get me some paper and a quill and ink from the cabin." He moved closer to the lantern hanging on the mast. It took five minutes for him to complete a rough sketch while the crew looked on.

"I believe you have an excellent idea, Tom. A wheel could be set in the stern. It would have a short thick axle. A rope wrapped around the axle would go below the deck, one end to starboard, the other to port, perhaps run through a couple pulleys, and then attached to the tiller, which is also below deck. The boat could then be controlled on deck by one man operating the wheel. Perhaps the spokes could be extended a bit past the wheel's rim somehow to serve as handles."

With excitement in his voice, John said. "Set the compass in front of the wheel and something for the pilot to sit on behind it, and you're ready to run a true course!"

Then, Griggs issued a directive. "After this run, we'll try to fashion one for the *Prudence* to see how it works."

Then he added, "Tom, what's the Scottish word for wheel?"

"That would be 'roth', Captain."

"Fine. If it works, we'll call it 'the roth' in honor of Thomas Hughson, its Scottish inventor, mariner, and oarsman!"

John Dobbs chimed in, "Tom, take over the roth for a minute. I'm going to the head!"

The crew chuckled.

Not to be outdone, Tom replied, "Not again, John! Whatever did you have to eat in that tavern last night?"

The crew laughed again.

Minutes passed after that, mostly in silence, and Tom found himself at that final choice point of deciding whether to let his eyelids drop when his attention was drawn to the land by a light. It went away immediately…there it was again…Fire!

Chapter 16

Block Island Fire

October 31, 1691

One of the buildings on the western rise beyond the beach was on fire.

"Look over on the hill!" Tom alerted his shipmates, and all his sleepiness evaporated. "One of those cabins is on fire!"

The three men switched their gaze from the stove to the western horizon. All four were immediately on their feet. The fire was easier to see now. The left side of the structure appeared to be in flames on the far side of its chimney.

John Dobbs was the first to speak.

"Let's go help 'em." He looked at Tom. "Captain, can Tom and me take the skiff and a couple of those canvas buckets and go over there?"

"Alright. But be careful and, for Heaven's sake, don't go into any burning buildings."

Tom went to the stern and pulled the skiff around. He unlashed the oars from their place along the rail, and John grabbed two buckets from where they hung beside the cabin. Both young men quickly lowered themselves into the skiff. John set the oars in their locks and dug their blades into the water. It was clear to Tom that John knew what he was doing. He expertly brought the small craft about and, with arm and back muscles in graceful and powerful coordination, drove the skiff rapidly toward the beach, its bow coming out of the water with each powerful tug on the oars. Tom watched the reflections of moonlight as the water ran off the oars between John's strokes.

In no time, it seemed to Tom, the skiff's bow scraped up onto the beach pebbles. John leapt out and pulled the craft higher up onto the beach. Tom, who had been sitting in the stern, scrambled forward with the two buckets, and the two then pulled the skiff to greater safety.

"Let's fill these buckets here, Tom, in case there's no water up there."

They dipped their buckets into the salt water, and then, each loaded down with the 40 extra pounds that the water contributed, they quickly began their ascent across the beach and up a sandy path that appeared to lead in the direction of the house, another 80 yards away. Tom was in the lead.

"Slow down a bit, Tom," John panted. "It won't do for you to trip and lose that water."

Tom checked his pace, and his shipmate caught up with him. For a moment, the two lost sight of the house as they made their way through a stand of jack pines. Then, reaching a clearing, they could see the burning structure. They noticed a woman in the front yard frantically trying to draw water from a well. Tom yelled at her.

"Please help us," she pleaded. "I don't know where they are!"

"Who?" Tom yelled.

"Virginia Luckstead and her infant daughter! They should be here! Mr. Luckstead and my husband, Caleb, are off fishing. I'm her neighbor."

John took the two buckets of seawater around behind the building and tossed the water on the flames at the back of the house. Tom ran to the open front door and yelled inside.

"Mrs. Luckstead! Hello! Is anybody here? Virginia!"

The fire had already broken through the back wall of the one-room structure, and the roof on that end of the house was ablaze. He tried to peer through the smoke and flames as best he could. He did not see anybody. He yelled again. A large table was turned over on its side. There was a loft on the other side of the room, apparently used for sleeping, but it, too, was empty. Tom ran back over to the well where John was lowering its bucket to refill his canvas.

"I couldn't see much through the smoke, but I'm sure there's nobody in there."

"Where could they possibly be?" The woman asked herself. "It wouldn't be like her to go far from the house this time of night with her husband, George, out fishin' the way he is."

"What about some neighbors?" Tom asked.

"I'm her closest neighbor, and I didn't see her walk by...I'm worried...Are you certain you didn't see anything?"

"No, Ma'am, nothing." Tom grabbed the well bucket and poured its contents into the second canvas bucket. John rushed them around to the rear of the house in a fruitless attempt to control the flames.

"Lord, please protect Virginia and her baby," the woman prayed. There was a pause..., and then she screamed, "The root cellar! They must be in the root cellar!"

"Where?" Tom shouted.

"In the house. There's a large trap door in the floor. George dug a small cellar to store vegetables!"

"Show me!" Tom yelled as he pulled the woman by the arm back to the front door. They both looked into the developing inferno. The smoke had engulfed the entire room, and the flames were spreading from the back wall to the roof. Somewhere in the corner of the room, a flash of gunpowder ignited.

"There!" the woman pointed. "In the center...The table fell over on the door."

The heat was too intense for Tom to enter. He spotted an overcoat hanging on a peg to the right of the door. He grabbed it and ran back to the well, where John was pulling up a bucket of water.

"John...on the coat! Throw the water on the coat!"

Tom raced the dripping garment back to the door and, throwing it over his head and upper body, he got down on his hands and knees and low-crawled to the trapdoor. He shoved the table off the door with his feet and grabbed the ring used for a handle. As he lifted it a crack, he heard an infant whimpering. The door wasn't hinged; rather, it rested on a molding into which it fit snuggly. He threw the door back and down in the hole he saw a woman crouched in the corner, clutching an infant.

"Come out, quick, Mrs. Luckstead! The place is on fire!" he yelled, but she remained motionless and stared up at him. He grabbed the edge of the molding and swung into the cellar.

"No! ...Please! ...No!" she pleaded.

Tom lunged toward her, grabbed her arm and waist, and shoved her up the six steps to the top. He tossed the wet overcoat over her and the infant and, following her through the opening, pushed her across the floor and out the front door. At the door, John dragged her to her feet and rushed her away from the flames and smoke. The neighbor took charge of the baby, who was, by this time, screaming.

With a loud crash, the burning roof caved into the structure, causing the whole house to be engulfed in just a few seconds. Flames reached thirty feet up into the night sky—brilliant, beautiful, terrifying. There was nothing that could be done now. All would be lost. The two young men stood there, staring into the inferno, stunned by their own sense of frustration and yet thankful for the rescue. Their trance was broken by the neighbor, Lydia Littlefield, her name was.

"Help me take them to my house. It's just over that rise."

With Lydia carrying the baby and John and Tom supporting Virginia Luckstead by her elbows, the group started down the path. They could hear men coming now. Shouts of "Fire!" and "at the Lucksteads' place!" filled the night air. In a minute, the two groups met on the path, and Tom gave them a brief account of the situation. The brigade continued on to the fire, partly out of some hope that they could still be of help but mostly out of curiosity.

Another twenty yards and Mrs. Littlefield, still holding Virginia's baby, guided the rescuers and the rescued into her cabin. "Hold Bridget, will you while I get everyone some hot tea and olykoeks."

Tom took the child and tried to console the sobbing young mother.

"Thanks to God's Providence, you and your baby are safe now, Mrs. Luckstead." He passed the now-quiet Bridget over to her.

In a few minutes, Virginia began to speak between hitching breaths. "I was so frightened." I saw three strange men come up the path, and I took Bridget and hid in the root

174

cellar. They came into the house and found George's rum." She took some quick breaths.

"I could hear them around the table. They were drinking and being profane and talking about all manner of terrible things. Oh, Lydia, I thought they would kill us!"

"There, there, Child; you're safe now," the older woman assured her. "Thanks to these two young men, you and little Bridget are unharmed. The men of the island will soon rebuild your home, and until it is finished, you can stay with us."

"They must have been some of the sailors we saw go ashore from the *Adventure*. How did the fire start?" Tom inquired.

"As the rum began to affect them, one of them told another to put wood on the fire because the night air was making him cold. It must have gotten too big because, in a few minutes, I heard them shouting about how the chimney was ablaze. They got up to leave, and, in their haste, they knocked the table over. I heard it crash to the floor. Its weight kept me from opening the door." She began crying again, and Lydia put a blanket around her.

In a minute or two, she gathered herself and resumed. "I prayed to the Almighty Father to deliver us…and then you came. I'm sorry for the way I acted, but I didn't know who you were."

"Well, you can thank Mrs. Littlefield. She told us about the root cellar. Were it not for her, we never would have known."

"Who are you boys, anyway?" Lydia interjected. "Where did you come from?"

"We're from the smaller of those two ships anchored off the beach. We came in late this afternoon to take shelter from the storm. We're taking a load of goods and produce to Boston. I'm John Dobbs, and this is Tom Hughson; he's fresh from Scotland. The captain is John Griggs from Gravesend. In fact, we should be returning before he sends out a search party for us."

"You saved my life," the young woman said, looking up at Tom. "What's more important, you saved Bridget's life. You were an answer to my prayers, and I will never be able to repay you." She couldn't have been over 19 or 20, no older than he was.

"Think nothing of it," Tom replied. "We saw the flames from our ship, and we came over to see if we could do something. We're glad we could help. We really must be going. You'll be safe now."

With that, the two left. They retraced their steps to where John had left the canvas buckets, thence to the beach. At the beach, they noticed that the longboat from the *Adventure* was gone. Tom wanted to row the skiff back to the *Prudence*. The trip took a little longer than when John manned the oars, and

176

the course wasn't quite as straight, but at least Tom was learning. He put his back into the chore, and periodically, an oar would slip from its lock under the strain of a misdirected tug.

"Don't pull so hard on the oars, Tom. Rowin' a boat is like makin' love; you've got to take it easy and be gentle."

"Aye, and what would you know about that?" Tom scoffed. The two laughed. All in all, it had been a successful evening. The lives of a young woman and a baby girl were saved. Not in his wildest imagination could Tom have foreseen the terror the Luckstead family would someday wreck upon his life.

Chapter 17

Dr. William Griggs

Salem, Massachusetts

November 1691

It was 8:30 in the evening, and rain was falling, a cold, drizzly rain typical of Salem in November. It had been raining all day. Dr. William Griggs sat in his favorite imported English chair, dozing in front of the fireplace. As usual, he had been reading when sleep overtook him. This time, it was a treatise on exorcism written by a Presbyterian minister in Scotland. The minister's thesis was that real exorcism was impossible, that only the purification of death would release the devil from his indwelling an afflicted earthly being. The tract lay on the floor by the doctor's chair, where it had fallen when he succumbed to the relaxing sounds and warmth of the crackling fire.

By the standards developing in Massachusetts society, Dr. Griggs was successful. His medical practice, combined with some clever investments over the years, had made him a wealthy man. He was a pillar of the Salem community and one of its most notable churchmen. He was also its physician. A good-looking man, he had a full head of gray hair and a few extra pounds that he carried with an air of distinction. One could easily have mistaken him for a member of the House of Lords. Like others in the Griggs family, the good doctor had aged well. He was content with his station and glad that he had not followed in his father's footsteps and become a builder of boats.

Furthermore, his second wife, Rachel Hubbard Griggs, was glad, too, for she shared in his fame and good fortune. She was known throughout the community as a good Christian woman and an ardent defender of Puritanism. In fact, she was obsessed with evil and the power it held over humankind and, specifically, over some of the residents in Salem whom she could readily identify for anyone who might ask her. Throughout their marriage, Rachel had supported her husband and his ambitions; she worked hard to help him achieve them, and now, in her later years, she was reaping the benefits. She lived in one of the nicer homes in Salem, a home that contained many furnishings from France and England. Her children married well, she had her friends, her husband, her position, and, thus far, her health.

Rachel had been a close friend, her husband thought perhaps a little too close, of the Reverend James Bailey. It was all those trips Rachel made to the Bailey home to give aid to the Reverend's sickly wife that made the doctor suspicious. Bailey had been the first Minister appointed to Salem Village twelve years prior in 1679. Ten years into his pastorate, a political tempest within Salem's church community led to Reverend Bailey's being replaced by the Reverend Samuel Parris, an ardent and wealthy Puritan who was also a slaveholder. Rachel harbored a deep dislike for Reverend Parris, an emotion she shared with no one except the ousted Reverend Bailey during those very rare occasions when she found an opportunity to be alone with him. By now, Parris had been Salem's minister for two years, but time had not cooled Rachel's negative emotions toward the man.

Rachel relaxed in her own imported chair in the sitting room. As she knitted on an Afghan that was to become a Christmas present for her daughter, she cast an occasional eye in the direction of her sleeping husband. She smiled to herself at the noises the 70-year-old made as his chin bobbed up and down on his chest. She was about to get up and remove his reading glasses when there was a knock on the door. The doctor alerted immediately. Whoever it was, it would probably mean a late-night journey through the rain. He got up and approached the door.

"I'll get it," he informed his wife.

The visitor was Reverend Parris. He was wrapped in a cloak that was soaked through with the rain.

"Come in, Reverend. Let me have that cloak. Please come over by the fire."

He nodded to Rachel as he handed her his dripping cloak.

"Doctor Griggs, I'm sorry to bother you this late in the evening, but our house girl, Tituba, is down with a fever, and she has turned delirious. She won't answer Mary or me, but she rambles on about dead chickens and snakes and a magic amulet she wants from her home in Barbados. She begged our daughter, Elizabeth, to go get it and bring it to her. It scares us that she is out of her head, so. I know it's late, but would you be able to come look at her?"

"Certainly, Reverend. I'll get my coat and satchel and be right with you."

Rachel Griggs went into the back room and retrieved a garment that, a century later, people would know as a poncho. It was made of oilcloth and virtually waterproof. She handed it to Parris.

"Put this on, Reverend. There's no sense in the doctor having to treat you, too."

"Thank you, Mrs. Griggs. I'll return it by way of your husband."

With that, the two men ventured out into the rainy night for the five-minute walk to the parsonage.

Samuel Parris guided Dr. Griggs around behind the parsonage to a cabin where Tituba lived. Even before they opened the door, they could hear her ranting, speaking words but making little sense. In between spurts of words, she coughed deeply, coughs that signaled severely congested lungs. The two men entered the room, illuminated by the light from the fireplace and a single candle on a small table next to the bed in which the stricken girl lay. Mary Parris sat in a chair next to her.

"How long has she been like this, Mrs. Parris?"

"For about two hours, Doctor. She's very hot."

Griggs placed a palm on the damp skin of the stricken girl's forehead. She was, indeed, very hot. He guessed that she was about 16 years old.

"We have to get her fever down before it damages her brain and proves mortal. Strip her to her waist, Mrs. Parris. Reverend, bring me a bucket of cold water and some towels quickly."

"Mrs. Parris, we're going to lay cold, wet clothes over her head and chest. We'll rinse them every five minutes and reapply them until the fever breaks. We'll have to prop her up with some pillows and blankets. Her illness has attacked her lungs, and I am afraid she may die if she remains in her prone position."

In her delirium, Tituba did not resist the efforts of Griggs and Mary as they removed her shift and propped her up with pillows. She merely continued to cough and ask for her amulet. The parson returned with a bucket of water and towels. Mary Parris immersed them in the water, rung them out, and she and the doctor covered Tituba's torso and head with them.

"There's not much we can do for her now but wait and keep changing the towels. As soon as the fever breaks, we'll get her dressed, keep her warm, and tap her back to keep her lungs clear. I have a herb in my satchel that the Indians use

182

for clearing lungs. I believe it's effective. When her fever breaks, you can make a tea of it, and we'll give it to her."

"Doctor, do you think she may die?"

"We'll do the best we can, Mary. The rest is in God's hands."

"But she's a pagan, Doctor. She believes in the island witchcraft of her home."

Griggs did not answer.

For three hours, the doctor and the pastor's wife watched the delirious slave, changing towels at regular intervals and listening to the strange combinations of words she uttered at irregular intervals, frightening words of evil beliefs and evil rites practiced by the Caribbean blacks; a strange and satanic mixture of African voodoo and warped pieces from Christianity. "Da cat's blood on me...his claw be on me...his fang be in me...his eye in my amulet...where my aaammmulet?...Runah, I die...Runah, I die!"

Nine-year-old Elizabeth Parris stood in the corner, staring at the slave, mesmerized by her delirious rantings. The doctor asked her to leave the room.

At one point, Tituba opened her eyes...wide. Then she closed them. She opened them again and stared directly into Griggs' eyes. For a moment, he thought he saw Satan staring at him...into him. His gaze was transfixed by the reflections of firelight dancing on...or was it in?...her black pupils. A cold chill shot down his neck and across his shoulder blades. It passed. "Could she possibly be possessed?" He wondered to himself.

Sometime after midnight, the patient's fever broke, and her ranting and delirious talk subsided. They got her dressed, propped her into a sitting position, and began tapping her back. Mrs. Parris made the herb tea and enticed Tituba into drinking some. More tapping. Finally, the coughing decreased a bit, and Tituba fell asleep. The doctor propped her up on the pillows.

"I've done all I can do," he informed the pastor and his wife. I'll come back later in the morning and look in on her. Give her some more of that tea when she awakens. Keep her propped up and have her breathe some steam from a kettle if you can."

"We will, Doctor. Thank you for all you did. I'll settle with you tomorrow."

"That'll be fine, Reverend."

Griggs stepped back out into the night. The rain had stopped, and it was cold. On his walk home, he saw those glaring eyes out there in the night sky in front of him…those black, glaring eyes that seemed to possess their own internal fire. Had he encountered Satan? He shivered.

Chapter 18

Voyage to Boston

November 1691

As dawn arrived over Block Island, the four men aboard the *Prudence* were already at work, scampering around the deck, making ready for their departure. In contrast, no one appeared to be moving on the *Adventure*, save the one chilly sailor who was standing watch. Captain Griggs was anxious to catch the outgoing tide because, as usual in those parts, there was little wind in the morning after a storm front blew through. Once they got out of Great Salt Pond and into the ocean, he was confident that the west wind that now barely moved the tell-tales on his sails would pick up and usher them on their way.

As the line of yellow-orange sunlight worked its way down the rise on the western shore of the Pond, it eventually illuminated the scene of the fire. A thin smoke rose from the ashes of what had only yesterday been the Luckstead home. Tom thought again about the young woman and her little daughter, Bridget. He thought about George Luckstead's return from fishing and the panic he would feel when his boat first brought him into viewing distance of what was once his home. He wondered how long the poor man would have to wait before he found out that his wife and child were safe. If

Tom only knew how his life would cross paths with theirs far in the future. But, of course, he didn't.

Once they cleared the entrance to Great Salt Pond and the sandy point that marked the northern end of Block Island, the west wind picked up, and the *Prudence* began to make meaningful headway toward Boston. By noon, the voyagers were already in Muskeget Channel, flanked by Martha's Vineyard and Nantucket Island. As evening descended, the ship had rounded the northern point of Cape Cod, and Captain Griggs decided to drop anchor for the night in its bay. He judged that the next day would afford an easy sail past Marblehead and into Boston harbor. Under the influence of that same westerly breeze, the *Prudence* swung around on its anchor chain, pointing its bow toward Plymouth Bay and the plantation that, 70 years before, had gotten the great New England adventure started.

As Tom prepared the evening meal, it was becoming a tradition, John Dobbs offered to help, the stove being a partial antidote to the dropping temperature. The two young men talked about Scotland and Gravesend and John's mother and his strong-willed sister, Maria. During the after-dinner pipe, Tom leaned back on some canvas and contemplated the host of brilliant stars scattered across the sky. He marveled at how the three stars in Orion's belt could form such a straight line. It was cold that night aboard the *Prudence*; cold and very clear. Winter was on its way.

Early the next afternoon, the *Prudence* was tied up at the wharf in Boston harbor, more accurately, in Charlestown, which was just across the Charles River from Boston and the location of the Griggs shipyards. While Captain Griggs finalized payments with various businessmen and traders, Richard oversaw the offloading of the cargo and the loading of the cargo they would be taking to Salem two days hence. Temporarily relieved of their duties, John and Tom strolled down the wharf and found a merchant where, at John's insistence, Tom purchased a fearnought jacket and a Monmouth cap and put both of them on.

"Now you look like a real mariner, Tom, me boy. I'm no longer embarrassed to be seen in public with ye."

"Aye, aye, Sir," Tom responded in an exceedingly false display of deference. He wondered where the dense fearnought wool got its name. Perhaps those who wore it didn't fear the cold wet weather that sailors had to endure in the winter.

In another fifteen minutes, the two young salts found themselves in the Three Cranes Tavern, each nursing a pewter tankard of ale. They tried valiantly to affect the demeanor of real seadogs; they were clearly having a good time. One hour and two tankards into their animated discussions of pirates and Indian fighting, Richard appeared at their table.

"Ah, I thought I'd find you two salts here! You'd better not be imbibing too much of that ale because the captain has a chore for you boys in the mornin'. Tom, how are you at handlin' a horse?"

Tom, mellow from his ale, stared into Richard's eyes and held his gaze for two or three long seconds.

"Richard, my good man, you are addressing a Scotsman. Why, your very question is an affront to my breed. There is not a Scotsman born whom God, in His Providence, did not make one with the horse. The horse and the Scotsman are blood brothers, spiritual kin, fashioned by God to bring strength and beauty to the earth."

John slapped his shipmate on the back. "Tom, the ale has made you eloquent. But, please, hold your tongue and let the Brit speak to us of horses."

Richard had a grin on his face. "Fashioned by God, indeed! Ain't you confusing your breed with the Irish, Laddie? Me thinks those kilts you wear have allowed the winter winds to damage your brains."

"Richard, you have never seen me wear a kilt. I am currently among heathen and, being among heathen, I dress as the heathen do; I wear britches, and I've even taken to eating cheese! But at more than that, I draw the line!"

"Well, listen, you two cavaliers," Richard went on, "the captain has a business associate who imported two fine thoroughbreds from England for a man named John

Hawthorne in Salem. The associate engaged two men to ride the steeds to Salem to deliver them. The men, however, failed to appear." He paused. "They were French…what can I say?" He paused again for effect.

"Griggs offered your services, gentlemen, to deliver the animals to Mr. Hawthorne in Salem tomorrow. You can then rejoin us after two days at the Salem dock. We have a passenger who knows the sea, and the three of us can manage the *Prudence* for that short voyage. Of course, you will be paid in advance for your effort."

With that, Richard removed from his pocket twenty shillings and gave ten to each mariner. The two young seamen-turned-equestrians examined the coins and pocketed them. Life was good!

"You'd better come along with me so you won't fall off your chargers in the morning," he said with a laugh. The two did as they were told and, with a rather loose gait, followed their older shipmate down to the wharf and back to the *Prudence*.

Chapter 19

Salem, Massachusetts

November 4, 1691

Captain Griggs awakened his horsemen at dawn the next morning. It was very chilly, but the morning portended a bright and beautiful fall day.

"The horses are ready for you at Chaffin's livery. The road to Salem is clearly marked. It will be about 16 miles to Salem. When you get there, ask for Mr. Hawthorne. He is to receive the horses, as well as the saddles and tack. Make sure you obtain a receipt from him. He's already paid for them. Is there anything else you need to know?"

"What shall we do while we await the arrival of the *Prudence*?" John inquired.

"My older brother, William, is the doctor in Salem. He and his wife, Rachel, live in a fine home, and I am sure they would be glad to put you up for the evening. After delivering the horses, look him up, tell him you are devout Christians and two of my faithful employees, and I am sure you will find him and Mrs. Griggs to be gracious hosts. Act like gentlemen and don't partake of any spirits or do anything else that would place my good name and reputation in jeopardy."

The two assured Captain Griggs that they would mind their deportment. The horses were indeed beautiful, each a bay and over 16 hands tall. In ten minutes, they were tacked with brand new expensive English saddles, and Tom and John were on their backs.

"Remember, boys, don't run 'em hard," Chaffin cautioned. "We want 'em lookin' full of spirit when old man Hawthorne lays eyes on 'em. He paid a pretty penny for those horses, that man did."

With that bit of instruction from the livery owner, the two were on their way, headed east out of the city. The wagon road to Salem was in moderately good condition. It meandered through marshy areas and majestic expanses of hardwood forests, which had all but lost their leaves for winter. Deer and wild turkey seemed to abound. The riders walked abreast along the road, making occasional small talk.

"So, Tom, how do you like America so far?"

"So far, I am well pleased, and I'm very thankful to God for the luck I've had finding a place to fit in. My mother must be praying for me…that's all I know. Peter from the *Victory* was a great help to me, and now you are, John. I really appreciate your friendship."

"Think nothing of it, Shipmate. That's how we Americans treat all Scotsmen…at least the ones who don't wear kilts and flash their backsides at us."

Chuckles.

"I do have one question, however, perhaps you could help me with it."

"Which is…?"

"Peter assured me I would enjoy meeting some of the wenches in New York, but the only ones I've seen up close are a few barmaids, and most of them have been downright frightening. Where does a fellow go to find more appealing ones?"

"Tom, you're not contemplating holy matrimony already, are you?"

"Of course not. I just thought it might be pleasurable to talk to someone a little more appealing to the eyes. Where does one find them?"

"Be careful, Tom. That's how it all starts, and the first thing you know, you're a husband, your woman outweighs you by three stone, and you have six little ones to feed." He paused and then added, "But, if you want to meet young ladies who are appealing to the eyes and able to appreciate your overwhelming Scottish intellect, I recommend that you attend church."

John laughed at his own wittiness, and Tom eventually joined in the mirth.

Then John continued. "If you want to meet a girl who appeals to the eyes and is willing to talk, I can always introduce you to my sister, Maria. But you'll have to be careful; she's headstrong and opinionated. And, she occasionally wears my worn-out britches."

They both chuckled at the thought and rode on in silence, but Tom stored away that information for future reference.

From time to time, they encountered other travelers, most of them farmers in oxcarts or wagons, bringing their produce to Boston for sale at the market. At Swampscott, they stopped at a small inn and enjoyed an early lunch of beef stew, bread, and cheese. John suggested a tankard of ale, but Tom prevailed on his fellow horseman on the need to remain in the saddle and alert for their meetings with Mr. Hawthorne and Dr. Griggs.

By late afternoon, they had arrived in Salem, located Hawhorne's home, and delivered the two stallions in good repair. Hawthorne, a pompous yet friendly man, insisted on riding each of them before he would sign the receipt. Tom noticed that the man's equestrian skills left something to be desired, and his rather large frame did not make things any easier. The horses, however, were professionals, and they held him well. He was wonderfully satisfied with his rides, and after one last detailed inspection of hooves, joints, and teeth, the receipt was finally executed. With the paper in their possession, Tom and John set out for the Griggs residence, which, Hawthorne told them, was on the other side of Salem Village.

The two travelers quickly discovered that Dr. and Mrs. Griggs met every expectation the captain had set for them. They welcomed the young men as though they were long-lost sons. John Dobbs, being the one with information about the Long Island branch of the family, was interrogated in detail about how Elizabeth was faring and what the children and grandchildren were doing. They were particularly interested in the plans that Benjamin and Samuel had for moving to New Jersey and building a mill. When John had related everything he knew about the Griggs family, it was Tom's turn to be examined by Rachel Griggs. Of course, the topic was Scotland.

"So, Tom, tell us what brought you to America?" Rachel inquired.

In an accent perhaps a little more Scottish than usual, Tom began his story. He told about his father, the fighting in the Scottish Highlands and Outer Isles, his indenture, MacFie's death aboard the *Victory*, his trip with Peter to the tavern…

Tom had reached the point where he was describing the fire when there was a rapid knock on the Griggs' front door. The doctor answered it.

It was William Hobbs. "Doctor, please come quickly! There's been an accident at the new barn we're building for Squire Corwin. It's Isaac Eastey. He came over from Topsfield to help us, and a post fell across him, and he's trapped by his legs. He is losing much blood! His wife and daughter are visiting at Corwin's. Should I go get them?"

The doctor grabbed his coat and satchel. "Yes, don't frighten them, but bring them over to the barn. Come along, boys; I may need your help!"

The three men moved at a quick pace during the twenty-minute trek to the site of the new Corwin barn. In a few minutes, Tom noticed that the elderly doctor was becoming winded. He reached for the doctor's satchel, which the physician gladly handed over. In five more minutes, they arrived at the accident scene. Eastey's wife, Mary, and his youngest daughter, Hannah, were already there inside the partially framed structure, huddled around Eastey, a heavy twelve-foot oak post pinning him to the ground and up against some framing. Upon seeing the doctor, the men cleared the way for him. Hannah knelt beside her father and wiped his face with a wet cloth. Although she was crying and clearly terrified, she attempted to comfort and reassure her father.

The doctor knelt beside the injured man. One of the carpenters briefed him.

"His leg is bleeding badly, and we didn't want to remove the post for fear of making it worse."

"That was good thinking, Simon," the doctor replied as he tried to probe the extent of the wound. "We've got to stop the bleeding."

As though he had worked with the doctor for years, Tom pulled one of the onlookers out of the way and dropped to his knees by Eastey's waist. He placed the heel of his palm in the man's groin and, with one hand on top of the other and both elbows locked, he leaned down with all his weight. Immediately, the bleeding subsided.

The doctor looked at him, "Where did you learn that, boy?" he inquired in a soft voice.

"My father," he replied. "It's one of those things you learn when you're a Scot living by the sword."

The doctor turned to the men. "His upper leg is broken, and an artery is punctured. On my command, I want you to lift the post from his legs. Enoch, is there any water here?"

"There's some in the kettle at the fire, but it is still warm from making tea."

"Bring it to me quickly!"

The doctor tested the water. It was warm but not too warm. God was with him.

"Enoch, after the post is removed, I'll cut his britches away from the wound. Then, when I tell you, pour the entire contents of the kettle over the wound."

"John!" The doctor turned to his other houseguest. "Kneel down by his foot and grab his shoe. After the water is poured, I will tell you to pull and pull you must. Lean back and put your weight into it. You will be there for a few minutes. Do not stop until I tell you!"

"I'll do my best, Sir," John said as he got into position.

"Alright, Gentlemen, lift the post."

The men gingerly removed the post, taking care not to hit the doctor or Tom. Griggs immediately cut away Eastey's upper trouser leg, exposing an ugly wound of blood, muscle, and bone. For 30 seconds, he probed the damage.

"Alright, Enoch, pour the water over the wound. Clean as much of it as you can."

Enoch did as he was told.

"Now, John…pull on his leg!"

As John began to apply the traction, Eastey uttered a loud yell. Of greater interest to the doctor, however, was the protruding white broken femur of his upper leg, which now slowly receded down into the muscle.

"Good, John, good! Keep up that tension. You're doing fine! Tom, he's still bleeding. Bear down a little harder," the doctor commanded.

Tom maneuvered his body weight to get more of it over his arms. Understanding the need for more pressure, Hannah knelt next to Tom. She put her hands on top of his and leaned forward. The bleeding eased.

"That's better, Tom…that's better. This wound will never close by itself. I'll have to sew it. John!" he said to one of the men standing by. "Go quickly to my house and tell Mrs. Griggs I need some of her heavy sewing thread and three needles. Bring them back as fast as you can! Does someone have a horse here?"

"Take mine." Peter Fuller said. "He's behind the barn, already saddled."

Appreciating the urgency of the situation, John Proctor broke into a run, mounted the horse, and galloped down the wagon road to the Griggs home.

Isaac Eastey groaned. "Be patient, Isaac," the doctor counseled in a calm voice. "There's a chance that God will make you whole again. Be patient, and we'll try to assist Him."

There wasn't much for Tom and Hannah to do except to bear down. For the first time, Tom took notice of the young woman. She was, he observed, exceptionally pretty, and she had a sensuous frame that her bodice and now-soiled skirts could not conceal. The bonnet she had been wearing was pushed back, hanging down her back from its strings, and Tom's attention was drawn to her light brown hair and dark blue eyes. Her face was dirty, and Tom noticed the streaks her tears had made as they rolled down her cheeks. But she had stopped crying by now. Her breast touched the back of his arm as the two pressed down together. She was very feminine yet determined. Periodically, she consoled and encouraged her father.

In fifteen minutes, the thread and needles arrived, and the doctor began his repair. Tom and Hannah continued to apply pressure. Hannah's position produced a gap in the front of her bodice, and Tom could not keep himself from stealing occasional furtive glances at her breasts. He noticed that her left breast had a small dark pigmented spot on it, shaped sort of like the moon when it was three-quarters full, he thought. At one point, Hannah caught him engaging in one of his visual excursions, and she smiled as he blushed and turned away.

The sewing finally completed, Dr. Griggs dressed the wound and then directed Tom and Hannah to release their pressure. "Let's see if the artery holds," he said, almost to himself.

A very long minute passed without the appearance of any fresh blood. Clearly relieved at the outcome, the doctor then directed the application of a splint on Eastey's broken leg. During the process, Tom took over the traction from John, who, by this time, was suffering much discomfort caused by the long duration of his fixed kneeling posture.

"Now, we must gently carry him to a nearby bed the doctor ordered.

By this time, Squire Corwin had arrived. "You can take him to my home since he lives in Topsfield. They can stay with us for a few days."

"Be careful not to move his leg along the way," the doctor admonished. "If he starts bleeding, we've lost him."

Tom, John, and four other men carefully picked up Eastey, and Hannah supported his head. In a few minutes, they had their patient in bed at the Squire's. Eastey's wife, Mary, and the doctor went about the task of making him comfortable and readjusting the splint.

"I want everybody to leave except you, Mrs. Eastey. Give him a chance to rest. Hannah, Tom, and the other men left the bedroom, and Hannah offered to show Tom to the well behind the house, where they could wash the blood and dirt off their hands and faces. Tom drew a bucket of water, and they began removing the evidence of their harrowing afternoon. In a few minutes, Mrs. Eastey appeared at the back door.

"Hannah, Doctor Griggs wants someone to go to his house and bring back a bottle of laudanum. He says that your father's leg may cause more pain later during the night, so he wants us to have some here in case he needs it. Will you go, please? Tell Mrs. Griggs what you need, and she'll get it for you."

"I'll go right now, Mother." And then to her new friend, "Tom, will you come with me? It will be getting dark by the time I return."

"Aye, Hannah. It's twenty minutes away."

"A bit less than that if we take the path by the millpond."

Then, she added, "Thank you so much for helping Father this afternoon. Do you think he will recover, Tom?" she inquired with a tentative voice.

"If his leg doesn't get infected, he may. It seems like his leg looked fairly straight in the splint," Tom encouraged. "It is in God's hands now."

"You speak different from the rest," She changed the subject.

"I'm from Scotland. In fact, I've been in America only a few days."

"Is your family here?"

"No, I'm alone. My father and mother are still in Scotland. But I've made some good friends quickly, and I'm working for Captain Griggs. He is a younger brother to your Dr. Griggs, and he lives on Long Island, where he owns several trading ships. He'll be here tomorrow with the *Prudence*. We will then sail it back to New York."

As they walked along the path, early evening was arriving, and there was a chill in the air. Hannah stepped closer to Tom and slipped her arm under his.

"Are you cold, Hannah?" he asked.

"Not now," she answered with a giggle.

There were pauses in their communication as they continued along the path arm-in-arm. Hannah would occasionally look up at him and smile.

What beautiful blue eyes! he thought to himself. Tom felt something course through his body, a new and warm, pleasant feeling. He could tell that Hannah was experiencing something similar.

At one point, Hannah giggled and said, "Tom, back in Corwin's barn, I saw you looking down my bodice. Before he could respond, she added, "It's alright; I don't mind. Did you see my brown birthmark? Mother says it is good luck, and it means I will marry a good man."

Tom had never been around a girl like this before. Not only was she very pretty, but she was funny and forward in a pleasant sort of way. He experienced strange twinges running up and down his spine. Not knowing how to respond to the birthmark comment—he thought it would sound foolish to deny it—he said, "I'm just glad I was there to help your father. When I write my own Da, I'll tell him about how his instruction may have saved a life."

In a few minutes, they arrived at the doctor's home, and with the laudanum in hand, they retraced their steps along the path, again arm-in-arm. When they reached the millpond, Hannah stopped. It was getting dark, and the moon, two nights past full, was rising in the sky, its beams shimmering on the water's surface. A few hardy crickets and frogs added to the scene, creating their own cacophony, and somewhere a whip-poor-will called out into the growing darkness.

Hannah paused and looked up at her handsome Scottish escort.

"Tom, I am so grateful to you for saving my father's life. I don't know how to express how I feel." She hesitated for a moment. "Will you kiss me?"

Did he hear that right?

She repeated her request. "I'd like you to kiss me, please." She turned in front of him and put her arms on his shoulders.

With a surge of adrenalin coursing through his veins, he wrapped his arms around her and kissed her. "That felt very good, Tom; could you do it again?"

He did. This time, she opened her mouth, causing him to do the same. She took his hand and moved it up to her breast. The kiss was a long one, and finally, they had to breathe.

"Tom, will I see you again?" she asked, holding both his hands in hers.

"Aye, Hannah; I will make it happen. I'll likely continue to work for Captain Griggs. In the early spring, I am sure we will bring cargo to Salem. I'll be here then. I will write to you, Hannah."

"I'll do the same. Until then," she said, smiling, "We will think of each other." She put her hands on Tom's face, and he bent over and kissed her once more. In five minutes, they were back at Corwin's house. The doctor thanked them for the laudanum and gave Mrs. Eastey instructions for its use. A neighbor offered to take the doctor and his two young visitors home in his cart, and after all his exertions of the afternoon, Griggs was glad to accept.

The conversation around the Griggs' dinner table that evening was animated as the doctor and his young assistants relived the afternoon's medical events and details. Tom contributed his share of comments, although his mind was somewhere else, on someone else. Did Hannah really like him, or were those kisses just some emotional reaction to his part in her father's survival? He hoped it was the former. Surely, he had been faerie-struck!

Chapter 20

Long Island

November-December 1691

Two days later, the *Prudence* was once again underway, this time toward New York. It was cold, but the wind was fair, and the ship made excellent progress. Tom, cozy in his new fearnought jacket, devoted a good portion of the trip to thinking about Hannah. He thought about how she looked, every word she said, the kisses, and even the little three-quarter moon on her left breast. He fanaticized about the future, about marrying her, maybe even in the spring. He wondered if he could be well situated by then. Being unable to control himself, he shared many of these thoughts with his young shipmate. Because it seemed like the most entertaining thing to do, John adopted a cynical position toward his moon-struck friend.

"Tom, you were taken up by the moment, lad. And she was taken by your accent. Once she gets used to your accent, she'll see how truly ugly you are."

At that, Tom laughed. "I don't know, John. I think God may have brought us together."

"I believe you've been struck by one of them Irish love faeries they talk about. What you need is another tankard of ale!"

After the *Prudence* had tied up in New York harbor and her cargo unloaded, Captain Griggs paid his three seamen. He then called Tom aside.

"Tom, you did a fine job for me on this voyage for no more experience than you have. I believe you have an eye and a heart for this business."

"Thank you, Sir."

"Furthermore, my brother, William, told me that you performed a good service for him during that accident at the barn in Salem. I am impressed with you, Tom, and I'd like to give you a permanent position with my trading business. I'll give you board and room in Gravesend and pay you eleven pounds a month. Do we have a deal, Tom?"

"Aye, Sir, we do! And thank you, Sir; thank you very much."

"Good. It's settled, then. And, Tom…don't call me 'Sir.'"

No, Sir, I won't," the young Scotsman replied.

Griggs chuckled.

That night, Tom wrote a letter to his father and mother detailing his recent adventures and good fortune. He even mentioned Hannah. He thanked God that his mother had taught him to read and write. "You must do it, Tom, to become an important man," she would tell him.

****

Winter was coming, and with it, the seas would grow less hospitable to ocean voyagers. Of course, ships still came and went in New York harbor, but Griggs' attention was given more to the landside aspects of his business and to shorter trips into Long Island Sound and to Philadelphia, which was another quickly growing city brimming with trade possibilities. That winter, he built a barn on his property with the help of both John Dobbs and Tom Hughson. The young men also worked on the mill that Griggs was constructing in Gravesend. For thirteen years, the Bolting Act prohibited the milling or packaging of flour anywhere but in New York, a very successful attempt to stimulate the city's economy. There was a movement to repeal it, however, and John Griggs wanted to be ready to take advantage of that business opportunity.

John Dobbs took Tom to his home and introduced him to his mother, Mary, and sister, Maria. The Dobbs family lived four miles to the east of Gravesend on Barrent's Island. Tom spent Christmas at their house. It had been two years since Walter Dobbs had passed away, and it was apparent to Tom that the family missed their husband and father. Christmas was not the same without him. John hoped that Tom would take a liking to his seventeen-year-old sister, and, in fact, the two did seem to get along rather well. They talked quite a bit, and that evening, Maria confessed in private to her brother that she thought Tom was special.

"He is tall and very handsome, John, and he is easy for me to talk to. He is very polite, but he also has a sense of humor. He's adventuresome, too. And I love his accent! It's too bad he has that Hannah you told me about."

John uttered a little snort. "He hardly knows her, Maria. He spent a part of one afternoon with her, and most of that was devoted to stopping her father's bleeding. I believe you're still in the horse race, Maria, if you want to be. You'll be seeing more of him."

"John. Stop being crude! I was merely saying that I admire your friend, that's all."

"Maybe I'm crude, but I think you're in love!"

"John!"

As for Tom, he had to admit to himself that Maria was, indeed, very pretty, with long blond hair, blue eyes, and a figure that was appointed with sensuous, yet subdued, curves. Furthermore, she was very animated and made Tom feel immediately at home in the Dobbs household.

It was Hannah Eastey, however, who constantly occupied his thoughts. He could not wait to get back to Salem. He saved every pound and shilling he made. He repeatedly calculated how much income it might take to provide for a wife. He wondered if her father, assuming he lived through his ordeal, would ever approve of him.

Chapter 21

Salem, Massachusetts

January-May, 1692

It was Sunday, and before church began, nine-year-old Elizabeth Parris and her eleven-year-old cousin, Abigail Williams, were huddled in a corner pew. "Tell me again what Tituba said," Abigail begged her young companion.

"She said that where she comes from, lizards crawl into little girls and eat them if they don't mind their parents. She said Satan takes the form of dogs and pigs, and they eat you unless you have your amulet."

"What's an amulet?" the other girl inquired.

"It's a little bag made of leather, and you keep the eyes of dead chickens and other things in it. She says the evil spirits cannot come near when you wear an amulet."

"Did she let you look inside her amulet?"

"Nooooo. She said nobody can look in, or its magic spell is broken."

"Do you believe anything she says about the evil spirits and lizards and amulets, Elizabeth?"

"Of course, I don't. It wouldn't be Christian. It's like when you and me played with the Venus Glass to see what our future husbands would work at. It's not real. But it's fun to think about, and sometimes, I like to scare myself by thinking about chicken eyes and lizards inside me. You should have heard Tituba the night the doctor came. She was screaming and moaning, and her eyes were rolling around in her head. She talked about all kinds of crazy things. I stayed and watched her until Dr. Griggs made me leave her room. It was fun."

"I think I would be frightened."

"It was kind of scary, but it made me feel excited, and I liked that. You should try to frighten yourself sometime, Abby, it's really fun! I like to do it after I've gone to bed."

Their conversation ended abruptly as parishioners began entering the church for the morning service. As usual, Reverend Parris was to preach on Satan.

That night, both girls were in their respective beds, thinking about their morning conversation. Images of lizards, wild dogs and pigs, and chicken eyes flashed through their minds. Elizabeth began crying and called for her mother. Abigail fell asleep but then awoke screaming from a terrible nightmare. Her parents comforted her. Receiving attention for their strange behavior only prodded them to engage in more and more of it. When they got together, they compared experiences and giggled about the fun they were having. As the days went on, their behavior became more bizarre: ranting, raving, trances, blasphemous curses. And with the increasingly strange behavior came increasing parental attention until Dr. Griggs was finally called in.

The doctor examined them thoroughly, but he could find nothing physically wrong with them. Abigail was entering puberty, which was a little early, but nothing in the doctor's experience led him to believe that those strange behaviors could be caused by the onset of womanhood. He questioned the parents about where the girls had been, what they had eaten and drunk. Nothing provided any clues.

One evening in mid-February, while sitting in their favorite chairs and watching the fire, the doctor and his wife discussed the girls' cases.

"The strange thing about it, Rachel, is that I can find nothing wrong with either of them. I almost think that if their parents were to pay less attention to it, the behavior would go away."

"William, you are forgetting that the Parris girl comes under the constant influence of that slave, Tituba, and her Caribbean spiritualism. She is of the devil, and I fear that she has brought Elizabeth under the influence of Satan. Elizabeth, in turn, has infected little Abigail Williams. I believe, Dr. Griggs, that you will find your cure by doing something about Tituba. She is a woman possessed; she is a witch!"

"You may be right, Rachel, but...I don't know...you should have seen her the night she was sick. I admit that she frightened me a little."

"Possessed, William. Those girls are possessed, and it's your moral obligation as a Christian to do something about it…to rid our community of this curse."

"Perhaps you're right, Rachel; perhaps you're right. They may be afflicted by an evil hand. I will pray about it tonight."

The next day, Dr. Griggs, feeling very unsure of himself, informed the Parris and Williams families that he believed their daughters' symptoms resulted from their being possessed and under the influence of Satan. Nothing else that he knew of could explain their mysterious behaviors.

Under the guidance of Reverend Parris, the Salem community entered into a period of prayer and fasting to rid itself of the satanic influence. John Indian, an ardent Puritan, and churchman, baked a witch cake comprised of rye meal and Elizabeth's and Abigail's urine. He maintained that the cake had special magic that would allow the girls to identify their witch tormenters.

When that wasn't successful, the girls were extensively interrogated by church fathers, who beseeched them to identify the witches responsible for their condition. Finally, on February 29th, they produced three names: Tituba, Sarah Osborne, and Sarah Good. All three were arrested and interrogated on March 1st by Magistrates Corwin and Hawthorne. Sarah Osborne and Sarah Good fervently maintained that they were not witches, but Tituba made no such denial. In fact, she asserted that the devil did, indeed, appear to her and that there were other witches in Salem to whom he was doing the same.

Over the next few weeks, witch hysteria spread among the people of Salem. Many came forward to tell of how they were being tormented. Names and accusations flew, suspects were interrogated, and their bodies were examined for the presence of witch marks.

****

In early April, Josiah Forbes told Magistrate Hawthorne that he was certain that Eastey's wife, Mary, was a witch. He told the magistrate that he had seen Mrs. Eastey in the woods petting a dead raven and talking to it in a strange tongue. On April 19th, she was arrested and interrogated along with three others. Much to Mary's horror, one of the women, Abigail Hobbs, confessed to being a witch. Mary was sent home and told to not leave the village.

Obtaining John Griggs' address from the doctor, young Hannah Eastey wrote a letter to Tom, telling him about what had been happening to her mother.

It was two weeks later, and Tom had spent the day on Barrent's Island helping John prepare one of the gardens for the spring planting. He returned to Gravesend in the late afternoon, and Mrs. Griggs met him by the well, where he was washing off the evidence of his hard work.

"Tom, a letter came in the post for you today. It looks like it's from Salem."

He dried off his hands and opened the seal quickly, again silently thanking his mother for teaching him to read.

"May 24, 1692

Dear Tom,

I hope you don't think it forward of me to write you and, indeed, I am not certain this letter will ever reach you. Thanks to God's Providence, my father's leg is healing. Although he still limps, he can work, and he is grateful to God for the gift of health that He has given him.

On another matter, however, we are not so lucky. Last January, two young girls in the Village were acting strangely. Dr. Griggs concluded that they were under a satanic influence because he could not find anything else wrong with them. The girls named three women whom they accused of satanic influence, and one of them, a slave named Tituba, confessed that she was a witch. Since that time, the Village has become obsessed with discovering more witches and other people under the influence of Satan. Several women and a few men have been examined by the magistrates and found to be witches. In April, my mother was arrested and examined. John Indian, young Ann Putnam, and Mary Walcott all testified that Mother's specter choked and bit them. Mother's sisters, Rebecca and

214

Sarah, were also arrested and examined. They locked Mother in jail for a month and then let her go after she promised to not leave Salem. Two days later, they arrested her again, and now she is in jail. They say she will be tried in September.

I do not know what all this will lead to, but I am frightened. I am told that once all the witches have been discovered, Reverend Parris will lead the village in a week of prayers and fasting to eliminate the curse they believe has fallen on some of us. They believe that then we will be purified, there would be no need for a trial, and we can go back to our normal lives.

Tom, I swear to you, as I swore to them, that Mother is no witch, and she does not consort with the devil. The Putnams have been fighting with Father for years over land ownership. That is why Ann said what she did about Mother. Father is worried about my birthmark. He thinks that if they find out about it, they will arrest me, too. Tom, I am no witch. No demon placed that mark on my breast. I pray to God daily, and I read my Bible. I want this terrible thing to be over with, and I hope that it will soon be. There is no way you can write me, but I will write you as things change. I am looking forward with great fondness to seeing you when you next come to Salem.

Respectfully,

Hannah Eastey"

Tom read the letter again. His heart began to race, and he felt a level of panic rush through his body. John Griggs sat on the front porch smoking his pipe and waiting for dinner. Tom took the letter to him.

"Captain, do you remember me mentioning Hannah Eastey, the young woman in Salem?"

"How could I forget, Tom? That's all you talked about on the voyage home. You gave John quite a bit of pleasure over it; you did! He thinks that lass turned your mind to porridge." He let out a chuckle.

"Here's a letter I received from her today. What do you think it means?"

Griggs took the letter. He, too, read it twice and then handed it back to Tom.

"What do you think it means, Sir?"

"I don't know, Tom. I imagine it will pass, and your Hannah will be alright. Those Puritans certainly are a peculiar bunch, though. Witches!… There is no such thing as witches. I don't imagine they would let any real harm come to Hannah or those other women, but" he paused, "I just don't know."

John Griggs thought a minute.

"I'll tell you what I will do, Tom. It seems like my brother, William, got the whole affair going with his satanic diagnosis. He's a leader in that community up there, and perhaps he'd be able to put a stop to it. I'll write him a letter and see if I can bring him to his senses. His wife, Rachel, is a problem, though. She's a wonderful woman, but she's an ardent believer in the Faith, and I imagine she supported him. I imagine she encouraged him."

"Perhaps I should go to Salem," Tom suggested.

"No, Tom. Wait until I contact my brother. I think everything will work out. I'll write him tonight."

That night, Griggs devoted two hours to composing a lengthy letter to his older brother, William. He implored him to reconsider what he was doing and the effect it was having on the community. He talked about young Hannah Eastey, how Tom had met her, and how he felt about her. He reminded William of his stature in the village and how the elders would certainly listen to him. He enlisted memories about their parents and how George and Alice Griggs would feel about William's part in all the unhappiness that was occurring. It was a good letter. Elizabeth read it and thought so, too. He posted it the next day.

Two weeks later, John's letter to his brother arrived in Salem. Rachel was the first to see it. She opened it, read it, and threw it into the fireplace. It was May 23rd.

****

John Griggs' plan was to wait until mid-September to hear from his brother, but early September came and went, and still, there was no letter from him. Then, on September 19th, he spoke with a mariner on the New York docks. The man had just come from Salem. He told Griggs that a special court had been convened by Massachusetts Governor Phips to try those accused of witchcraft in Salem, and he thought that some defendants had already been convicted and condemned to hang. John reluctantly shared this news with Tom.

"I have a load of wheat and molasses that is supposed to go to Salem, Tom. I was going to take it there later in the month, but given the circumstances, we can leave tomorrow if we get the *Prudence* loaded."

"Would I get there any faster if I took a horse along the Boston Post Road?"

"No, Tom," he answered. "I'm afraid the quickest way is aboard the *Prudence*."

The four men worked long into the night, stowing cargo and making the ship ready for the voyage. The next morning, they left with the outgoing tide.

At 1:00 PM two days later, September 23rd, the *Prudence* glided up to the Salem dock. Tom, with the bow line in hand, leapt from the deck, secured the line to the dock with three quick cleat hitches, and sprinted up the hill toward the town's livery to secure a horse for the eight-mile trip to

Topsfield. Panting heavily, he saw a crowd off in the distance; it seemed to be in the process of dispersing. An elderly man was walking in his direction, and Tom stopped him.

"What is going on over there?" he demanded.

"They hanged another witch, lad. Her soul is now purged and purified, and she can go to Heaven."

"Who was it? Who did they hang?" he demanded.

"It was Isaac Eastey's wife."

Tom panicked. "Where's her daughter, Hannah? I've got to find her!"

"That won't be easy, Son. She's gone. She left yesterday for Boston or some other place south of here with her uncle. I don't think she's coming back 'cause her father fears for her life if they decide to examine her. I ain't from these parts, myself. Don't plan to stay either! These people are demented!"

Tom immediately thought of Hannah's birthmark, and he knew her leaving was the right thing. He thanked the man and slowly walked back toward the dock. He began to cry; he couldn't help himself. In ten minutes, he was aboard the *Prudence*; he told Griggs what he had learned about the hanging and Hannah's escape.

Griggs' first response was to console Tom.

"She may write you again, Tom, and tell you where she is. I wouldn't give up hope yet."

But then anger welled up in him. Why didn't his brother answer his letter? It could have made a difference. He could have made an earlier trip to Salem.

"Damn that brother of mine and his crazy wife! His name will go down the generations as the one who started all this witch lunacy. I can't stand this place. Why doesn't the Governor put a stop to these crazy people? I should go see William and confront him, but I guess it wouldn't help at this point." He paused, then added,

"Let's get the cargo off-loaded and leave this town before I kill somebody!"

Chapter 22

Western Long Island

Spring 1693

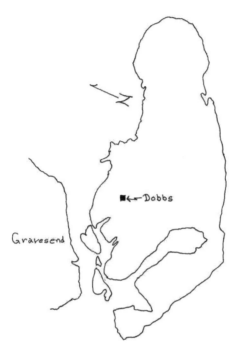

Barrent's Island

It was now early May; no letter from Hannah Eastey ever arrived, and over the past months, John Dobbs had done his best to lift Tom's spirits. His primary strategy was to ask Tom to spend some of his free days with his mother, his sister, Maria, and himself, helping out on their small farm on Barrent's Island. During the spring, Tom made the short trip to the island several times. Because of his own upbringing in Scotland, he knew farming, and he enjoyed the hard work he put in on the Dobbs' crops. Furthermore, John's mother and

221

sister always rewarded him with a good meal and the warmth that comes from being part of a family.

As the weeks passed, John began to see progress in his friend. After all, Tom didn't really know Hannah; he had met her for only three hours, and, more than anything else, it was the loss of his fantasies about her that he had to deal with. It was clear to John and Tom that time was, indeed, working its healing magic.

It was Saturday in late June, and once again, Tom found himself on Barrent's Island helping John, his mother, and Maria work their fields. Tom's obsession with Hannah had been fading over the past few months, and he began to look forward to seeing Maria.

Although not yet July, it was a hot and humid Long Island summer day. The sun beat down on the four as they worked at weeding and cultivating. Seagulls floated on the currents overhead in their lazy, effortless way, and cicadas seemed to be everywhere, filling the air with their raspy buzz. Somewhere, a meadowlark was calling to its mate. Tom finished hoeing a row of young squash, and he went over to the bucket under an oak tree to quench his thirst with a dipper of water.

Seeing him move in that direction, Maria took a break from harvesting lettuce and made her way toward the oak tree. Tom noticed her approaching, and something inside him wiggled ever so slightly. Much to her mother's chagrin,

Maria's farming trousseau consisted of a pair of her brother's hand-me-down britches, the legs of which she cut off at mid-calf, and a hand-me-down linen pull-over shirt with two buttons at the top, which she never buttoned. Over time, her mother had become used to that outfit on her daughter, but Tom never did. Whenever the opportunity arose, he stole surreptitious glances at Maria in her farmer togs, her slender yet athletic frame evident underneath. This day, she had tied her long hair back with a green ribbon, and a blond mane hung from her bonnet down to the bottom of her shoulder blades. She was barefoot, and her britches were dirty from the kneeling she had been doing. The back and the front of her brother's old shirt were wet with perspiration, something Tom found intriguing, or was the word arousing?

"Thomas, I suppose you never experienced heat like this in Scotland."

He filled the dipper and passed it to her.

"Nay, Scotland is much easier on a man's and a woman's clothes." He gave her damp shirt a quick glance, and she smiled at him.

"When Father died three years ago, we had a difficult time keeping things up. Of course, the wages John earns from Captain Griggs help a lot. We used to hire men to work our fields, but without Father, we were unable to. My Uncle Isaac wanted to send one of his slaves to work in our fields,

223

but Mother would have none of it. Then, after Mother married Nathaniel Pitman, her situation improved when she and my little brother and sister moved to Mr. Pitman's in New York. John and I stayed out here."

She continued the story. "Before Mother married Nathaniel Pitman, she transferred this land to my older brother, William. Poor William is trying to become successful with his brewery in New York, and he isn't able to help much with the fields or with the money. Mr. Pitman is a trader, and it carries him back and forth to the Caribbean Islands. Even my mother doesn't see much of him. He tells her that will change in a few years. Maybe it will."

She paused and then added, "That's why Mother still spends much time out here with us."

"From the way they seem to be enjoying themselves, your little brother and sister must like it on the island."

"Both of them love it here. Walter, especially, is not happy living in Mr. Pitman's house. It's a very nice home on Pearl Street, but it's not the same. I think Margaret likes the farm better, too. I know I certainly wouldn't enjoy being there. This is my home, Thomas. I love the feel of grass under my feet, not cobblestones."

"Aye, this is, indeed, a beautiful place, and I'm glad to help with the crops, Maria. John and your whole family have been good to me. And I still think about that delicious Christmas dinner."

There was a pause in the conversation, and Maria changed the subject.

"Thomas, what was it like up there in Salem?" she asked in a way that seemed to Tom at once bold but also, he knew, came straight from her heart.

"I don't know how to think about it, Maria. I guess I really didn't know Hannah, but over that winter, I thought a lot about her. I had never done that before. When we got to Salem, it was such a shock; Maria…she had gone away with her uncle." he paused and looked at the ground.

"I'd wager she was a fine lookin' lass, wasn't she, Thomas?"

"Aye, she was very pretty."

"Those people in Salem are evil, Thomas. God will surely punish them."

"At least they've stopped holding trials. Governor Phipps put an end to it."

Maria changed the subject. "Do you like working for Captain Griggs?"

Tom broke off a long stalk of grass and began chewing on the end.

"I consider myself very lucky, Maria. He's been very kind to me these past months, and I feel I owe him something in return. Your brother, John, has been a real friend, too. I've learned much from them, and I've saved a tidy sum of money already. Sailing the ships and working on the docks in New York is honest labor, and I love being on the water, but I don't think it's how I wish to spend my life."

"What do you want to do, then, Thomas?" she inquired.

He leaned over and picked up a clod of dirt. He squeezed it and let it fall through his fingers. "I believe I want to farm. I know somethin' about farming. We have a farm in Scotland. We grow wheat, rye, potatoes, and other vegetables. We also have some sheep, a cow, and horses. My father was a soldier, but he was home enough to see that our crops got planted and harvested. Of course, my brother and I did much of the work." He paused.

"Is your brother there now?"

"No. He was killed in battle, fighting the Lowlanders. He wanted to be just like our Father, and when he was 18, he got his wish. Two years later, he was dead."

"What was his name?"

"Richard…his name was Richard." Another pause. "My mother died three months ago, and my father is now there by himself, but he told me he'd come to America once I got established."

"Do you think he will ever come here?"

"Nay. He is a son of the Isles, and I believe it's there that he wants his bones to rest…next to my mother's." Another pause.

"I think I could make a life at farming, Maria. There's something about the smell of the earth and the sight of the young plants first coming up in the spring that makes me feel good. I must think about a way to do it. I'm saving all my money, and I'll just have to see what opportunities God brings me."

Maria looked at him and smiled. He smiled back.

"You're a good man, Thomas Hughson." She put her hand on his arm. "I believe you'll get your farm and become a wealthy gentleman, too."

Her blue eyes locked onto his blue ones and lingered there. Something wiggled again...down deep in his gut.

That evening, Mary Dobbs laid out a big dinner for her hard-working children and the hard-working young man who came to help them in their fields. She arranged the table so Tom sat across from Maria. There was much small talk at dinner about farming, ocean voyages, and Scotland. Tom thought he was doing a good job of masking his growing interest in John's sister; he kept the conversation flowing. But his performance wasn't good enough to get by Mary. She saw their glances lingering on each other, and she knew that something was brewing. She liked this young man; she especially liked his accent.

Soon after dinner, Tom was ready to leave. He still had a half-hour's walk to Gravesend after he got off the island.

"The tide's in. I'll row Thomas across, Mother," Maria announced in a determined voice.

Mary and her son, John, glanced at each other.

"She's well able to row the skiff, Ma." He had a twinkle in his eye.

"Alright, then, but come right back, Maria. I don't want you on the water after dark."

At the water's edge, Tom insisted on rowing the skiff across the short expanse of Jamaica Bay that made Barrent's Island an island. Maria sat in the stern, and during the trip, they didn't say much, but they did look at each other, long gazes that would have been impossible at the dinner table. The sun was beginning to set, and somewhere in the trees toward which Tom was rowing on the bank, a mourning dove began giving voice to his evening vigilance.

"I'm glad you came today, Thomas, and not just because you helped with our crops, either."

"I'm glad I came, too," he returned.

The boat slid up onto the sand and came to a rest. Tom shipped his oars and climbed out. Somewhat to his surprise, Maria climbed out, too.

"You're a good oarsman, Thomas," she said with a smile.

"Your brother taught me well, Maria."

There was a pause.

"Will you come back soon?"

I can come in one week if your mother will have me."

"She likes you, Thomas. She told me so."

He looked down at her bare feet, not knowing quite what to say next.

Then, he took a leap of faith.

"Can I kiss you, Maria?"

"Yes, I want you to kiss me goodnight so I can kiss you back."

He bent over and kissed her. She put her arms around his neck and said, "That was very nice. Would you please kiss me again, Sir?"

He did.

"I like you, Thomas," she whispered in his ear.

"I like you, too, Maria…very much."

They released their hold on each other. Tom was speechless as Maria turned, stepped into the skiff, and took her place at the oars. She turned around and looked at him with a huge grin.

"Will you kindly push me off, Mister Hughson?"

Tom pushed the boat out into the water and shoved the bow to the side to help her reverse direction. She expertly swung the boat around and bent to the oars.

"Come back soon, Thomas Hughson, or I'll miss you," she yelled as the boat slipped out into the bay.

"I will…I'll come back soon," he promised.

He stood there on the shore and watched her guide the craft toward the small dock on the opposite shore. Tom started down the path toward Gravesend.

Wow! Maria!

John was right. His sister certainly was strong-willed. "Forward" was the word. The girl knows her mind and acts on it. His heart was pounding. He was in love, perhaps real love this time!

Those blue, blue eyes!

Those lips!

The little wiggle down inside had grown into an earthquake as he shouted "Maria!" to the noisy cicadas and tree frogs. He quickened his pace toward Gravesend as Venus, already visible in the darkening sky, led the way.

Chapter 23

Tom and Maria

1693-1694

Throughout the summer and into the fall, Tom did come back many times, in fact. In the middle of October, Maria's mother took her younger children back to the Pitman residence in New York, and Tom became a frequent visitor there, too. When they were in New York, John or Mary conveniently invited him on one pretext or another, and he and Maria cherished those occasions to develop their relationship.

Tom worked hard for John Griggs. He lived frugally and saved every pound, shilling, and farthing he earned. By Christmas, it was well understood by all that Tom and Maria would eventually be married, but first, Tom had to have enough money to make into a reality the farm both wanted. He worked for Griggs another six months, and the pounds, shillings, and farthings accumulated. In May 1694, during a Sunday evening dinner, Nathaniel Pitman announced that he had arranged with Frederick Philipse, the wealthiest man in New York, the possibility of two land lease holdings on his manor in Westchester County.

"He's a very rich man, Tom. He started out as a carpenter for the West India Company and then became a trader. Thirty years ago, he married a rich widow, Margaret

Hardenbroeck de Vries. He's combined her wealth and his shrewdness to make himself the richest man in New York. There's hardly a venture he's not involved in, from windmills to pirates. I've had many business dealings with him. He has a 92,000 acre land grant in Westchester County, and just last year, he was even given exclusive rights to the King's Bridge. Now, if you want to enter or leave Manhattan by land, you must pay his toll. He's a tough old Dutchman, but he's always been fair with me, and he's willing to make you and John a good deal on two leases."

Pitman told Tom that if he and John wanted to farm, this would be an excellent opportunity. The rent would be a portion of the crops, and Philipse was even willing to consider some arrangement so the two could eventually own the lands they would be farming.

Later that evening, Tom and Maria walked back into the small apple and cherry orchard that grew behind the Pitman home. They held hands as Tom discussed the opportunity. She pulled him behind the gardener's shed.

"Sit down, tall Thomas, so I can reach you."

Tom sat down on the stump of what was once a very large chestnut tree. Maria dropped into his lap and put her arms around him. They gave each other a long hug.

"Thomas, I am ready to be a farmer's wife," she said softly into his ear. "I am ready to help plant crops, keep a house, take care of you, and raise lots of children...our children."

"She rubbed her nose back and forth across his a couple of times. "I love you, Thomas."

They kissed. "I love you too, Maria. And as for me, I want to be married to a farmer's wife as soon as possible, especially one who occasionally wears britches."

Another long kiss.

****

A trip up to Westchester County to the location of the holdings and a meeting with Philipse's solicitor finalized the arrangement. Tom's leasehold was a 279-acre parcel, much of it in hardwood forest but a good bit in meadows that would make farming easy. There were several brooks and three fair-sized ponds on the land, a good place for some livestock. Best of all, it was only a short distance from the North (i.e., Hudson) River, and it afforded easy access to the wagon road down to New York. The other leasehold, which John Dobbs would be farming, was a little distance to the south, and it boasted a similar geography, one that would be very appealing to any young farmer. Tom felt blessed; it would be a good place for Maria and him to begin their lives together. When he got back to Gravesend that night, Tom wrote a letter to his father:

"Da,

In my last letter, I told you about Maria Dobbs. She is a wonderful girl, beautiful, hardworking, and intelligent, and when I am around her, we are constantly laughing. She reminds me of Mother, with her blond hair, blue eyes, and slender carriage. She calls me Thomas. Also, I find her mother and brother, John, to be very compatible with me. We are planning to get married soon. Her stepfather knows a rich Dutchman who will give me a land lease up the North River about 25 miles from New York. It's a good piece of property, about 280 acres, with meadows and forests and a flowing spring near where I'd build our home. Maria's brother, John, is going to farm the land next to mine, so we'll be close to each other when we need assistance. The land is near the North River, and John wants to start a ferry service over to New Jersey. I may get involved in that, too. Da, please do consider coming to New York to live with us. I know you would like it here, and eventually, there may be some bairns for you to play with and instruct in the art of swordsmanship. Write me when you can.

I remain-----

Your respectful Son

Tom

Between the money he had saved and the cash he received from the sale of MacFie's gunsmithing equipment,

Tom was able to purchase a horse and wagon and some construction and farming tools. With the occasional expert assistance of John Griggs' son, Benjamin, Tom and John devoted the next three months to building two log homes on their holdings. Much to Tom's delight, he found Benjamin Griggs to be a very amicable and skilled craftsman. A year younger than Tom, Benjamin exhibited a keen interest in anything that had to be designed and built. He had a good eye for space and how to use it, and on more than one occasion, his builder's insight, which seemed to come naturally, saved Tom and John from making some architectural blunder.

Knowing how impatient Tom and his sister were to be married, John insisted that they build Tom's home first. It was a substantial structure, built on a rise and containing four rooms, a back entryway, and a porch on the front. Its centerpiece was a huge stone fireplace that dominated one wall of the largest room. A short distance from the back door, a spring bubbled out of a rocky crag, its water meandering down to a brook. The house was in a clearing surrounded by tall chestnuts and oaks, a very cozy place, indeed, to begin a life together.

As soon as the structure neared completion, Mary and Maria made regular visits to the homestead and added their labor to create the dream. Beside the new home, they planted some vegetables that would satisfy the newlyweds' needs during the upcoming winter. With each wagon trip came more furniture and other necessities for the house, much of it from the farm on Barrent's Island.

By late August, everything seemed to be ready, and Tom and Maria were married on a Saturday evening in a log church in Gravesend, surrounded by family and friends. The minister, an elderly Presbyterian named William MacGowen, assured the gathering that Tom and Maria had been ordained by God to meet, to love each other, and to be fruitful and make the world a better place. Much to everyone's relief, Tom finally got to kiss the bride. After the service, a reception was held at the Griggs home, and to see the effort she put into it, a casual observer would have thought that Tom and Maria were Elizabeth Griggs' own children.

"Tom," Captain Griggs said, putting his hand on the groom's shoulder, "you're a fine young man, and I hate to lose you. But, you're choosin' the life of a farmer over a mariner, which means you'll probably live to an old age and die in bed. I'm happy for you, Tom. You've got a fine lass there in Maria. If I can ever help you, be sure and let me know."

"Thank you, Captain," Tom replied. "You've been very good to me, and I will not forget your kindness."

The young couple spent the next two nights in Nathaniel Pitman's home on Pearl Street. They had the house to themselves. By the fifth evening, they were in their new log farmhouse in what would eventually be known as Dobbs Ferry on the eastern shore of the Hudson River. Life was good!

****

A month went by, Tom and Maria had begun to settle into the routine that nature and reality demanded of any couple intending to devote their lives to growing things. The barn was nearing completion, and the new hen house boasted 13 hens. "He's for Sunday dinner," Tom announced when he brought a rooster home.

Maria was quick to react. "Thomas, you wouldn't really eat the father of all the rest of our Sunday dinners, would you?"

"I guess not. Let's give him a name so we'll be sure to not invite him to dinner."

Maria chuckled.

"How about James, after your famous Scottish king?"

"Aye, that's a good name, Lass. It would be hard to eat a Scottish rooster named James. I can see it now. 'Goodbye, Momma.' 'Goodbye, children. Have a wonderful day at school, and when you get home, Mamma will have somethin' real tasty for your dinner tonight. COME HERE, JAMES! BAWK!' Nay, that would never happen here!"

Maria laughed so hard she had to sit down. "Thomas, I love you a bunch. You make me laugh, and you make me feel good at night, and I'm very glad we're married."

"Aye, Maria, me, too. I'm glad we're married, and, in case I haven't mentioned it, I, too, enjoy our evenings together." She giggled and slapped him on his rump as he rose from the table.

The crops that everyone had planted earlier in the spring were thriving, and a good part of Tom's days was devoted to helping John finish his house a quarter mile to the south. Returning one evening from a trip to Philipsburg Manor to sell some cabbages, Tom added a beagle puppy to the growing Hughson estate. He declared the little hound to be a late wedding present for Maria to keep her company when her husband was in the fields.

"Do you think he'll hunt rabbits when he grows up?"

"I'll take him next time I go."

"Thomas, I'm coming with you. You can teach me to hunt rabbits, then he and I can be Nimrods together."

What's a Nimrod?"

"I think it means hunter in some language. I heard Mr. Pitman use it a few times." She paused. "That's it, Thomas. I'll call him Nimrod."

She picked up the puppy and hugged him to her breast. "Would you like to be called Nimrod, little fellow?"

The puppy licked her on the end of her nose.

"That means he likes the name Maria. Nimrod, it is then." Tom enveloped Maria and Nimrod in a big group hug and kissed each of them on their cheeks.

****

One warm early October afternoon, Tom showed up at the door a little sooner than usual.

"Come with me, Maria, he said, "I have something to show you."

He took her back on the property to a clear rocky stream that meandered through the woods. They walked north up the stream to a point where the land began to rise on either side. Because of the shade cast by the huge chestnuts, elms, and oaks, the forest floor was clear, and the pair found the going easy. The draw through which the brook ran veered off to the right, and when they turned that corner, Tom stopped.

"Well, what do you think, Lass?" he asked.

In front of Maria lay a beautiful little pool perhaps 30 feet in diameter, created in a clearing by a dam of stones and gravel that stretched from one side of the small rocky canyon to the other. At the upper end, the stream fell over a rocky ledge, and a small waterfall splashed its way into the pool. On either side, flat rocks protruded out of the canyon sides

239

just above the water, creating a perfect setting for a picnic or a relaxed meditation in the sun.

"Thomas! It's beautiful! Did you make this?" she exclaimed.

"Aye. John and I found the stream when we were hunting for squirrels. When I saw the waterfall and how the land rises on each side of the stream, I thought I'd try my hand at damming it. There was already a small pool here. I just had to make it bigger."

"How deep is it?"

"About four feet in the middle. Of course, it's shallow around the edges, and it drops off gently. Do you like it, Maria?"

"I absolutely love it. Is it on our property?"

"Aye, that it is. But I don't ken we'll have it all to ourselves because your brother knows about it. Certainly, he'll make use of it. I thought it would be a good place to picnic or perhaps go swimming."

"Do you think he may bring Elizabeth Hyatt up here for a picnic?"

"He may, but not if her father has anything to do with it. I know they're sweet on each other, but old man Hyatt wants his daughter's suitors to already be established."

"Maybe she'll wait for him to prosper. You help him with his farm, Thomas, and perhaps you'll have nieces and nephews before you know it."

There was a slight pause as she dipped her hand into the water and asked, "There aren't any leaches in the pool, are there?"

"Nay. No leaches, no fish, no turtles."

"Well then, let's try it, Thomas!"

"Now?" He looked at his young bride.

"Why not? Now, it seems perfect to me. Come on, Thomas!"

She was already in the process of unbuttoning and unfastening, and her clothes fell, one by one, to the forest floor. Tom, now energized, added his to the pile. He stared at her in wonderment. Her blond hair and blue eyes, her slender frame, her beautiful breasts, her cute, round derriere. And her constant smile. Was she really his wife? How God had blessed him! They waded into the water, which was a little chilly but invigorating. Tom noticed that Maria's nipples rose to the occasion. He also found himself rising to the occasion despite the cool water. Maria dropped into the water immediately, while Tom felt his way a little more cautiously.

"Just dunk yourself quickly. You'll get it over fast, and then you'll feel warm."

She was right. The strategy worked, and in a moment, they were wrapped in each other's arms, bodies, and lips pressed together. Maria's hips squirmed back and forth. "What's that down there, Thomas?"

"That's a rather personal question, Mrs. Hughson."

"Well, then, you must give me a personal answer, Mr. Hughson."

Seven minutes later, Maria broke their embrace and began laughing.

"What's so funny?"

"I was just thinking. Have you ever noticed how when a cat approaches another cat, it knows they greet each other by bumping their heads together?"

"Aye, I saw that as a child in Scotland."

"Well, we humans do the same thing, only we kiss instead of bumping heads. Perhaps we should bump heads before we kiss."

"Maria, you have an entertaining mind."

"Let's try it."

"I'm willing, but I think our head bump should come after the kiss. It seems more appropriate."

They kissed and then bumped their foreheads together.

"I like it, Thomas. It seems to communicate something special. Do you think we may be part cat?"

"I wonder if lions bump heads when they greet."

"They probably do."

"Aye, then we'll do it, too."

And so they did, for the next twenty-three happy years. The last thing Maria said to her husband on her deathbed was, "Thomas, let's kiss and bump heads one more time." They did.

Was that little swimming hole ever a good idea! Thank you, John, for helping to build it. Ten minutes later, the young couple walked back to the house and the waiting Nimrod. Nine months later, on June 14, 1695, little Thomas was born; Nimrod and James had a baby brother! Life was good!

Chapter 24

Elizabeth

New York, 1694

Measured in acres, Tom and Maria's first harvest was not large, but what grew, grew well. They worked hard, and Maria's bother, John, and Tom helped each other with the cultivating and harvesting. Both young men were maturing quickly under their new role as planters. John's house was built, and his barn was almost completed. Maria teased him about having to find a wife, maybe that pretty Elizabeth Hyatt, but John protested that he was too busy to be encumbered with a woman in his life.

"A wife will have to wait, Maria, for a year or two until I am a wealthy gentleman!"

"Well, go clear some more land then, Squire Dobbs," Maria chided good-naturedly. "Maybe Miss Elizabeth will wait, little brother."

By the middle of November, Tom was ready to make his second trip to New York with a wagonload of produce from their farm, along with some cured skins from bears and cougars that he had shot and beavers and otters he had trapped. This time, Maria accompanied him on the 25-mile excursion. It was a bright, crisp autumn morning for their adventure, one that made you glad for your coat and wrap. Steam issued forth from the horse's (Maria named him

"Jonas") nostrils as Tom led him out of the barn and hitched him to the wagon.

The road south to New York was a narrow wagon trail that meandered through the hilly forests along the east side of the Hudson River. This time of year, the road was muddy in places but still easily passable for any travelers who were not in a hurry. Maria remarked how pretty the woods were against the bright blue sky, now stripped of their leaves and awaiting the winter snow. Deer and other wildlife seemed to be everywhere. Occasionally, the road crossed a stony brook, still flowing freely to the Hudson, not yet encumbered by the ice that was soon to arrive.

The road took the young couple past occasional farms, with their friendly smell of wood smoke, and down through Yonkers, eventually joining up with the Kings Bridge Road. At the north end of Manhattan, they paid Mr. Philipse's toll at the bridge over Spuyten Duyvill Creek.

"You'd think that Patroon Philipse had enough money without the toll bridge, too," Maria mused.

"Rich people are just like poor people, Maria. There's never enough money for either of 'em."

"I feel rich already, Thomas." She leaned over and kissed him on his cheek. "God is good to us. Just look at the bounty in this wagon."

Tom had to agree. God was, indeed, good to them.

They continued south on the Kings Bridge Road until it ran into Broadway, a wide road that went south into New York, mostly dirt with not a small amount of mud this time of year. As Tom negotiated the wagon round the worst of the ruts, they passed the small farms, fields, and orchards that stretched from the west side of the Broadway down to the Hudson River. Two gristmills greeted them along the way, their circular sails rotating lazily in the afternoon breeze that was floating off the river. There were also a number of taverns and tippling houses along the road, and Tom half-jokingly suggested that they stop at one for a tankard of ale, but Maria vetoed the plan. She was ready to get to her mother's and the hearty dinner she knew would be in preparation.

As they drew closer to the city, the east side of Broadway became increasingly dotted with cottages, small business establishments, and other buildings. Shortly, they reached the intersection with Maiden Lane, and the city was upon them. Tom turned Jonas east on Maiden Lane and then south on Nassau Street. At the gate in the old wall, the street changed its name to Broad Street.

They continued south and ran into a traffic jam at the green. Hundreds of people, horses, wagons, and carts were gathered around a gigantic bonfire. Many of the revelers were intoxicated, and several fired guns into the air. Tom experienced a moment of panic as the thought entered his mind that there had been a rebellion in the city, but a passing reveler informed him that Governor Benjamin Fletcher had ordered the celebration in honor of the King's birthday. It had been only three years since ex-Governor Leisler had swung from the gallows and then lost his head to the block for his papist ways, and the new Governor wanted to impress on all his subjects that William and Mary were now the legitimate monarchs of England and its possessions.

Tom eventually extricated Jonas and the wagon from the fray and continued south. Maria brought up the subject of Leisler's demise.

"Why do you think they cut off his head after they hanged him and then went to the trouble of sewing it back on again before he was buried?"

"Who knows, Maria? What can I say? They're English, and I'm Scottish. I don't think like them."

She laughed. "Perhaps they wanted him to have his head for the Second Coming. That's probably it. You see, Thomas, you Scotsmen have it all wrong; the English are civilized after all!"

"Aye. It wouldn't do to be headless at the resurrection. He needs to see what Hell looks like when he gets there!"

They both laughed at that comment.

Almost to the fort, Tom turned Jonas west on Bridge Street and over to Pearl Street, where the Pitmans lived.

Pearl Street was a fashionable area of town. The street was paved with pebbles and cobblestones, and the homes were large and well-kept. The fact that Pitman owned a house here attested to his wealth and prominence in the city. The young couple would spend two nights at the Pitman's and the day in between, Tom would devote to selling his produce at the market over on Dock Street.

His early morning trip to the market was short and easy, one block from the Great Dock on the East River. Each time Tom went to New York, it seemed to him like it had grown. The market was teaming with hundreds of people buying and selling farm produce, animals, clothing, spices, glass, farm implements, shoes, house wares, and even furniture. Bustling would be the word to describe it. People of all descriptions, aristocrats, freemen, indentured servants, and slaves, young and old, mingling, buying, selling, bargaining, and all in over a dozen tongues. There were tradesmen everywhere, advertising their services: wheelwrights, carpenters, coopers, sail makers, the gunsmith who bought MacFie's tools and, for the first time, a glassblower.

Tom found a good place to park his wagon. The skins sold almost immediately and for much more than he ever dreamed possible. Wealth was accumulating in New York, and the wealthy were increasingly able to spend their money on things that would set them apart from the commoners. Fur adornments were one of those items.

By late morning, Tom's wagonload of turnips, squash, onions, and potatoes was moving quickly. In between sales, he consumed his lunch of bread, cheese, and apples that Maria had assembled for him in her mother's kitchen. He was in the middle of finishing up the last of the cheese when a young black woman approached his wagon. Tom thought she must be a slave, but she was well dressed, and she carried herself and her wicker basket with a dignity uncommon among the slaves in New York. Tom hesitated.

"Elizabeth?" he asked tentatively.

"Mr. Hughson? Mr. Hughson from the *Victory*?" she exclaimed.

"Aye. The same one. You explained to me about the light in the water coming off the ship's bow."

"I remember. You were nice to me, Mr. Hughson. You made me feel better." There was a pause while she petted Jonas.

"What happened to you, Sir? I see you're a farmer."

"Aye. I spent some time as a mariner for a merchant named Griggs, but now I have a leasehold near Philipse Manor in Westchester County."

"You don't farm it by yourself, do you, Sir?"

"No, I am married to a girl named Maria. Her brother, John, has another leasehold south of mine, and we help each other. We've just started out, but the land is good, and we're going to grow. And please call me Tom or Thomas or something, Elizabeth. I'm neither old enough nor wealthy enough to be 'Sir.'"

"I'm glad you found something to do, Thomas." She smiled at him. "I'm sure your wife is very pretty."

"Aye, she is...as pretty as they come." Again, Tom was struck by how refined this slave girl was, how articulate. She spoke better English than he did, and it was certain that she had read more.

"How about you, Elizabeth? What happened to you? Did you go to those people to help with their children?"

"Yes. The Verplancks on Stone Street. I mind their children; I teach them to read and do sums. I help with chores around their home and go to the market for food."

She gestured toward the basket she was carrying.

"They're fair, but Mrs. Verplanck is strict. I have the freedom to come and go, and they give me some money to spend on myself. I guess I could be worse off."

They looked at each other for a few seconds.

"In fact," she smiled, "I'd like to buy some of your onions and potatoes for the Verplancks' table."

Tom picked through his remaining produce, selecting the best specimens to fill her basket. An emotion welled up inside him.

"I don't like slavery, Elizabeth. It certainly is not in God's purpose for men to own other men. Slavery is of the devil…it's wrong!"

"I know, Thomas. But the Bible says that we should endure the present with joy and place our hope in the eternity we will spend with Jesus. That's what I try to do."

Responding to an emotional impulse, Tom asked, "How much would it cost to purchase your freedom, Elizabeth?"

Elizabeth smiled at him. "I don't think the Verplancks would let me go, Thomas." Then she added. "If I were free, there'd be nowhere for me to work or live anyway. In some ways, the freed slaves are worse off than the rest of us. There's a group of them just north of the city, but they are very poor, and they have a hard time just staying alive. No one in New York wants them, and if they go somewhere else, they'd probably be enslaved again."

She picked up a turnip and put it in her basket. "I am afraid that's what's going to happen to William," she said quietly, almost to herself.

"Who's William?"

"The Verplancks own him. He does carpentry and gardening, and Mr. Verplanck contracts him out to other people to work. Mr. Verplanck inherited him in his father's will. But the will also said that after ten years, he was to be freed. The time will end this month, and Mr. Verplanck will honor his father's wishes and free William, but he's forty-two, and I fear he'll have no place to go. He isn't lazy, and he's very good with his hands, Thomas. He even knows how to make shoes. He's been very kind to me, and he's helped me when I didn't know what to do or how to act."

There was a short pause while Tom thought.

Another impulse.

"Do you think William would come to Westchester County and live on our leasehold? I need help up there, Elizabeth. We could build a cabin for him, and he could help me with the farming. I wouldn't be able to pay him very much at first, but he could have a portion of next year's crops when we sell them. Maybe he could make some shoes."

Elizabeth became energized. "It's very kind of you to offer that, Thomas. I'll tell him about you. If he comes, you'll not be sorry. William is a fine man. I'll tell him you are a Scotsman and that you'll treat him fairly," she said with a smile.

Then she added, "What's the way to your farm in Westchester? I'll give the directions to William."

Tom described the route to her.

"How much do I owe you for the vegetables?"

"Nothing, Elizabeth. I want to give them to you."

"I insist on paying, Thomas. After all, it's Mr. Verplanck's money anyway."

The two laughed.

"In that case, you owe me a half shilling."

"You're a good man, Thomas. I won't forget you."

With that, she turned and walked back toward her master's residence.

That evening at dinner, Tom told Maria and his in-laws about his encounter with the slave girl from the ship and the possibility that they would soon have a hired hand to help with the farm.

It was four weeks later, cold and snowing. Tom and Maria had just sat down to supper when there was a quiet knock on their door. Tom rose and opened it. A black man stood in the doorway, snow in his hair and on the shoulders of his worn coat. He was clutching a sack that contained all his worldly possessions.

"Mr. Hughson?" he inquired.

"Aye. I would be Thomas Hughson."

"My name is William. Elizabeth told me you needed some help, Sir."

"Yes, William. Come on in out of the cold."

Maria took his coat and set him a place at their table.

William spent his first night at the Hughson farm on a bed of quilts Maria made for him by the fire in the kitchen. The next morning, Tom and William began the construction of his log cabin, which they located between the house and the barn. William turned out to be very skilled with his hands. In short order, trees were felled, logs hewn, and the cabin began to take shape. It was completed in seventeen days; a cozy structure, 12 feet by 20, with a fireplace in one end and a loft in the other. Tom supplied it with a chair. The rest of the furniture William fashioned over the next two weeks during the evenings after he spent his days helping Tom clear away the forest to make more space for crops in the spring.

William was a quiet man. He was not used to being free, and he showed Tom a great deal of deference, which made the young farmer uneasy.

"William, you will have to stop calling me "Sir," Tom told him one day in the fields. "I have no title, and you are not a slave or my servant. My name is Tom, William, just plain Tom…although for some reason Maria insists on calling me Thomas."

The two men chuckled.

"Then I'll be callin' you 'Tom,' but I'll keep callin' your wife 'Mrs. Hughson.'"

"Well, if you wish. It will probably help her get used to that name herself!"

They chuckled again.

William paused and then changed the subject. "I have no last name to call my own. I'm just 'William.' When I was owned by the elder Mr. Verplanck, sometimes I was called

'William Verplanck,' but I don't like that name. I'd like a second name…a name that would sound like I'm a free man in America. What would a good name be?"

Tom leaned on his axe handle and thought for a moment. "How about MacIntosh?" he suggested in a spurt of nostalgia. "MacIntosh is a fine Scottish name, William. The Scots are brave men and warriors. They are slaves to no man. And all their women are beautiful. 'William MacIntosh'…the name sounds like you should be a clan chieftain. No one would dare bother a freeman named 'William MacIntosh.' I'll have Maria make you a kilt!" Tom poured on his Scottish accent.

The black man drew up to his full height. "'William MacIntosh.' Yes, I like the sound of 'William MacIntosh.' I'll be called 'William MacIntosh.' Will you show me how to write it so I won't have to make my mark?"

"Aye, William MacIntosh, that I will." Tom glanced over at the brook meandering through the ice-covered rocks ten yards away.

"Come with me, William."

The two men walked over to the stream. Tom bent over and gathered some of the cold water in the palm of his hand. He reached over and placed his hand on the black man's head.

"I christen thee 'William MacIntosh' Lord of the Isles, Chieftain of all MacIntoshs, gallant Scotsman, dark warrior, and servant to no man."

Tom was grinning as William caught his gaze and stared into his eyes for a long moment. A tear rolled down his cheek. "Thank you, Tom,…thank you."

That evening around the Hughson dinner table, the three celebrated the arrival of a fellow Scotsman. Tom broke out a special supply he kept for just such occasions. Maria declined to partake in the spirits, however. She said she hadn't felt that well during the morning, although she was better now. William shot Tom a quick glance; there was a twinkle in the old Scotsman's eye.

A week later, when William arrived for the evening meal, he presented Maria with a small bundle.

"For you, Ma'am." He said. "You can open it."

Inside, she found a pair of Indian-style soft deerskin moccasins William had fashioned out of a hide Tom had cured.

"I hope they fit alright," he said.

"William…they're beautiful!" She started to try them on when William added, "There's more in the sack."

Maria reached in and withdrew another pair of deerskin moccasins, a very little pair.

"Just in case you ever have need of them, Mrs. Hughson," he said with a smile.

Maria blushed. "Oh, Thomas, look at them. Aren't they cute? And they're so tiny! William, thank you very much!"

Tom took them in his hand and examined them for a moment.

"Aye, they are indeed bonnie...and well made, too. You're a very talented cobbler, William. Perhaps we should purchase some tools and set a place for you in the barn."

"I'd like that, Thomas. You would never have to buy boots again."

"Then we have a deal, William!"

The two men shook hands.

Chapter 25

Elizabeth and Bartholomew

Christmas 1694

With the manumission of William, the Verplancks circulated the word within their network that they wanted to purchase a slave to take over his duties. Karl Verplanck was not the sort to buy a slave at a public auction; he wanted some independent confirmation that the one he was purchasing would be contrite, obedient, and hard-working. He hated to lose William, but he was a man of honor, and that extended to honoring his father's wishes. One of his business associates knew of a baker, Jacob Bratt, who owned a twenty-year-old slave named Bartholomew. Bratt's bakery business on King Street was growing, and he wanted a worker with more experience. Upon interviewing the young man, Verplanck thought he would do well. Furthermore, he calculated, he might be able to breed him to Elizabeth and eventually recover his investment. A signed contract and £85 pounds later, Bartholomew was delivered to the Verplanck residence.

After a short lecture to Bartholomew on what he would and would not tolerate, Verplanck turned the new servant over to his wife, Margrietje, who oriented him to his duties and then showed him to his quarters in the back. They were William's old quarters, next to Elizabeth's. She introduced

Elizabeth to the young man, and they immediately recognized one another from the *Victory*, although they did not let on in front of Mrs. Verplanck.

A short time later, Bartholomew came to Elizabeth's door to get some embers to light his fire. It was turning into a very cold evening. He was of average height but muscular and rather good-looking, Elizabeth thought. He exhibited a certain alertness that attracted her attention.

"I need some coals in this cup to start my fire," he said. "Can I take some from yours?"

"Help yourself," she answered. He went over to the fire.

"I remember you from the ship, and I wondered what happened to you."

"No need to wonder about me, woman. I can take care of myself."

"Is it true that you worked for a baker?" she asked, trying to create a positive tone for their conversation.

"A man named Bratt. He was pretty good to me. I worked ten hours a day, and he let me off on Sunday. I could come and go pretty much as I pleased. What's it like here?"

"Much the same. Mrs. Verplanck is quite strict. But they don't treat us lowly or mean."

"That's good because I ain't used to no chains or padlocks."

She chuckled. "You won't find any chains or padlocks around here. Just do the work you're told to do, and you'll be alright."

"You sure do talk uppity for a slave girl," Bartholomew observed. "What do you do here, anyway?"

"I learned to read and write and cipher in Jamaica. They wanted someone to mind their children and teach them some. That's mainly what I do...and other housework, of course. Mrs. Verplanck doesn't stand for rough language from her servants. It would be good for you to mind that."

"Well, I'll do the best I can, Missy. Maybe you can teach me to talk good like you."

"Maybe I can, and my name's not Missy; it's Elizabeth," she replied a little stiffly.

"Then 'Elizabeth' it'll be if that's what you want."

"You should know that I'm also a Christian woman," she added.

He moved toward the door; then he turned and added with a smile, "Elizabeth, you sure are a fine-lookin' Christian woman."

"Good night, Bartholomew." she shot back.

"Good night, Elizabeth."

****

As Elizabeth and Bartholomew were to discover, the Christmas season was a big event at the Verplanck residence on Stone Street. The highlight was a Christmas Eve dinner party for some of Karl Verplanck's business associates, their wives, and others whom Margrietje Verplanck thought it would be appropriate to invite. She invited eighteen guests to her gala this year, and she expected that all would come. They would eat, drink, and socialize until it was time to attend the midnight service at the Dutch Reformed Church. Both Elizabeth and Bartholomew were to help Moriah attend to the guests' needs. The mistress of the house lectured them on exactly what to do and how to act.

One positive benefit for the three slaves was that they each received a new set of clothes so they would be presentable for the evening. Bartholomew looked quite handsome, Elizabeth thought, in his new blouse, knee britches, white stockings, and shoes with buckles. Bartholomew was having similar thoughts about Elizabeth in her blue dress with buttons and a white collar and cuffs. Moriah, in her new gray and black dress, was definitely the servant-in-charge, and the other two treated her with appropriate deference.

"You two look real pretty, and I seen you admirin' each other. You keep your mind on your business and make Mrs. Verplanck proud. Ya here me? I'll have no messin' up this evenin'!"

This year, Margrietje Verplanck had outdone herself with decorations, candles, and an assortment of delicious foods: a main course of duck and ham, several side dishes, sweet breads, mince pie, pumpkin cake, and even a variety of candies. Of course, for the men there would be brandy and pipes after dinner.

Elizabeth helped Moriah prepare the dinner and then serve the guests and freshen their drinks. Bartholomew's primary duties entailed greeting them at the door, taking their cloaks, and ushering them into the festivities. He was also charged with keeping the fireplaces going in the dining room and the two adjoining parlors and, as the dinner progressed, removing plates and dishes from the table. The table was an extravagant delight: a fine white linen tablecloth and napkins in silver rings, silver flatware, and wine goblets, and her finest dishes imported only last year from Staffordshire, England. Three silver candelabras on the table, each with six expensive spermaceti candles, completed the ambiance of the room.

As the evening approached, a light snow began to fall, but it wasn't enough to deter most of the guests. Only old Heinrich Van Ness and his wife failed to appear. The couple was getting on in years anyway, and they wouldn't be missed.

The dinner progressed without blemish; the food and conversation were excellent and, much to Mrs. Verplanck's relief, her three servants deported themselves in keeping with her high standards. After dinner, the men adjourned to one of the parlors to enjoy their brandy and pipes. They struck up a lively conversation about New York politics, business problems and opportunities, and the growing issues related to slavery in the city. Because she was charged with attending to their needs, Elizabeth was in the room quite a bit and heard much of their conversation.

The parlor was, indeed, filled with influential men, mostly Dutch merchants who (or whose fathers) had survived the city's transition from New Amsterdam to New York back in 1664. They shared business connections but also several concerns. The English mercantile policy of not allowing trade with any other foreign countries, for one. Furthermore, although most of them were slave owners, some foresaw the difficulties caused by the rapidly-growing slave population, many of whom were engaged in the trades, a fact that discouraged working-class immigrants in Europe from coming to New York as artisans and indentured servants.

"New England is managing quite nicely without much slave labor," protested Cornelius Van Cortlandt. "And the English, Scottish, and Irish are creating a steady flow of immigration up there."

"That they are!" added Jon Kierstide, the son of New Amsterdam's first physician and a close friend of Governor

Fletcher. He had been instrumental in arranging the excessive hospitality the Governor had shown of late to the notorious pirate Thomas Tew. "Those people work hard. They possess Christian morals, and most importantly, they trade with the merchants. Boston is flourishing."

"Even William Penn's Philadelphia just west of us is attracting immigrants," interjected Johannes de Peyster. "The city's only been in existence for twelve years, but they seem to have no shortage of labor, like we do here in New York. Their port is beginning to create major competition for us."

"Which one of you will be the first to free his slaves and send them up Bouwerie Lane to live with the others?" Verplanck weighed into the conversation with a cynical laugh. "The city's commerce depends upon African labor, even if it is of low quality. The English clearly see the need for slavery. They've protected our property rights to it, haven't they?"

"Aye, they have, but I'm afraid we may have trapped ourselves, Karl." Van Cortlandt again. "Especially with the type of blacks we've been importing of late. The seasoned slaves from Barbados are rebellious and Catholic." There were chuckles in the group.

"And the slaves from Angola are sickly and untried. And even some of them are bringing rebellious attitudes with them."

William Hall, the only non-Dutchman in the room, piped up. "Well, there certainly is a need in this city for stricter laws to control the Negroes. That's one thing the British have helped with a bit, but there's no doubt that the blacks in this city have too much freedom to come and go. And they're growin' more insolent, too! They're allowed to roam at night without their lanterns. On Sundays, they gather in some of the taverns by the dock and on upper Broadway and dance, drink, and gamble until the early morning. Who knows what else they're up to? We catch more and more of 'em stealing, and it's those damned tavern owners who are fencing their booty! It's becoming a disgrace. I don't trust 'em, I tell ya, I don't trust 'em at all."

"Come, come, Squire Hall." This time it was Dederich Van Twiller. "I fear the brandy is softening your brain. The city's slave trade is prosperous and growing every day, thanks to the English, and the slaves are helping us get rich. They've been here for sixty years, ever since they were imported to help build the fort. They'll be with us for two hundred more. As far as rebellion is concerned, it's amazing what a trip around the city tied to an oxcart and receiving a dozen lashes at each corner will do to quell insolence and a rebellious attitude."

"Well, perhaps for a hundred years, but not two hundred, Dederich."

"Who cares? By then, even I will probably be dead!"

265

There was hearty laughter among the group at that comment. Feeling the effects of his brandy, one of the guests glanced over at Elizabeth, who was removing some glasses from a table. He slowly eyed her up and down.

"Come here, girl."

She approached him.

"You don't look like one of those rebellious and insolent slaves to me. You're not, are you, girl?'

"No, Sir." She responded.

"She better not be," Verplanck interjected, "or it will be the lash upon that bare brown back of hers!"

Everyone knew that the host was just talking through his hat. However, Bartholomew entered the parlor with an armload of firewood just in time to hear that comment. He hesitated for a moment and stared at Verplanck. He had an urge to kill him right there in front of his friends. Verplanck expected his warning to Elizabeth to draw more laughter from the group than it did. He paused, then added,

"Come on, gentlemen. It's time to go to the midnight church service."

The guests and their hosts filed out the front door and into the waiting sleighs for the short trip to the Dutch Reformed Church. A light snow was still falling. Margrietje Verplanck left the cleanup to her three servants, and Moriah immediately took command. As soon he got an opportunity to talk with Elizabeth out of Moriah's earshot, Bartholomew cornered her in the parlor where the men had been.

"Did you hear what Verplanck said, Elizabeth? Did you hear him? He's a devil! I'll kill him if he ever whips you. I mean it, Elizabeth, I'll kill him! I don't care what they do to me!"

Somewhat taken aback by Bartholomew's apparent feelings for her, she just looked at him for a moment. His countenance was intense. He didn't look like a slave; he looked determined...and capable. Then, she gathered her thoughts.

"No, you won't, Bartholomew. You'll do no such thing. You shouldn't talk that way, even if you don't mean it. I can handle myself. And besides," she added, "he was just talkin' big in front of his friends. You just mind what you do and stay out of trouble yourself." She paused.

"But it does please me that you want to stand up for me. Thank you for that."

Bartholomew took her hands in his. They looked at each other for a long moment.

"Elizabeth, I..." His head dropped and he let go of her.

"Thank you, Bartholomew. Thank you for caring for me," she whispered. "You're a good man."

He turned and walked back into the kitchen. He, too, was a bit surprised…surprised at the hatred he felt for Verplanck and surprised at the growing intensity of his feelings for Elizabeth. God, he wished they weren't slaves!

An hour later, the place was cleaned up, dishes washed, and leftover food put away.

"You two go on to bed," ordered Moriah. "I'll wait up to let 'em back in. No tellin' how long that service will last." Then she added, "You fold those pretty clothes nice so they don't wrinkle, you hear me?"

"Yes, Ma'am." They replied in somewhat patronizing tones.

Outside the rear entrance to the house, the snow was gathering, and the backyard was thick with the muffled stillness that snow always brings. The night air was cold, very cold, and it stung their noses as they breathed it in. The snow quietly crunched under their feet as they made their way down the path to their cabins. When they reached the well, Elizabeth stopped. She touched Bartholomew's arm, and he stopped, too.

They stood there in the snow, holding each other's arms and looking into each other's faces.

Elizabeth broke the silence.

"I'm glad you were here tonight, and I'm sorry that I snapped at you, but I'm afraid that you'll say something or

268

do something that'll get you in trouble." More silence. Then she added, "You'll never make a good slave, Bartholomew, because down inside, you're a free man...as free as any white man."

He slid his hands up her arms and gently held her head.

"I've been thinkin' about you a lot, Elizabeth. I don't want nothin' to happen to you, girl."

He slowly leaned over and kissed her. She kissed him back.

Chapter 26
Westchester County
Spring 1695

The winter set in on the Hughson farm, but it was a mild one, and the fair weather provided Tom, William, and John Dobbs a welcomed opportunity to clear more land and get ready for spring planting. Occasionally, Benjamin Griggs would appear at the door ready to put in two or three days of hard work. Everyone enjoyed his company; he was very energetic, talkative, and funny, and his light-hearted attitude made everyone feel more optimistic about everything. It seemed to Tom that Benjamin could design and build anything. Together, they added a room to the back of the farmhouse. It was needed, Maria said, because a little Hughson was on the way. She said that he was going to be a boy. Tom wondered how she could be so sure, but he was agreeable with her prediction.

"We'll name him Thomas," she announced.

Tom was agreeable with that, too.

In March, the men cut ten cords of wood off John's leasehold, and John sold them to his neighbor, John Hyatt. Maria took advantage of the occasion to renew her friendly chiding of her brother, John.

"John, when you go over there with your wood, don't forget to spend some time with Elizabeth. Now that you're a landed squire (she chuckled), it may be time to pursue that young lady."

It wasn't long before John Dobbs began frequenting their farm on one pretext or another.

"John, my boy, it's plain to see that you have an eye for my Elizabeth and she for you, I'm glad for your attention to her. Both Mrs. Hyatt and I think you are a fine young man. However, you will make the two of us very happy if you put off thoughts of matrimony for another year until your farm is established."

"That was my plan, Mr. Hyatt. I want to be a good provider, Sir." There was a pause. "And I certainly want to keep up with my brother-in-law. Otherwise, my sister, Maria, would never let me hear the end of it!"

The two men laughed, and John Hyatt put his arm around the young man's shoulder.

"It's settled, then. You and my daughter have our blessings, John. Let me know if I can help get your farm on a sound footing."

That evening, a very happy John and Elizabeth sat on the Hyatt's front porch in a swing her father had made and hung by two chains from the porch ceiling. She was very pretty, with a flowing mane of dark red hair and blue-green eyes. The two got along very well. She made him laugh, and she always seemed to be in a pleasant mood.

"John, whatever am I going to do for a year while you work on your estate? Maybe I should go up to Philipse Manor and learn how to be a refined country squire's wife. If I learned how to set the table correctly, maybe I wouldn't embarrass you in front of Tom and Maria when they come for Sunday dinner."

They laughed.

"Elizabeth, my brother-in-law wouldn't know which fork to use, and he'd probably drink the water out of the finger bowl. You'll do fine, and besides, I'd miss you if you went to the manor."

"Alright then, I'll stay here so you can visit me and tell me how much fun it will be when we get married. Maybe we can even visit that swimming hole in the woods you boys made, but only if the water is warm enough for us to get in it while we plan our wedding."

He looked around to make sure they were alone, and then he kissed her, a long kiss during which the swing temporarily stopped swinging.

On one of John's visits, Mr. Hyatt asked the young lovers if they would drive the wagon down to the North (Hudson) River to pick up some farm implements that would be arriving that afternoon on a boat from New York. Of course, they both jumped at the chance, and, with the lunch Mrs. Hyatt had packed for them, they started out on their adventure. It was a beautiful, warm spring day. The leaves were beginning to emerge, here and there, rhododendron were blooming, and all around, the birds were serenading them with a constant springtime chatter. Best of all, the road was dry and easily passable.

When they got to the dock, the boat had not yet arrived, so John unhitched the horse and hobbled him with a rope so he could munch on the new grass. Then Elizabeth joined him with an old blanket in her arms. "Look what I found under the seat, John! I must have put it there early this morning before you arrived. I wonder why I did such a thing."

The two laughed. "Maybe it's for ole Hawk over there, in case he gets cold."

"No, I think it's for you to spread on the ground so we can eat the lunch Mother sent along."

John spread the blanket, and they settled down next to each other, bodies touching, and dove into the basket. Pieces of fried chicken, biscuits, and a wooden canteen filled with apple cider. In between bites of chicken, John seemed to be staring across the river in a contemplative mood.

"Whatever are you starring at, John?" she inquired.

"You see over there on the far side? There's a dock and some activity and a building. You know, a person might be able to make a tidy sum of money with a good-sized rowboat, ferrying people back and forth. I haven't heard of any ferry crossings around here. Surely, there are folks over there who would have business on this side and would pay to get across. And the other way around, too. The current isn't very fast here, so it wouldn't be much effort to cross."

"Well, thanks to your Mr. Griggs, you certainly know how to row a boat."

Several years later, John and his cousin, William Dobbs, did, indeed, start a ferry service. They built two boats, hired and trained two men to help him and set up a business relationship with the Snedens on the other side of the river. People began calling the general location "Dobbs Ferry," which eventually became a town with the same name; it is currently situated on the original Hughson land lease.

****

Spring was passing on the Hughson farm. Tom and William worked hard at cutting wood, clearing more fields, and building an icehouse. In late March, two young Scotsmen, the brothers Samuel and Philip MacAllister, fresh from the Highlands, showed up at the Hughson's front door "ready and willin' to work hard for a Scottish farmer." In their early twenties, hardy looking, and each with a thick crop of shoulder-length blond hair, they did, indeed, look able to work.

"We found out about ya, Mr. Hughson, Sir," Samuel began, "from an Englishman named Benjamin Griggs, whom we chanced to meet in a tavern on Dock Street. He said you were a fine intelligent man, for a Scotsman, he said, and that you may have a place for us on your farm."

The three men laughed.

"Well, I don't know about intelligent, but a Scotsman I am. Come in, gentlemen." Maria entered the room.

"This is my wife, Maria. Maria, this is Samuel and Philip MacAllister. They're Scotsmen, but they're willing to work anyway. I thought we might discuss it over a cup of tea."

More chuckles.

"I'm pleased to meet you gentlemen," she replied. "Come in. I'll brew some tea, and I just made some bread."

The MacAllisters were a light-hearted pair, but they seemed to Tom to be of good character and, indeed, willing to work. They had come to America for adventure and to learn the skills of a farmer in a land where it was possible one day to actually own their own farm. An arrangement was agreed upon amid much laughter and talk about Scotland.

After their negotiations over bread and tea, Tom took the young men out to see their accommodations and to meet William, who was busy fashioning a pair of boots.

"William, I'd like you to meet Samuel and Philip MacAllister. Benjamin sent them up, and they're going to work for us. Boys, this here is William MacIntosh.

"Pleased to meet ya, gentlemen." The black man extended a hand.

Philip was the first to grasp it.

"William MacIntosh. Good," he said. "Another Scotsman. It appears like this farm will be worked entirely by Scotsmen! It should be very successful."

"Aye, he's a Scotsman and a free Scotsman at that," Tom added, affecting his brogue. "He comes and goes when he wants, and he's beholden to no man."

Over the next two months, the four went at farming with a vengeance. Tom bought another horse for pulling stumps and plowing, and before long, several more acres were available for planting. The wheat and potatoes, of course, could be planted early, but other crops had to wait until the threat of frost was over, around the end of April, Tom was informed.

In addition to the plowing and woodcutting, Tom, Philip, and Samuel hunted and trapped. Thanks to William's tanning expertise, the hides were of very high quality and would bring good prices at the market in New York.

****

The seasons passed quickly, and by 1705, John Dobbs had built his land lease into a productive farm, and he and Elizabeth were married. They also must have enjoyed a productive romantic life that, by the time they celebrated their 16th anniversary, resulted in seven children: William,

John, Mary, Thomas, Walter, Abigail, and Michael. Not to be outdone, however, John's sister, Maria and Thomas Hughson, produced, by their 19th anniversary, nine little bairns: Thomas, John, William, Richard, Mary, Abigail, Benjamin, Walter, and Nathaniel. For their holiday family get-togethers, it took three tables to feed everyone! Furthermore, all the overlapping names among the cousins caused some degree of humorous confusion, especially when Christmas gifts were passed out. Unlike many families in the early 18th century, all these cousins lived into adulthood, sending their descendants into the future by the thousands.

Chapter 27
Trip to New York City
April 1712

The winter of 1711-12 seemed to fly by and, before they knew it, the Hughson family was hard at work preparing the farm for another spring planting. Young Thomas was 15 and of considerable assistance to his father in helping run the affairs of the farm. John, five years his junior, was turning into a young man, and he also pulled more than his weight with the farm chores. He was especially interested in the shoe-making enterprise William conducted out of his cobbler's shed. John spent many hours watching the black man tan leather, cut out the shapes, and fashion them into shoes and boots, most of which eventually ended up on the feet of the ladies and gentlemen in New York and Philadelphia. William enjoyed the boy's company and nurtured his interest in the craft by instructing him in the skills of a cobbler. He was getting on in years, and his eyesight wasn't what it used to be, so he appreciated John's unofficial apprenticeship, especially with the stitching.

"Oooo-Weee! Look at dem straight stitches!" he would tell the boy. "Someday you gonna make a fine cobbler, young John...yes, Sir, a fine cobbler."

Thomas and Maria's third son, William, had not yet turned eight. Although he did his part with the farm chores, the henhouse being under his charge, he seemed to be developing into the intellectual of the family. Already, he could read almost as well as both his older brothers, and Maria encouraged his scholarly interests. For Christmas, she gave him an old seaman's Bible, which he read nightly and stored in a safe place under his bed. When discussing her children, Maria would always say, "Will's going to be a preacher or a lawyer when he grows up. Of course, I would prefer the former."

All the children seemed to have the Hughson look: brown hair, fair complexion, and sturdy build. Unlike his older brothers, however, young Will was born with hazel eyes, a trait that his father thought somehow explained his penchant for reading. Despite his tender age, Will was an excellent shot with a rifle, an ability that his father also attributed to his son's hazel eyes. The young lad would be adding significantly to the family's income from the fur trade.

It was early April, and some of the farm's remaining stores of wheat and turnips had to be taken to New York to sell. Of course, there was always the load of furs and several pairs of boots and shoes that also had to be converted into currency. The Hughson farm produce often left by boat, but this time, it would fit in two of the wagons. This trip would be a milestone for the family because it was to be the first time Tom and his sons would make it without the accompaniment of William or the MacAllister brothers. The excursion began Sunday, April 10th. The family got up earlier than usual, but Maria, quite pregnant with yet another Hughson, who would be named Nathaniel, arose earlier than the rest and presented her men with an extra hardy breakfast consisting of beans, eggs, ham, biscuits, and coffee.

In his role as wagon master, Tom began issuing directives to his sons as the boys were downing the last of their meal.

"Tom, harness up Sherry and Jonas to the new wagon. You'll be driving them. I want you to stay behind me the whole way. Do you understand, Son?"

"Yes, Sir," the boy replied.

"If something spooks those two critters, I don't want to give them any place to run."

Then he added, "John, you ride with your brother. And as soon as we're out a spell and the horses have their wind, John, I want you to take over the team for a little while. It'll be a good experience for you. And, Tom, you keep an eye on him."

John shot a big grin in his brother's direction, the latter receiving it with a look of slight aggravation at having to share his control of the reins on such a momentous occasion.

The wagon master continued. "And John, you hitch up Baldy and Peggy to the old wagon for me. Will, you and I will ride in that one together."

"Can I drive the team, Father...maybe just for a little bit?" the seven-year-old pleaded.

"Aye, Will, that you can. This trip will make a teamster out of you," his father grinned.

Twenty minutes later, the boys announced that the wagons and teams were ready. Tom and Maria stepped out on the porch. It was a still morning, warm for early April. The sun was just making its appearance, flanked on either side by hills poking through a blanket of ground fog that covered their fields to the east. Everywhere, peeper frogs created a constant racket, assuring any would-be listeners that spring, indeed, had gained a foothold. Adding their own reassurance, two mourning doves cooed at each other in the meadow in front of the house.

"Isn't it beautiful?" Maria sighed as she held onto her husband's arm. "I'm so glad I chose to be a farmer's wife."

Tom put his arms around her. "Maria, I, too, am glad for your choice...God has been good to us." Then he added, "I love you, Mrs. Hughson."

"Be careful, Thomas. Take care of our boys."

"I will. And you be careful, too, Maria." He patted her lightly on her stomach, and Nathaniel gave a little kick in return. "William will look after your needs. We'll be back in five days."

The wagons, loaded with produce, furs, and shoes, were lined up, the young teamsters impatient at the reins. Tom climbed aboard next to Will, gave the word, and they were on their way.

For the first leg of the trip, the teamsters headed for Frederick Philips' manor, where Tom could sell some wheat and purchase a few sacks of flour. In mid-morning, their two wagons rolled into the entrance road to the manor, a gigantic complex that stretched from the road down to the Hudson.

For a carpenter and a Dutchman, Philipse had done well for himself in New York. He survived the British takeover in 1664 and found such favor with William and Mary that he received a land grant of 52,000 acres along the Hudson. It was 237 of those acres that Tom Hughson now farmed. Although Yonkers had been founded by a Dutch nobleman (that is, a "youncker") named Adriaen van der Donck, what came to be known as Yonkers really got its start with Frederick Philipse's grist mills. The "Lower Mills," as they became known, provided a very substantial income for the Lord of the Manor and, after his death in 1702, to his young grandson, Frederick Philipse II. It was to this young man's trustees that Tom Hughson paid the annual rent on his farm. And it was to his gristmills that Tom was obligated to bring much of his wheat.

Young Tom had seen the Philipse Manor before, but this was the first time for John and Will. The approach to the manor took them over a long wooden bridge spanning a portion of the millpond. The mill itself was beyond the bridge on the left and at the edge of the dam. An elaborate system of races and gates controlled the water and made it run either over the giant wheel or down a fall into the lower pond. At the moment, it was not turning. John was especially fascinated. Past the mill were several other outbuildings and, standing majestically on a spot overlooking the Hudson, was the manor house, a large, two-story brick edifice with four dormers facing the front and an expansive captain's walk on the roof.

There seemed to be slaves everywhere, dozens of them engaged in the myriad activities necessary to the care and feeding of such an enterprise. The Hughson boys had never seen so many slaves in one place. They stared in amazement. The wagon master called the caravan to a halt in front of the mill, and he took notice of the scene that had gained his sons' full attention.

"Pretty amazing, isn't it? And to think that Mr. Philipse started out as a lowly carpenter. When he landed in New York, all he had was a few tools."

"A carpenter, like Jesus," Will added.

"Except Jesus didn't own any slaves," John interjected.

"You're right about that, Son; Jesus wouldn't own any slaves."

Will piped up again. "We wouldn't ever own slaves, would we, Father?"

"No, Will, we wouldn't."

"William's not a slave, is he?"

"No, William is a free man. Once a long time ago, he was a slave, but now he's as free as we are."

Young Tom noticed several white men armed with muskets and perched in various locations around the manor grounds.

"What are those men with the muskets doing, Father? Who are they guarding?"

"I imagine the Philipse trustees engaged them to keep an eye on the slaves. Young Master Philipse would be in a fix if all his Negroes attempted to gain their freedom."

"Do you think they'll ever try?" his eldest son asked.

"Nay. They know what their fate would be once they got caught. New York isn't like those Caribbean Islands. There are too many armed white men in this colony who'd catch 'em and hang 'em. Nay, it won't happen here."

He changed the subject.

"Boys, unload the wheat sacks from the wagons while I negotiate for a price and buy a couple sacks of flour. Tom, you and John make sure the horses get some water."

With the help of a Philipse slave named Elijah, young Tom set about the task of emptying the wagons of their sacks of wheat while John watered the teams with a nearby bucket used for that purpose. Will strolled over by the dam to investigate the water wheel. There wasn't much to watch; the great wheel stood idle, and the water meant to drive it, diverted down a shoot to fall without purpose into the pond below. Then one of the miller's assistants appeared and lifted a wooden gate that redirected the water down a race to the wheel. With the water quickly filling its wide wooded troughs, the huge wheel began to turn, slowly at first but then picking up speed. Will heard the noises coming from inside the mill as the wooden gears engaged, and the heavy millstone began to turn in response to its watery engine. For a moment, Will wondered if some similar mechanical arrangement with four wheels could make a wagon go, but then he considered the problem of where the water would come from, and he dropped the line of mental inquiry.

Just as the last sack of wheat was lifted off the wagon, Thomas Hughson reappeared with the shillings from his transaction jingling in his pocket. He had negotiated a fair price, and there was a smile on his face.

"Climb aboard, men, and let's repair to New York!"

Will ran over from his viewing spot by the dam, scampered up onto the wagon seat and grabbed the reins with the confident air of a seasoned teamster. His father slid in beside him and, going along with the moment, ordered his son into action. "Get 'em movin', Will."

"Mup, Baldy, mup, Peggy!" the boy shouted at the horses as he pulled expertly on the right reins to make the team reverse direction. His father chuckled to himself. 'Mup;' short for 'Move on up.' Already, the boy was learning to talk the talk. The second wagon fell in behind, this time with John at the reins and Thomas cradling the musket, just in case they encountered any road agents.

The road down to New York was much easier to travel than it had been when Tom and Maria first brought produce to market seventeen years before, and the signs of civilization much more apparent. The road generally followed the crest of the hill that sloped off on the right down to the Hudson. At several places, the river was visible through the still-barren trees, exposing its beautiful vista and, below them, the docks and wharfs extending out from the clearings and fields of the ever-increasing numbers of farms.

Late in the afternoon, the Hughson caravan approached Yonkers, a place that had barely existed when Tom made his first trip to his farm. Now, however, it had grown into a thriving village, or should it really be called a town, with people everywhere going about their business. America was growing, Tom mused...growing fast. In Yonkers, Tom noticed that one of the larger farmhouses along the road had been converted into a tavern and inn. A freshly painted sign identified it as the "Black Boar Inn" underneath was written "Bed Board and Stable." And below that, "George Luckstead, Proprietor." On a whim, Tom directed his teamsters to pull up in front of the establishment for dinner and a room for the night. A woman met Tom on the porch, and a boy and girl ran from the front door and offered to tend to the horses. Tom ordered his teamsters to help with the horses and make sure they got their water and feed.

"Good evening, Ma'am. Are you the proprietor's wife?"

"That I am. Virgina Luckstead's my name."

"I'm Thomas Hughson, and these are my boys. We're on our way to New York City, and we'd like some food for our stomachs and a room for the night."

"That can certainly be arranged. Come on inside, Mr. Hghson."

Luckstead…Tom racked his brain. Why did that ring a bell? They entered the inn, which was not crowded, but there were other patrons, and the aroma of cooking food made Tom realize how hungry he was. The four Hughsons sat down at a long, heavy oak table laden with an assortment of very appetizing things to eat. The other diners at the table were engaged in animated conversation about some recent goings on in New York, but Tom couldn't catch the gist of their discussion.

As the boys dove into the variety of vegetables, ham, beef, and chicken, Tom returned to the proprietor's name. Luckstead. Where had he...at that moment, Virginia Luckstead appeared from the kitchen, bringing a freshly baked loaf of bread and some current jam to the table. She seemed to be in her early-forties, nice looking, and with a pleasant demeanor. She set the bread down directly in front of Tom and said, "Something for your boys, Sir... and you, too, if you like. If there is anything else you need, please ask." Then, she added, "You've got some fine sons there, Mr. Hughson."

"Aye, Ma'am, they are. This here is Thomas, and those two are John and Will."

"They're fine lookin' lads, too." Turning to them, she said, "If there's anything you boys need, just ask. I'll have some pie for you in a few minutes."

Turning back to Tom, she said, "My husband and I just opened this inn last year." She seemed to be eyeing Tom strangely. "I haven't seen you before," she said with a slight hesitation in her voice. "You must not be from around here."

That's it! Virginia Luckstead! The fire on Block Island! It all came back.

"My name's Thomas Hughson...Did you once live on Block Island about twenty years ago?"

"Yes...I...You're Tom Hughson! You saved us that night in the fire! You pulled Bridget and me out of the root cellar!"

"Aye, Mrs. Luckstead. I was there with John Dobbs, who is now my brother-in-law. 'Tis a strange world, indeed. And here you are preparing a meal for me and my sons."

The Hughson boys looked perplexed at this development, and Virginia Luckstead proceeded in animated tones to tell them the story of the pirates, the fire, and their father's bravery. Her tale attracted the attention of the other patrons at the table. When she finished, she said to Tom. "I want you to meet George, Mr. Hughson. He's out back in the smokehouse."

She retrieved her husband, and introductions were made, followed by animated conversation. Four years before, George had tired of trying to scratch out a living fishing off Block Island. He brought his family to Yonkers to work with his brother-in-law, an arrangement that did not thrive. It was then that he and Virginia decided to become innkeepers. The first year had worked out well, and he was optimistic about the future.

"You and your three sons will dine at our table and stay the night as our guests, Mr. Hughson," he announced.

"Thank you very much, Mr. Luckstead, but I insist on paying you."

"Nonsense! You have paid me a thousand times over. You gave me back my wife and my daughter. You've no idea of the thoughts that passed through my mind when I returned from fishing and saw my home at a distance, burned to the ground. I beached the boat and ran up the hill, fearing the worst. But there they were with Lydia, safe and unhurt…thanks to God's Providence and to you, Mr. Hughson. Yes, Sir, I owe you more than I can ever pay."

"Well, I'm obliged to you for your hospitality, Mr. Luckstead."

"Think nothing of it. I'm glad to serve you and your boys. Every time you come through Yonkers, you must sit at our table as our guests."

"Were those your children who helped tend to my horses?"

"Aye, that's young Isaac. He's ten. And Sarah is his little six-year-old sister. She has a mind of her own…sort of like her mother." He chuckled and nudged his wife. "She says she can do anything her brother can, and I almost believe it!"

Then he added, "Bridget, our oldest, is married to a merchant in New York…a man named Schuyler. I would think that he also owes you a huge debt of gratitude." George cast a big smile at Tom.

Changing the subject, Tom said, "I'd like to ask you something. I couldn't help overhearing parts of the conversation at the other end of the table. Has something special happened in New York recently?"

"You mean you haven't heard yet?" George replied.

He continued. "Four nights ago, a band of around twenty-five Negro slaves recently brought from Africa gathered at night in the middle of the city in Crook's orchard. They armed themselves with muskets and knives and conspired to kill their masters because they had worked them too hard. They set an out-building on fire, and when the citizens came to extinguish the flames, the band slaughtered nine of them. Then, they escaped into the surrounding woods north of the city. Governor Hunter had the militia drive the island to flush 'em out. Most of them were caught, although some took their own lives. One even killed his own family first! Other conspirators were also arrested by the militia. They're all to be tried, beginning today."

Concerned for the welfare of his sons, Tom asked George, "Is the city safe? Are people in any danger? What word have you had?"

"Oh, I reckon it's perfectly safe now. I imagine those conspirators will meet a cruel and certain fate…the gallows or the stake…and that'll make the rest of 'em think twice about tryin' anything similar for a while. Continue your trip to New York, Thomas. You'll be fine."

Then he added, "Bringin' all them blacks to New York was a terrible mistake. They should 'a listened to those

Quakers. It's un-Christian greed, pure and simple, that's caused these difficulties. Free men make better laborers. And they don't plot in the dark of night to kill you and your wife and children. And those that think that Negroes from Africa are more docile than the ones from the Caribbean need to reconsider their position. They're all a danger, I tell ya, and slavery is a threat to our way of life. Someday, I'm afraid we'll all pay for their greed."

Tom pondered George's statements for a moment.

"Well, thank you for your information. We must be off to bed. We'll stop on the way home, but only if you let me pay."

"Alright, Tom. You are true to your name; you're a stubborn Scotsman, and that's all there is to it. You can pay for your meal, but your boys are my guests. I absolutely insist!" Then, reverting to his earlier life on the sea, he added, "There was a red sky this mornin', Tom. You might be runnin' into some rain tomorrow before you and your boys dock those two wagons in New York."

After the Hughsons enjoyed a hardy breakfast early the next morning and harnessed their horses, Virginia Luckstead produced a bundle containing lunch and a pie. Handing it to her young daughter, she told her to give it to the boys. Sarah, who had been eyeing John all the while, thrust the package into his hands.

"Here," she said, flashing him a big six-year-old smile.

With a curt "Thanks," John turned and, giving his best impression of a real teamster, climbed aboard the wagon, stashing the bundle under the seat.

As the wagons rolled away from the inn, young Tom turned to his brother and, with a big grin, said, "I saw that, John. Little Sarah likes you." He laughed. "You sure have a way with the little women!" He laughed again.

"Shut up!" was the sole reply.

Chapter 28

New York City

April 1712

It was late afternoon and clouding over when the Hughson caravan paid the toll at King's Bridge and crossed over onto the island of Manhattan. Once again, Tom was in awe of the growth that had taken place, even since his last trip. The little houses and shacks along the road where the free blacks lived seemed to be growing into their own town. A few taverns had sprung up along the road, apparently to serve their social needs despite the laws prohibiting such activities. Tom noticed, however, that the establishments did not appear to be open for business. In fact, the entire community of blacks seemed to be ensconced inside their pitiful shacks. Virtually none of them could be seen on the roads or going about their daily routines. Tom surmised that they had been driven inside by fears emanating from the recently failed revolt in the city or, more likely, from fears of retribution at the hands of white citizens who, in their lust for revenge, could not be counted on to discriminate between the few who participated in the shedding of white blood and many others who didn't. Reflexively, he glanced back at his eldest son and the musket he held across his lap.

The thought surged through his mind that he and his sons should have turned around after their night at the Black Boar.

He pulled his pistols out of the satchel beneath the wagon seat and thrust them into his belt, one on each side, the grips pointing toward the front. Will looked at him nervously. Before the boy could inquire, however, his father reassured him.

"Don't worry, Will. I always carry my pistols when I come to New York. It's sort of a tradition among us Scotsmen."

In the approaching darkness, the wagons continued past the spot where the old wall used to stand and on down Broadway. A misty rain began to fall, accompanied by a chilly east wind that caused the four Hughsons to don their coats. Tom considered turning left on Maiden Lane and then right down Nassau Street to avoid the areas of the city where people tend to congregate, but then he let the thought pass, opting instead to stay on Broadway, the shortest route down to Pearl Street and the Pitman residence. The wagons passed Trinity Church on the west side of Broadway, just below Wall Street. The fifteen-year-old imposing structure was clearly visible in the evening sky, its front and impressive spire illuminated by a score of torches carried by men in a crowd that had formed for some purpose in its yard. They were armed, and Tom could tell from their shouts that they were about to embark on a hunt for more rebellious slaves. Some had dogs with them, which kept up a continuous yapping that only served to further energize the crowd into action. Tom took the reins from his son and clucked Baldy and Peggy up into a trot. Behind him, John followed his father's lead and urged Sherry and Jonas to keep pace, snapping the reins on their rumps.

Just then, someone, mounted on horseback in the crowd, noticed the two wagons. He broke from the crowd and galloped toward the wagons, drawing rein in the road in front of Tom, so he had to bring his team to a stop. Tom shot a quick glance at his sons in the wagon behind, opened his coat, and put a hand on a pistol.

"You're blockin' my way, Sir! What do ya want?" He demanded in a forceful voice that rang of command.

"Who are ye and where are ye goin?" the rider demanded a middle-aged man with an unkempt beard and rough demeanor, rainwater dripping off the brim of his hat.

"Now, I don't suppose that's any of your business, is it?" came Tom's retort, along with a measure of Scottish brogue.

The rider backed off a bit. He could see that the wagons contained only white men, a musket lying across one's legs, and the Scotsman with his hand concealed inside his coat.

By way of explanation, the rider reported, "There's been a slave riot in the city, Mister. Eight white people are dead, and twelve more wounded, shot and stabbed by those murderin' black bastards. We've already caught most of the ones responsible. They've been tried and convicted, and eighteen of 'em are dead or soon will be, but we think there's more out there, and we aim to get 'em before they kill again." Then he added, "Which way did you come from?" this time in a more civil tone.

"Down from Philipsburgh," Tom answered.

"Did you run into any blacks along the road goin' north?" he inquired.

"Just some old people in farm wagons or walkin' along the road. Nobody who looked like a conspirator or a murderer." Then he added, "We're headed down to Pearl Street for the night, and I'd be pleased to have you remove your horse from our way."

The rider hesitated for an ego-saving instant and then guided his horse to the side of the road. As he turned to go, he warned, "I'd be careful with those boys, Mister. New York is not a safe place to be tonight!" Then he galloped back to the crowd.

Tom changed his mind about continuing down Broadway, and at his command, the two-wagon caravan swung around and proceeded east on Wall Street. Tom thought there may be fewer crowds gathering in that direction. His plan was to go down Broad Street and then over to Pearl. Pearl Street was east and a bit south of the fort and had become one of the more aristocratic neighborhoods of the city. It was where the Pitman's lived and was still the residence of the widow Mary Pitman, Maria's mother.

Tom's hopes for a quiet passage through the rest of the city, however, were soon laid waste. In front of the new City Hall at the corner of Broad and Wall Streets, the Hughson wagons came upon another crowd, this time formed around a bonfire that had been laid in the street. What appeared to be at least a hundred people, men, women, and children, were milling around and watching some activity that was taking place by the fire. A large wagon wheel lay flat on the ground, and on it, a black man, stripped of his clothes, was lashed hand and foot, face up, in spread-eagle fashion. It was clear from his screams that he was in pain, although he also sounded like he was beginning to succumb to whatever torture he was enduring. It was also apparent from their gross deformities that his right arm and leg had been broken. A man dressed as a sailor and yelling and cursing in Dutch was dancing around the poor retch, brandishing a metal pick.

"Break 'em on the wheel! Break 'em on the wheel!" the crowd chanted, at which the sailor brought the pick down on the man's left foot, breaking the bones and causing yet another scream. For a moment, Tom stared in shock, a blank mind providing him with no immediate direction. His son, John, interrupted his trance from the other wagon.

"Father, MAKE 'EM STOP! They're killing him!"

Tom's first impulse was to get his boys out of there.

"Break 'em on the wheel! Break 'em on the wheel!" the crowd chanted. A woman's voice screeched above the crowd. "Murder a white man, will ya, you black devil! Break 'em again, Dutchman. Break his other leg!"

As though filling a special order, this time the sailor chose the left tibia, crushing it with one swift flick of the iron bar. Another series of screams from the pathetic human strapped to the wheel. The crowd roared its approval through the misty drizzle.

"FATHER, MAKE 'EM STOP!" came the cry again from John. But Tom made his decision. He would be helpless against that crowd. He picked up the reins and was about to slap his team into action when someone in the crowd threw a small pine tree on the bonfire. It flamed up, and in the increased light it gave off…what was that? There she was. A black woman in the crowd, clutching an infant to her chest and staring, transfixed, at the poor slave on the wheel who was having the life broken out of him one bone at a time. Some burly white man dressed as a longshoreman said something and grabbed at her. She pulled away, but in the process, the hood of her cloak fell from her head.

"ELIZABETH!" Tom yelled involuntarily. "ELIZABETH!"

She didn't hear him. The longshoreman knocked her down into the mud, and she tried to get up, still clutching the infant.

"Hold the team, Will!" Tom yelled to his son as he jumped to the ground. He pulled one of his pistols and ran

299

toward her. He momentarily lost sight of her in the crowd, and he pushed his way through the throng in what he thought was the right general direction. There! There she was, still on the ground, the baby crying. The crowd was cheering again, another successfully broken bone.

"Elizabeth!" He leaned over and pulled her to her feet. She looked at him as if in a daze. "Claus, Claus." She murmured weakly. And then, "Mr. Hughson? Mr. Hughson, is that you? Please, help me."

"Elizabeth! Come on! You've got to get out of here!" He thought about picking her up but then decided it would attract too much attention. "Come on, Elizabeth!" He grabbed her around the waist and pulled her toward the wagons. As he approached, he saw young Thomas, his musket at the ready to cover his father's retreat.

"Hurry, Father, Hurry!" Will cried, his hands grabbing the reins.

When Tom reached the front wagon, he heaved Elizabeth and the baby in the back and jumped in after them. "Let's go, Will! Let's go!" he shouted at his seven-year-old teamster.

Will snapped the reins on the horses' rumps. Mup, Baldy! Mup, Peggy!" he yelled. The team broke into a trot, and the second wagon followed suit. Tom crawled up into the seat next to his young son and took the reins from him as the team proceeded down Broad Street.

"You did good, Will," he panted. "Get in the back with the woman and child and stay down!" Then he added, "Keep your head below the sides of the wagon, Will. Do you understand?"

"Yes, Sir, I will." He crawled into the back of the wagon.

When they reached Pearl Street, Tom brought the horses down to a walk. It was not a great distance to Pearl Street, but, in terms of their safety, it seemed to Tom to be all the distance in the world. In a couple more minutes, father and sons brought the wagons to a halt behind the Pitman house, and Tom's racing heart finally began its descent to normalcy. He climbed out of the wagon and went around to the back.

"Elizabeth. Are you alright?" He asked. His three sons gathered around.

"Yes, Mr. Hughson, thank you so much." She paused, and then her mind returned to the scene. "Did you see how they were torturing Claus? They broke him on the wheel. Poor Claus. My God, why are they so cruel?" She began to sob uncontrollably. "He had nothin' to do with those killings." Tom took the baby from her arms and passed him to his second son.

"John, take the baby into the house. Tell your grandmother what happened. We'll be in shortly."

John carefully took his charge and disappeared up the back stairs and into the house.

Tom gave another directive. "Boys, take the wagons into the barn and see to the teams. I will be out to help you shortly."

Then he turned to Elizabeth. He picked her up and carried the still-sobbing woman up the stairs and into the house, where Mary Pitman took over.

"Put her in the front bedroom," she ordered. Tom carried her up the stairs, and Mary Pitman followed with the infant.

"I don't think she's hurt physically, but…do you have any idea what's going on out there?" he inquired of his mother-in-law. "A crowd is in front of City Hall chanting while some Dutch sailor tortures a slave to death. That's where I found Elizabeth. She'd been knocked on the ground and couldn't get up."

"They're executing the slaves condemned for the revolt and murders they committed last Tuesday," Mary replied. "He must have been one of those." Then she added, "Do you know this woman, Elizabeth?"

"When I came to America, she was in a group of slaves we picked up in Jamaica on our way to New York. I saw her once in the market several years ago, and she told me she worked for a family named Verplanck. That's all I know. That child must be hers."

"Verplanck, yes, I know that family. When she calms down after a bit, perhaps she can tell us what is going on. I can tend to her. You go out and help the boys."

Tom and John returned to the barn to help his sons. In silence, the four of them took the tack off the sweat-soaked horses, rubbed them down, and finally, once they were cool, put them in two vacant stalls with grain, hay, and water for the evening. Finally, on their way back to the house, Tom broke the silence.

"I'm sorry that you had to see that, boys. No man deserves to be treated that way, not even a murderer." A pause. Then he added.

"We should have turned around at the inn. But I suppose what's done is done, and we'll have to deal with our thoughts as best we can."

"But Father, we were there to save Elizabeth," John countered softly. Then he began to cry. His father put an arm around him.

"Aye, John, we were there for Elizabeth."

"Is she the slave on the ship you told us about?" young Tom inquired.

"Aye, Tom, she's the same one. She must have known that slave on the wheel. She called him 'Claus.'"

"They won't come here tonight to get her, will they, Father?" Will asked.

"No, son, they won't come here. She and the baby will be safe with us. In the morning, we'll determine what to do."

Then he changed the subject. "You boys handled the wagons very well tonight. And, thank you, Tom, for the rifle cover. You boys are real Hughsons!" He paused, then added, "Your grandfather would be very proud of you."

They went into the house, where Mary Pitman met them in the back entryway.

"I made Elizabeth some tea, Tom. She's upstairs nursing the baby. She said she'll come down by and by."

Grandma Mary looked over the weary travelers. Her kith and kin now safe under her wing, she said, "Come on into the kitchen, and let me get you boys something to eat while we wait for Elizabeth to come down."

She extracted the remains of an apple pie from the pie safe in the corner and set it out on the table, along with plates, forks, and mugs for tea. She placed the pie in front of young Tom, shot a sly grin at him and said, "Tom, will you please cut this pie in four equal pieces for me? When you're done, Will can choose the first piece, John the second, your father the third, and you can have the last piece, Tom."

The four pieces couldn't have been more equal in size if they were measured in the king's own counting house. Tom chuckled at the precision with which his eldest son approached his task.

"Hurry up, Tom," Will admonished. "Don't take all night!"

Twenty minutes later, Elizabeth descended the staircase and timidly walked into the kitchen, her baby boy in her arms.

"Come in, Elizabeth," Mary entreated. "Sit down here at the table and let me get you something to eat."

Elizabeth sat in an empty chair next to John. The baby looked at John, and John looked at the baby. Mary noticed this silent communication and said, "John, take that baby so this poor girl can get somethin' in her stomach!" Then she added, "What's that baby's name?"

"Caesar. His name is Caesar. We named him after Bartholomew's brother." She paused. "Bartholomew's my husband. He belongs to Verplancks, too. He's gone to Philadelphia with Mr. and Mrs. Verplanck. They been gone six days and won't come back for three more."

"What were you doing out there tonight, Elizabeth?" Tom asked.

"Claus…" she paused a moment. "Claus was a friend of Bartholomew's. They worked together layin' brick for the new City Hall."

"What did Claus do, anyway?" Young John broke into the conversation.

"They say he was one of the conspirators who burned a barn and killed the white folks last week. But I don't believe he did it. Claus would speak against slavery when he got the chance, and he gave his master, Squire Denison, some trouble. That's why he turned him in. When he'd worked for the Squire for seven years, he sued him for his freedom, but the court said he was a slave, not an indentured servant. That was two years ago, and Claus has been frettin' about it ever since. But he wouldn't kill anybody, Mr. Hughson, not even for his freedom. He was a good man, really he was." She began to cry again.

You stop talkin' now and eat." Mary Pitman ordered. Then she asked, "Is there anyone at the Verplanck's tonight, Elizabeth?'

"Yes, Ma'am. Moriah's there. She cooks and keeps the house."

"Elizabeth, you and Caesar can stay here tonight. Tom, why don't you saddle a horse and go over to Verplancks and tell Moriah what's happened. We'll get you back home tomorrow morning, Elizabeth. Come, I'll show you to a bed."

Elizabeth, physically and emotionally exhausted, dragged herself out of the chair and retrieved the sleeping Caesar from John's lap.

"They live on Stone Street, Mr. Hughson," she said. "There's a small oak growing by the front door. Moriah will likely be 'round back behind the house in her cabin."

"You go now, Tom. I'll take care of the boys," his mother-in-law said. "Take our horse; he's fresh."

Five minutes later, and with both of his pistols stuck in his belt, Tom was once again on the streets of this possessed city. The drizzle had let up, and light from a three-quarter moon through the broken clouds reflected off the puddles and wet paving stones. Scattered here and there, small groups of people had gathered around their torches and lanterns and were engaged in animated talk. Tom went out of his way to avoid most of them. He tried to keep off the cobblestone paving as much as possible to reduce the sound of his horse's hooves and the attention it may bring to him. In ten minutes, he was on Stone Street, and he identified the Verplanck residence by the small oak tree next to the front steps. There was light from a candle visible through an upstairs window. He rode around behind the house and reined in his horse by the cabin, dark, except for a faint glow through its one window, perhaps from some dying embers in a fireplace. He dismounted and knocked on the door several times. No response. As he thought about trying at the main house, he knocked one last time.

"Moriah, open the door! I come from Elizabeth, and she has a message for you."

He waited. Movement inside. The door opened a crack.

"Who are you!"

"I'm Tom Hughson. My boys and I pulled Elizabeth and her child from a mob in front of City Hall, and she is now safe at my mother-in-law's on Pearl Street. She wanted you to know."

His name rang a bell with the elderly woman. She opened the door further and stepped out.

"Yes. I know who you are, Mr. Hughson." There was some relief in her voice. "Elizabeth told me 'bout you. Is she alright?"

"Aye, she and little Caesar are fine; just very tired, that's all. We'll see that they get back here tomorrow."

"I told her not to go out there, Mr. Hughson. I told her. She couldn't help that Claus, nohow. This city ain't safe for no black folk to be out, not since them killin's. They gonna take their revenge on us now, that's for sure. Even the slaves and freemen that didn't know nothin' 'bout it." She began to whimper.

"Moriah, will you be alright here?"

"Yes, Sir, I'll be alright. I lit a lantern in the Verplanck's bedroom so folks will think someone's home. Nobody'll bother me. You go on now." She glanced at the pistols in Tom's belt and added, "Be careful of those folk out there, Mr. Hughson. Some of 'dem is crazy."

Tom mounted his horse, ready to take Moriah's advice. But as he proceeded down Stone Street, his curiosity took command, and he turned back toward City Hall. As he approached, he saw a small group of men standing around the wheel to which Claus was still lashed. He took a firm grip on one of his pistols. Between the moonlight and the torches, he could clearly see that the black man had finally succumbed to his torture and was now mercifully rescued by death. Vacant eyes stared up into the night sky, eerily reflecting the flickering light of the torches.

When Tom got within a few feet of the group, one of the men recognized his presence and, as if by way of apologetic explanation, said, "This here's one of them murderin' Africans. He's killed his last white man, Mister. We saw to that, yes, sir!" Then he added, "Maybe it'll be a lesson to the rest o' them black heathen."

"Perhaps," Tom answered. "Perhaps."

With that, he turned his horse back into the night.

****

The next morning, after a big breakfast personally supervised by Mary Pitman, Tom and the boys hitched the teams to their two wagons and took Elizabeth and young Caesar back to Stone Street and the Verplancks. During the ride, Tom told her of how he had returned to City Hall the night before and that Claus had already died. She was silent during the ride, clutching Caesar to her and rocking back and forth. When they arrived at her cabin behind the main house, she finally broke her silence.

"Thank you, Mr. Hughson...thank you for saving Caesar and me and for all your kindness. And please thank Mrs. Pitman, too."

"I will, Elizabeth. And you keep off the streets 'till all this trouble is over. D'ya hear?"

"I will...I'll stay right here. And Bartholomew will be home in a few days with the Verplancks."

She passed little Caesar to John while she climbed out of the wagon. He handed the child back to her, and she disappeared into the cabin. The men climbed back in the wagons and headed toward the market. It was a warm sunny day, and life must go on. Tom was concerned about what his sons had experienced during the past fifteen hours. He was especially worried about John, who seemed to be the most troubled by what he had been through. He sat, silent, next to his father in the wagon.

"Take the reins, boy. Let's see what kind of a city teamster you are!"

A few minutes passed.

"Father, did that man really kill white people?" the boy inquired.

"Aye. They say he did, John. He and some other slaves set a building on fire, and then when folks came to fight the blaze, they shot 'em and beat 'em to death."

"Why did they want to do that."

"I don't know, John. Maybe they thought they were being mistreated by their masters."

John adeptly guided the team around an oxcart stopped in the middle of the road, its owner patiently waiting while the ox relieved himself.

"If they were mistreated, that doesn't give 'em the right to kill other white people, does it?"

"Nay, John, it wouldn't justify murder."

"Did that man go to Heaven?" the boy inquired further.

"Well, that's a hard one to answer." Tom paused for a moment. "I suppose if he repented of his sins and accepted Jesus before he died, he most likely went to Heaven."

"Then, slaves can go to Heaven?"

"Anyone can go to Heaven if they accept Jesus, black men included."

"Are black men just like us?"

"Aye, John, they're just like us, 'cept they're a lot less fortunate than we are. They were unlucky enough to be captured by other blacks in Africa and sold to Arabs, who sold them to other men, who brought 'em here."

"Are they dimwitted?" the boy continued his inquisition.

"Nay, John. I don't believe they're dimwitted; they just don't have any learnin'. Just because you're a slave doesn't mean you're dimwitted. Remember, the Jews were slaves once in Egypt. And Jesus was a Jew. He wasn't dimwitted, was he?"

The boy chuckled at the absurdity of the thought. "No, Father, Jesus was smart! He was the smartest man who ever lived."

"Besides," Tom deftly drove home his point, "you don't think William is dimwitted, do you, John?"

Another chuckle. "No, Sir...not William. He's very smart!"

Chapter 29
The Hughson Farm, Westchester
Fall 1717

The next five years on the Hughson farm passed quickly. More fields were cleared, more crops were grown, and more shoes and boots were made. Maria gave birth to one more son, Nathaniel, who increased her brood to nine children: seven boys and two girls. Down the road at the Dobbs farm, John and Elizabeth added two more children to their growing brood to bring their total, so far, to four boys and one girl. Maria prepared the Easter Sunday dinner for the two families, which meant that there were 21 hungry mouths to feed that day, counting William and the MacAllisters. It was a good thing that God provided a warm sunny day for the occasion; Maria took advantage of the weather to make space at the table by consigning several of the cousins to the porch for their meal. As usual on these occasions, the food was plentiful and delicious, and, once again, Thomas sent a silent prayer Heavenward, thanking God for his precious wife. Little did they all know that it would be the last Easter meal Maria would ever prepare.

In September, Maria's mother, the widow Mary Pittman, decided she needed more help with maintaining her large and elegant home on Pearl Street. Her plan was to purchase a slave, probably a young woman, immediately free her, and employ her in the capacity of an indentured servant. On September 9th, Mary read in the newspaper that the slave ship *Rose* had just docked, and its captain, a man named Gulick, had sixty-seven slaves for sale at the Meal Market at the foot of Wall Street. Mary decided to launch her plan. Accompanied by her solicitor, she rode to the Meal Market, and two hours later, she had purchased a young black woman named Ella, a pretty girl with only a rudimentary command of English. On the ride back to the house, Mary carefully and slowly explained her plan for the girl, who seemed to understand the main point: she was free, but not exactly.

A week later, the plans for the new servant were disrupted when Ella woke up with a severe headache and chills. As the day progressed, she became nauseous and vomited. The next day, she was worse and experienced back pain. Mary Pittman was concerned enough to have the doctor visit the girl. Caleb Rulon was an elderly man who had been practicing in New York for twenty years, before the New York Yellow Fever epidemic of 1702. He knew the signs and symptoms; His diagnosis was that she had contracted what he called the plague. There was not much he could do except to admonish Mary Pittman to isolate her and pray. He knew that she should be kept away from people, but, of course, he had no idea that mosquitos were part of the problem. In fact, he told Mary to open the windows to let in the fresh air, which she did. Five days later, Ella had gone to meet her

314

Maker. Mary posted a letter to her daughter to inform her of the sad developments.

September 15th 1717

Dear Maria and Tom,

In my last letter to you, I informed you of my plan to obtain help in managing the house by purchasing a slave girl, freeing her, and employing her as an indentured servant for three years. I carried through with this plan and purchased a young woman named Ella at the Meal Market. I freed her and executed a three-year indenture contract for her. About a week ago, however, she took sick and died four days later. The doctor thinks it may have been the plague, but he isn't certain.

The whole episode was very troubling for me, and I hope I haven't caught whatever it was she suffered from. At present, I feel fine, and I pray I stay that way. I did want you to know what happened, however, but I am currently in no need of your presence here. I will post a letter to you in a few days to let you know how things are.

Much love,
Mother

Three days later, Maria received her mother's letter. She showed it to Tom.

"What do you think it means, Thomas? Could the girl have really died from the plague?"

"I ken that it's possible. I guess we'll just have to wait and see."

"If she takes sick, I should go to New York and nurse her."

"It would be dangerous, Maria. What if you got sick, yourself? Isn't there someone else in New York who could help her? Perhaps we could hire someone."

"Do they know how people catch the plague, Thomas?"

"Nay, they don't, but it's probably some invisible vapor in the air that enters a person through his nose or mouth."

"If it is a vapor, where does it come from?"

"I don't know, Maria. Maybe a person with the plague breathes it out and then someone else breathes it in." He paused, then, "In any event, let's hope you don't have to go. If you do, I will come with you."

"No, Thomas. You stay here. There is no sense in both of us getting near the vapors. We have a family here to care for. I'll go alone. You can take me in the wagon, but then drop me off by her door and leave. Promise me, Thomas."

"Aye…I will drop you off, but you will have to kiss me."

She smiled at him. "You know I will, my handsome Scotsman."

The next day, Maria received a second letter from her mother. Mary was sick and had taken to bed. Mary wrote that she awoke one morning with a headache and pain in her back.

Marie went to her side, and after six days, the woman had begun to improve, so the Pittman gardener was engaged to drive her daughter back to the Hughson compound. Four days after her return, she awoke with a terrific headache. Tom's worst fears were borne out, and eight days later, the couple kissed and bumped foreheads for the last time. Tom was devastated.

William fashioned a pine coffin for her, and three days later, she was buried, the first one in what would become known as the "Hughson Burying Ground". Over forty mourners were present during that warm and sunny afternoon, Tom's children trying in vain to console him. She was 47.

In 1717, the Yellow Fever outbreak in New York was a minor occurrence compared to the one in 1702, in which 570 people, eleven percent of the city's population, perished. Nobody knew at the time that mosquitos, and not vapors, were the culprits.

Chapter 30

Sarah Luckstead

Westchester County

May 1725

Eight more summers came and went on the Hughson farm. It was almost summer again and, once more, time to haul Hughson produce, cured skins, shoes, and boots to the New York market. John volunteered for the job. Now 25, he was a man in his own right; taller than his father and possessed of the Hughson look, muscular, square-jawed, and handsome. He was already tanned by the spring sunshine, and he looked fit and able. He planned to take his young brother, Will, with him to drive the other wagon. Although still thinner of frame than John, Will had the same Hughson look, and even the most casual observer could recognize them as brothers.

Of course, the whole family was aware of why John was so eager to make the trip. It would give him a chance to stop at the Black Boar Inn in Yonkers and visit with Miss Sarah Luckstead again. Over the last twelve years, the Black Boar Inn had become a regular stopping point for the Hughsons on their many trips to and from New York, and young John and Sarah's friendship had grown from pulling pigtails and adolescent teasing to extended conversations and mutual

318

gazing into one another's eyes in the quiet nooks of the inn and on the forest paths behind.

The evening before the trip, John brought up the topic of marriage at the dinner table.

"Father," he began, "I'd like to ask Sarah Luckstead to marry me and live here on our farm. Between the section I plant and my cobbler business I know I can provide for her. Of course, I'd have to build a house first, like Tom did before he got married. I figure it would take the summer with Tom and Will helping me."

The young man paused and awaited his father's reaction.

"Well, Son," his father began with a smile. "I reckon you need to follow what your heart is tellin' you. That young lass is headstrong and very pretty, a lot like your mother, I'd judge. She ought to make a good farmer's wife."

He put his hand on his son's shoulder. "John, you have my blessing and I, too, will help you build your house."

In a tentative voice, John asked, "Do you like her, Father?"

"Of course, I do, John. She'll make a fine wife, and I'd love to have her in the family." Then he added, "Do you think she will like being a farmer's wife?"

"Aye. We've already talked about it. She said it would suit her just fine as long as she could buy a few new things every once in a while."

"I ken that's a reasonable request for any woman to make, John." His father reassured him. He continued. "Are you going to ask her mother for her hand?"

"I guess that would be the right thing since her father died. Aye, I'll do it on the trip down."

"Well, good luck to you, John." His father added, "I hope she says 'yes.'"

"She will, Father, she already told me she will."

With a relieved look on his face, John got up from the table. "Come on, Will, let's get ready for our trip to New York!"

Early the next afternoon, John and Will found themselves at one of the tables at the Black Boar Inn, getting their fill of what seemed to be an extra special spread. While Will launched into a third helping of ham and cabbage, John and Sarah retreated out the back door. Fifteen minutes later, they returned, and John approached Virginia Luckstead, who had been conveniently and expectantly waiting in a quiet corner of the dining room, a look of contentment on her face. Virginia was fully prepared to marry off her daughter. Sarah had just turned 22, and in her mother's eyes, she was fast approaching the dangerous age of spinsterhood. John Hughson would do fine!

It took only four minutes. Did he really love Sarah? Aye, that he did! When would the wedding be? In the fall, after the house was completed. Would it be on the farm? Aye, on the farm. Did his father approve? Aye, he approves. Was John making a good living? Aye, he worked as a farmer and a cobbler and was doing well. With that, she gave him her blessing and announced the existence of a £40 dowry, to boot! Both Sarah and Will had been listening from around a corner. They gave each other a hug. "Welcome to the family, Sister," he whispered.

The summer raced by, and with the help of his brothers, father, and old William, the house was completed by the end of August. It was a four-room log structure with a veranda around the south and west sides that was wide enough, John said, to find shade in the summer any time of the day. The house was located near the road and about a stone's throw from the cobbler shop. As it neared completion, Sarah and her mother made several trips up to oversee construction and add their feminine touches to the structure.

"I think you're going to love this home, Sarah. Just look at that view off the front porch! Leaded windows, and did you notice they built two bread ovens into the fireplace? What a wonderful place to raise children." She winked at her daughter.

"Yes, Momma, it will be." Sarah blushed.

In mid-September, the couple was married during the Sunday service in the new Dutch Reformed Church in Yonkers, the Rev. Archibald Vandermere officiating. The Reverend told the young couple that, although he is the head of his house, a husband must also be a servant to his wife, as Christ was a servant to those He came to redeem. Out of the corner of his eye, Tom noticed Virginia Luckstead nodding in fervent agreement.

After the service, a grand party was held at the Black Boar Inn. In addition to many well-wishers from Yonkers, all the growing Hughson clan, including William MacIntosh, attended, along with John Dobbs and his wife and children. Even Benjamin and Samuel Griggs made the trip from their mill in what folks were beginning to call Griggstown in New Jersey. It actually wasn't much of a town yet, but the mill was beginning to attract people, and business interests were steadily developing. Someday, Griggstown might even deserve its name.

Tom was delighted to see the Griggs brothers. The three friends sat on the porch and reminisced about the old days on Long Island when he worked for their father.

After some small talk about gristmills, Samuel changed the topic with a chuckle and said,

"Tom, we never could figure out how you were able to show up on Barrent's Island and whisk Maria out from under us. We were both totally charmed by her, and she was friendly enough but, despite our Griggs good looks and well-bred manners, she was able to resist our attentions. We finally decided that it must have been your Scottish accent that fogged her judgment."

That caused some laughter, after which Tom, effecting his best Highland brogue, said, "Me Lads, it is well known that women, especially English women, are enchanted by our Scottish accent because it signals that the man behind it will make a far superior companion at night. Or, in the afternoon, for that matter!" he added.

"But surely not both, Tom," Ben asserted.

"Nay, Ben, I fear ye have been misinformed. Both, also!"

After some laughter, Sam asked, "Well, Ben, do you think Tom speaks the truth? Or, is he just trying to make us feel inferior?"

Tom answered for him. "Truly, I speak the truth, but be assured I intend no insult to fine English gentlemen, like yourselves."

"We take no offense, Tom, that another tankard wouldn't dissolve."

"Laddies, I can certainly arrange that."

It was early evening before Tom and his oldest son, Thomas, found themselves alone on the front porch, escaping some of the body heat from the crowd in the dining room.

"Well, Da, two married and several yet to go."

"Aye, Tom, but we're off to a good start." He paused. "I hope John doesn't find his bride to be an overly demanding wife."

"What do you mean, Da?"

"I believe young Sarah has developed her mother's eye for fine things…things that may not be too plentiful in a life on the farm."

"It's plain to see that she loves our John," Tom reassured his father. "I believe things will work out." Then he added, "God must have led you to save her mother and sister from that fire for a reason."

"I hope so, Tom, I hope so."

Chapter 31

John and Sarah

New York, 1735-1737

For several years, life on the farm for John and Sarah Hughson progressed rather smoothly. As these years passed, John devoted more and more time to the cobbler's trade and less to tending the fields. He made an adequate living and was content with his station in life and with having his extended family around him. His other brothers were all engaged in helping their father on the farm. They had added property to the original land lease, and there was enough acreage under the plow to provide for all. The area, once known as Wysquaqua, was growing. People were moving in, and the cobbler business was brisk. In the years since John Dobbs and his cousin, William Dobbs, established a ferry service across the Hudson in 1730, the place lost its Indian name and came to be called "Dobbs Ferry". John Hughson was the man to see for shoes, boots, saddles, and saddlebags in Dobbs Ferry.

Sarah was another matter, however. Although a devoted wife and mother, she had never quite taken to life on the farm. She had given birth to four children: Sarah (1726), Mary (1727), William (1728), and Jane (1730), and, in February 1734 found herself pregnant again, this time with Elizabeth. She wanted more out of life, more things, and she began to view New York as the place to get them. Her mother, Virginia Luckstead, was still alive, and she encouraged her daughter in her aspirations. Being familiar with the inn and tavern business herself, she thought that would be an excellent choice for her daughter and son-in-law.

"Sarah, there is always room for another tavern. You and John could do very well in that business, and Sarah and Mary are already old enough to help serve the patrons. You could become rich with a tavern in New York, Sarah. You could have the things you've always wanted." She paused for effect. "You should talk to John about it."

She did, and John finally succumbed to Sarah's pressure. On a trip to New York to sell a stock of shoes and boots, he found a building for rent on the north end of the city along the East River he thought might be suitable. They could live upstairs, and there were no other taverns in the immediate vicinity. He signed a contract and paid the first month's rent. Three weeks later, in late October 1735, the family moved, and John was now the proprietor of a tippling house. The sign he hung over the tavern door simply read,

Hughson's
Good Food
Good Spirits

John's mother-in-law was actually a great help in getting things organized, setting up the books, making arrangements with brewers, and purchasing all those items necessary for a tavern. The tavern's location and ambiance were not suited to attracting the better clientele of New York. It was a little too far north. But, much to the new proprietor's satisfaction, there was a very thirsty crowd of mariners, longshoremen, cartmen, artisans, and laborers who patronized the establishment almost from its opening day. The first floor of the tavern contained three rooms: one large room that was furnished with five long trestle tables and benches and a counter in the corner, behind which were stored the spirits, mugs, and the various plates, bowls, and utensils required to feed those who came hungry as well as thirsty. A huge stone fireplace dominated the rear wall, its massive mantel adorned with candles, several long-stemmed clay pipes, and a supply of tobacco for those patrons who wished to indulge in two vices at once. The low ceiling, with its exposed rough-hewn beams and dark, smoke-stained plank walls, created an ambiance of rustic coziness. The second, smaller room was used as a kitchen and storeroom. It had its own fireplace and

327

a rear door that opened on a small yard containing a barn, a shed, and a well. The third room was also smaller; it was furnished with a table and benches to be used for overflow crowds or for those who wished to meet in relative privacy.

Soon, John was, indeed, making money with his tavern, much more than he could ever hope to make at the cobbler's bench in Westchester County. As it turned out, it was Sarah who had the head for business, and it wasn't long before she took over the books, the ordering of supplies, and the hiring of the barmaids and a cook who soon became necessary. With this part of the business under control, John's time was freed to be the gracious host, laughing and joking with the patrons, listening to their troubles with their greedy employers, and generally making them feel at home. In November, little Elizabeth was born, and Sarah secretly felt good that perhaps her daughters would not have to grow up to marry farmers. There were a lot of men in New York, and many of them were becoming very rich.

"We've done it, John." She told her husband late one evening, just after they had closed and barred the door to their establishment. "We've made a future for ourselves and for our children." And then she added, "A few years here, and we'll be wealthy enough to buy a house on Pearl Street."

Although he muttered agreement, John knew that his wife's fantasies would never come to pass. There would never be enough money for Pearl Street, and even if there were, the legitimate merchants and their wives who made their homes on Pearl Street would never accept the likes of John and Sarah Hughson, tavern keepers to the rough and vulgar. He didn't care about them anyway, those haughty Dutchmen and Englishmen who considered themselves superior to everyone else in New York, white and black, who existed merely to serve them and indulge their whims. No, thank you. He'd live somewhere else.

By May 1736, the business at Hughson's Tavern had grown to the point where Sarah was obliged to take on additional help. She hired Phillis, the 32-year-old wife of a black freeman named Frank, to cook. Phillis had taught herself to read, and she was interested in political affairs in New York. Phillis talked about local politics, the plight of the slaves, and the things that were wrong and should be made right. Sarah considered her uppity but had to admit that she was a reliable worker. John enjoyed listening to Phillis' opinions. He found her to be amusing and informative. And it wasn't long before Phillis had convinced him to serve black customers on Sunday afternoons and evenings "in the small room," she said, "where they wouldn't be noticed, but they would bring in good money."

At that time, there were perhaps fifty taverns and tippling houses in New York, and although there was a law against it, a few of them served alcohol and food to blacks, both slaves and freemen. They came mostly on Sunday when their masters gave them a day of rest from their labor. They would eat, drink, and dance to the fiddle, sometimes until dawn. Furthermore, they would pay in hard coin, money they had made on the side, spending money their masters gave them as a reward for good behavior and, occasionally, money they had made from fencing stolen goods. Certainly, no self-respecting tavern owner would serve blacks, free or slave, that is, not if he wanted wealthier and better-known clientele to patronize his establishment. The Hughsons, however, found their self-respect in other ways, and by the summer of 1736, John and Sarah gave in to Phillis' persistent requests.

"You be on the north end, Mr. Hughson," she said. Dat's near where da free black folk live over by Great Pond. And there ain't no tavern near here that'll serve 'em. They be comin' here, Mr. Hughson. Yes, Sir, they be comin' here wit dare money. Jus' you wait and see!"

In preparation for their venture into this new source of income, Sarah encouraged John to build another door into the smaller of his taprooms so the African clientele could have their own entrance in the rear.

"It wouldn't look proper havin' 'em come in the front door under our sign," she exhorted.

By the middle of August, the new door was finished, and John told Phillis to spread the word that blacks were welcome on Sundays only and that there would be no tabs run, cash only.

Despite Phillis' efforts, it was three weeks before the first patrons of color cautiously stepped through the rear door of Hughsons—Good Food, Good Spirits. Four of them, in fact, all freemen and all related to Phillis or her husband. With tentative steps and his wife looking on, John showed them to a corner table and took their orders, ale it would be, three tankards. When the pewter mugs arrived, the oldest of the three, a brick mason named Josiah, immediately withdrew a shilling from his coat pocket and placed it on the table. John dropped it in his apron and gave the man his change. He felt his tension subsiding. These men might be black, but their money is plenty good. Phillis may have guided him to a real windfall after all! As rounds two and three were served up, the new patrons also grew more at ease. Their conversations became louder and less guarded, and John and Sarah found themselves eavesdropping as the four talked about a stable they were building for the governor and what a big rear end his wife had.

"Man, dat woman is real broad in the beam, kinda like a good fishin' boat, big beam but stable in a storm!"

The others laughed, and one said, "Josiah, whatda you know about women with broad beams or fishin' either, for that matter?"

"Well, I know dat both of 'em are stable and you ain't gonna fall overboard!"

More guffaws. Even John chuckled, and Sarah elbowed him in the ribs.

"You aren't thinkin' about MY bottom, are you, John?" she wondered out loud.

"Nay, Woman. Not I. I don't know nothin' 'bout no fishin'."

Some sailors and longshoremen came in the front door and dropped down at one of the tables. They also heard the black voices in the back room. One of them got up to investigate, and he reported his discovery to his drinking partners. When John came over to take their orders, one of them chided him good-naturedly about serving heathen on the Sabbath, but then nothing more was said, and the seamen went about their business of loud talk and libation. John and Sarah breathed a sigh of relief. This might work, after all. Sarah thought about living on Pearl Street.

****

After that first Sunday afternoon, the ice was broken; the blacks came through Hughson's back door, slave and freeman, male and female alike, and, much to the Hughsons' relief, their Sunday reveling did not seem to affect the weekly white trade at all. Rather, it seemed to grow for some reason. Of course, the sheriff came by with a few church leaders to express their feelings on the matter, but it seemed to John to be more of a formality that did not pose any real threat to his growing enterprise, especially since he was astute enough to cross their palms with a small gratuity. "In appreciation," he said, for the fine work they were doing to preserve community safety and standards.

As time went on, John Hughson grew to like these Africans who frequented his establishment. They were an animated, optimistic, and forgiving bunch of souls. They laughed and sang and danced to the fiddle. The women were lively and uninhibited. In some ways, they seemed to be the ones in charge. It was often from their skirt pockets that the coins were produced for the food and drink. John joined them, listened to their stories, and developed a growing sympathy for them and their state of servitude. He began to detest slavery, not so much as it was practiced in New York, but the stories of what some of those poor people endured when they were in Barbados, Trinidad, St. Croix, or those other Caribbean islands made John want to kill the first Portuguese, or Spaniard or Iberian Jew he could lay his hands on.

New York, he told himself, was different. Sure, some of these black patrons were enslaved and forced to work for nothing under the fear of brutality or even death. But in reality, they didn't have it that bad. They weren't much different from the hundreds of white indentured servants in New York...only they wouldn't be freed in seven years like their European brothers and sisters. They came and went pretty much as they wanted to, even at night if they carried a lantern with them. True, they were more restricted under English rule than they had been when the Dutch owned New York, especially since the 1712 uprising in the city. But they weren't in chains, they had Sundays off, and there were laws against treating them cruelly. They had spending money, a roof over their heads, and two meals a day. Things could be worse; in fact, they were certainly much worse off back in Africa. And they could come to Hughson's tavern and drink and socialize, couldn't they? Their lot could be much worse, indeed.

One Sunday afternoon in early December 1737, a new face appeared among the revelers in the back room, the "African room," is what John's children began calling it. A handsome, well-built young black man in his mid-twenties, John judged. He was animated and carried himself less like a slave and more like an important city merchant. He dressed better than the others in the room. He seemed to be acquainted with most of them, as he called each by name. At first, John thought he must be a freeman, but he wasn't. Despite his condition of servitude, he had the air of one who was in charge. He bought a round of rum for the other eleven blacks in the room, and then he got up and approached John, greeting him respectfully but as though they were equals.

"Mr. Hughson, Sir. My name's Caesar," he said, extending a hand to the proprietor. "I work for John Vaarck, the baker, and I want to thank you, Sir, for letting us share a tankard together in your establishment. You'll find that I'll make no trouble, and I'll pay promptly for my food and drink."

John was taken aback. 'I work for...'? He never heard a slave refer to his master in those terms. Where did a slave learn to speak like that, he wondered. While he considered exactly how to respond, Sarah chimed in, "Welcome to Hughson's, Caesar."

"Yes," John added, "Welcome to Hughson's."

John intercepted Phillis on her way back to the kitchen. "Do you know that one called Caesar standing over there by the fire?"

"Yes, Sir; he be owned by Mister John Vaarck. He do the bakin' and deliverin' for him. He also hire himself out to do jus' 'bout anything. He's a dandy, that one. He don't really consider himself a slave, and he be gettin' into trouble for it all da time. Sometimes, he don't show da proper respect to white folks, but he don't mean no harm. Mr. Vaarck don't really know how to deal with him, so he mainly jus' let him be, so long as he do his chores. He always into somethin', dat boy is...him an' his friends, Cuffee, Prince, and Cambridge." She chuckled and continued. Dat Cambridge is trouble. He's owned by Mr. Christopher Codwise, Sr., but he don't keep a tight rein on him. Dat boy'll steal anything he can. I'd keep an eye on ole Cambridge if I was you."

She continued. "Jus' last summer Caesar and Prince was caught one night makin' off with six barrels of Geneva from Baker's Tavern. Cambridge was with 'em, but he didn't get caught. They was whipped on the green for that one. Ole Mr. Baker sure was glad to get that gin back. It come all da way from Holland. I expect Caesar learnt his lesson, alright. He ain't been caught stealin' since, that I know of."

"Where did he learn to talk like that?"

"His mama; she could be a school mistress if they'd let her. She be owned by Mr. Verplanck over on Stone Street."

At that instant, John made the connection.

"Of course, Elizabeth's son," he said in a voice that aroused Phillis' curiosity.

"You mean, you know him, Mr. Hughson?" she inquired.

John proceeded to tell her the whole story, beginning with how his father had met her long ago on his voyage to America. He told her about the terrifying night back in 1712 when his father and brothers had pulled her and young Caesar from the mob and rushed her in their wagon to the safety of his grandmother's.

"I've thought about 'em some over the years, but I haven't seen either of 'em since then," John concluded. "Not until this afternoon, that is."

When the group of slaves and freemen began to disperse for the evening, John found the opportunity to corner Caesar and share the connection with him. Over the next two hours and a tankard of ale, the two men shared a great deal of information about each other. During the course of their conversation, Caesar brought up the Baker's Tavern incident and quickly assured John that he had learned his lesson. The look in the black man's eyes led John to silently question the veracity of that statement, but something about him made John trust him anyway. At midnight, Caesar finally left through the Africans' rear door.

Caesar became a regular at Hughson's on Sundays and sometimes during the evenings. He was usually accompanied by his three friends, Cuffee, Prince, and Cambridge, each a slave and each, like Caesar, testing the limits of his station in life. It seemed to John as though his presence breathed life and spontaneity into the other black patrons. When he arrived, the laughing, storytelling, and singing began in earnest. And he always seemed to have money, money to spend on food and drink for himself and others, and money to tip the server, a tradition still uncommon in America. The tip, he told John one evening, was "to insure promptness. T-I-P," that's what it was for, and he appreciated the prompt and respectful service he received at Hughson's. John was intrigued by Caesar. He just didn't think of himself as a slave; rather, he was a man with a job to do and an impact to make on the world.

Chapter 32

The Second Tavern

1737-1738

Life progressed at John Hughson's establishment. The weekly number of patrons, including black patrons, continued to grow, and John and Sarah realized they needed to expand the tavern. Hearing of their idea, Caesar offered to help them, and a price for his weekend labor was decided upon. The next night, Caesar arrived with detailed drawings of how the addition might look. Caesar explained his concept to the very impressed proprietor.

"You can make your main room bigger to the south and build another fireplace at the end. On the west side of the new room, you can also make the room bigger for the Africans and build a second fireplace. The second floor can be expanded over both rooms, and you could put in stairs in the southeast corner and build in six rooms for boarders up there. See, I've sketched out what they'd look like." He produced the drawings on the backs of three letters he had picked up somewhere.

Caesar was excited. He paused and looked at John with anticipation. John picked up the drawings and took them over by the fire for a better view. He poured over the designs for three or four minutes and then passed judgment.

"Aye," Caesar. "'Tis some good sketches you've made. I believe we'll do it." Then he added, "Where did you learn to draw like that?"

"Since I was little, I liked to draw. My mama showed me some tricks about drawin' buildings. She'd tell me I was going to be good carpenter someday."

Caesar proved to be a great help to the project. He knew where to purchase good but inexpensive lumber and supplies, he uncovered sources of labor, both slave and freeman, for carpenters and stonemasons, and, much to Sarah's pleasure, he and others spent a good portion of their earnings on food and drink at Hughson's.

In eight weeks, the expanded establishment was completed. The new sign read:

John and Sarah could not have been more pleased. The new Hughson Inn attracted ever-increasing crowds, black and white. Even the rooms began to fill with boarders, not exactly the caliber that Sarah would have hoped for, but paying renters, nonetheless.

As the weeks and months wore on, John's and Caesar's relationship developed, both on a personal level and in terms of the business opportunities that the black man brought to the tavern keeper. In the summer of 1738, Caesar approached John with a plan to start a timber business. There was a growing need for timber and firewood in New York, and there was plenty of forest for the taking across the Hudson over in New Jersey. If John bought the necessary provisions, Caesar would gather a small weekend workforce of slaves and freemen who could cut the logs and haul them back to the city. John, being the white man and, therefore, the legitimate partner, would sell the loads to the brokers at the wharves. After paying the men, Caesar proposed that he and John split the profits 50-50. John considered the proposition over a tankard of ale, and the two men finally settled on 60-40, a figure John thought was more appropriate because Caesar was, after all, a slave. Furthermore, to oversee the cutting crew, Caesar knew just the man, his friend, Cuffee, owned by Adolph Philipse. Cuffee was trustworthy; he'd make the others work for their pay. But just to make sure, Caesar proposed that Cuffee be paid on commission, 7% of the broker's price for each load.

"Caesar, I believe I'm gonna like working with you. If it weren't for that skin of yours, I'd swear you were a Scotsman!" The two men laughed heartily. Again, John marveled at his command of proper English. Elizabeth taught her son well.

Throughout the summer and fall of 1738, the wood business thrived. Cuffee kept the men working, and John and Caesar began accumulating a sizable profit; at least it was sizable by their standards. John hired three cartmen to help deliver the orders for firewood throughout the growing city…all white cartmen, of course. No black, even a free black, could be a cartman unless he was driving personally for one of the influential city fathers. It wasn't long before John's wood was even being delivered along Pearl Street to the most elegant homes in the city. He also delivered to the Verplanck's. In fact, Caesar saw to it that his mother's owners received a ten percent discount.

"It's only right, Mr. Hughson," he insisted. "They're family."

****

One Saturday evening in early November, John and Sarah Hughson were enjoying a rare respite from the normal crowds that frequented their tavern, the dearth of patrons undoubtedly caused by a tremendous thunderstorm that had enveloped the city. The rain fell in an absolute downpour, the kind of storm that rolls in off the ocean and drops water an inch a minute, making so much noise that a person has to shout over it to be heard. With the additional noise from the constant claps of thunder, it was nigh impossible to talk at all, so the couple sat by the hearth, enjoying its warmth and sipping two tankards of ale Sarah had drawn for the occasion. They were, therefore, startled when the front tavern door (for whites only) flung open, and in stepped Caesar, a flash of lightning silhouetting the large oil cloth draped over his head and shoulders.

"Caesar, in Heaven's name, what in the world brings you out on a night like this? Drop that canvas on the floor," Sarah ordered, "and get over here by the fire before you catch your death, and we'll have to bury you with the rest of 'em over in the African burial ground!"

Caesar did as he was told and pulled a small bench up to the fire. He was clutching a brown cloth bag with something in it.

"Why are you out on a night like this, Caesar?" John asked. "Is the sheriff after you again?" he inquired with a chuckle.

"No Sir. I've been leadin' a Christian life, I have." He responded in a faux-hurt voice. And then, mimicking the slave dialect that he normally didn't speak, he added, "I jus be tryin' to act like da slave, dat they wants, but it ain't easy, Massah Hughson, no Suh, it ain't easy!"

At that, Sarah snorted through her nose, all the time eyeing that brown bag with the interest of a little child at Christmas. Caesar noticed her anticipation out of the corner of his eye but, feigning oblivion, did nothing to assuage it. In case the bag contained something for her, Sarah decided to be congenial.

"You want a tankard, Caesar?" she asked.

"Yes, Ma'am, thank you," he said, resuming his polite and diffident manner. By now, steam was rising from his socks and knee britches that had been soaked by the rain. It presented a humorous picture, causing John to laugh. Sarah returned with a pewter tankard and handed it to Caesar. She could stand the suspense no longer.

"What's in the sack, Caesar?" she asked.

"I brought you somethin,' Mrs. Hughson." He hesitated, "somethin' I found and I thought you might like."

He reached into the bag and produced a fine silver creamer and sugar set, complete with a silver tray to place it on.

"I found 'em down by the river. I think the tide washed 'em in last night." He chuckled and added, "They must have come off of some sunken ship."

"Caesar, they're beautiful!" she exclaimed, taking possession and immediately polishing them with her apron.

"Alright, Caesar," John demanded in an accusing tone, "Where did they really come from…who did you steal them from? They're gonna hang you, boy!"

"John!" Sarah interrupted.

"Mr. Hughson, I swear I found 'em on the riverbank in the tideline. They were all washed up together amongst the kelp."

While John contemplated that improbable image, Caesar got down to business.

"Mr. Hughson, I find lots of stuff in the kelp. So does Cuffee and some of the others. They're just good and findin' stuff. We don't know what to do with it, the ships already bin sunk and all, and if we try to sell it, they'll accuse us of stealin', and it'll be the whip or even the gallows for us."

Caesar let that soak in a moment. Then he added, "We were thinkin' that maybe we could sell what we find to you at a cheap price and you, being a white man and an upstandin' member of the city's merchants, could find a good place to sell it at a profit."

John thought a moment. "A fence, Caesar, you want me to become your fence? They'd hang you and me both!"

"There's no fencin' to it, Mr. Hughson, 'cause there ain't no stealin' involved since the stuff is lost and we just find it. Not only by the river, but sometimes over in New Jersey in the woods when we're loggin' or sometimes on the side of the roads, or on the dock when it falls off some wagon. You never heard me talkin' about no stealin,' did you, Mr. Hughson?"

Caesar shot a pleading glance toward Mrs. Hughson. He and Prince and Cuffee already had a fence for large quantities of merchandise they purloined, a lawyer and upstanding member of the business community named John Romme. They could use another fence for the small stuff, however.

Sarah could see the possibilities.

"What kind of merchandise do you and your friends find, Caesar?" she inquired in a tentative voice.

"We find silver, like that right there. And we find cloth, lace, tools, coins, glassware, hardware, like hinges and nails, window glass, buckles, muskets, sometimes kegs of flour or powder, medicine, even furniture, once in a while. We find just about anything. Most of it could be sold in Boston and New England if we had a way to get it there. That's our problem, no way to get it there without bein' hanged."

He dropped his head, assuming a dejected aspect but keeping Sarah in view.

She inquired further, "You mean to tell me that none of it, the lace and the cloth, gets ruined by the seawater, or the kelp, or the other elements?"

"No damage, Mrs. Hughson, no damage at all."

She continued, "Who knows you find these things?"

"Nobody but us, and now you. We keep it secret for fear of being called thieves. We keep the stuff well hidden. We're very careful, like tonight. I came in the storm, so nobody'd know I was here to talk business."

The rain was beginning to let up.

"Caesar, you'd better leave now, and Mrs. Hughson and I will discuss your proposition."

Without uttering another word, Caesar smiled, got up, took one final gulp from the tankard, donned his oilskin, and slipped out into the night. He knew he had closed the deal.

Sarah broke the silence that had followed the slave's departure.

"John, this could be very lucrative for us. My mother has connections with the merchants who stop at the Black Boar on their way to and from New England. She could get a good price for the stuff, and it would be out of New York, where there would be no suspicion. Let's try it, John," she encouraged. "We'll keep it on a small scale. That way it'll be safe from detection."

"If we get caught, we'll be jailed or worse," her husband cautioned. "No one will believe us if we say we thought the stuff was found. If those slaves get caught in the act," he added, "they're sure to tell the sheriff about us."

"If we keep it small, we keep it safe, John. And Caesar is no fool; we both know that. It's a small risk we'd be taking, John."

She continued her argument. "We'll keep none of the stuff at the tavern. And we'll not utter a word to Caesar about what we do with it. If he implicates us, there will be no evidence."

"I don't know, Sarah," he countered. "We're already on slippery ground as it is, sellin' liquor to those slaves and freemen."

Her tone grew insistent. "John, there are more than ten taverns in this city that let the blacks in their doors. They all do what we do; they cross the sheriff's palm whenever he visits. They'll think nothing of us. Believe me, John, it's a very safe plan."

"Receiving stolen property from slaves and disposing of it for profit is not a safe way to live, Sarah," he remonstrated, albeit weakly.

"John," she retorted, "you know we want to have a better life for us and the children. This is a way to help achieve it. We're going to do it. We'll do it safely, John; we'll do it safely."

A clap of thunder punctuated her declaration as her husband sat immobile, staring into the burning embers.

In a fortnight, two bolts of cloth from England made their way to the Black Boar Inn in Westchester, thence to New England, and silver coins dropped into the pockets of Caesar, the Hughsons, and Virginia Luckstead. It wasn't much, but the whole venture worked, and it gave the Hughsons a measure of confidence. As time went on, there would be more lost items making their way to the Black Boar.

****

A year later, the Hughsons were ready to expand. Taking Caesar's advice, they sold their establishment on the East River and, in 1738, rented a building at the end of Liberty Street, next to the North (Hudson) River and a block from Broadway. It was closer to where the freemen lived and, therefore, offered a greater potential for more patronage and increased opportunities for dealing in lost items. Plus, it was that much closer to the road and the Black Boar. Broadway was becoming a major thoroughfare, and the tavern business for both white and black customers was lucrative. The new establishment was a bigger, three-story building, which provided much roomier accommodations for lodgers and their own four girls, one boy, and a baby on the way.

With the food, drink, lodging, and fencing, the Hughsons were doing quite well, at least quite well by their standards. They would never live on Pearl Street or be invited to one of the Verplancks' Christmas parties. But as far as Sarah was concerned, it beat the life of a farmer's wife in Westchester County. John was not that averse to the farming alternative, and he was a clobber, after all, thanks to old William. But Sarah ruled, so John resigned himself to his lot.

As time passed, John felt increasingly at home with the slaves and freemen who patronized his establishment. The fencing business was not as lucrative as John and Sarah had hoped, largely because there wasn't nearly as much to fence as the optimistic Caesar had predicted. Nevertheless, an occasional item or two came their way, which they usually sent on to Virginia Luckstead for disposal. The trade at the tavern, both African and white, was plentiful, however, and John's firewood operation was expanding. Although much larger than the first Hughson Inn, the design of the new one by Broadway was essentially the same as the one on the East River. There were four large rooms on the first floor, three for white customers in the front and the fourth for black customers in the rear, complete with its own entrance. The six small rooms for rent were on the second floor. The Hughsons, themselves, lived on the second floor of the "L" shaped extension off the north end of the main building. A stable and some outbuildings behind the tavern completed the picture.

Because he now had the money to hire more help, John was becoming more the man of leisure, and he spent much of his time in conversations with the patrons, both black and

349

white. Caesar and Cuffee were frequent visitors, and as time went on, they brought other young male slaves to the tavern to imbibe and discuss their lives, their masters, and their discontent with their station in life. Among the many slaves who became regular patrons, a few stood out in John Hughson's mind. There were Quack, Prince, Wan, Albany, Fortune, Cato, Othello, York, Will, and Venture, all basically good men, as good as any man but repressed by a social system that had not yet run its course.

As time went on, John became increasingly sympathetic toward these men and the conditions they had to endure. Of course, they had it a lot better than their brothers and sisters on the plantations in the Caribbean Islands or in the southern colonies of Virginia, the Carolinas, and Georgia. And none who could remember their homeland was interested in returning to the squalid conditions and terror that most of them had to endure back in Africa. John found these men to be ignorant and superstitious, and yet they were also lively, expressive, and friendly. They thought about life in a philosophical way that somehow made them his equals. They were ready to voice their opinion yet eager to learn; they asked questions and contemplated the answers. They valued relationships more than things, and they supported one another in their mutual lowly state. John knew the Quakers were right; it was indeed a sin to deprive such men of their freedom.

As these black patrons got to know John and Sarah, their trust levels grew, and they felt at increasing liberty to discuss their hopes for freedom in open conversations around the tavern's tables. What were the avenues to freedom? What about running away to Canada, to the Indian nations, or to Kaintuck? Why couldn't they work for their freedom like the indentured servants? What would they do if they were free? Why weren't New York's current freemen any better off? What about the blacks in the Caribbean who rebelled and won their freedom? How were they surviving? What about the 1714 slave uprising in Carolina? Why did it fail? For that matter, what about the 1712 slave revolt in New York? What went wrong there? Why did it fail? Could a successful uprising happen in New York? Would the Spanish arrive, side with the blacks, and release the city from its British domination? What would keep the Spanish from re-enslaving them if they did come?

Caesar had the answers to many of these questions. He was quick-witted and knowledgeable, and he seemed to have endless information networks throughout the city. He knew what he was talking about, and the others deferred to him. John could see that he was a natural-born leader; only his slave condition kept him from becoming one of New York's success stories.

John knew that giving these men a place to meet and drink was wrong, let alone allowing such talk of freedom to

351

go unfettered. He was breaking the fundamental rule for members of the slave-holding class. They must report and suppress any manifestation of resistance among the oppressed, no matter how small, for a spark could ignite a blaze, and a blaze could produce a deadly conflagration. But the discussions were lively and entertaining, and John was at once amused and enlightened by the discourse. Perhaps what he was doing for them was illegal by British standards, but on a higher plane, John decided that he was serving God's purpose to "remember the poor," and his reward would be great in Heaven, if not on Earth. However, his earthly reward was growing.

Chapter 33

Peggy Kerry

New York, April 1739

February 12th, 1739

My Dearest Peggy,

I have arrived safely in the New World. You would not believe how big New York is. Pretty soon, it will be bigger than London itself. Thousands of people, many speaking tongues totally strange to me. Everywhere men and women scurry about, conducting business, buying and selling anything you can imagine. My regiment is stationed in Fort George at the very southern tip of New York, where the two rivers meet. There are places to live nearby for soldiers' wives, Peggy. We can get married as soon as you arrive.

Contact my brother, Paul, about your passage. I left enough money with him, and he will make the arrangements for you. Write me as soon as you know which ship you'll make the crossing on. You can be sure I'll be there on the wharf to give you the greatest kiss you can imagine. If, for some reason, I cannot make it as soon as you arrive, inquire about me at the fort. All will be well. Come quick, Peggy. I love you, and I cannot wait to hold you in my arms again.

Your Obedient Servant,

Cpl. Richard Sorubiero,

Nineteen-year-old Margaret Kerry—everyone called her Peggy—stared at the letter, the letter she had been praying for over the last five months. Sitting on her bed in a tiny room in Plymouth, England, she read it again and then again. The afternoon sun streamed through the tavern window and made her red Irish hair all the more brilliant. Now, she could leave her employment with old man Whitacker as a barmaid and servant girl. Life with Richard in America. The dream she had been dreaming was now to become reality. Richard! She loved him the minute she laid eyes on him, handsome in his red uniform. A Fusilier, too...not just any old soldier. Maybe someday he would be an officer.

Her devotion to Richard was matched only by his love for her. Despite her Irish heritage and her working-class station, she was beautiful by anyone's estimate. Had she been the daughter of a duke or viscount, she would have attracted the romantic attention of many a young English gentleman. As it was, she had no fine clothes, no dowry, no servants to do her bidding, and, when Richard met her in the market purchasing mutton for the tavern, no family to call her own. Something about her captivated him immediately, and it wasn't long before she was the center of his plans and dreams for the future. When his time was up in the army, they would stay in America. He would go into business and become successful. He would provide for Peggy, they would live in a big house, they would have servants, and they would become aristocrats together in America.

The next morning, Peggy walked the mile and a half to Paul's glass-blowing shop on Stratton Lane. She watched him finish an ornate glass decanter and tap it off his blowpipe onto the bench. Then, he turned and greeted her warmly.

"Dearest Peggy, how's my favorite future sister-in-law?"

"I am about to burst with joy, Paul. I just received this letter from Richard." She passed it over to him. He read it and then hugged her.

"Great news from America, Peggy. I'm very happy for the both of you. When Richard gets out of the army, perhaps I'll join him in America in some business venture. When those Americans stop drinking their ale out of pewter goblets, animal skins, and gourds, they may have need of my talent!"

They both chuckled at Paul's confirmation of the low British view of American refinement.

"I'll make the arrangements for you straight away. I'll go down and purchase a passage for you in the morning. You go home and pack your belongings."

"I want to be on the very next ship, Paul! Do you hear me? The very next ship!

"Aye, aye, Missy; the very next ship it'll be."

It turned out that the very next ship was the *Raven*, scheduled to sail with the tide in two days. There was, of course, no sense in sending a letter to Richard, for it would get there the same time she did. Peggy resigned herself to not being met at the wharf in New York for that kiss Richard promised. She'd have to wait for it until she got to Fort George. No matter. She would surprise him, and in five weeks she'd be Mrs. Sorubiero!

Five weeks later, Peggy gazed out over the rail of the *Raven* as it eased up to the wharf at the end of Broad Street in New York. Richard was right. What greeted her on the dock below was a bustling pageant of sailors, merchants, stevedores, carts, horses, oxen, barking dogs, and people of all shapes, sizes, and colors. A score of people stood on the dock waiting to meet their relatives and friends who had just survived their voyage to the new world on the *Raven*. She thought briefly about the elderly woman, Mrs. Waverly, who had died from pneumonia during the crossing and would not be coming down the gangplank to hug her recently widowed son and his two young daughters. Of course, Richard wouldn't be there to embrace his Irish love, but she'd make her way to the fort and fix that soon enough.

The quartermaster told Peggy her trunk would be offloaded in the morning, so she grabbed the two carpetbags that held her clothes and few worldly possessions and dragged them down the gangplank and to a waiting cartman who offered to deliver her and her bags to the fort for a half shilling. He motioned to her to get up beside him and then clucked the old horse into a very slow walk.

"Well, Lass, from that red hair and the dress you're wearin', I'd make you out to be an Irish wench. Am I right about that?

"Yes, Sir, I hail from Tipperary, but I spent some time in Plymouth."

He looked at her out of the corner of his eye. "Plymouth, huh? And what were you doin' there, might I ask?"

"She hesitated and decided to tell the truth. "I worked for an innkeeper, doin' whatever he needed."

"It didn't include providin' him pleasure, now did it, Lassie?" he inquired with a sneer.

"No, it did not! And you're a might too inquisitive! I'll thank you to treat me like the Christian woman I am!"

"Christian, huh! More likely you're a Catholic than a Christian. New York is gettin' more and more of you Papists. Pretty soon we'll be no different than Spain!

There were several minutes of silence, finally broken by another inquiry from the cartman.

"What brings you to the fort, Missy?"

"I am to marry a soldier there. He sent for me, and I came by the very next ship, so I'm to be a surprise to him."

"A surprise, huh?" grunted the cartman. "Likely as not you'll find him in one of the tippling houses, drunk and with a wench on each arm."

He chuckled at his insightful commentary on the life of a British soldier in New York, but Peggy remained silent, failing to see the humor. Instead, she studied the beautiful homes along Pearl Street, wondering what the people were like who lived in them and if she and Richard would ever live in a house like those. Well, certainly not for a while, not on a soldier's pay. But anything was possible in America, and she was certainly willing to work hard, to save, and to plan. Who knows what wonderful things lay in store for Richard and her? In the meantime, they had their love for each other. That would be enough for now.

The cartman unloaded Peggy and her carpet bags and collected his fare.

"Good luck to ye, Lass," he said, for the first time showing a softer side to his demeanor.

"Thank you, Sir," she replied and turned toward the gate.

There were no guards, and Peggy walked inside, dragging her bags. She approached a sergeant who was sitting on a barrel smoking a clay pipe and cleaning his nails with a penknife.

"Excuse me, Sir. How can I find Corporal Sorubiero?" she inquired of the man.

He gave her a quick visual once-over and sneered.

"Ye better be gone from here, ya little red-haired trollop, before the guard locks ya up. Go ply your trade somewhere else!"

Peggy thought quickly.

"Sir," she said in as forceful a voice as she could muster, "I am Margaret Kerry Sorubiero, the wife of Corporal Sorubiero. He sent for me, and I have come from Plymouth to be with him. Would you kindly tell me how I may find him?"

At that, the Sergeant's attitude appeared to adjust somewhat.

"I'm new here myself, Missy, and I don't know any Corporal Sorubiero, but I'll inquire for ye."

He rose slowly from the barrel as if the task he was undertaking would overwhelm him, and he made his way toward one of the buildings. In about five minutes, he returned, and as he approached, Peggy noticed that something in his countenance had changed. He appeared more business-like, as though he had a purpose.

He paused for a moment, looking her in the eyes. Then he said, "I'm sorry, Missy, but your Corporal Sorubiero won't be comin' to meet you. You see, he was killed three weeks ago down on the docks. They was unloadin' gunpowder, and somehow he dropped a keg he was carryin' and it went off. Terrible shame that was."

All Peggy could do was stare; she stared at the man—vacant eyes—her reality torn away from her in the flash of a moment. Then it all crashed down around her, and she collapsed to her knees and then prostrate in the dirt…sobbing. How could it be? Richard…gone. What was she to do? Where would she go? A surrealistic combination of grief and panic welled up and overcame her.

For the longest time, the sergeant felt helpless to assist the young woman. Finally, he lifted her back to her knees and, in his own gruff manner, attempted to calm her.

"I'm sorry Ma'am. They say he was a good man and a good soldier, too. You bein' his wife and all, you're entitled to his effects, his last month's wages and ten pounds. Come with me to the paymaster and we'll get it for you."

He pulled her to her feet, and, with one arm around her to support her, they made their way to the same building where he had gone before. Fifteen minutes later, Peggy left the fort, dragging her two carpetbags, headed she knew not where…or why. Her life was over. She hadn't gone very far when she couldn't bear it any longer. She dropped her bags against a building, fell onto them, and began again to sob. Passersby ignored her, stepping clear of her and pretending she wasn't even there. That is until a black woman came upon the pathetic scene. She was middle-aged, and she carried herself with a certain dignity. She had been to a bakery and was holding a sack with six loaves of bread, still warm from the oven. It was Elizabeth. She set the bread down and knelt beside Peggy.

"Whatever is the matter with you, child?" she asked in a sympathetic voice. "Are you sick? Do you need some help?"

Between sobs, Peggy told Elizabeth her story. Not wanting to get into trouble for taking the money, she continued to refer to herself as Richard's wife. Somehow, it made her feel better, anyway. At least as Richard's widow, she was somebody; she had some identity to cling to.

"Well, Peggy, honey, this street is no place for you to be. Come with me to the Verplanck's, where I work. We'll clean you up, give you something to eat and put you to bed. Tomorrow we'll worry about what to do. Carry this bread for me, will you, child?"

Elizabeth picked up the two bags and, with Peggy in tow, headed for Verplanck's. The panic that had so thoroughly overtaken Peggy began to subside as she let the black woman take charge of her. She wondered if Elizabeth was a slave. She certainly didn't fit the Irish girl's conception of what a slave in America would be like. She was articulate, sure of herself, and she had the carriage of a lady. Peggy stopped crying. Maybe she would survive this ordeal after all.

A few minutes later, Peggy found herself in the kitchen in the rear of the Verplanck home. Elizabeth prepared a plate of sliced bread and cheese and placed it in front of the Irish girl.

"Here, Peggy. Eat some of this. It'll make you feel a whole lot better."

Peggy ate in silence, head bowed, as Elizabeth sat across from her, silently reflecting on the young woman's situation and what some alternatives might be. In a few moments, she had a plan.

"Peggy, have you ever worked for a household?"

"Just for my own mother and father, but I worked in a tavern for a while as a maid and a server for a man named Whitacker back in Plymouth. I did some cookin' for him, too."

"Did you ever have to take care of old people?"

"While I was still home, I helped my mother tend to my grandparents for three years before they died of the fever. They couldn't do much for themselves and needed us to help them with their daily affairs."

Peggy looked at Elizabeth expectantly.

"How would you like to work here for two months, Peggy? The Verplancks are getting on and Mrs. Verplanck is growing infirm. Her daughter and husband are moving here from Philadelphia in June so she can help her mother, but until that time Mrs. Verplanck might need your assistance. Would you like me to inquire?"

"Oh, yes, Ma'am," the young widow exclaimed. "Please ask her. I'll work for my keep. That's all I would want!"

Elizabeth chuckled. "Oh, I think she'll also pay you for your service. The Verplancks are kind people."

There was a moment when neither woman said anything. Then Peggy added, "I have a small trunk on the *Raven*. Tomorrow it will be offloaded, and I need to get it."

"We'll send someone to pick it up. Is your name on it?"

Peggy hesitated. "Yes, my maiden name, though. It says 'Margaret Kerry' on the tag. It's brown and old looking."

"I am sure James can find it. We'll send him," she said reassuringly.

The next day, Peggy, bathed, appropriately attired, and coached by Elizabeth, was introduced to Mrs. Verplanck, who quickly assented to the new girl's hire. Now gainfully employed, Peggy threw herself into the task of familiarizing herself with the Verplanck household chores and duties. Bartholomew, Elizabeth's husband and one of the Verplanck slaves, built her a bed, a chair, and a small table and furnished a tiny room in the corner of the barn. It would do, and it certainly beat sleeping on the street. Peggy was a survivor, and she was, indeed, surviving.

Peggy's two months stretched into several more because the Verplancks' daughter, Juliann, and her husband, John Gregory, were delayed by their affairs in Philadelphia until

November 1739. Also, Peggy's employment had decreased the pressure on them to come to their mother's aid. John was still eager to move to New York, however, because he would be taking over his father-in-law's business.

In June 1739, Peggy moved from the barn into a spare bedroom in the house to be closer to Mrs. Verplanck. It was in that same month that she met Caesar, Elizabeth's and Bartholomew's 27-year-old son, who was owned by a baker named Vaarck. He came by to deliver a load of John Hughson's firewood and to help his father remove a tree stump in the yard beside the house. Peggy brought some water out to the two perspiring men.

"Thank you, Ma'am," Caesar said in his best courtly manner.

Bartholomew broke in, "This here's my son, Caesar. He's a baker".

"Hello, Caesar," she responded. "I'm Peggy Kerry." She had taken to using her maiden name again. "I work for the Verplancks, thanks to your mother. She talks about you often."

"I hope she says only good things," he said with a grin.

"Well," she paused and smiled, "she actually says that you're a rascal and that you create much aggravation for Mr. Vaarck and the authorities."

All three servants laughed.

"I guess she's right about that. It ain't easy always actin' like a good slave, so most the time I don't even try. I learned that from my father here."

Bartholomew smiled and winked at his son.

"How'd you end up in New York?" Caesar asked, changing the subject. "Your red hair and your tongue give you away as an Irish lass." He knew the Verplancks never took on indentured servants.

Peggy recounted a shortened version of her sad saga about coming from Ireland to England, meeting Richard, and sailing to America to be with him, only to find that he had been killed. She expressed her deep appreciation to Elizabeth for rescuing her and to the Verplancks for taking her in, at least until Juliann and John arrived.

Caesar listened intently to her tale, taking advantage of the opportunity to study the young woman and her red hair, freckles, and blue eyes. The impermissible thought shot across his consciousness; if only he were white…

As for Peggy, Caesar immediately struck her as being different. He was articulate, like his mother, handsome and finely built. Indeed, she had difficulty thinking of him as a slave. He was his own man, self-assured and with an inner freedom of spirit that transcended any subservient station fate may have assigned him. Peggy didn't think of Caesar as beneath her. There were no slaves in her past experience, and she never acquired the attitude of feeling superior and distant from people with different skin. Thus, she did not have to overcome such emotions in her appraisal of this black man.

The two talked for some minutes while Bartholomew, keeping an ear on the conversation, feigned busyness with the stump. Finally, she went back into the house. A minute or two passed, and Bartholomew broke the silence.

"Boy, I know what you're thinkin' but it ain't gonna happen. She's white and you're black and she's free and you ain't. So leave it at that!"

I ain't thinkin' nothin', Papa. I just feel sorry for her, that's all."

"Well, that's good 'cause I don't want you gettin' in any more trouble than you're already in. That sheriff would be more than glad to send you to the Caribbean, or worse. Vaarck seems unable to make you do right, no how. He'd probably be glad to let the sheriff take you off his hands."

Caesar laughed. "Papa, everyone knows I work hard for Vaarck and anyone else he loans me to. And I got legitimate business dealings with Hughson, too. They ain't gonna mess with me."

He paused, then added, "But don't worry, Papa. I'll stay away from the white women." He shot his father a wink.

Caesar was unable to keep his promise to his father, however. As the weeks went by, he found more and more reasons to go to the Verplanck home: firewood here, medicine for his mother there, or a project with his father on a Sunday afternoon, or any number of other excuses. Each time, he sought ways to run into Peggy, and she sought ways to make it easy for him.

When John and Juliann Gregory finally arrived in November 1739, and Peggy's services were no longer needed, Caesar had a solution for the young woman. He arranged for John Hughson to take her in as a barmaid in return for her board and a few shillings spending money. Caesar, for his part, would pay for her rent for one of the rooms above the tavern. All parties agreed to the arrangement, and on December 1st, Peggy moved to the new Hughson Tavern off Broadway.

Over the next few months, Caesar and Peggy found themselves in a burgeoning romantic relationship. He would come to the tavern at night and have his friends boost him up so he could climb through her window. It was only a matter of time, however, before the Hughsons discovered their trysts. Sarah was particularly chagrinned at the thought of miscegenation taking place under her own roof.

"John, do you realize people are calling her a whore? She's going to ruin our reputation and our customers will vanish!" Sarah had some standards, after all, even if she was just a Scottish tavern owner's wife who was willing to serve slaves at her establishment and fence the articles they stole.

John was less concerned, in part because he didn't want to jeopardize the fencing relationship they had developed with Caesar and his friends. "Calm down, Sarah. She's been here several months, and our patrons are still coming. She's a good barmaid, and everyone seems to be friendly toward her. She doesn't mind the occasional slap on her rump, and she always has a smile on her face for our patrons. I for one don't mind Caesar sneaking up to her room, and I don't think you should, either. He pays the rent every month on time, doesn't he?"

Sarah didn't answer him; she brushed past her husband and stalked off toward the kitchen. As the weeks wore on, however, she got more used to the idea. Peggy, after all, was a good worker, and Caesar was faithful with the rent, not to mention the lost items he brought to Sarah for disposal.

****

By 1740, John and Sarah were beginning to accumulate significant wealth from their tavern receipts and the fencing operation. John began to think of himself as a burgeoning pillar of the community, and Sarah was anxious to insert herself into what she considered to be the wealthy gentry of the city. She longed to be invited to the receptions and galas and wear expensive gowns imported from France. John thought it was time to enter into society by joining the Free Masons of the city. He made an inquiry of Abraham Abrahamse, a wealthy merchant and important figure in the Free Masons. His meeting did not go well.

"I'm sorry, John, but you would be unacceptable to the members. You run a tavern that serves Negroes, you allow a whore to stay in your rooms, and you don't attend church. Furthermore, from what I have been told, your wife is not very refined. She would not fit in with the other wives when we have our functions. You are basically a good man, John, but you are reaching too high if you want to be a Free Mason."

John was devastated. His rejection would not sit well with Sarah. In fact, he thought she would be furious. She was, but he had a plan and approached Caesar and Prince with it.

"Boys, I am going to start a Black Free Masons lodge. All your friends will be invited. We'll be just like the city's Free Masons; we'll have secret oaths and initiation rites.

We'll elect leaders and governors. We'll have rules and be loyal to each other. We'll punish any members who give up our secrets and plans to any outsiders. We'll make fun of the white Free Masons, and we'll drink a lot and eat a lot and dance with the women."

The idea was an immediate hit. The Black Free Mason meetings would be held at Hughson's tavern once every two months on the third Sunday. John elected himself Grand Master of the Lodge. He established policies and issued orders and generally felt much better about his place in society. Sarah, on the other hand, was not at all impressed.

"John, do you realize how foolish you appear? The venerable head of a bunch of enslaved Free Masons. You should call yourselves the 'Not-So-Free Masons'." She laughed at her own joke.

John didn't laugh. "You're just jealous, good Wife, because you aren't allowed to join or be privy to our secrets." What John failed to recognize was that secrets can morph into conspiracies, and conspiracies can lead to very deadly outcomes.

****

Despite its various occasional nuances, life for Sarah Hughson was rolling along smoothly until one evening in August 1740 when Peggy came to her. She fidgeted and hesitated, causing Sarah to demand, "Speak up, girl. What's your problem? Did you break a dish or something?"

Peggy's eyes were riveted to the floor. "No, Ma'am. The fact is that I missed my time for the last two months." She began to whimper.

"You did what?" the older woman demanded.

"My visitor hasn't come for two months," she repeated. "I think I'm gonna have Caesar's child." Peggy broke into sobs.

"Girl, I might of known! And with a slave, too! You're nothin' but an Irish slut! I told John this would be a bad arrangement! I told him at the time it wouldn't work!"

Peggy cried even more, causing Sarah to soften a little.

"I'll talk to Mr. Hughson about this, and we'll decide what we're going to do about you. For now, get out there and take care of the customers. And keep this quiet! Do you hear me?"

John, it turned out, was much more understanding. After Sarah briefed him on the crisis, he issued his decree.

"We'll leave her be for now, Sarah. She's a good worker and Caesar is making us some money. She won't be the first white woman to birth a dark bairn. I can name you any number of black women owned by respectable men, both Dutch and English, in this town who've birthed light babies. Tell me how that came to be, Mrs. Hughson."

"By the way," he changed the subject, "I've located an indentured servant, a fifteen-year-old named Mary Burton, who might make a good servant for us. She's at the beginning of a seven-year contract for a man named Richard Carson. He's moving to Massachusetts and wants to sell the girl's contract to me for twenty pounds."

"I do need someone else around here to help with the work. Bring her around, John, and I'll interview her."

Chapter 34

Conspiracy

New York, 1741

As the Christmas season approached, Hughson's tavern was very busy, with patrons and travelers filling the available rooms on the second floor. On Sundays and some evenings, the slaves and freemen continued to patronize the establishment. Caesar was a regular, as were his friends, Cuffee, Prince, Cambridge, and Quack. Usually, another eight or ten would accompany them, mostly men but a few women, also. As the weeks passed, however, there seemed to be less boisterous activity, less singing, dancing, and gambling among the group. The women stopped coming, and the evenings were spent in drinking and conversation, sometimes in hushed voices. Furthermore, the group wanted to be served only by Peggy. They said she treated them the best. Sarah Hughson acquiesced to their demand, but she was becoming increasingly uncomfortable with the group's demeanor. Nonetheless, she continued to act friendly toward them, taking their coins and the stolen property Caesar and Cuffee brought her. Mary Burton was especially unhappy at not being allowed to serve the blacks because Caesar and Prince tended to place tips on the table when they left for the evening.

John Hughson, too, noticed the change in the group. With the memory of the aborted slave insurrection of 1712 in the back of his mind, one Sunday evening after the group left, he confronted Peggy for an interrogation.

"Those blacks have been awfully quiet in there the last few weeks, Peggy. Do you know what's going on? What are they talking about, anyway?"

He noticed that she hesitated for a heartbeat. "They talk about the same things every week, Mr. Hughson. Stories about their masters and their masters' wives, how they're being treated, who ran away and who got captured, and what they'd do if they were free. Their talk doesn't change much."

"Peggy, I'm sure you noticed that the women don't come anymore and that they don't sing or gamble or laugh as much. Something seems different with them. They seem too quiet. They aren't planning anything, are they, Peggy? I'll not have them conspiring in my establishment. I swear, I'll report them to the authorities if I thought that."

"Well, they talk about rising up and gaining their freedom, but it's just general talk. They aren't planning anything."

Hughson's threat seemed hollow, even to him. He had to worry about the stolen property he'd been receiving from them. Yet, none of it was kept at the tavern. His habit was to send it immediately up to the Black Boar for disposal. There was no evidence, and if it came to that, who would believe some slaves over him, anyway? They aren't even allowed to testify against a white person in court.

Then he added, "Why do they insist that you be the one to serve them, anyway?"

"I think it's because they know about me and Caesar and that I'm going to have his child. Also, they don't like Mary because they say she is rude to them."

"Well, you be sure to let me know if they talk about anything I should be worried about. Do you hear me, Peggy? There will be severe consequences if I find out there's something you are not telling me. Now go up to bed with you."

Peggy didn't answer him. She just turned and left the room. Peggy was, indeed, carrying Caesar's child and had been for over eight months. Three weeks after her talk with John, and after seven hours of very hard work, she delivered a healthy and light brown baby boy. Peggy was attended by Sarah and her two eldest daughters, 16-year-old Sarah and 15-year-old Mary. Peggy named the boy Michael after her deceased father.

****

In fact, the blacks were, indeed, conspiring in the Hughson's back room on Sunday nights. Caesar, Cuffee, and Prince were the ringleaders. Cambridge, the Codwise slave, was also present at those gatherings, but he typically didn't have much to say. They talked about the uprisings of the

Caribbean slaves and what it would be like to be free. They discussed what a revolt in New York would be like and whether it could be successful. Could the 2,000 slaves in the city subdue the 9,000 whites and those others who may come to their aid? Would the French or Spanish assist in a revolt? How many of the 9,000 whites in the city would be sympathetic to their cause?

Cuffee and Prince thought that a massive fire in the city might weaken the English hold enough to allow the French or Spanish to sail into the harbor and throw them out. Even if all that didn't happen, a scorched New York would at least teach their masters a very important lesson. Maybe during such a conflagration, the slaves could escape to Long Island and make that 120-mile stretch of land their own, sort of like the slaves in the Caribbean Islands. Caesar wondered if the slaves in the other colonies would join them. And how about the Indians? Since King Phillip's War, they have endured the continual sting of losing their land and livelihood to the English. He wondered if they could really make Long Island into their own country. He thought not.

Caesar was very skeptical that any such revolt would be successful; he couldn't envision a good outcome. As time went on, however, he succumbed to the notion that, at least, a big fire and its aftermath would be interesting to experience, as long as he and his fellow conspirators didn't get caught. In the ensuing weeks, there were more discussions about setting fires, what buildings, how many and how fast, how to set the fires, how to escape from the scene, and who should do it. There was also some talk about whether people coming to fight the fires should be shot. At that, Caesar put his foot down.

"No! We'll not be doing any of that! It won't help us, and it's too easy to get caught. They'd slaughter every black man in the city! If no one gets caught setting the fires, they won't know for sure who did it. It could be the Spanish or even the French or Indians. It would be smart to start with one of the military buildings at the fort. That way, people may think foreigners did it. We can burn down the town and hope the Spanish or French arrive."

Then he added, "And hope that they don't enslave us, too!"

With that, Caesar got up and stalked out of the tavern.

****

The planning, such as it was, continued on Sunday evenings in the back room of the Hughson tavern. Ten to fifteen slaves trudged through the snow to the meetings, their thin garments no match for the sub-freezing temperatures that had plagued the city all winter. They spoke in hushed tones as they sipped ale from their tankards. Nobody seemed concerned about the endgame. What will the ultimate outcome be like? Despite Caesar's earlier warning, some still talked in hopeful terms about killing all the white men

377

and ravaging their wives and daughters. Prince and Cuffee thought that Caesar's notion about starting with a building at the fort was a good idea.

"The location won't set the whole city ablaze, but that can come later."

Prince agreed, and Cuffee volunteered to carry out the initial deed. So far, so good.

What should be next to burn?

Cuffee spoke up. "Let's burn down Captain Warren's home. He's still at sea, but when he's here, he's very hard on his slaves. He sold Anna's seven-year-old boy to some slavers from Trinidad. We should repay him for that."

"When should we do it?" asked a slave named Isaiah.

Cuffee had an idea. "Let's wait one week after the first fire so the city's white folk will have time to think about it."

There was general agreement.

Up to this point, Caesar had been quiet, but he finally spoke up.

"You know I think the plan is a good one. But, if any of us gets caught, he'll be tortured, and, before he dies, he'll give up the rest of our names, and we'll all be looking at our own guts. One mistake and it'll be all over, boys, for every one of us. I'm still with you, but I sure hope you know what you're doing."

As they were all leaving the tavern through the rear door, Caesar stopped Cuffee, Prince, and Cato in the yard. It was a freezing cold night, part of the coldest winter ever experienced in New York. The four men weren't dressed for it, but Caesar insisted on a word with them.

"You know I support our plan, but I think it'll end in disaster for us and for many of the slaves in this city. Somebody will get caught, and you know the rest. We have to stop coming to Hughsons for our meetings. They're not involved, and I don't think they know anything about what we're doing. And, we've got to stop bringing them the goods we steal, too."

Cuffee spoke up. "Stop worrying. Caesar, we're not going to get caught. Your woman, Peggy, and your little high yellow baby will be safe if that's what you're thinking about."

Caesar glared at Cuffee in the half-moonlight but ignored his comment. "Have you seen the way that Mary Burton tries to hang around when we're here? She could get out of her indenture if she ever testified against the Hughsons. She must know that they fence our stuff. There's lots of this I don't like."

Prince tried to lower the heat. "Alright, Caesar. No more meetings at the tavern and no more loot. I'll tell the others. Let's get outta here. I'm freezing."

****

Meanwhile, the fencing operation continued unabated. On February 28th, Caesar and Prince ventured forth into the cold night for yet another burglary. This time, it was for money. A young sailor, Christopher Wilson—his buddies called him Yorkshire—was in Robert Hogg's establishment on Broad Street the day before. He bought some items, and when Hogg's wife, Rebecca, opened a drawer to give Yorkshire his change, the sailor noticed that she had several pieces of eight. Yorkshire went straight to Hughson's tavern, where he found Caesar, Prince, and Cuffee. The men hatched a plot to retrieve the coins, and the plan was afoot.

That night, Caesar and Prince retrieved the money. The two slaves kept to the alleys as much as possible, avoiding the bright light from the moon, just two nights from full. Twenty minutes later, they were again at the rear of Hughson's tavern laden down with silver, cloth, and other merchandise from the store. Once again, Caesar clambered up through Peggy's window with his share of the loot and spent the night with the young mother and her newborn son. Early the next morning, he was the first one up. He crept downstairs and helped himself to a piece of mince pie left on the counter.

"What are you doing here?" Mary Burton demanded as she descended the stairs. "You here to see your lover Peg again and your little high-yellow kid, she whelped?"

Surprised by her sudden appearance but not shaken, he said, "I just came by because I have some business with Mr. Hughson. Do you know if he's awakened?"

"No, he hasn't," she retorted. "The sun isn't even up yet. What do you expect?"

She paused and then added, "So, you just arrived, did you? You mean you just arrived from Peggy's room, I expect."

Ignoring the comment, he smiled at her and reached in his pocket for a Spanish piece of eight fresh from the Hoggs. "I brought you something, Mary, and I want you to have it because I like you."

She took the coin from him and asked, "Is this so I won't tell anyone you spent the night here, Caesar?"

"It's for you to buy something pretty for yourself. Maybe a new nightshirt. I see that one has a few holes in it. I wouldn't want you to catch your death of cold because a draft blew in there and chilled your little chest."

She thought of something nasty to say about the cold shrinking something on him, but she felt the coin in her hand and thought better of it.

"You best leave and return this evening when people won't see you sneaking up the alley."

"Farewell, me, Lady." With that sarcastic comment, Caesar turned and exited through the slaves' door in the rear of the tavern.

Later that morning, when Rebecca Hogg opened her shop, she immediately saw that it had been burglarized. She ran to the cubby where she left the sack of cash. Gone. Gone, too, were some bolts of cloth, and a few other items. She ran upstairs to notify her husband.

"Robert, we were robbed last night! The money is gone, as well as some other items. This is terrible! Go get the sheriff! We need that money, Robert. We need to get it back!"

Robert did as he was told, and an hour later, the sheriff arrived along with one of his six constables. He took a cursory look around the shop. "They got in through that window, I suppose? What all was taken?"

His constable made a list and handed it to the sheriff. He read over it quickly to make sure it was complete. "We'll see what we can do," he said. "Maybe those candlesticks will show up somewhere." With that, the two men left.

Rebecca was furious. "I'll wager that's the last we'll ever see of them!"

Robert let out a long sigh. "I bet some of those slaves did it. I sure wish their masters would keep a closer eye on 'em. But I guess they don't care as long as the work gets done.

One sheriff and six constables certainly can't watch all two thousand of 'em, in spite of the law."

"Do you mind if I make a few inquiries among the other shop owners? I want to get that money back, Robert, and someone may know something."

"I guess it wouldn't hurt. But don't make a spectacle of yourself, and we'll tell the sheriff if you find out anything."

Rebecca Hogg pursued her role as a criminal investigator with a vengeance. Furthermore, she met with success. Prince had failed to show up at the appointed time and place to give Wilson his share of the loot. Miffed, the sailor returned to Hogg's shop and told Rebecca that he may have seen some of her missing Spanish coins at Hughson's tavern in the possession of a man he identified as John Guin.

"Yes, Ma'am. I was there with some of my crew members from the *Flamborough*. We was havin' a tankard or two when I saw John Guin pass a Spanish coin, like you described, to the barmaid to pay for his drink."

Mrs. Hogg informed the sheriff, who went to the tavern to investigate.

"Hughson, we're looking for a man named John Guin. We were told that he was here last night. He could be the one who broke into Hogg's store and stole money and some merchandise. Mrs. Hogg thinks this Guin might be a sailor."

At first, nothing came of the sheriff's investigation; nobody at the tavern seemed to know anyone named John Guin. Finally, the sheriff learned that "John Guin" was an alias sometimes used by the slave Caesar. Wilson confirmed that "John Guin" was, indeed, a black man, but he thought the man didn't act like any slave.

Being very familiar with Caesar's history as a petty criminal, the sheriff found him at Hughson's tavern that evening and arrested him. He was questioned but admitted nothing.

"He's close friends with that slave, Prince," the sheriff told his constables the next day. "Let's bring him in and see what he knows." But Prince, too, said he knew nothing about the burglary.

"We could arrest Hughson for allowing blacks to drink at his establishment. Let's bring him and his wife in to see what they know. The threat of losing their tavern might make them nervous enough to loosen their tongues."

It didn't; the Hughsons professed complete ignorance. The sheriff wasn't convinced. Hoping to discover some of the stolen property, he sent his constables to search the tavern, but they, too, came up with nothing.

Caesar, Prince, and the Hughsons all breathed a sigh of relief. Once again, they had covered their tracks. The merchandise that Caesar brought through the window was already well on its way to Yonkers.

The next day, Sarah Hughson sent her indentured servant, Mary Burton, out to buy some candles and sewing thread at a shop owned by a woman who was a good friend of Rebecca Hogg. During a conversation with the shop owner, Mary hinted that the sheriff missed something during their search of the tavern the previous day. The shopkeeper, Anne Kannady, pressed the girl.

"Mary, you realize that if you report what you know to the sheriff about what is going on with John Hughson in that tavern, you might even be released from your indenture." She paused for the effect and then added, "You'd be a free woman, Mary. You should think about it. You'd be a fool not to."

Mary left without saying any more, but the prospect of freedom began to occupy her thoughts with increasing frequency.

Anne's husband, James, was one of the constables, and two days later, they returned to the tavern to search it again and interrogate Mary further. She talked, implicated Peggy, and gave them the coin she had received from Caesar. As events unfolded, the Hughsons, Peggy, and Prince were arrested and then released on bail pending the April court hearing. But Caesar remained in custody.

****

The whole situation was getting out of hand. Prince was nervous. On the evening of March 9th, he met with Cuffee.

385

"We need to start our plan for the fires. It'll stop the sheriff from worrying about Caesar and the Hughsons."

"I don't think the fires will work to get us freedom, Prince, any more than they did when they tried it before. The Spanish won't come to our aid, and even if they do, they'll probably keep enslaving us anyway."

"Maybe, Cuffee, but it'll save our friend. We need to do it."

"If we get caught, we'll be hanged…or burned."

Prince was insistent. "We won't get caught. We'll be careful. Tell Quack to do the fort. He'll want to burn it because the Governor won't let him visit his wife down there anymore, and he's mad about that. Tell the others to be ready. Tell 'em, all we're gonna do is burn; no killin' and no ravaging white women. If we start that, we're sure to get caught and burn ourselves. They'll know what to do and when."

Very early in the morning of Saturday, March 18, 1741, Quack was on his way to Fort George with a small pot of red coals in his hand. The sun had not yet risen, and it was very cold. The frigid air stung his nose as he slipped silently and quickly through the empty back streets and alleys. When he reached the fort, all was quiet; not even a dog was up at this hour. His target was Lieutenant Governor Clarke's mansion. The governor and his family were at home in their beds, but Quack guessed that they would be able to escape from a fire started on the roof. It was made of cedar shakes and would burn nicely. A two-story porch on the rear of the house, complete with stairs to each level, provided easy access to the roof. Quack climbed the stairs and, standing on a railing, he managed to carefully dump the coals into the wooden gutter by the edge of the roof. Then, he quickly and silently descended the stairs and made his escape.

The fire was a good one; the home was gutted, and the fire managed to spread to the enlisted barracks and eventually even to a home outside the fort. The family escaped the blaze, and no one was hurt, but for the entire morning, the fire burned out of control despite the efforts of a bucket brigade and several citizens. Finally, a rainstorm blew in and put an end to the destruction.

As expected, the fire did not further the conspirators' cause. The authorities and people of New York attributed the blaze to an accident, something about a workman's fire. No one seemed to be concerned about rogue slaves or a Spanish or French insurgency. The conspirators pressed onward. Captain Peter Warren's home was next.

Exactly one week later, it went up in flames. This time, however, the bucket brigade and the city's newfangled Newsham fire engines saved most of the structure.

Another seven days, the next Wednesday, Van Zant's warehouse burned down for a total loss.

Three fires on three successive Wednesdays. The people of New York were beginning to get suspicious. The sheriff temporarily lost interest in Caesar and the Hughsons. Three days later, a stable fire broke out, and a house that same day. On April 6th, four more fires, one of them a warehouse owned by Frederick Philipse. But this time, the authorities got a break. A fireman saw Cuffee running from the warehouse and sounded the alarm. A large group of citizens gave chase, and he was captured. Caesar's worst nightmare was about to unfold!

The city was in panic mode. The Negroes were revolting! Lieutenant Governor Clarke called out the militia to patrol the streets. Arrested blacks began pouring in by the dozens. The sheriff crowded them into stone cells recently built into the basement of City Hall. There were no more fires. Meanwhile, Caesar didn't set any fires; he had the perfect alibi. He was incarcerated the whole time in the basement of City Hall. As he sat in his cell, he wondered what would happen to him if Cuffee talked.

On April 21st, a grand jury was empaneled to investigate the recent fires and the conspiracy that was suspected. The grand jury was aware of the friendship among Cuffee, Prince, and Caesar and that they were all known to frequent Hughson's tavern. Someone also implicated Codwise's slave, Cambridge, as another one of the conspirators, although the court took less notice of him.

Three days later, a visitor came to the tavern very early in the morning. Hughson had to get out of bed to answer the door.

"Mr. Hughson?"

"Yes. What is it?"

"My name is Christopher Codwise, Sr. I own the slave, Cambridge, who I believe frequents your establishment on occasion."

"Yes. I know the man. Why don't you come in."

Codwise entered the establishment, and Hughson directed him to a chair.

"I'll get right to the point, Mr. Hughson. Cambridge has been implicated in this whole conspiracy mess that's being investigated by Judge Horsmanden and the grand jury. He made the mistake of admitting to some prior knowledge of the plot, but he swears to me that he did it under duress during an interrogation where they threatened him with being sold to the islands or burned at the stake. He swears he's innocent. I believe that Horsmanden knows his confession was not legitimate, but I am here to ascertain what your testimony will be regarding Cambridge if it comes to that. As you can well imagine, I am concerned about my reputation as a businessman in this city, as well as the fact that Cambridge is a good worker and he represents high-value property, which I can ill afford to lose."

"Mr. Codwise, I am here to tell you that I know absolutely nothing about any effort to instigate a slave revolt in the city, and I certainly have no knowledge of your Cambridge being involved in such a thing. Of course, I will testify to that if it comes to it. I am a little concerned about the forthcoming testimony of my indentured servant, Mary Burton. I know she wants to get out of her indenture, and Horsmanden might offer her that opportunity in exchange for her desired testimony. But I am certain everything will eventually turn out to our satisfaction."

"Thank you, Mr. Hughson. You have relieved my concerns. If it does come to anything, I will certainly be indebted to you."

With that, Christopher stood up, shook Hughson's hand, and left the tavern. Little did the two men know that their families would cross paths decades in the future.

****

The first person to be interviewed by the court was Mary Burton. Before her testimony, she was told that she might be able to have her indenture terminated. At first, she didn't disclose anything of value, but when she was being taken to the jail, she changed her mind. The more she talked, the better her memory became. She testified that a conspiracy was, indeed, hatched at the Hughson tavern, that the Hughsons and Peggy Kerry knew about the fencing activities and the conspiracy. In fact, she finally "remembered" that

390

John Hughson was directly involved in the plot, which included plans for setting fires in the city, killing the white men, and ravaging the white women. Furthermore, once the revolt was successful, the blacks promised to make John Hughson king of New York.

Of course, the Hughsons denied any knowledge or involvement, but it didn't help. At first, Peggy Kerry also denied any knowledge of a conspiracy, but on May 7th, motivated by the hope for mercy, she finally confessed to her knowledge of the plot but maintained that none of the planning ever took place at Hughson's tavern.

Convictions began to pile up. On May 30th, Quack and Cuffee were burned at the stake. In May, the court found John and Sarah Hughson and Peggy Kerry guilty and sentenced the three to be hanged. Later, a Catholic priest, John Ury, was also found guilty and sentenced to hang, mostly because he was a Catholic priest who was seen at Hughson's and, they thought, may be a spy for the Spanish. Also condemned to the gallows or the stake were 30 slaves who were accused of participating in the revolt. Scores more were deported to the Caribbean. Caesar and Prince were hanged in May, not because they were conspirators, but because they were convicted of burglary.

When the constables arrested Peggy Kerry at the tavern, they let her take her three-month-old son, Michael, with her because she was nursing him. She was convicted of participating in the conspiracy on June 4th. A week later, Sarah, the Hughson's oldest daughter, went to visit her in her stone cell in the basement of City Hall, which she shared with two other women arrested for prostitution and theft.

"I brought you some fruit, Peggy. You should eat it for the babe. You don't want to dry up." Then, she added encouragingly, "I expect you'll soon be out of here. They won't believe that little lying witch, Mary Burton."

Peggy changed the subject. "Sarah, if they should hang me, will you take my little Michael and raise him up like he was one of your family?"

A tear came to Sarah's eye. "Of course I will, Peggy, but don't talk like that. Everything's going to be alright, and you can raise him yourself."

"Caesar and me…we didn't mean no harm to anyone. He was a fine man, Sarah…it's just he was a slave and didn't have a chance. He didn't act like a slave, did he, Sarah?" a smile emerging through her tears.

"No, Peggy, he certainly did not. He acted like a proud free man."

"Maybe my little Michael will act like a man, too." She paused.

"What will happen to him, Sarah? Will you save him?"

"Of course I will, Peggy. I think, no matter what happens, we'll be going back to the farm in Westchester to live with my Hughsons. We'll take Michael with us. I expect Michael can grow up there."

"Will your family accept him…will he be a slave?"

"Goodness, no. He would be free, and yes, if I know my grandfather, everyone will accept him. The babe is half Irish, after all, and the Irish are like the Scots." She paused for a couple seconds. "Well, not exactly like the Scots, but you know what I mean. Their families stick together."

The two young women laughed. Then Sarah continued, "A black man named William MacIntosh lived on the farm until he got old and died. He's the one who taught Father how to make shoes. But there's no need for us to talk like this, Peggy. Everything will be fine."

Everything was not fine, however. The Hughsons and Peggy were convicted of conspiracy and running a fencing operation. They were hanged together on Monday, June 12, 1741. During the solemn cart ride to the gallows on the city green, Sarah and Peggy sat quietly in the straw, accepting their fate and praying. John, on the other hand, kept up a continuous sobbing, wailing, and moaning, all the while maintaining his innocence and providing entertainment for the crowd gathered to watch justice at work.

Early in the morning, before their hanging, young Sarah went to say goodbye to Peggy and retrieve little Michael.

"I think he's old enough to eat food, Sarah. Be sure to mash it up so he can swallow it." With that bit of final advice, she kissed her son and, amidst a wash of tears, passed him over to the crying Sarah. Sarah didn't say anything. She wasn't capable of saying anything. She just turned and quickly ascended the stone steps to the street, clutching the infant to her chest.

On June 13th, news of John and Sarah's execution arrived at the Hughson farm in Westchester in the form of the sheriff, who was armed with a court order to incarcerate Thomas and four of his sons, Nathaniel, William, Walter, and Richard, to prevent their possible escape, in case Judge Horsmanden discovered any complicity they had in the plot and wanted to bring them to trial. The sheriff apologized but said he was obligated by Horsmanden's warrant. He tried to encourage the aging patriarch.

"We've known each other a long time, Tom, and I know you had nothing to do with the events in New York. This should be all over soon, and you and your sons can get back to farming." Then he added, "Do you want me to notify John Dobbs about what's happening?"

"I would appreciate that, Jacob. Ask him to come see me."

"I'll be back in a week, Tom."

"Thank you, Jacob."

John came the next day.

"Tom, what's going on? How long will they keep you? What about the crops?"

Tom briefly filled him in on the latest developments, and then he had a request for his brother-in-law. "They hanged John and Sarah a few days ago. Their children are still living in the tavern, and we need to get them up here right away. John, could you do that for me?"

"Of course, Tom. I'll leave immediately. They can stay with us for now until this mess gets straightened out."

As it turned out, father and sons sat in the Westchester County jail all summer. Finally, in September, Thomas sent a petition to Horsmanden requesting that they be pardoned or at least allowed to make bail so they could tend to their families and their crops. A month later, Horsmanden finally responded; he decided to pardon them, with the stipulation that they leave the county. They were released on October 21st and began that day to make preparations for the Hughson clan to move out of Westchester County.

The storm clouds had darkened over Tom Hughson's family. The aging patriarch was glad that his beloved wife, Maria, was not there to suffer through the family's tragic turn of events.

Chapter 35

On to Dutchess County

October 1741

They had lost everything, so they would have to start anew somewhere, but where? Uppermost in Thomas Hughson's mind was the future of his children and their families. The day he and his sons were released, he called them together for a conference. He had an idea.

"Boys, Horsmanden agreed to our offer to move out of the county, and I don't see any way to change his mind. We have to leave all we've built here and start afresh somewhere."

The patriarch paused to take a breath, and Richard spoke up. "We've got John and his wife, Sarah, to thank for this mess. I always knew that woman was no good for him," he blurted angrily.

His father reacted, "Richard, whatever happened was in God's Providence, and there's no sense in going over it now. Our task is to settle on a future for our families." He continued.

"I've made the acquaintance of a man named Adolphus Brewer. He is moving from Yonkers to new land north of here in Dutchess County. It's in the west part of the county next to the North River." He says there's land available up there, and the province is giving away 100 acres to farmers who will live on it, improve it, and pay the taxes. There are five of us, which means that we can have 500 acres, all in one large tract. After five years, we would own it outright. Indians still live in that area, but according to Brewer, they are peaceful and work their own farms and trade. He said the piece we'd have is good land; it runs along a creek and includes land on the North River. He said that he'd like to have us as neighbors."

"Exactly where is it located?" William asked.

"It would be about 45 miles north of here along the North River, a few miles west of a village about 50 years old called Fishkill. Brewer is up there now on his tract. We could go up and look at the land to see what we think."

All four sons agreed, and the next morning, they were on their way. Two days later, they arrived at Brewer's cabin.

"I'm glad to see you gentlemen and to know you may be my neighbors. I'll saddle my horse and show you your new farm."

Brewer and the Hughson men devoted the next five hours to walking over the land. The further they walked, the more excited they grew. It was a beautiful piece of property. The lay of the land included forests and open areas, creeks and rivers, and a wealth of game. Evidence of deer, beavers, rabbits, and turkeys seemed to be everywhere.

The decision was easy to make.

"How soon can we take possession, and what's involved?" Tom inquired.

"The sheriff has the documents; it's merely a matter of you men signing them. You could probably see him tomorrow. The land would be yours, and next year, you can pay the taxes."

Always the detail man, William brought up the issue of timing. "We wouldn't have time to build the houses and barns before winter."

Tom was already planning. "Nay, we couldn't, but I think Horsmanden would allow us to stay until spring. We could come up here and get started on the buildings at least through December. With Benjamin and John, there are seven of us to work on the construction. I ken that we could get a lot done. Also, I noticed that there are several meadows on the land, which would make it easy for us to put in some crops in the spring."

Lots of hard work paid off, and by the middle of March, the Hughson clan was ready to make the move. It took four trips to convey people, furniture, farm implements, and animals up to the new homestead. Their land was in Dutchess County, near where Wappinger's Creek flows into the Hudson, about sixty miles from New York. Their brother, Benjamin, was still in Westchester County, apparently now of little interest to Judge Horsmanden. The same was true of their sister Abigail and her husband,

William Boddy, who also avoided being swept up in John's notoriety. Thomas's other daughter, Mary, came with the family, intending to keep house for her father. Before the move, Tom met with his son, Benjamin, who remained in Westchester.

"We'll miss you, Benjamin, and your lovely young wife, but I understand why you and your Mary have chosen to stay. We'll continue sending you our produce so you can get it to the merchants and ship captains in New York."

"Aye, Da. And we'll do more each year, so we'll all become rich and buy big homes overlooking the North River!"

Both men laughed. "Well, I don't know about that, but we'll do our best, anyway." Tom paused and then added, "We'll have Peggy Kerry's baby, little Michael, with us. Your sister, Mary, will be living with me, and she wants to help raise him."

"I know you'll see to it that no one will ever force him into slavery, but he needs a last name to go by to be really free. I wonder if you could give him your name to grow up with, Da?"

"Of course I will, Ben…besides I know that your mother would have had it no other way!"

The two men chuckled. "Then, Michael Hughson, it is."

Tom thought for a second.

"How about Michael Kerry Hughson, Ben?"

"Aye, Da, 'Master Michael Kerry Hughson.' That will do just fine! You'll get him baptized, then?"

"Of course we will." Tom paused and then added, "I believe he looks a bit like you anyway, Ben…same brown eyes."

"For Heaven's sake, don't tell Mary!"

The two men laughed again.

So, with John and Sarah's nine children and little Michael Kerry Hughson in tow, the Hughson clan repaired to Dutchess County and settled in what would eventually be known as Hughsonville; the hamlet is still there to this day. Among the other structures in the new Hughson compound, Thomas and his sons built two homes, a small one for himself and another house a few yards away for the orphans. It was a large structure with six bedrooms and a long trestle table in the main room that could accommodate the whole crowd. Tom kept a close eye on the children, and it was common for him to take his meals with them and spend time in the evening by their fire.

Being the patriarch, Tom had overseen the construction of the homes and barns, the clearing of land for the spring planting, and the purchase of livestock. The family thought he was working too hard, but their admonitions to slow his pace fell on deaf ears. Mary was especially concerned.

"Da," she pleaded, "let the boys do the work. They can have this place put together in no time. We will all be fine. Look at the progress you've all made already."

Tom knew she was right, and he had noticed that he was getting shorter of breath when he exerted himself. He felt it most while splitting wood. He was seventy-one, after all, but he had to keep going until he knew his family was secure in their new lives. Well...he did keep going, but only until August 22, 1742. Of course, he was splitting logs for his daughter when he dropped dead of a massive heart attack, axe in hand. Mary found him. She grabbed little Michael, ran the short distance to William's house, and, between sobs, told him about their father's passing.

William mounted his mule and, with Mary and Michael behind him, galloped back to where his father lay, only to confirm his sister's report. With the mule's help, he and Mary carried their father back to the house and laid him on his bed, covering him with a quilt.

"I'll go tell the others, Mary. We'll bury him tomorrow. You and little Michael can stay with us tonight."

Then he added, "I guess you'll have to tell Abigail when she returns...where is she, anyway?"

"She went over to see the Vail's new baby. I'll be alright, Will. We'll be over by and by."

The children buried their father the following afternoon. Richard dug the grave the evening before behind the homestead on a little knoll, and Walter found an appropriate stone to mark the spot. Thomas and Walter worked late into the night, fashioning a suitable casket. The boys laid him in it, closed the cover, and carried him up to the spot Richard had prepared. The family and a few neighbors gathered around, and Mary read from her mother's Bible...the 23rd Psalm. There was no preacher available, so William volunteered to say a few words.

"All I know is that yesterday was one of the worst days for all of us, but I am also certain that it was the best day for our father because Da is with the Lord, Ma, and... John. He loved us, he put bread on our table for more than forty years, and he found us a new home after our tragedy of last summer. I suppose it's now for us to carry on, to put bread on our tables, love each other, raise our children and little Michael, and make him and Ma proud...because I know they are looking down on us. The Lord is, indeed, our Shepherd. He will carry us through this valley and all the valleys that may yet come. We love you, Da."

Will's emotions overcame him, and he stepped back while his brothers lowered the coffin with two ropes into the grave. The Scottish brothers, Samuel and Philip MacAllister, stepped forward, and each tossed a handful of soil onto Tom's coffin. One by one, the other mourners followed, tossing in their handfuls; then, the party made its way slowly back to the house. Thomas and Richard remained behind and, shovels in hand, finished the job of committing their father's body to the earth.

With all the food and the gathering of family and friends in the house, spirits generally rose a bit that evening. The "Thomas" stories began circulating…fond memories surfaced, and there was even some laughter.

Will probably had the best story. "Remember all those times when Ma and Da went up into the woods together in the summertime and told us they'd be going for a little walk and to not follow them? Well, a couple years ago, Da told me what they were doing. They went up to that little pond Da made, and they took their clothes off and went swimming together!"

"Is that really true, Will?" Mary was brave enough to ask.

"It certainly is."

Richard chimed in, addressing his brothers. "Maybe we should build one of those here, gentlemen. I wonder if my Elizabeth would be interested.

Mary retorted, "Don't count on it, boys. You should keep your minds on higher things, like farming."

Everyone laughed, but Walter was still thinking. "What stream did you have in mind, Richard?"

Everyone laughed again.

All-in-all, Tom had a good life. Over those seventy-two years, he survived his voyage to America, and he married a wonderful girl. He was able to support his large family, and although he didn't know it, he would become the progenitor of thousands of Hughsons in America. God was good!

The day after Tom's funeral, Will had a talk with his sister, Mary.

"Mary, my Mary and I discussed it this morning, and we want you and Michael to live here with us. We really do, Mary. The boys and I can build two additional rooms off the side of the house."

"Thank you so much, Will. I would love that. I hope little Michael grows up to be just like you."

"I am sure he'll become a good man, Mary. After all, he's a Hughson, isn't he?"

Chapter 36

War

John and Michael Hughson

April 1775

The next thirty-plus years were good ones for the Hughsons of Dutchess County. The family members farmed; a few became coopers, others bred horses and cattle, and they had lots of children, most of whom made it to adulthood and had their own children. In short, the family became pillars of the community. The males in the family who were of age fulfilled their civic duty by joining the Dutchess County Militia. Once a month, they would meet, march, shoot, and practice various maneuvers. Indian raids were now rare in that section of the country, but stories from parts of New England and the western frontier of the colony of New York served to maintain a heightened level of vigilance among the county's farmers and tradesmen. Will's son, John, born in 1733, was an especially active member of the militia, and by 1770, he was serving as the unit's quartermaster. His wife, Catherine, would occasionally tease him about his enthusiasm for things military.

"It's a good thing you don't have a uniform, John, because it might be really hard for me to get you to do your chores."

"When you speak to me in that tone, Woman, I'll thank you to salute first and then address me as "Sir'.""

"Yes, Sir. Don't forget, Sir, you promised me you'd clean the chicken coop this morning, Sir."

"I know, I know. I'll do it right away."

"Very well, Sir. Now, give me a big kiss so I know you're a trustworthy soldier."

After a long kiss, Catherine released her hold and said, "Not bad for a quartermaster militia man."

"How many quartermasters have you kissed, anyway?"

"Numerous, but most of them were French and a few Spanish that I can recall."

"Really?" He paused, then, "What, no English?"

"No English. They have yellow teeth and smell like codfish. Now I'm going to bake you a pie."

"What kind?"

"Apple, of course, your favorite."

"My heart felt approbation, Madam. I'll be in the chicken coop if you need me."

"You're dismissed, Private."

"Aye, aye, Ma'am!" He saluted her.

One afternoon in late March, while taking his flintlock down from its place over the mantel, John announced, "Catherine, I'll be in the back field looking for a turkey for Sunday. I'll return shortly."

"John, be sure to keep an eye out for Indians, too." She laughed. "They may be out there gathering turkey feathers. Perhaps you could take Will with you in case you get surrounded."

"Good idea! Let's go, Will, you can carry my gun, and we'll discuss military strategy along the way."

Sporting his most military demeanor, young Will fell in beside his father. "Can I join the militia when I'm seventeen, Da?"

"We'll see, Boy, we'll see."

By 1775, Michael Kerry Hughson was thirty-three years old, a proud and free Hughson, married to Rebecca and father of Josiah and Will. He farmed with the other Hughsons and had become quite skilled in the construction and repair of equipment and farm implements. In 1760, he was introduced to the gunsmithing profession by an elderly neighbor who had worked in the trade while in the British Army. Being a free man, Michael had also joined the Dutchess County Militia, and when John was appointed Quartermaster, Michael became the company's gunsmith and armorer. It wasn't long before men from miles around brought their weapons to him for repairs and adjustments. John set up a location in the hay barn for him to use. Michael constructed a workbench, shelves, and drawers for his tools, and he put in a window over the bench to let in more light.

Within a couple months, weapons were lined up against the wall, waiting for Michael's expert attention.

One afternoon, John was watching him rebuild a trigger lock on Abraham VerPlanck's birding gun.

"Michael, what do you know about rifled barrels increasing a gun's accuracy?"

"Rifling increases the accuracy because it makes the bullet spin, like the feathers on an arrow make it spin, causing it to fly true. They cut a spiral groove inside the length of the barrel. It's hard to do, and it takes a lot of time, but a ball coming out of one of those barrels is spinning, causing it to go where you aim it, even at great distances. But it takes a man longer to load the weapon because the rifling slows down the process. Some of those rifles can be accurate for over three hundred yards."

"Do you know how to put rifling in a barrel?" John asked, a bit of excitement showing in his voice. He was already thinking about the militia and how much more deadly their unit would be if the men were equipped with rifled guns.

"I believe I could do it, but I would need some special tools."

"Would they have them in New York?"

"Perhaps. If not, I would have to order them, probably from France."

"I'll be going to the city next week with a wagonload of yams. Why don't you come along, and we'll see if somebody has what you need."

A week later, the two men were on Fulton Street in New York. John, always prepared, had a pistol in his belt and a hickory axe handle under the wagon's seat. The street was crowded with men going about their business and others skulking in corners and huddled in small groups, looking for work or probably up to no good. John stopped the wagon in front of a harness shop.

"Wait here with the wagon a minute, Michael, while I see if I can purchase some buckles for the plow harness."

Five minutes later, John exited the shop to find three men huddled around the front of his wagon.

One of them ordered Michael, "Get down from that seat, Boy, and put some of your nice lookin' yams in this here sack."

Michael hesitated.

"I said get down and fill this sack, nigger!"

John's heart started pounding. He walked quietly up behind the one doing the talking. He pulled his pistol from his belt and jammed the muzzle between the man's shoulder blades.

"Move, and you're dead, Friend," he said softly as he pulled back the cock. The man froze.

"Now, kneel down on the ground, very slowly...Don't make me nervous."

The would-be yam thief did as he was told. John yanked the man's pistol from his belt.

"His name is not Boy or nigger; it's Mr. Hughson. Now, you will very politely apologize to Mr. Hughson for your crude behavior, and you'll do it immediately."

The other two thugs backed away, slack-jawed, not knowing if they should stay and help their friend or run. Then they saw Michael pull the axe handle out from under the seat, and they decided to run.

"I apologize," the thug mumbled weakly.

John responded, "I'm sorry...I did not hear you, my friend. You will speak in a loud voice, so all these people watching us can hear. You will say, 'I apologize to you, Mr. Hughson, Sir, for being so rude to you.' And you'll remove your hat while you're doing it."

He removed his hat.

"I apologize to you, Mr. Hughson, Sir, for being so rude to you."

"Much better. Now get up and be gone with you!"

The thug got to his feet and was gone in a flash, disappearing through the small crowd of people who had gathered to watch the excitement.

John climbed back into the wagon.

"Let's get out of here and take these yams to the dock."

"Thank you, John, for that. I must say that you were pretty good there. Weren't you a bit scared like I was?"

"My heart's still pounding, but it was kinda' fun, though."

"Would you have shot him?"

"Probably not unless he went for you or me. You want his pistol, Michael?"

"Can I really have it?"

"Don't see why not. You earned it by saving the yams. But, put the axe handle back under the seat before I hand it over to you so it won't look bad in case somebody's still watching."

The two men chuckled. Michael passed the reins over to John and took the weapon.

"My goodness! This is a beauty…made in France! Look at the engraving on the sides. Whoever he took this from must have had a lot of money."

"Well, if we find him, you'll have to give it back, but I don't reckon that's very likely."

"I hope not."

"Michael, shame on you!" John answered with a laugh as he clucked the horse into a walk.

Over on Broad Street, they found a gunsmith shop and inquired about rifling equipment.

411

"I happen to have a set I'll sell you. The rod and guides are made of wood, except for the blades, of course. It works fine. I used it for quite a while until I got my new one, all the way from Switzerland. The spiral progression I carved in the wood rod seems to be a good design for accuracy. It'll cut barrels up to three feet long if that's what you plannin' on."

"How much do you want for it?" Michael asked.

"Three pounds, and it's yours."

The deal was struck, and in five minutes, the men were back on their wagon, with the rifling set wrapped carefully in burlap and placed under the seat next to the axe handle. God was Good!

****

It was April 23, 1775, and John and Michael were on their way home. They spent the evening at the Blue Heron Inn in Westchester County. It had begun to rain, and they found the establishment to be a cozy sanctuary from the elements. After their meal, they joined a small group of travelers relaxing around the fireplace, nursing tankards of ale and passing around a clay pipe.

John addressed the men.

"Evening, gentlemen. I'm John Hughson, and this is my adopted brother, Michael Hughson. We're on our way back to Dutchess County."

John's eyes darted quickly around the group to see if anyone had a problem with that. Nobody seemed to, and one man said, "Take a seat, gentlemen, and perhaps you can help us settle our debate over the current situation with England."

John chuckled. "I don't know about that, except to say that we Hughsons are Scottish, and we're born with a basic distrust of anything English. I should say, however, that my mother was English, and Michael, here, is half Irish, so we don't rightly know what to think. Maybe you gentlemen can point our views in the right direction."

That got a corporate laugh from the group.

"Well, at least you Hughson boys should be able to see both sides of the debate."

"Aye, perhaps we can, but we've been too busy growing crops to think much about it." Then John added, "I do know one thing, however. That Currency Act Parliament passed nine years ago eliminating our own paper money has driven the colonies into poverty. There's not enough money around to support our commerce. That includes those Bank of England notes for which we'd have to pay 'em eight per cent a year for the privilege of using."

One of the men spoke up. "I read in the *New York Gazette* a while back that Parliament got rid of that Act last year."

"You might be correct, but the damage has already been done to our prosperity. We can't allow them to ever put it back."

Another man entered the conversation. "You're right, Mr. Hughson. Until '67, my son and I had a cooper shop. Our customers were growing, and we even hired four men to work for us. Then, the bottom fell out. Folks told us that they lost their own customers and had no need for our barrels until things got better."

"Everybody is talking about the evil tea tax. Do you know what that tax cost my family last year? I'll tell you…about one dollar. That's all…one Spanish dollar. Hardly worth complaining about."

For the next hour, the political give-and-take continued. It was common that spring for conversations to gravitate toward politics. There was much to talk about. The British had levied taxes on the colonists, the "Indians" in Boston had thrown a shipment of tea into the harbor, the British had sent soldiers to control the population, British soldiers in Boston had shot and killed citizens demonstrating in the street, and citizen militias were stockpiling weapons and ammunition. Men advocating independence were surfacing in the colonies, especially in Massachusetts and Virginia.

Americans were taking sides; some wanted independence; others wanted a restoration of good relationships with King George III. And so it was with this group of sojourners at the Blue Heron. At inns and taverns throughout the colonies, travelers from both sides attempted to convince each other with their opinions and their own versions of the "facts." Phrases like "rights as Englishmen," "disloyalty," "treason," and "independence" peppered discussions in taverns, churches, mills, and farms.

Likewise, a few of these phrases surfaced among the travelers that night as they debated, pewter tankards in hand. The discussion at the Blue Heron went on until 8:45, when they were interrupted by a rider entering the tavern, soaking wet and covered with mud. The tavern owner, Cornelius Van Ness, approached him.

"Welcome, Friend. Come in out of the rain."

"Can someone tend to my horse?" the traveler asked with excitement in his voice.

"Certainly, take off your coat and come over by the fire. I'll get you something hot to drink."

"I can only stay for a little while. I've come from Boston with news."

He had the immediate attention of everyone in the room, especially the group sitting around the fireplace.

"On last Wednesday, the 19th, the militia outside of Boston engaged British soldiers in two battles, one at Lexington and one at Concord. Several lives were lost, and it means that we are at war!"

"What is your name, Sir?"

"I'm Timothy Wickham, and I'm in the Lexington militia. We call ourselves the Minutemen. I volunteered to ride to New York and notify them of the battles. I need a fresh horse. I have a fine animal to trade, but he is worn out."

Isaac Treadwell rose to the occasion. "You can have mine, Sir. But tell us the details."

Wickham stood with his back to the fire, steam beginning to rise from his wet clothes.

"We've been storing weapons and ammunition in a barn in Concord, which is about 25 miles from Boston. We knew the British were aware of it and that they planned to destroy the cache. Last Wednesday, they made their move, and the word was spread during the night to the Minutemen by two of our men, Revere and Dawes." He paused a moment and then continued.

"The British had to pass through Lexington on their way to Concord, so we assembled on the green and waited for them. When they arrived at sunrise, we confronted them and refused to obey their command to disperse. Shots were exchanged, and eight of our men were killed. We dispersed immediately and went to Concord and were joined by other Minutemen. When the British arrived, we confronted them again at the Concord bridge. This time, we drove them back, and they marched back to Boston. Along the way, we shot at them from the woods and caused several casualties. I'm afraid this means we are at war. I must get to New York with the news! Then, they'll have to send riders to Philadelphia and Williamsburg."

Van Ness intervened. "Wickham, stay here and rest at least until the rain lets up. You're not that far from New York; it's pouring outside, and it won't do if your horse slips and kills you. Please, sit down and have some pot roast. I'll get you a tankard and something dry to wear."

The other men concurred with Van Ness, and Wickham relented.

"Alright, but if I fall asleep, wake me before dawn so I can be on my way."

****

The next morning brought a clear, sunny day, and John and Michael were back on the road, deep in conversation about the recent events.

"Does this mean we're actually at war with England, John?"

"I don't imagine you could call it war just yet. Maybe some cooler heads will prevail, and some accommodation can be reached. Those men in Philadelphia may arrive at a plan. But, that conflict in Massachusetts will certainly give the fire eaters some fuel."

"What does it mean for our Dutchess County Militia?"

"It means that we've got to be ready, but, God willing, this little crisis will melt away, and reasonable men will prevail."

"Well, John, we're certainly no match for the British army if King George decides to teach us a lesson."

"How fast can you make fifty rifled weapons?" John asked with a chuckle.

"Not fast enough, I'm afraid."

"I imagine Colonel Brinkerhoff will order the militia to assemble and try to get us ready in case we're needed, Michael."

"He's going to have trouble because some of the men won't be partial to fighting the British, or becoming independent of them, for that matter."

"Probably the colonel's first step will be to demand that we sign loyalty oaths in case there's a war. He'll want to clear his ranks of men he can't depend on. Can you make two rifles, one for each of us?" John asked in jest.

"I can probably do that. I'll get started right away."

Colonel Abraham Brinkerhoff did call the militia together, he did discuss the recent events in Boston, he did call for loyalty oaths, and a few men left, maintaining that the whole thing was treasonous. The militia's training took on an increased energy and focus; weapons and ammunition were stockpiled. Twenty-seven men from the militia traveled to Boston to join the thousands of other militiamen from New England who were pouring into the area to surround and box in the British troops in the city.

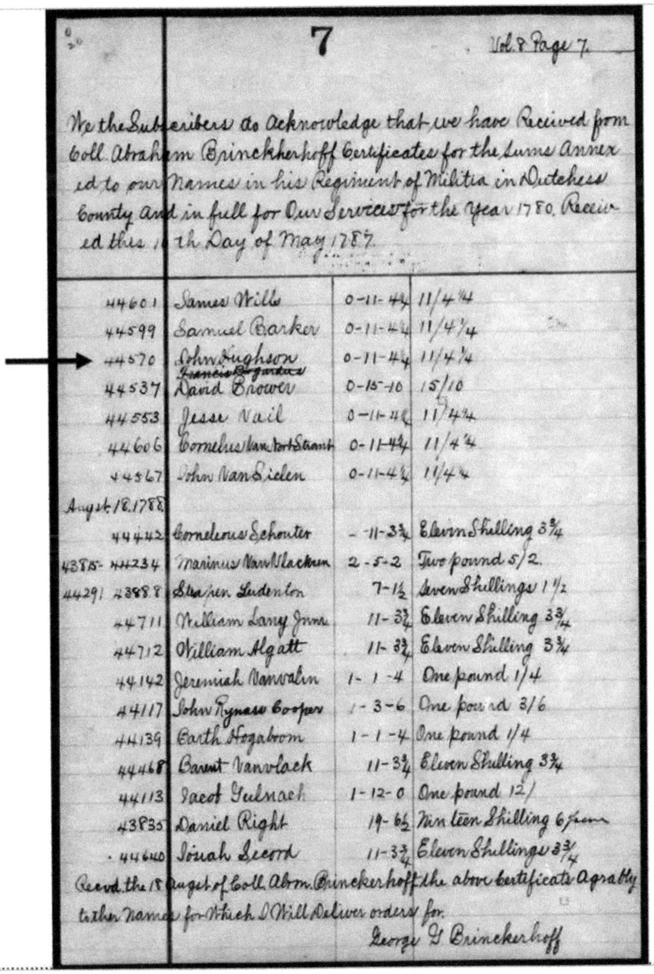

7   Vol 8 Page 7.

We the Subscribers do acknowledge that we have Received from Coll Abraham Brinckherhoff Certificates for the Sums annexed to our Names in his Regiment of Militia in Dutchess County and in full for Our Services for the year 1780. Received this 1th Day of May 1787.

44601	James Wills	0-11-4¾	11/4¾
44599	Samuel Barker	0-11-4¾	11/4¾
44570	John Hughson (Francis ...)	0-11-4¾	11/4¾
44537	David Brower	0-15-10	15/10
44553	Jesse Vail	0-11-4¾	11/4¾
44606	Cornelius Van Port Saant	0-11-4¾	11/4¾
44567	John VanSielen	0-11-4¾	11/4¾
August 18 1788			
44442	Cornelius Schouter	-11-3¾	Eleven Shilling 3¾
4385-44234	Marinus VanVlacken	2-5-2	Two pound 5/2
44291-23888	Stephen Sudenton	7-1½	Seven Shillings 1½
44711	William Lany Junr	11-3¾	Eleven Shilling 3¾
44712	William Algatt	11-3¾	Eleven Shilling 3¾
44142	Jeremiah Ranvalin	1-1-4	One pound 1/4
44117	John Rynaw Cooper	1-3-6	One pound 3/6
44139	Garth Hogaboom	1-1-4	One pound 1/4
44468	Barent Vanvlack	11-3¾	Eleven Shilling 3¾
44113	Jacob Gulnaeh	1-12-0	One pound 12/
43835	Daniel Right	19-6½	Nineteen Shilling 6
44640	Jonah Secord	11-3¾	Eleven Shillings 3¾

Received the 18 August of Coll Abrm Brinckerhoff the above certificate agreably to the names for which I Will Deliver orders for.

George G Brinckerhoff

Dutchess County Militia, 2nd Reg't Pay Voucher

During the next few months, things developed rapidly. On June 17, 1775, the British attempted to break the siege of Boston by attacking the Americans on Breed's Hill (erroneously called "Bunker Hill" by history). They gained the hill but at a terrible loss of their own blood. Nine months later, during the night of March 4, 1776, General Washington armed Dorchester Heights with some of the heavy cannons Colonel Knox had retrieved from Fort Ticonderoga, causing British General Gage's army to evacuate Boston and head for Halifax. On July 4, 1776, the world was informed that the Second Continental Congress had declared the thirteen colonies free and independent of England. The British army, now under the command of General William Howe, appeared in New York Harbor and invaded western Long Island on August 27, 1776. Washington was there to meet him at Brooklyn Heights, but he was defeated. Luckily, 9,000 of his soldiers escaped in the fog, but what followed during the next four months was a series of lost battles and skirmishes and the Continental Army's retreat to Bucks County, Pennsylvania, by the Delaware River near a place known as McConkey's Ferry, not all that far from Trenton, New Jersey.

Chapter 37

The Codwise Family

1683-1776

Although he was born in 1683 in Manheim, Germany, where his parents were at the time, Jan Koenaet (John Conrad) Codwise was Dutch. The family home was in Utrecht, Netherlands, where Jan's father was a schoolteacher, but by 1700, it was getting harder to make ends meet. Back in 1648, the Dutch Republic had finally gained its independence from Spain, and for a while the tiny country enjoyed a degree of prosperity. Until the end of the century, that is, when a weakening economy began turning life into a struggle, especially for the Dutch working class. The situation deteriorated even further when Poland lost Ukraine to Russa and was no longer able to export grain to feed the Dutch people.

By 1701, the Codwise family arrived at the same decision made by countless other families who found themselves in similar circumstances. They would send 18-year-old Jan and a cousin, Willem, who lived with them, to America. America was prosperous; its economy was flourishing, and opportunities abounded for industrious young men. Jan and Willem would sail to New York. There were thousands of Dutch in that colony, and surely, they could pursue some lucrative opportunities. Jan was studious, like his father; he was accomplished at reading and handling numbers, and he had a clear hand. His mother was not at all worried about his prospects. As soon as the young men got established, perhaps the rest of the family could join them.

"Jan, you have a second cousin in New York, Peter Van Ness. When you arrive, contact him, and I am sure he will help you get started. I've written a letter for you to give him when you arrive. He works at the customs house, which is probably near the docks. I'm sure he will be easy to locate."

With that, the cousins walked down the dock and onto the gang plank of the Dutch fluyt, *Vrijheid* ("Liberty"), bound for New York.

Five weeks and three days later, the young men found themselves on the crowded dock in New York. As they waited for their trunks to be off loaded, they were amazed to find a great number of people who were speaking Dutch. The two immigrants went to the customs house and contacted Cousin Peter, who gave the young men a warm and enthusiastic welcome. John passed him his father's letter; Peter read it twice and placed it on his desk.

"It says here that you are quite learned for a young man, John. Is that true? By the way, in America your name is 'John' and, addressing his cousin, your name is 'William'".

"Well, Sir, I have done quite a bit of reading. I taught myself some English so I could read their books, too. And I have some familiarity with mathematics, geography, and astronomy."

"Hmm…how would you like to teach school, like your father? My sister informs me that there is an opening in a town called Newark, across the river in the colony of New Jersey. They are looking for a school master who speaks both Dutch and English. It is a one-room school, and most of the children are Dutch. You can live with my sister's family. Her husband is a farmer, and he also runs a grist mill." He paused and then, "What do you think, John?"

"I would like to do it, Sir."

Fine. You boys can stay at my home tonight, and tomorrow, I'll take you over there." Turning to Cousin William, Van Ness said, "Will, I am sure there would be something for you to do over there. You come along, too."

After a boat trip across the North (Hudson) River and a wagon ride into Newark, the three arrived at Peter's sister Rutje's home, where they received a Dutch welcome. The next day, John met with five community leaders who declared him fit for the position of school master. His board and room were to be provided on a rotating basis by the parents of the children.

Three months later, on one of these rotations, John met Margaret Stillwagon, born in New York in 1684, serving as a governess; she was very pretty, witty, and conversant in both Dutch and English. Their mutual attraction was immediate, and they were married in New York City on a cold January day in 1704.

After two years in Newark, the couple moved to New York City, where John continued his teaching career. The couple had a son, Christopher, Sr. (1709-1742), who became a felt maker in New York. He married Petronella Van Giessen in New York in 1730, and by 1741, the couple had two boys and four girls. Their son, George Codwise, was born in 1736 and Christopher Codwise, Jr. in 1740 (Jeff Hughson's sixth great-grandfather). As his felt-making business grew, Christopher Sr. needed more help, so he purchased a slave named Cambridge, who quickly learned the trade and became a valuable economic asset to his master.

Christopher Sr. had a head for business and began accumulating wealth, an effort that was cut short by his death in 1742. His sons, George especially, inherited their father's entrepreneurial drive, eventually transforming the Codwises into one of New York City's more prosperous families. They became successful merchants, owning ships involved in the coastal trade and a sugar plantation in St. Croix in the West Indies. George was known as "Captain Codwise," and during the Revolutionary War he provided money and supplies to the Army.

Christopher's other son, Christopher Jr., graduated from Kings College (now Columbia) and participated in the family business. He married a woman named Catherine Ditmars, and together they enjoyed a prosperous life in New York City, raising their son and two daughters, Christopher, Penelope, and Catherine.

When the British occupied New York City in August 1776, after winning the Battle of Brooklyn Heights, thirty-six-year-old Christopher Jr. moved his family 75 miles north to Fishkill in Dutchess County, a town he thought would offer a better sanctuary from the Redcoats. He planned to use his trading and logistics skills to assist the Cause by dealing in supplies for the Army, but three months later, those plans were to change.

Chapter 38

The 2nd New York Regiment

1776

In November of that year, the 2nd New York Regiment was reorganized and undertook a major recruitment effort. Regimental recruiters came to Dutchess County with the mission of incorporating some of its militia into the regiment's ranks. Being between 16 and 45 years old, both John Hughson and his adopted brother, Michael Kerry Hughson, were in the Dutchess County Militia. The two men met with their Colonel Brinkerhoff to discuss the recruitment.

"John, I understand the 2nd New York's need for soldiers, and, indeed, it looks like I will be losing over forty men from our ranks. Because of your leadership role in the regiment, I would really hate to lose you. We'll have a great deal of training to do with all the young men who will be joining us over the next few months. I will need you, John, to stay and assist with the militia."

The colonel then turned his attention toward Michael. "Michael, I would also miss you and your ability with weapons repair, but I suppose General Washington is in greater need of your skills than we are. So, if you wish to join the 2nd New York Regiment, you have my blessing…but only if you promise to come back in one piece!"

Faint chuckles.

"I promise to come back, Colonel. I'll keep my head down."

But then, in a tentative voice, Michael asked, "Can black men serve in the Continental Army, Colonel?"

Of course, they can. There are hundreds of them already, scattered all throughout the regiments, and I expect there'll be a lot more, too, before this war is over. Just remember everything you learned in the militia, obey your officers, and offer up your gunsmithing skills. You'll be fine."

Michael drew himself up to his full height. "Yes, Sir, I will do all that. I promise."

"Very well. You men are dismissed."

As they walked back to their homes, Michael said, "John, I must tell Becky and the boys about this. It will be different for them when I'm gone. How long do you think the war will last?"

I don't know, Michael…maybe a year or two. The British can't afford to keep this up forever. It seems to me that all Washington has to do is keep his army from being defeated, and King George will eventually empty his treasury. That's how I see it, anyway."

"John, will you watch over Becky and my boys while I'm gone?"

"Of course I will, Michael. No need to worry about that. The Hughsons take care of their own."

Michael paused, then added, "Even if I don't come back?"

"Even that, too, Michael. But you'll be coming back...I'm certain of it. You already promised Brinkerhoff, didn't you?"

"I did!" Michael felt better, and he picked up his step.

A week later, the Hughson clan gathered among tears, hugs, and well-wishes to say "goodbye" to Michael. He climbed onto the wagon, with young William at the reins, anxious to make the short trip to the dock. John passed his favorite rifle up to the soldier. Take my fire stick with you, Michael. With those grooves you cut in the barrel, it's accurate past 300 yards. It may just come in handy."

"Thank you, John," He bent over the side of the wagon and gave his adopted brother a final hug.

Recovering his command voice, Private Hughson said, "Let's go, Will."

Among the other residents of the Fishkill-Hughsonville area to meet the recruiters was Christopher Codwise, Jr. When the recruiters discovered that he was a graduate of Kings College, they approached him with an offer of a commission. Four days later, on November 26, 1776, Christopher received his commission as a 1st Lieutenant in the 2nd NY and was on his way with forty-three other men and boys to join the regiment, one of whom was Private Michael Hughson. The recruits finally caught up with the 2nd NY and the rest of the Continental Army two weeks before Christmas…just in time to cross the Delaware.

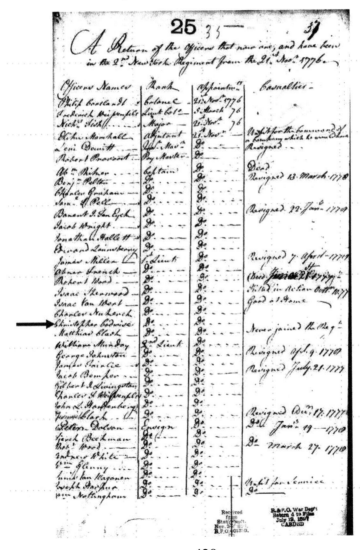

During the trip south, the recruits rode in wagons or walked, depending on the day and terrain. Being a lieutenant, however, Codwise rode his own horse. The lieutenant in charge of the recruits, a man named Robertson, decided when and where to stop for the night. He was adept at locating barns and stables for the men, who were grateful for the comfort during those cold December nights. Cooking fires were started, and the men gathered around, smoking, chewing, and talking. On one of those evenings, Codwise took the opportunity to approach Michael Hughson and inquire about his rifle. The weapon appeared to be finely balanced and possessed a beautifully shaped and finished stock and ornate lock.

"That's a fine weapon you have there, Soldier. Where did you get it?"

Michael passed it over to him and said, "I made it myself, Sir. The barrel is rifled, making it very accurate to more than 300 yards."

Christopher hefted the rifle and raised it to his shoulder, aiming at a tree. "It's a beautiful weapon. What balance! If what you tell me is true, you're a very skilled craftsman. What's your name? Mine's Christopher Codwise. They tell me I'm a lieutenant."

"Michael Hughson, Sir. My name's Michael Hughson," showing the other man the proper respect for his newly earned rank.

"You from over there in what they call Hughsonville?"

"Yes, Sir."

"You free?"

"Yes, Sir. Never been a slave."

"How did you get the Hughson name?"

"My mother died when I was a baby, and the Hughsons took me in and raised me. They gave me their name. I guess I'm what you'd call a black Scotsman."

Codwise chuckled. "Well, I come from New York City. When the British invaded last August, I took my family to Fishkill to move them away from the trouble. Now, here I am, a new Lieutenant, and I have to learn quick what lieutenants are supposed to do."

"I am sure you will do fine, Sir."

"And you, Private Hughson, should be an armorer for the Regiment. When I get a chance, I'll let Colonel Van Cortlandt know about you. They tell me he's in charge of the regiment."

"Thank you, Sir. I brought a few tools with me here in this sack in case they want me to work on firearms."

The 2nd New York Regiment joined Washington and the Continental Army a few days before Christmas, just in time

431

to participate in the Battle of Trenton. As part of a last-ditch effort to save the Patriot Cause, Washington crossed the Delaware River on Christmas Eve 1776 and struggled all night through an ice-clogged river and a cold winter blizzard to rout an outpost of German Hessians at Trenton. The army marched to Princeton a few days later and defeated a small British force stationed at the college. From there, it marched into winter quarters in Morristown, New Jersey, where Christopher, Michael and the rest of the 2nd New York endured the cold and lack of provisions. True to his word, the new lieutenant was successful in having Michael designated as an armorer for the regiment.

Chapter 39

Penelope Codwise

Fishkill, 1777

While the Army was at Morristown, Lieutenant Codwise was placed "on command" by Colonel Van Cortlandt and sent back to Fishkill for the month of March to recruit for the regiment. The colonel reasoned that Codwise would be a good choice because he was familiar with the area since he moved his family there from New York the prior September. Also, the lieutenant was adept at reading and writing, and he had a "clear hand" with a quill and ink, skills that were valuable and not all that common. Christopher left on the 75-mile trip early the next morning in the falling snow, and two days later, he arrived at his rental home in Fishkill, to the welcomed surprise of his wife, Catherine, and three children, Christopher, Penelope, and Catherine.

Catherine ran to her husband and embraced him with a huge lingering hug.

"Oh, Christopher, I'm so happy to see you! Thank you, Jesus!" But, then, an immediate look of concern. "You weren't wounded, or you're not sick, are you?"

"Nay, nothing of the kind, my Love, I'm quite well. The army is in winter quarters in Morristown, so there's not much happening. Howe and the Brits are doing the same in

New York. So, the colonel ordered me to Fishkill for a month to recruit for the regiment."

"Well, take off that wet cloak and sit at the table. As you can see, we were just about ready to eat."

"Smells wonderful! I'll be right back after I put Lucky in the barn."

Penelope piped up. "I'll take care of him, Father. You can start without me."

Without waiting for her father's assent, she grabbed a cape off the peg and was out the door.

****

After a hardy homecoming breakfast the next morning, Christopher ventured forth to begin his recruiting effort. He made some initial inquiries about the 2nd Regiment of the Dutchess County Militia and was told that they were currently gathered at John Hughson's farm engaging in drill practice, so he headed in that direction. Colonel Brinkerhoff was away on an errand, so the visitor was directed to John Hughson.

"Good morning, Sir. I'm Lieutenant Codwise from the 2nd New York Continental Line."

"Yes, Sir. I'm John Hughson. We already know of you. If I am correct, your family is staying in Fishkill."

"That's right. We came up last September when the British occupied New York City." He continued. "The regiment is with General Washington in Morristown, and they sent me up here for a month to recruit."

"We'd be most honored to assist you all we can, Sir, but, as you probably already know, our militia was pretty much depleted by the 2nd New York last November, and we are just now getting our own batch of new recruits into some military form."

"Well, I would certainly appreciate any help you could give me, and perhaps you can help put out the word to the town that I am looking for a few good men for the Cause. We pay a recruiting bounty."

"We'd be very glad to assist you, Sir." John paused and then asked, "Do you know of the black soldier, Michael Hughson?"

"Yes, I do. He's a fine soldier."

"Is he well?"

"He's very well. I learned that he's a gunsmith. I intend to speak to Captain Hallett about having him serve as one of our armorers."

At that point, John's young son, William, walked up, and his father introduced him to the lieutenant. "This is my son, Will. He's too young to be a soldier, but I'm sure he'd be glad to assist you should you need it."

"Pleased to meet you, Will."

"Yes, Sir, I'm ready to help you if you need me, Sir." The young man said, in his best military voice and pulling himself to his full height.

Fifteen-year-old Will was an ardent patriot. When he wasn't in school or doing his chores, the lad spent all his time hanging around the militiamen training on his father's farm. To anyone who saw him, Will was clearly his father's son. He was tall, "strapping," and mature for his age. He had his father's brown eyes and his head of thick brown hair. He was already an excellent marksman and horseman, and he made himself available to the regiment for tasks, which mostly involved carrying firewood and cleaning weapons. Occasionally, there were exceptions, however.

It was a cold winter Saturday morning in March 1777. As usual, Will had arisen early and made his way over to the soldiers, who were cooking breakfast, drinking coffee, and generally complaining about the snow.

Codwise was already there, talking with a few men on the verge of joining the 2nd New York. When he spotted Will, he approached him.

"Will, I have a task for you if you'll be kind enough to accept it."

"Yes, Sir?"

"I forgot to bring the recruit muster roll with me this morning, and I need to add some names to it. Could I get you to ride into Fishkill and ask my wife to give it to you? You can take my horse. He's good in the snow."

"Yes, Sir. I'll leave right now, Sir!"

"Do you know where I live?"

"Yes, Sir; you stay at the Van Houlton house."

"That's right. Be careful in the snow and ice, Will."

"Yes, Sir."

Wow! A real mission! Will was energized. Wait 'till he tells his father about this! Today, he felt like a soldier.

A soldier brought up the lieutenant's horse, saddled and ready to go. Will mounted in his best military posture and was off into the light snow that was falling.

Half an hour later, he reined his horse to a halt in front of the Codwise home and tied him to the hitching post. He stepped onto the porch, stomped the snow off his boots, knocked on the door, and stood at attention. In a moment, the door opened, not by a wife, but rather by a girl, a very pretty girl. Will recovered quickly from his surprise.

"Good morning, Miss. I'm Will Hughson. I've come from your father, Lieutenant Codwise. He sent me to bring him the recruit muster, which he left here this morning."

"Yes. I'm Penelope, his daughter. Come in out of the cold, Will, and wait over by the fire. I'll get my mother.

437

She'll know where the muster is." With that, she left the room.

Wow! Penelope! She was a pretty lass! Blond with blue eyes—of course, she's Dutch—and sporting a lean but feminine figure under her green smock. She was about his age, maybe a tad older. Being a soldier on a mission had its rewards. In a couple minutes, Mrs. Codwise appeared with the paper rolled up and in a cloth sack to protect it from the elements.

"Good morning, Mr. Hughson. Here's the muster roll. And thank you for coming through the snow to retrieve it for the lieutenant."

She called him "Mr. Hughson". That made him feel even more soldierly.

"Thank you, Ma'am. I'll take it to him right away." He started to turn toward the door.

Penelope demurred. "Tom, won't you stay a few minutes and warm up?"

"Please do." Mrs. Codwise encouraged. "Have a cup of tea with us and a piece of fresh-baked sweet potato pie. Penelope set a place for him." Then she added, "It wouldn't do to send you out into this weather on an empty stomach!"

Both women flashed him encouraging smiles.

"I suppose a few minutes more won't hurt anything. Thank you, Ma'am. I'll put the lieutenant's horse in your barn."

Will was back in less than five minutes, and they sat down to the tea and pie. Penelope started the conversation.

"Do you like Father's horse? His name is Lucky."

"I do. He's a fine animal. I think he was glad to get in the barn."

Penelope's mother picked up the table talk. "We'll have you back on the road in a few minutes, Will. You must be related to the Hughsons over in Wappinger's Falls?"

She called him "Will!"

"Yes, Ma'am, I'm John Hughson's son. He's in the Dutchess Militia. He helps train the recruits. When I'm seventeen, I plan to join them."

"How old are you, Will?

"I'm fifteen, Ma'am."

"I'm sixteen." Penelope volunteered. Then, she added, "We were living in New York, but when the British occupied us, Father moved us up here to Fishkill, where it would be safer. I like it here. People are much friendlier than they are in New York, and they don't talk nearly as fast."

Will chuckled, "That's what everybody says. I like it here in Dutchess County, too."

Ten more minutes of small talk, and Will was out the door and on his way with lots to think about as he and Lucky trudged through the snow. He was already planning how he might get to see Penelope again. Military life was pretty good!

Later that morning, Will handed the muster roll to Codwise.

"Thank you very much, Will. How did you find my household? Did Mrs. Codwise give you something to eat and drink?"

"Yes, Sir, she did, tea and sweet potato pie. She's very nice."

"And…what about my daughter, Penelope? Was she nice, too?" He chuckled.

"Yes. Sir. She was very pleasant."

"Pleasant, huh?" He chuckled again.

"Yes, Sir," Will replied, looking down at his boots.

Because his father was occupied with the militia, Will and his younger brother, John, had plenty to keep them busy on the farm. As the weeks dragged on, however, Will did find numerous reasons to travel into Fishkill on "business," and on several of these trips, he had occasion to spend some time with Penelope. He began thinking that they might even have a future together. As time went on, he thought more and more about that. When Christopher came home on short

440

furloughs, he seemed to approve of Will's growing presence in the family.

Life was good!

Chapter 40

Private Michael Hughson

2nd New York Regiment, 1777

A week after Will met Penelope, Lieutenant Codwise repaired to Morristown with 53 recruits in tow. He reported to his company commander, Captain Hallett, in the 2nd New York and took the opportunity to tell him about Michael Hughson, who had also been assigned to Hallett's company.

"Captain, I have observed the black soldier, Michael Hughson, for a while; he is a good man and an excellent marksman. Furthermore, I am told that he is a skilled gunsmith, and he's especially acquainted with the rifling process to increase accuracy. I think he'd make a good armorer for the regiment."

"Fine, Lieutenant. On your recommendation, I'll talk to the colonel about assigning him to that task."

Captain Hallett wasn't disappointed. Michael Hughson was assigned as one of two regimental armorers, and he continued displaying his gunsmithing skills, much to everyone's satisfaction. In addition to his ability to repair weapons, it wasn't long before his prowess as an excellent marksman was well-known throughout the regiment. In fact, he became an assistant instructor on the firing range, a very unique position for a black man. It wasn't long before he was called "Dead Eye" around the camp, a moniker he took as a great compliment. Around the campfire in the evenings, some of the soldiers would ask him about his background. One evening, the conversation went like this:

"No disrespect, Dead Eye, but how'd you, a colored man, get here, and where'd you pick up your smithing skills? Also, we've noticed that you don't talk like most black folk...more like you've had some schoolin'."

Michael chuckled. "Well, first of all, I'm not colored. No, sir. I'm told that I was born this way!"

He let that settle in for a few heartbeats; then, everyone began to laugh.

Things quieted down, and Michael continued. "I've never been a slave if that's what you're wonderin'. My father was, but my mother was Irish. They died in 1741, when I was a few months old, and the Hughsons took me for their own and raised me. My wife, Becky, was a slave until she was two when her mom was freed in a will after her owner was killed in a duel. She was raised by some Quakers in Westchester. We have two boys, Josiah, he's thirteen, and Will's ten."

One of the soldiers interjected. "I'm not for this slavery business. I think it's pure evil. It's against the Bible!"

Another soldier cut in. "Surely, if we win this war and free ourselves from Britain, those men in Philadelphia will ban slavery from the whole country."

"I don't know, Sam." a third one added. "Those southerners on their plantations will fight it, for sure. It could be a real mess before it's over."

"I'll tell you one damn thing, Joshua," another soldier chimed in, "if our new country allows slavery, we'll eventually be in another war, but this time, amongst ourselves. We may not live to see it, but I reckon it's sure to happen."

That brought on a few seconds of silence.

Then, Sam turned the conversation. "So, Dead Eye, where did you learn your gunsmithing skills?"

"When I was young, we had a neighbor who was a gunsmith. He learned his trade years before in the British army. He let me visit his shop, and I began helping him more and more, making parts and assembling pistols, muskets, and rifles. He was getting old, and one day, he quit working, gave me his tools, and sent me out on my own. I've been makin' and fixin' firearms ever since."

Sam capped off the conversation. "Well, Hughson, we're glad you're a soldier and one of us, ain't we, boys?" Grunts and words of agreement emanated from the group. Then, always the group comedian, he added, "And this evening, we learned that you ain't colored, neither. No, Sir. Turns out that you came out that way!"

There was general laughter as Michael reacted to the comment, "That would be correct. Also, as you can see, I

444

came out a shade lighter because I'm half Irish, which means I also have a natural tendency to fight, drink, dance, make babies, and despise the English."

Considerable laughter, then someone's final comment. "Hughson, in that case, I believe you'll fit right in!"

There was more laughter as the group got to their feet to return to their tents.

That evening, Michael walked back to his tent with the comfortable feeling that he was actually accepted as one of them...a brother soldier fighting for Washington and the Cause. Those men gathered around the fire weren't judging him based on his skin color or curly hair. Rather, they gave him respect as a man, as a member of their brotherhood. He felt encouraged and ready to do his part.

Chapter 41

Saratoga, Freeman's Farm

September 1777

At the end of July 1777, General Putnam relieved the 2nd New York Regiment of its duties in White Plains and two weeks later, he ordered the regiment "to march immediately to the northward" to counter the threat posed by British General Burgoyne's 7,000 troops descending from Canada in an attempt to split New England off from the rest of the colonies. By August 22nd, the regiment had reached Louden's Ferry on the Mohawk River and was camped with General Poor's brigade, to which the 2nd had been assigned.

That evening, Lieutenant Christopher Codwise found himself sitting on a log by a campfire, drinking coffee from a tin cup. He was in the company of a half dozen other lieutenants from Poor's brigade gathered around the fire to fend off a slight chill in the air and the omnipresent mosquitos. A lieutenant named Nathan Peterson from Massachusetts turned to address the newcomer.

"You're lucky you boys missed our shameful midnight skedaddle from the British at Fort Ticonderoga, Codwise. We'll never live it down."

"What happened up there, anyway, Peterson?"

"It's a long story. To my way of thinkin', we were doomed from the very beginning. The generals couldn't decide who would be in command of the fort. Gates never did show, Schuyler tried to command with letters from Albany, and St. Clair was as useless as teats on a boar hog. We all knew that we'd be goners unless we dragged some cannon up Mt. Defiance. The engineer begged 'em to do it…we all expressed concern. But…No…the good General Schuyler had us dig trenches, instead, in which we'd all die if the Brits ever got THEIR cannon up on that dammed hill."

"Did they?"

"You bet they did. That's the first thing they did, and we knew it was all over. That evening, our generals had a VERY short meeting, and the next thing we knew, the whole garrison was running around in a disorganized mass, trying to evacuate everyone while it was still dark. We spiked a few of our 58 artillery pieces, and in the middle of the night, we got the order to evacuate. We got outta there as quick as green corn goes through the new maid, leaving behind piles of food, equipment, hundreds of muskets, and barrels of powder. The Brits and Germans must have thought it was Christmas when they entered the gates the next morning! They took the fort without hardly firing a shot! It was shameful…yes, Sir, shameful…that's what it was. I imagine General Washington was a might bit miffed when he got the report."

Peterson continued. "And since then, St. Clair and Schuyler have us runnin' from the Redcoats but tryin' to stay between them and Albany." The soldier snorted, spit into the fire and picked up his story.

"There is one piece of good news among it all. General Stark clashed with some Brits and Germans over at Bennington. His militia walloped 'em and sent 'em runnin' back to Burgoyne with their tails twixt their legs. According to their stragglers, they suffered over 200 dead and another 700 captured."

"What's the word on our next move, Peterson?" Codwise inquired.

"Well, four days ago, General Gates arrived to take command. St. Clair and Schuyler must be back in Albany looking for somethin' to do. Gates don't have many options. The Brits are headed for Albany, so we got to stay in between and stop 'em. Washington can't let 'em march clean down to New York and cut off New England from the rest of us. If that happens, it's all over. Hopefully, Gates will locate a good place for us to make a stand. When he does, you men in the Second are sure to be in the middle of it with the rest of us. General Poor is a fighter. I don't reckon he'll have his brigade in the rear guarding the wagons and tents."

When Washington got word of Ft. Ticonderoga, he was, indeed, miffed. Not only did he put General Horatio Gates in charge, but he also ordered General Benedict Arnold and Colonel Daniel Morgan, with his regiment of sharpshooters, north to lend their assistance to the effort to stop Burgoyne's advance.

****

To thwart the British advance southward toward Albany, General Gates moved his Army of 10,000 men north and established a defensive position near Saratoga on hilly terrain that he thought was conducive to withstanding a British assault. By the third week of September, Burgoyne, commanding 7,200 men, had crossed over to the west side of the Hudson and was camped within four miles of Gates' defenses.

On the morning of September 19th, the two armies faced each other in line of battle. The British right flank was commanded by General Simon Fraser, perhaps the most competent British field commander in the Revolution. The 53rd King's Regiment of Foote was part of this line, and it happened to include 31-year-old Private William Jones from Broseley, a town in Shropshire, England. It would turn out that Private Jones was to become the fifth great-grandfather of police Lieutenant Jeff Hughson.

Facing Fraser was the American left flank, commanded by General Benedict Arnold, one of the best American field commanders of the war. The line included Poor's Brigade and the 2nd New York. 1st Lieutenant Christopher Codwise, another 5th great-grandfather of Lieutenant Jeff Hughson, was there. The action began at 3:00 in the afternoon when General Burgoyne ordered a frontal assault on the American line. What resulted was one of the most intense hand-to-hand confrontations of the entire war. During one of the British assaults, the withering firepower from General Arnold's men forced part of the British troops into a disorganized and frantic rout.

All that is, except for one brave soldier, who turned around, faced the oncoming Americans, aimed his Brown Bess directly at Codwise and pulled the trigger. The lieutenant heard the ball whiz past him a few inches from his ear. Amazingly, the soldier stood there and began to reload his musket. Codwise saw his chance; running as fast as he could to cover the twenty yards separating the two, he charged the man and tackled him just as he finished priming the weapon's pan. Producing a six-inch blade, Codwise screamed at the soldier, "Move a muscle, and you're a dead man!"

For a moment or two, neither man moved as three soldiers from Christopher's company approached on the double.

"You alright, Lieutenant?" One of them inquired.

"Yeah." He paused for a breath. "Take this man to the rear. Lucky for me, he's a terrible shot." With that, the lieutenant jogged back toward his company, still breathing hard from his exertion.

"Get on your feet, Bloody Back. You're goin' for a walk to meet some of your friends." Two of the soldiers grabbed the prisoner by his arms and jerked him to his feet, while the third picked up his musket. The Brit was a good-looking fellow with light brown hair and muscular.

"Shoot at our lieutenant, will ya? You're lucky he didn't gut ya with that pig sticker of his. What's your name, Puke?"

"The name's Private William Jones. I'm in the King's Fifty-Third Regiment of Foot, and that's all I'm gonna say."

Effecting his best English accent, one of the soldiers said, "Well, ya won't be seein' your regiment tonight, Lobster Back." He paused and then added, "I'll allow one thing for ya, fella; you showed a lot of grit, standin' your ground for one last shot like you did. And all without gettin' nary a scratch on your bloody arse."

"Thank you, Sir." Was all William could think to say.

"You're most welcome, Sir," came the retort.

The battle lasted until dusk, when the Americans finally retreated to their defensive line, leaving Burgoyne on the field, thus giving him the technical victory. However, the Redcoats paid a very high price for the honor: 600 killed, wounded, and captured. Private William Jones was among the prisoners.

****

That evening, Jones and the other British and German prisoners were in a holding area in the American camp and under the watchful eyes of men from the 2nd New York. The captives, together with some of their guards, were gathered around several campfires to ward off a chill in the night air, discussing the unfortunate events of the day and reminiscing about their lives back home. As he was making his rounds through the groups of men, Lieutenant Codwise overheard a British soldier mention King's College in New York. He recognized him as the soldier who took a shot at him that afternoon. He walked over to the man, who stood up when he saw the American approaching.

"What's your name, Soldier?"

"William Jones, Sir." He immediately recognized the lieutenant he had shot at and added politely, "My apologies for shootin' at you, Sir. Had I known it was you, I'd been more respectful."

Codwise smiled.

"I'd like to thank you for your poor marksmanship. Sit down. Where you from, Jones?"

"Broseley in Shropshire, Sir. My kin's been there for many generations."

"I Just heard you talking about King's College in New York."

"Yes, Sir. That would have been me."

"What caused you to mention King's College?" Christopher's interest was peaking.

"I have a cousin, Isaac, who went there. When he was just a wee thing, his parents moved to New York back in '43 to establish a carriage business. Our mothers wrote to each other, and Aunt Ann always bragged about how smart her little Isaac was. I think he became a preacher."

"Was that his name…Isaac Jones?"

"Yes, Sir, Cousin Isaac."

"Move over and give me some room to sit down."

William scooted over on the log, and Christopher took a place by the fire with the other prisoners. He grew quite animated.

"I attended King's College, and I knew an Isaac Jones. A real smart lad, especially in Greek and Latin, but he also knew how to enjoy himself. We used to frequent an establishment called Fraunces Tavern on Pearl Street, and Isaac would always buy the first two rounds. He had quite a sense of humor, too. He would keep us in tears laughing at his impersonations of the various professors." He paused, then, "Do you know what he's doing now?"

"He never did come home. The last we heard, he was a preacher with a parish in some place called Setauket on Long Island."

Isaac was, indeed, in Setauket...and what Private Jones didn't know was that his cousin was also working with Washington's spies, "the Culper ring," as they reported on the British Army's activities in New York City.

This short conversation made both Codwise and Jones and the other prisoners more comfortable with each other, and Jones changed the subject.

"Lieutenant, Sir, when we were told that we'd be shipped over to America to put down a rebellion against the King, they told us how Washington's army was composed of a bunch of farmers and shopkeepers who would run at the first sight of our red uniforms. At first, that was pretty much the case, like in Brooklyn. But, today, those farmers and shopkeepers of yours taught us to be a mite more respectful of 'em. They stood up under fire better than we ever could if I do say so myself." Several of the other prisoners around the fire mumbled their agreement.

"Well, thank you, Jones. Coming from you, I consider that a real compliment. Despite our lack of your military training and your pretty uniforms, we're fighting for our freedom and for our families, and you men are fighting for your eightpence [$2.13] a day. That makes a real difference."

He continued. "By the way, why do you wear those bright red uniforms anyway? It just makes you easier to see and to shoot at."

One of the other prisoners piped up, "We know, Lieutenant, and we've brought it up more than once. That's why many of our recruits want to join the rifle companies. They wear those green uniforms, which makes 'em harder to draw a bead on. Our red uniforms are supposed to hide the blood so we don't panic and run away under fire."

"Does that work?"

"Not to my way of thinkin'. When we're lined up shoulder to shoulder thirty yards apart shootin' at each other, I don't think our uniforms are of much account."

Another one inserted a comment. "As for me, I'd rather be dressed like one of your Indians. I could lie down and disappear in the grass if I had to."

A few chuckles and grunts of agreement around the fire provided him with encouragement.

"Furthermore, if I were an officer, I sure wouldn't want to ride a white horse, not the way you Rebels seem to fancy shootin' holes in 'em. In Europe, it's considered bad manners to shoot at officers. It's not civilized if you don't mind me sayin'. It ain't right to my way of thinkin'."

There was some more general grunting among the men around the fire. Then, one of them, a man named Elijah, spoke up. "Lieutenant, what's the story behind those men on your left today, the ones in those light-colored shirts? They stayed behind those trees that must have been over two hundred yards away from us, and yet they were able to drop our officers like flies. We've never seen anything like it."

"Those are Colonel Morgan's men. They were hand-picked from woodsmen living on our frontier, and they're used to the woods, hunting for their livelihood, and fighting Indians. They carry their own rifles, which have spiral grooves in the barrels that make the ball spin and fly true. Also, they're commanded by a man who is truly fearless and able to infect his men with the same courage. They're very dangerous, and I'm glad they're on our side."

Codwise got up to leave, but he had one last question.

"Off in the distance I've been hearing the skirl of bagpipes this evening." He addressed a soldier wearing a Scottish uniform, sitting with the other prisoners.

"You there, in the Scottish uniform. What's your name?"

The soldier stood up. "Fergus Rankin, 21st Royal Scots Fusiliers, at your service, SIR."

"Those your bagpipes I'm hearing, Mr. Rankin?"

That would be correct, Sir. The regiment took a severe whippin' today, and they're playing a dirge to honor our dead and wounded."

"Are you men what they call the "Black Watch?"

"Yes, Sir. That's us."

"Where did that name come from."

"From the dark colors in our tartan, Sir."

"Well, Private Rankin, at least you made it through the day."

"That I did, Sir."

****

To assist Gates, General Washington ordered Colonel Daniel Morgan and 500 of his frontier sharpshooters to march north and join his forces. Morgan had gathered his men from the hills of Virginia, Pennsylvania, and Kentucky, men dressed in hunting shirts who knew how to fight Indian style and use their Kentucky and Pennsylvania rifles to great effect. Most of them were deadly at 200 yards or more. Michael Hughson, who, by this time, had his own wagon assigned to him to transport gunsmithing equipment, came to the attention of Colonel Morgan's armorer.

"Colonel, there's a black man named Hughson in the 2nd New York. Turns out, he's an excellent gunsmith and a crack shot. Perhaps you could ask to have him assigned to us temporarily. We could really use him. Jenkins took sick, and we had to send him back."

Morgan made it happen, and Michael quickly found himself and his wagon headed over to his camp. As he was leaving, Codwise gave the soldier an order. "Do good, and keep your head down, Private, and come back to us in one piece.

"Yes, Sir. I'll try my best."

An hour later, Michael was standing at attention in front of Colonel Morgan. "I hear you're good at smithing weapons. Is that true, Private?

"Yes, Sir. I reckon it is."

"I also hear that you're a pretty good marksman. Is that true?"

"Yes, Sir, Colonel. I can do fairly well."

"Well, let's see."

Addressing one of his sergeants, Morgan said, "Brewer, get a playing card from my tent and fix it to that tree over there," gesturing to an oak about 30 yards away.

Brewer took the card down to the tree and was about to hang it on a twig when Michael said. "No...stick it in a crack in the bark so the edge faces me."

Brewer hesitated and looked at Morgan. The colonel nodded, so Brewer complied with Michael's wishes and then stepped five paces to the side. Michael primed his rifle, licked his thumb and touched it to the front sight, aimed, let out half a breath and squeezed the trigger. The ball split the card in half. Brewer picked up the two pieces and brought them to the colonel.

"Mighty good shootin', Private. Where did you learn to handle a rifle like that?"

"I learned it from my father and brothers in Fishkill, but soon I got better than them."

"Well, very soon, you'll be able to put that learnin' to good use, Soldier."

Chapter 42

Saratoga, Bemis Heights

Battle of Bemis Heights

October 1777

On October 7th, eighteen days after the Battle of Freeman's Farm, Burgoyne made a second attempt to break through the American's lines, this time at a place called Bemis Heights, a short distance south of his last encounter with the Americans. General Benedict Arnold watched the British organizing for their assault through his glass. Realizing that the British and German soldiers required close command to form and maintain their assault and defensive lines, Arnold, who took command of the American left flank, ordered Colonel Morgan to bring his sharpshooters forward and told them to focus their fire on the British officers. During the British preparation, Arnold spotted General Simon Fraser, the brilliant Scottish officer who was mounted and not afraid to go into battle with his troops. Seeing his chance to take Fraser out of the fight, Arnold ordered Morgan to bring forward three of his best sharpshooters. Only two appeared, however. Morgan thought quickly and plugged the hole with Michael Hughson.

"Hughson, go with those men...quickly! Your target is that officer on the horse."

"Yes, Sir!" Michael answered, and he double-timed off toward the wood line.

One of the sharpshooters, Timothy Murphy, took charge. "When we get in position, we'll wait for our chance. I'll shoot first. If I miss, Palmer, you shoot second. If you miss Dead Eye, you shoot next. After you shoot, reload as fast as possible!"

The men took positions behind three trees. Michael's heart was racing, and he wondered if it would jiggle his rifle and cause him to miss. He braced himself against the tree, primed his rifle, licked his thumb, touched it to the front sight, and took aim at the mounted general over 250 yards away. Frazer was trotting back and forth in front of his men of the British 24th Regiment, a couple aids trotting behind him. He would be a moving target unless he reined in for a moment. Michael stared down his sights, the tip of his finger on the trigger.

"Stay calm," Michael told himself. "Breathe easy…in and out, in and out. You can do this." He began to perspire.

There…the general reined in his horse.

With a loud crack, Murphy's rifle discharged. Michael could see that his bullet cut the crupper on the general's saddle. Fraser collected his startled mount. A second explosion from Palmer's rifle, the ball harmlessly grazing the horse's mane. To account for the bullet drop, Michael placed his sights on Frazer's metal gorget below his neck so the bullet would strike him in the chest. He let out half a breath and carefully squeezed the trigger. Click...the cock dropped, and the flint struck the frizzen, knocking it forward, allowing the spark to ignite the powder in the priming pan. Then, a split second more...DON'T MOVE...BOOM! A .48 caliber spinning lead ball whistled through the air and struck the general in his stomach. Michael didn't even hear the report of his rifle, but he saw Fraser pitch forward and then fall from his horse.

"You did it, Hughson!" yelled Murphy. "Let's get the Hell outta here!"

The three men left their cover and scrambled through the trees, several rounds of British musketry whizzing over their heads. They got back into the line Morgan had established as the men were preparing for a British charge. But it wasn't forthcoming. With their general down, the rigid and highly choreographed lines of the British attack seemed to fall apart. The soldiers were suddenly leaderless, and confusion ensued. General Arnold and the Americans saw their chance and charged.

The final outcome of the Battle of Bemis Heights was that the British Army was routed, and General Burgoyne withdrew from the field. Surrounded and running out of supplies, he was forced to surrender his entire army a few days later, a devastating blow to the British effort in America and the turning point in the war for the Patriots. Generals

462

Burgoyne and Gates negotiated the final surrender terms. Over 5,000 British and German soldiers were marched off to eventually end up in a prisoner-of-war camp not far from Charlottesville, Virginia, and thousands of muskets, cannons, wagons, and other war materiel passed into the hands of the jubilant Patriots. As for Gates' troops, they marched south to join the Continental Army on its way to Valley Forge for the winter.

****

The evening after the surrender was signed, Morgan ordered the three marksmen to his tent.

"Thank you, men, for your excellent work here at Bemis Heights. Simon Fraser was certainly a good soldier and a good general, but he had to go. You seen what happened when those battle lines lost their leader."

Palmer spoke up. "Colonel, it was Hughson, here, who done it. Our balls merely scared his horse."

Yes, I saw that, but those balls made Fraser stop and hesitate so Hughson could get a shot."

Michael spoke up. "It was a team effort, Sir. I just got a lucky shot."

"Hughson, you made a perfect shot. I don't attribute it to no luck. Do you realize your shot may well lead to an American victory in this war? When news of this British defeat gets to Europe, the French may be persuaded to join our cause, and that'll settle it."

Morgan paused a moment and seemed to be transfixed by the candle taper burning on the camp table. A slight breeze entering the tent made the flame flicker, causing Morgan's shadow on the tent wall to dance. While Michael watched this performance for a minute, the colonel's thoughts finally became audible.

"It's a strange thing about Fraser. Here he is, a Scot fightin' in the British army just thirty years after the Bloody Backs slaughtered over 1,200 of his countrymen at Culloden. They say his father was a Jacobite, and he fought in that battle, and sometime after that, the British beheaded him. And here his son is fightin' in a red uniform for the Crown and gets himself killed. I don't understand it. You'd think he'd ah done somethin' else with his life. Fought for us, maybe."

He paused again, still staring at the candle; no one said anything. Then he broke his own spell.

"Regardless, he was still here to kill us, tear us apart with his musket and cannon fire and send forward his evil Germans to slaughter our men with their bayonets. And he'd ah done it without battin' an eye. Somethin' made him turn on his fellow Highlanders, and he turned on us. Well, thanks to you men and God's Providence, he's no longer walkin' this earth. And I expect he's not in Heaven, either."

464

The three marksmen uttered their agreement.

"How about a quick drink, Gentlemen? I just happen to have a little rum I've been savin'." He produced a bottle and four small glasses, poured a splash in each one and passed them around.

"Let's raise our glasses ...to General Washington!"

"Here, here...to General Washington!" went the corporate reply.

"Well, Gentlemen, I'm tired, and I need some sleep. You're dismissed...and thank you again. You've rid us of a devil, and you just might have saved the Cause."

The three soldiers rose to leave when Morgan added, "Hughson, please remain for a minute."

"Yes, Sir."

"Hughson, I want you to know that you've changed my thinkin' about black men. We Southerners have been raised to believe that the Negro is somehow an inferior, helpless being who must be led and directed by others for his own good. I see now that we may be wrong about that. You're a good man, Hughson. I'm glad you're free. It's just possible that you have single-handedly turned the tide of this war. I will mention you in my report to General Gates."

"Thank you, Sir," was all Michael could think to say.

"You're dismissed, Soldier."

As Michael walked back to his tent, he began feeling much better...better about Morgan, better about Fraser, and much better about himself.

General Gates had remained (some said "cowered") in his tent behind the American lines during the whole battle. After the fight, that's where Morgan found him to make his report. Morgan did report to Gates that the free black from New York, Private Michael Hughson, was assigned along with two of his own best sharpshooters, Murphy and Palmer, to dispatch Fraser but that it was Hughson's shot that found its mark.

Before finishing his report, Gates asked Morgan, "Colonel, can you tell me again who shot Fraser?"

"Private Michael Hughson, 2nd New York, Sir."

"A Negro, you say?"

"Yes, Sir, a freeman."

Gates gave Morgan a quick look of disgust. "Colonel Morgan, I am afraid you're mistaken. It was actually the other man...what's his name...Murphy. It was Murphy who killed the general."

"General Gates, that's not true, Sir!" Morgan protested. "I'm tellin' you that it was Hughson. The man is a tremendous marksman."

"Colonel Morgan, you're dismissed!"

Gates wrote his report. It included the statement that Murphy had killed General Fraser. Furthermore, Gates did not even mention General Benedict Arnold or the valiant and successful effort he led to save the day by personally reversing the potential rout at Bemis Heights. Finally, in an effort to enhance his own stature and his hoped-for possibility that Congress would replace Washington with him, he sent his report, not to Washington, as would have been proper, but rather directly to his friends in Congress. As for General Arnold, he rode back with the army to Valley Forge, where he signed the Loyalty Oath to the United States, witnessed by none other than General Knox. Three years later, and totally disgusted with his treatment, he tried to turn West Point over to the British.

When news of the victory reached Europe six weeks after Bemis Heights, it convinced the French to finally enter the war against England, which led to the United States' ultimate victory. Although he didn't realize it at the time, it could rightfully be asserted that the black soldier, Private Michael Hughson from Dutchess County, helped turn the tide of the war and changed the fortunes of the American Cause.

****

Two months after the battle, Colonel Morgan was told that, in his report to Congress, Gates did, indeed, attribute

Fraser's death to Timothy Murphy. He was so incensed by Gates' deceit that he immediately dictated a letter to General Washington. He summoned his aide, Captain John Palin.

"John, I want to send a letter to General Washington, and you are much better with writin' the words than I am. I'll tell you what I want to say, and you put it in proper English."

"Yes, Sir." Palin retrieved pen, ink and paper from the Colonel's chest and sat down at the camp table.

"I'm ready, Colonel."

Morgan began.

"General, I have learned that General Gates…"

The next morning, Palin took the final version of the letter to Morgan for his approval and signature.

"Read it to me, John, so I can hear what it sounds like." Palin read the letter:

His Excel. General Washington   *In the Field*

                                                          December 14, 1777

Your Excellency

 It has come to my attention that, in his report to Congress on the recent conflict at Saratoga, General Gates was in error as to who actually killed General Fraser. The facts are that General Arnold, commanding the left wing at Bemis Heights, spotted General Fraser on the field, and he ordered me to send my sharpshooters forward in an attempt to dispatch him. I immediately sent three men forward, Privates Murphy and Palmer, and a black freeman from the 2nd New York, Private Michael Hughson. Hughson was serving temporarily as an armorer, and he is an excellent marksman. All three men fired their rifles at Fraser, one after the other, but they agreed that it was Hughson's third shot that brought down the General over 250 yards away. This information was in the report that I submitted to General Gates the day after the battle. For posterity's sake, I feel that the record should be corrected.

I am...

Your Humble and Obedient Serv't

Daniel Morgan, Colonel

His Excel. General Washington

"Very well done, John. You certainly have a way with words."

Morgan signed the letter.

"Make an extra copy of the letter and see that Private Hughson receives it. I'll sign the copies, myself."

"Yes, Sir."

Michael cherished that letter for the rest of his life, and it passed through generations of his Hughson descendants before it was apparently lost. Unfortunately, the original letter never got into General Washington's hands at the time, and although historians have expressed some skepticism, it was Timothy Murphy who received credit for the deed. Strangely, Murphy himself never did claim that it was his shot that brought down General Fraser. He knew full well that it was actually Private Michael Hughson who helped open the way for the creation of the United States of America. It may not have been "the shot heard 'round the world," but it was certainly "the shot that changed the world" forever.

Chapter 43

President Washington

New York 1789

In September 1789, newly-elected President Washington accepted the advice of his cabinet and decided to undertake a tour of the northern states in an effort to help unify the young nation. While organizing some of his wartime letters and communications in preparation for the trip, the President discovered the unread 1777 letter to him from Colonel Morgan. Already in a state of confusion as to what, if anything, to do about the slavery issue, the discovery of this letter gave him yet another occasion to pause.

He thought again about his contempt for General Gates and the man's cowardice and traitorous ambition. He recalled the noble performance those 5,000 black soldiers in the Continental Army gave to the Cause. He thought about the black soldier from Marblehead, Massachusetts who helped row him across the Delaware River on that freezing December night. He thought about the 300-plus slaves at Mt. Vernon and how he would dearly love to be rid of them. That evening at dinner with Martha, he gave voice to his ruminations.

"My dear Patsy, as I have said many times before, during my eight-year absence from Mt. Vernon, you proved to be an accomplished and excellent manager of our estate during

471

what were exceedingly difficult times. I greatly admire and respect your management skills, and, as you well know, I hold your opinions in high regard."

"George, you're making me blush."

"I mean it, Patsy. You have been my valuable partner in this long endeavor, and I greatly value your thoughts and opinions."

"Thank you, George. I value your approbation." She answered as she looked down at her napkin.

"Regarding our slaves at Mt. Vernon, I am in a moral quandary as to what to do about them. Selling them is out of the question. Not only because I couldn't even legally sell the 153 dower slaves because they belong to the Custis estate but also because many of them have married into the 123 I do own outright, and I refuse to break up those families. Our slaves are terribly expensive to maintain; 30 per cent of them are too old or too young to work or otherwise add to the profitability of our farms. I suppose we could free my slaves and hire them back on a wage. But then that can't be done for the dower slaves and would, of course, eventually lead to trouble between the two groups."

He paused and then added, "It is a major conundrum that constantly weighs heavily on my shoulders. I wish the states would settle it by outlawing slavery altogether. Massachusetts already did, and I imagine the rest of the northern states will follow suit in short order. But not Virginia, the Carolinas, and Georgia."

"I certainly don't have a solution, George. It will most likely require another war to resolve it sometime in the future, one that the nation may not even be able to survive. But at least for now, perhaps you could put these thoughts on the back shelf and prepare for our trip into the northland."

"You're right again. I thought I was doing that by spending some time organizing my war correspondence when I ran into this twelve-year-old letter from Daniel Morgan for the first time. He extracted it from his vest pocket and passed it over to her.

"May I borrow your reading glasses, Husband?"

"Of course, but be careful with them." He chuckled. "They're the ones from Rittenhouse that I was obligated to use during my Newburgh speech to the officers, convincing them to not march on Philadelphia to demand back pay. They felt sorry for me because I said I was going blind in the service of my country."

While Martha read Morgan's letter, George poured himself another glass of cherry bounce—his favorite—and waited for her to absorb the letter's contents.

She put the letter down. "That's amazing, George. Killing General Frazer and winning the battle of Saratoga was what turned the war and helped us to win the Revolution. Isn't that what you told me?"

"It certainly was. It brought the French in, and the rest, as they say, is history."

"That poor man. I wonder who this Michael Hughson was and if he even survived the war."

She paused for a few heartbeats, and then, out of the blue, she received an inspiration.

"George, I have an idea. It says he was from New York. We'll soon be up there, and perhaps you could have someone locate him, and you can meet together and express your personal gratitude for his marksmanship."

"Patsy, you're a genius! That's an excellent idea. I'll ask Hamilton to try and locate him. If anybody can do it, Alex would be the man."

The next day, Washington composed a letter to Hamilton requesting his assistance.

President's Residence

New York City

September 5, 1789

Alexander Hamilton, Esq

My Dear Colonel,

I am enclosing a copy of a twelve-year-old letter from Colonel Daniel Morgan that has just come to my attention for the first time. It concerns the killing of British General Simon Fraser at Saratoga in 1777. Apparently, in his report to Congress, Gates did not state what he knew to be the truth regarding the soldier who fired the fatal shot. It was actually a black private from the 2nd New York, one Michael Hughson, not Timothy Murphy, a white soldier from Morgan's regiment. Gates didn't want the honor to go to a black man, so he lied in his report despite protestations from Colonel Morgan. I would very much like to meet with Pvt. Michael Hughson during my northern tour and to personally thank him for making America possible. Would you be kind enough to attempt to have him located without letting him know? I'd like our meeting to be a surprise.

I do not know what company he was in, but the 2nd New York was in Poor's Brigade, and I believe its colonel was Philip Cortlandt. The regiment was raised in the Fishkill, New York area, so that would be a good place for your men to start.

Please let me know if you're able to undertake this mission for me. If we are successful, Colonel, perhaps you could join me in my meeting with Private Hughson.

I remain,

Your Humble & Obed't Serv't

G Washington

Post to

Colonel Alexander Hamilton, Esq.

New York

Alexander Hamilton took on the task with his typical aplomb. He rounded up several Continental officers from the New York Society of the Cincinnati, arranged a quick organizational meeting in Fishkill, and sent them out to make discrete inquiries. Two days later, they had located their man in Hughsonville, a hamlet a few miles west of Fishkill, near Wappinger's Creek. They briefly surveilled Michael's home and determined that he did, indeed, live there with his wife and two sons, who worked with him in a thriving blacksmith and gunsmith business. Hamilton immediately replied to the President.

New York City

September 14, 1789

General,

Our mission is accomplished. With the assistance of four officers from the New York Cincinnati, we went to Fishkill, made some discrete inquiries, and found Michael Hughson living in Hughsonville, a few miles west of Fishkill on the Hudson. He is a free black with a wife and two sons. He has a blacksmith and gunsmith business where he and the boys work. They seem to be doing well. He appears to be closely connected with the white Hughson family in the area and a valuable member of the community. I await your word to arrange a surprise

meeting with him and his family. I would be honored to
attend the meeting with you, General.

I remain,

Your Humble & Obed't Serv't

Alexander Hamilton

Post to:

President George Washington

New York City

On Friday, October 2nd, Rebecca Hughson was busy preparing a ham she planned to cook for dinner when there was a knock on her door. She opened it to discover a handsome middle-aged and well-dressed gentleman.

"Good morning, Ma'am. Are you Michael Hughson's wife?"

"Yes, Sir. I am Rebecca Hughson. Can I help you?"

"Yes, Ma'am. I am Philip Cortlandt, a friend of President Washington, and I have some very good news for you, but first, I must swear you to secrecy about everything related to our meeting this morning."

"I can be trusted, Sir. I am a good Christian woman. Please come in and sit down. I'll brew you a cup of tea."

The tea was brewed and served along with two fresh breakfast muffins; Rebecca sat at her table across from Cortlandt while he began his story.

"During the recent war, did your husband ever mention anything about being in the Battles of Saratoga in '77?"

"I knew he was there with his regiment, but he spared me most of the details. He never talked much about being in the war. I just know it was a difficult time for him, but he was glad to have a small part in the creation of America."

"Well, Mrs. Hughson, your husband played much more than a small part, and that's why I'm here."

He paused and then continued. "Although it occurred four years before the end of the war, our victory at the second Battle of Saratoga was the turning point in our struggle because it led to the French officially joining our cause against the British. Their contribution of soldiers, ships, and materiel was what led to our eventual victory at Yorktown."

He continued. "Since the victory at Saratoga was so vital to our success, one could ask how we were able to win that particular battle. Well, one of British General Burgoyne's field commanders was a Scotsman, General Simon Fraser, probably the finest British field commander in America. During the last day of the battle, Fraser commanded thousands of British and German troops with the intent of breaking through the American lines and claiming victory. Our own General Benedict Arnold took command of our troops; he noticed General Fraser on his horse on the other side of the field. He ordered three of Colonel Morgan's sharpshooters to be brought forward in an attempt to kill Fraser."

Cortlandt paused and took a bite from his muffin. "Mrs. Hughson, you are an excellent baker!"

She smiled, "Thank you, Sir. Please have another," and pushed the plate with three more muffins in his direction.

"To continue. Your husband was one of them. They were told to take out the British general on his horse, over 250 yards away. The first two fired and missed. Your husband then fired, striking Fraser and knocking him off his horse. He died a few days later. When the British and Germans saw that their leader had fallen, they became confused and disorganized in their battle formation. General Arnold took advantage of the situation, launched a counterattack, and won the day. Burgoyne had to surrender his whole army of over 5,000 men to the Americans."

"Oh, My! Michael never told me a thing about any of that, Mr. Cortlandt."

"After the battle, General Gates wrote a report and sent it to Congress in which he said that another soldier named Murphy was the actual shooter. He knew this was a lie, but he didn't want to give a black man credit for turning the battle. General Morgan wrote a letter to Washington with a true account of the incident. Unfortunately, his letter never came to Washington's attention until a month ago, when he found it in a pile of war documents he was organizing."

"Why did you come to tell me all of this, Sir?"

"Well, Mrs. Hughson, the President will be in this area during his tour of the northern states, and he wants to stop by and personally thank your husband. Will he be at home on Monday, October 19th, at about 7:00 in the evening?"

"Yes, Sir, I expect he will be."

"I understand you have two sons."

"Yes, Josiah and Will."

"Can you arrange to have them here, too? They would not want to miss this occasion."

"Yes, I'll make sure they're here."

Rebecca paused. "Mr. Cortlandt, I don't know a thing about how to act around the President. Should I invite him in and offer him some tea?"

"That would be fine. Perhaps some of these muffins, too. Don't worry about acting appropriate. You'll find that the President is a very friendly and understanding man. He'll just have one other person with him, Colonel Alexander Hamilton. He doesn't require any special preparations. He just wants Michael to know that his contribution to the creation of America is duly recognized and appreciated."

"Do you know the President, Mr. Cortlandt?"

"Yes, I do. In fact, I was the colonel who commanded the 2nd New York Infantry, the regiment your husband was in. Believe me, Mrs. Hughson, you'll find the President to be very agreeable. Don't worry about a thing. And, remember that you promised to not breathe a word of this to anyone, not even your sons."

"My lips are closed, Mr. ...I should say, Colonel Cortlandt."

He smiled.

"Thank you, Ma'am. I will see you on October 19th. I'll be back by your barn, holding their horses. Perhaps your boys could bring me out one of your muffins then." He chuckled and then added, "Remember, do not tell a single soul of our plans. It could be a matter of the President's personal safety."

"I will see to it, Colonel," Rebecca said with a big grin.

****

Monday, October 19th rolled around quickly. Rebecca busied herself making preparations that would create a good impression with the important guests, but without tipping off her husband and boys. She rearranged her men's clutter as best she could, swept the kitchen and dining area floor, put on one of her prettier (but not church) dresses, and prepared a meal that could be cleaned up easily and quickly. Of course, she also baked a fresh batch of her special muffins.

As usual, her men showed up at 5:30 after ten hours of metal bending and firearms repair, and Rebecca received her regular kiss at the door. As usual, they washed up and then went directly to the kitchen table.

Michael cast a glance around the room. "Becky, I see you've been busy today. And how pretty you look! Also, the aroma of your famous muffins fills the room. What's the special occasion?"

"Nothing special, Michael. I just felt like making things a bit homier for my hard-working men."

"Well, we really appreciate it, don't we, boys?"

"Yes, Sir," they responded in unison. Then Will added, "Can we ask the blessing now?"

By 6:45, dinner was over, the dishes were washed, and tea water was warming in the kettle.

"Becky," Michael inquired. "When do we get to devour your muffins?"

"As soon as the tea is brewed. Patience, everyone." She checked the clock on the mantel; 6:55. She wondered if the President would be punctual.

7:00 o'clock and, sure enough, there came a knock on the front door.

"I'll get it," she said, her heart pounding. She opened the door.

"Mrs. Hughson?"

"Yes?"

The three Hughsons at the table alerted immediately.

"I'm Alexander Hamilton, and this is President George Washington. May we come in?"

"Certainly, Sir."

The Hughson men sprang to their feet, jaws agape.

"Good evening, Ma'am," the President said, erect and holding his hat in his hand.

"Ah, yes, and you must be Private Michael Hughson and these two young men, your boys."

"Yes, Sir, Josiah and Will," is all that came to his mind to say.

Rebecca interjected, "Please come in and sit down. It is indeed a great honor to welcome you to our home. Mr. President."

Michael finally broke into the conversation. "I don't understand, I am, indeed, honored, General. But why have you come to our home?" As he asked the question, he immediately figured out why his house was picked up, his wife in her pretty dress, and the smell of muffins' wafting throughout the room. She was in on the whole thing!

"Private Hughson, I am here to right a grave wrong perpetrated on you during the war. It concerns the death of General Simon Fraser at the Battle of Saratoga. It has recently come to my attention through a letter Colonel Morgan wrote me over a decade ago that it was you, and not Murphy, who killed the British General Fraser, causing his men to panic and lose the battle. Burgoyne was obliged to surrender his entire army of 5,000 troops. Hearing of the outcome, the French joined the conflict as our ally, allowing us to win the war. Gates knew you fired the fatal shot because Morgan told him, but Gates didn't want to give a black man the credit, so he lied in his report to Congress. My disapprobation for the man is considerable."

The President paused and then asked, "Is my understanding of the event accurate, Mr. Hughson?"

"Yes, Sir. It is. In fact, I have a copy of that letter."

"Dad," Will blurted out, "why didn't you ever tell us that story?"

Rebecca had the same inquiring look on her face.

Washington answered for him. "Will, it is not easy to speak of killing another human, even when it is justified in war. Fraser was a good field commander. But, he had seen to the deaths of hundreds of our patriots in battle. He would have killed many more before the war was over if he had not been stopped. Your father must have saved countless lives, including the lives of British and German soldiers."

He paused for a few seconds and then continued. "You must forgive your father for wanting to speak of other things. Nonetheless, it does not negate the fact that his marksmanship proved to be the turning point of the battle. I cannot be prouder of him."

The boys and their mother could not stop starring at Michael as he sat there with a pensive look on his face.

Rebecca broke the spell. "Gentlemen, please allow me to serve you some tea and fresh-baked muffins. Then, she remembered Cortlandt, who was probably holding the horses back by the barn. "I understand Colonel Cortlandt is minding your horses by our barn."

"Yes, Ma'am," Hamilton answered.

"My Colonel Cortlandt?" Michael asked in an excited voice.

"The same," responded Hamilton.

Michael issued his first order of the evening. "Boys, go out and untack their horses and put them in our stalls with something to eat. And ask Colonel Cortlandt to come in immediately and join us." Then he added in a questioning voice, "I'm sorry, General. Would that be alright?"

"Of course."

The young men sprang into action, and three minutes later, Cortlandt appeared at the door. The reunion between him and Michael was heartwarming.

Tea and muffins were served, and the conversation around the table became increasingly convivial. The General seemed to loosen up and actually enjoy himself. He inquired about Michael's background, and the latter told him all about his birth, the Negro Uprising of 1741, and how the Hughsons took him in and raised him.

"How did you become such an excellent marksman?" the President asked. "And I understand you have a thorough knowledge of firearms and served as a regimental armorer."

"When I was a lad, one of our neighbors in Wappinger Falls was a veteran of the British Army and had served many years as a regimental armorer. He taught me the gunsmithing trade and the amazing accuracy of the rifled barrel, like the ones carried by Morgan's sharpshooters. I was temporarily assigned to Morgan's regiment as an armorer, and that's why I was available when General Arnold called for assistance at Bemis Heights."

Michael walked over and took down a weapon from its spot over the fireplace. "This is the rifle I carried at Saratoga. I fashioned it myself according to specifications for the best barrel length and rifling progression I had worked out over the years. It's accurate up to 300 yards."

He handed it to Washington. "What a beautiful weapon! Perfectly balanced, easy to shoulder and sight, and intricate scrollwork on the plates. The stock is walnut, I assume, and hand-rubbed with oil."

"Yes, Sir."

He passed the rifle over to Hamilton. "Look at this weapon, Alex. Hughson, you are a true artist."

Hamilton raised the rifle to his shoulder and sighted down the barrel. "Beautiful. The balance is perfect." He passed it back to Washington.

Michael had an inspiration. "General, I want you to have it as a gift from me."

"I couldn't possibly…"

Michael interrupted him. "I insist, General. If what you say is true about the battle and the French entry leading to our victory, then this rifle helped create the United States. It is only proper that you should have it, Sir. Besides, I can always make another one for my hearth. Or, my sons can."

"Well, then, I accept it as a cherished gift from a true Patriot. Thank you so much, Private. A thousand times, thank you."

The General studied the rifle on his lap. He said in a quiet voice, almost to himself, "The gun that won the war."

Then Michael changed the subject. "You must be tired from your trip, General, and I don't mean to keep you."

Washington waved off his comment.

"Not so. I will let you in on a little secret. If the truth be known, I am having a very enjoyable and relaxing evening with you folks, and I am not yet ready to bring it to an end. My days and evenings are filled with hordes of people, cannon salutes, cavalry escorts, bands, fireworks, children with flowers, ladies dressed in their Sunday best, more people, and more cannons. This evening of quiet relaxation and talk among a few friends and patriots is such a relief that I cannot put it in words."

Then Washington turned his attention to Josiah and Will.

"Boys, you are very lucky young men because you have a wonderful mother and a brave patriot for a father who, in my judgment as a military man, helped turn the tide of the war and allowed us to create these United States. I thank Providence that you are free, and I pray for the day that the same will be said of all black men and women in America. I, myself, am personally caught in the snare of slave ownership, and it has been the bane of my life."

Washington continued. "Eventually, the evil of slavery will be resolved. Our new Constitution contains all the necessary provisions to make that happen, hopefully without an armed conflict."

The President reached for another muffin and sat back in his chair. "I apologize for the dreary discourse, but the issue weighs heavily on my mind. I thank the Lord that you Hughsons are free and strongly recommend that you do not move south."

The men uttered a slight chuckle. "You can be sure of that, General!" Michael guaranteed.

"I suppose we should be going, Alex, before someone notices our absence and sends out the alarm that I have been kidnapped. Thank you again, Michael, for your contribution to America and for this beautiful rifle. I am truly honored to make your acquaintance."

Then he added, "I'll send you a letter documenting our visit with you folks."

"Thank you very much, Sir; that's very kind."

Then, the hero of Saratoga issued an order. "Boys, please go out to the barn and saddle the men's horses. General, I'll get you a scabbard for the rifle."

In ten minutes, the horses appeared at the front door, saddled and ready and held by the young grooms, who were bursting with pride. The visitors rose from the table, said their good-byes, and rode off into the night.

Chapter 44
Sean and Bill Hughson
1998

In the four months following the incident at the Quick Stop, Sean Hughson became increasingly enthusiastic about uncovering his lineage. As he worked on developing his family tree, he knew, of course, who his parents were, both teachers for most of their adult lives. Luckily, his mother still had a copy of his father's birth certificate.

Calvin Patrick Hughson (1917-1996) was born in Chicago.

He knew his paternal grandfather, Michael Leonard Hughson (1892-1964). Michael's birth certificate was on file in the Orleans County, NY, County Clerk's office. Sean ordered a copy. It said Michael's father's name was Sean Hughson, born in New York.

At this point in his search, things got a little sticky. He called Bill for some advice.

"As a reasonable first shot in the dark, you can assume that the Sean Hughson family was still in Orleans County in 1900 because Michael was born there. Check out the 1900 census and see if a Sean Hughson as a head-of-household is there."

Sure enough, there he was, along with his entire family. It listed Sean Hughson, colored, born in July 1862 in New York. And there was young Michael L., colored, born in January 1892.

Now, what? Sean put in another call to Bill.

"Why don't you check out the 1865 NY state census to see if there were any three-year-old black males named Sean Hughson."

Two hours later, Sean reported back.

"Bill, I found one: a Sean M. Hughson, born in Dutchess County in 1862."

"I'll bet a fifth of Jack Daniels that he's your grandpa, Sean! What was his father's name?"

"John Hughson, colored, born about 1834 in Dutchess County. His mother's name was Rachel. Before that, however, I'm afraid it's a brick wall, Bill."

"Well, maybe." He paused and then said, "Let me think about this for a bit, Sean. I'll call you back."

Sean sat in his study, pouring over various genealogical and family history records, in search of any promising tidbits, when Catherine entered with a tray containing a teapot, two cups, sugar lumps, and some kind of tasty little almond cookies.

"How about a break, dear, while you tell me of all the exciting stuff you've uncovered."

"Sorry, honey, nothing new to report. I've got my Hughson line back to the 1830s in Dutchess County, but there, everything grinds to a halt. Bill's putting his brains to it as we speak. Maybe he'll come up with something."

She flashed him a sympathetic smile.

"If only I could run into an old newspaper article, a probate court record, land title, or even an old family Bible with some births, deaths, and marriages recorded in it, but no chance of that, I guess." He sighed.

"How about that old Bible on the bookshelf right behind you?"

"What Bible…?" He swiveled his desk chair around.

"Right there, in the zip-lock bag. The one your grandmother gave to you years ago for safekeeping."

Sean reached for the old leather-bound book, extricated it from its bag, and carefully opened it up.

THE

HOLY BIBLE

CONTAINING THE

OLD AND NEW TESTAMENTS

TRANSLATED OUT OF THE ORIGINAL TONGUES AND WITH
THE FORMAL TRANSLATIONS DILIGENTLY COMPARED AND
REVISED,
BY HIS MAJESTY'S SPECIAL COMMAND.

APPOINTED TO BE READ IN CHURCHES

CUM PRIVILEGIO

CAMBRIDGE:

PRINTED AT THE PITT PRESS;
BY JOHN W. PARKER, PRINTER TO THE UNIVERSITY

M.DCC.LXI

"Oh, my Goodness! And this has been right behind me
the whole time. Let me see... M.DCC.LXI. That would be
1761!"

Sean slowly turned the page over. "Kate, look at this!"
In what appeared to be a woman's hand was written

"This Bible was given to Rebecca Wells on Nov. 16, 1761, by the Rev. Henry Morris, 1st Presbyterian Church, Hughsonville, New York, upon the occasion of her becoming a communicant.

Rebecca Wells"

One page over, he saw the title, "Our Family," printed at the top. That page and the one following it were full of handwritten recordings of births, deaths, and marriages, the first several in the same hand as the first page. Sean and Catherine read it together. The record started with Rebecca:

Rebecca Wells was born on April 8, 1745, in Wappinger's Creek, New York. Daughter of Isiah and Patience Avery Wells.

Rebecca married Michael Kerry Hughson on May 22, 1764, in Hughsonville.

Note: Michael Kerry Hughson was born April 2, 1741 in New York City to a slave, Caesar, and an Irish woman, Peggy Kerry. After the Negro Revolt of 1741 in New York, his parents were hanged, and Michael was taken to Dutchess County by the Hughson family and raised by William Hughson and, after he died, by his son, John Hughson.

Michael Hughson and Rebecca had two sons, Josiah and William.

Josiah was born on March 3, 1764 in Wappinger Falls.

He married Frances Hawkins on December 25, 1793 in Fishkill.

William Hughson was born on November 14, 1767, in Wappinger Falls.

William married Martha Palmer on May 22, 1795, in Hughsonville. They had one son, Christopher, born on September 30, 1798.

In a different hand, was written the following:

Rebecca Wells Hughson, wife of Michael Hughson, died on April 24, 1821 in Hughsonville, age 76.

Christopher Hughson married Emily Schuyler on March 3, 1830, in Hughsonville.

Michael Hughson, husband of Rebecca Wells Hughson, died on December 24, 1833, in Hughsonville, age 92. He was a soldier in the Revolutionary War.

John Hughson, son of Christopher and Emily Schuyler Hughson, born on August 23, 1834, in Hughsonville.

In a different hand, was written the following:

John Hughson married Rachel Hopkins on March 23, 1858 in Hughsonville.

Sean M. Hughson, son of John and Rachel Hughson, born on September 10, 1862, in Hughsonville.

"I found this John Hughson in my line, Kate," Sean said in an excited voice. "And right below him is his son, Sean M. Hughson. That means Michael Hughson must be my…let me see." Sean quickly wrote the names down on a scrap of paper.

Sean, Calvin, Michael, Sean, John, Christopher, William, Michael, Caesar

"Michael was my fifth great-grandfather, and the slave, Caesar, was my sixth!" Sean's excitement was at a peak. "Wow! This is amazing, Kate! I have to call Bill about our discovery!"

Catherine said, "Let me see that Bible for a minute, Sean."

He passed it over to his wife, and she slowly leafed through it.

"What's this?" She asked in a surprised voice. There was a folded piece of old yellow paper tucked between the pages of the *Book of Revelations.*

"Wow! It looks like a letter! Open it, Kate, but very carefully," he directed.

Sean concentrated on the old brown handwriting and read slowly out loud. Catherine grabbed a yellow pad and pencil and began writing down the words as her husband deciphered them.

Fair copy

His Excel. General Washington   *In the Field*

December 14, 1777

Your Excellency

 It has come to my attention that, in his report to Congress on the recent conflict at Saratoga, General Gates was in error as to who actually killed General Fraser. The facts are that General Arnold, commanding the left wing at Bemis Heights, spotted General Fraser on the field, and he ordered me to send my sharpshooters forward in an attempt to dispatch him. I immediately sent three men forward, Privates Murphy and Palmer, and a black freeman from the 2nd New York, Private Michael Hughson. Hughson was serving temporarily as an armorer, and he is an excellent marksman. All three men fired their rifles at Fraser, one after the other, but they agreed that it was Hughson's third shot that brought down the General over 250 yards away. This information was in the report that I submitted to General Gates the day after the battle. For posterity's sake, I feel that the record should be corrected.

I am…

Your Humble and Obedient Serv't

497

His Excel. General Washington

Sean could hardly control himself. "Kate, do you know what this means? This free African American, Michael Hughson, my fifth great grandfather, was a soldier in the Revolutionary War, and apparently his marksmanship helped save the day at Saratoga, which eventually led to our winning the war! This letter is a copy made from the original that Colonel Morgan sent to Washington. Can you believe it? I must be a descendant of this Michael Hughson, or why else would my grandmother have possession of this Bible and letter?"

****

Five minutes later, Sean called Bill to apprise him of the fantastic news.

"Bill, I found something amazing! All this time, I've had an old family Bible my grandmother gave me years ago. I rediscovered it an hour ago, and it's full of births, deaths, and marriages. The bottom line is that I now know my lineage, and it turns out that my fifth great-grandfather, Michael Hughson, was an orphan, the son of a slave named Caesar and an Irish woman, raised by the Hughson family in

Dutchess County. It happened after some slave rebellion that took place in New York City. And…guess what…there was an original copy of a letter in the back from the Revolutionary War. A Colonel Morgan wrote General Washington to inform him that it was actually this same Michael Hughson who killed a British general at the Battle of Saratoga. Apparently, he gave Michael a copy of his letter to Washington."

"Wow! That's some story, Sean. I recently read a book on the Saratoga battles. The American general, Gates, reported to Congress that a soldier named Murphy shot Frazer, but for the rest of his life, Murphy never took credit for it. Also, strange you should mention that 1741 revolt in New York. A couple months ago, I bought a scholarly work on that incident, but I haven't read it yet. I'll take it off the shelf and see if the author has anything to say about Caesar."

Two hours later, an excited Bill Hughson dialed Sean's number.

"Sean, I plowed through the book, and sure enough, Caesar was a ringleader of that unsuccessful revolt in 1741. He knew John Hughson, my uncle. He and his friends frequented Hughson's tavern on New York's west side, and he paid John rent so Peggy Kerry could stay in his tavern. Peggy was pregnant with Caesar's child. The conspirators were caught; Caesar and Peggy were hanged, along with John and his wife, Sarah. Before her sentence was carried out, Peggy gave the baby boy to one of Hughson's daughters, who took him back to the Hughson enclave in Dutchess County. So, it all fits with your story, Sean."

He paused and then added, 'Wow, this is very exciting stuff! The son of a slave played a significant part in helping to win the Revolutionary War, and you descend from him!"

"Does this mean I'll be able to join the Sons of the American Revolution?"

"It most certainly does, Sean."

Bill was inspired.

"Sean, your Michael Hughson should have been hailed as a major patriot of the Revolutionary War, just like Paul Revere and Nathan Hale. Because of the times and a general with political aspirations, he was deprived of that honor. Why don't we try to right that wrong?"

"Whatdaya mean, Bill?"

"Well, first, we go to New York and try to find his grave. It would likely be a wild goose chase, but at least it would be an adventure."

"How would we ever go about that search?"

"If he does have a grave with a stone, it probably wouldn't be in any of the known cemeteries, where black burials weren't allowed. Maybe there's an African American cemetery in the area, or he could have been buried in a Hughson family plot on a farm somewhere."

"What if, by chance, we do find him? Then what?"

"Your letter from Morgan testifies to his contribution." Bill continued.

"If we do find his grave, we can go to the local Daughters of the American Revolution and Sons of the American Revolution chapters, show them the letter and Bible, and see if they are interested in honoring him with a grave marking ceremony. If they are...and they will be...we'll bring in the local press and television, and we'd be off to a good start. Also, the National Park Service at Saratoga would be very interested in this whole thing. I am sure they would love to be involved and maybe put up a display and memorial at the battlefield."

"Bill, you realize that this is all just a pipe dream. What are the chances..."

"Sean," Bill interrupted, "what else are you doing this summer? We can take a trip up there and have a look around. We'll take our wives and call it a vacation. I've always wanted to see Fishkill in the summer, anyway."

"Yah, right."

"Meanwhile, I'll do some cemetery research of the area and see what I come up with. As they say in the horseshow business, you can't win a ribbon unless you get in the ring."

****

Thanks to an email from a Hughson cousin, Bill discovered a Hughson researcher, Alan Bunner, who had been documenting the New York branch of the family for over thirty years. From him, Bill learned about a George Hughson, who owned a farm in Carmel on which he established a family cemetery. Carmel Town government knew about the cemetery; its historical documents indicated that George Hughson was buried there in 1769 and his wife, Susannah, in 1771.

Bill briefed Sean on his discoveries about the Hughson Cemetery. "When Michael died in 1833, the farm and cemetery were owned by George Hughson's grandson, Robert, who was, himself, a veteran of the Revolutionary War. Whadaya say, Sean? That would be a good place to start. I even have the address. 535 North Lake Boulevard, Mahopac."

****

A month later, Sean and Bill were standing in the Hughson Cemetery; it was close to the road, well maintained, and surrounded by woods. From the depressions in the ground, it appeared to contain about thirty burial plots, perhaps three-quarters of them with stones. Many of the stones, however, were just that, plane rocks with no inscriptions. They inspected all the legible tombstones:

various Hughsons and some other last names, probably subsequent owners.

They stopped for a rest and a few sips of their Gatorade. Sean let out a long breath, "Well, if Grandpa Hughson is here, we'll never find him. Maybe I should walk around this place until I feel a vibe from his spirit."

Bill chuckled. "I don't know about that. I believe Michael's haint is long gone."

"Haint?"

"I forgot. You were raised in the north. Haints are spirits from the recently deceased. They hang around for a while aggravating people by hiding their car keys, or reading glasses, or finishing off the remaining Jack Daniels in the bottle that's being saved for a special occasion. They're sorta like Irish faeries, except they are afraid of water. I guess they can't swim."

Sean laughed. Then Bill added.

"You know, Sean, I've read that in the old days when they buried blacks in the same cemeteries with whites, they often put them in the back, away from the rest of the departed, so their spirits wouldn't accidentally mix. Just for a lark, let's walk around in the woods behind the graveyard for a few minutes. We can look for stones and feel for slight depressions in the ground as we stroll around."

"Okay, Bill...just for a few minutes."

The forest floor behind the cemetery was relatively clear of undergrowth, due to a full canopy of huge trees and the resultant reduced sunlight. There were, indeed, a few depressions in the ground's surface but no stones. The men had been walking slowly back and forth for twenty minutes when Sean found something.

"Bill, come here for a second."

Sean pointed to a small flat stone protruding from the soil, perhaps six inches wide and four inches high. Furthermore, there was a grave-sized dip in the ground behind it.

"Whatdaya think?"

"I think it's a footstone. In the old days, they often put them by the foot of a grave to help mark it. They were usually accompanied by headstones."

"No headstone here," Sean offered the obvious.

"Maybe it fell over and was covered by years of leaf litter." Bill took a hunting knife from his backpack and handed it to Sean.

"Poke around over there with this and see if you hit anything hard."

Sean dropped to his knees and began pushing the knife into the soil while Bill looked on. After a minute, he struck something hard.

"I hit something!"

"Use the knife and dig away, Cousin. Let's see what you found."

In another couple of minutes, it was clear that the hard object was, indeed, a tombstone lying face-down. Sean freed it and turned it over.

"There's an inscription, but I can't read it."

A whiskbroom emerged from Bill's pack. He handed it to Sean.

"Man, you came prepared!" he commented.

"Boy Scouts always come prepared, Cousin. I also have a couple of Three Musketeers bars in there for emergencies. Do ya want one?"

"Maybe later." Sean gently swept away the soil and rotten leaf litter on the stone.

"Do you see anything, Bill? The stone is really weathered. I think I see a 'g' right there, and maybe that's an 'o' over there. Down lower on the stone, that might be a '8'." Sean paused for a few seconds and then said, "But that's about it".

A few more seconds passed, and Sean sighed, leaning back on his haunches. "I'm afraid this is a dead end. This stone is much too weathered." He handed the whiskbroom back to Bill. With another dejected sigh, he said, "I'm ready to go."

"Wait a minute, Sean," Bill interjected. "I have an idea. I had a high school buddy who became a State Department officer, and when he was in Thailand, he bought a temple rubbing for me. People place rice paper on stone temple carvings and raise the designs in the stones by rubbing some chalk-like material over the paper. Let's try that technique on the stone and see what happens." Bill was excited.

"Come on, Sean. We'll pick up the girls and find an art supplies store where we can get some tracing paper and charcoal sticks. We can be back here well before dark."

Forty-five minutes later, all four Hughsons returned to the cemetery and gathered around the afternoon's find. Sean took the tracing paper and laid it carefully on the stone. Catherine handed him the charcoal stick. He looked up at the three anxious spectators and said, "Here goes nothing...or maybe something."

Kneeling by the side of the stone, slowly, gently, and very lightly, he began to rub the black stick back and forth over the paper. The three spectators looked on intently, holding their breath. At the top of the paper, the capital letters "H" then a space, "GHS" another space, "N" took shape in the rubbing.

"That could spell Hughson!" Judy exclaimed.

Sean kept rubbing. Below those letters an "M" began to take form, next to it an "i" then a space, then an "h" then another space, then an "el". Next to these letters, a "Ke" appeared, then a space and, finally, an "ry" surfaced.

"Sean," Bill gasped, "That's him...Michael Kerry Hughson!"

Below these letters, Sean raised some numbers: "1 space 41-1833." Centered below those were the letters "RW".

Sean dropped the charcoal stick on the ground. A strange silence descended on the four as they stared at the paper and then at the stone and back at the paper again. Catherine knelt beside her husband and put her arm around him. Both Bill and Judy dropped to their knees. Judy put her hand on the stone, and Bill held her close to him. For several moments, nobody broke the silence for want of knowing what to say...how to put their feelings into words. They were overwhelmed by their emotions as they knelt by the grave of the black man who, yet unknown to Americans, had helped to make America possible.

Finally, Sean broke the silence. "What do you suppose the 'RW' stands for, Bill?"

"I imagine it stands for 'Revolutionary War'". He was a Revolutionary War veteran, after all. And very soon, the whole world will know this Hero's story and what he did for our nation.

The End

Historical Note

Most of the people in this story were real, as were many of the events, towns, geographical locations, ships, streets, and buildings. Peggy Kerry and Caesar did have a baby who was raised by the Hughsons. However, the subsequent story of this child, whom the author calls "Michael Hughson," is fictional. Below is a partial list of the people, places, and events that the author did not conjure up in his imagination. The information came from original documents, newspaper accounts, and published documented sources. Names in parentheses refer to the preceding individual's ancestral line, i.e., father, grandfather, etc. A few of the dates may be approximate:

- There was a student riot at Southern Illinois University in the spring of 1969. This author was there to witness it.

- George Griggs (1593-1660) and his wife Alice Sibthorpe (1593-1662) immigrated from England to Salem in 1635. He was a shipwright and the 9th g-grandfather of the author's wife.

- John Griggs (1634-1702), son of George, and his wife, Elizabeth, moved from Salem to eastern Long Island and thence to Gravesend. He was a mariner.

- William Griggs (1621-1693), son of George, married Rachel Hubbard (1628-1718) and served as Salem's doctor. He diagnosed the two young girls, Elizabeth

Parris and Abigail Williams, as bewitched, initiating the Salem Witch Trials era.

- Walter Dobbs (1644-1691) and Mary Merritt Dobbs (1648-1737) lived on Barrent's (Barren) Island. He was also a mariner and a farmer.

- Maria Dobbs (1670-1717), Walter and Mary's daughter, married Thomas Hughson (1670-1742) in 1694.

- John Dobbs (1675-1759), Walter and Mary's son and Maria's brother, farmed a land lease adjacent to Thomas Hughson in Dobbs Ferry, New York.

- Nathaniel Pitman was Mary Merritt Dobbs' second husband.

- Thomas Hughson (1670-1742) immigrated to New York about 1691. He married Maria Dobbs (1670-1717) in 1694. He was the author's 7th g-grandfather.

- Isaac Eastey (1627-1712) lived in Salem, Massachusetts, and married Mary Towne (1633-1691), who was executed as a witch.

- Hannah Eastey (1670?-1741) was Isaac and Mary's youngest daughter.

- Thomas, John, William, Richard, and Benjamin Hughson were all sons of Thomas and Maria Hughson. They farmed on a Philipse land lease in what is now Dobb's Ferry, New York.

- Wading River, Port Jefferson, Block Island, Sag Harbor, and Gravesend are real historical places on (or near) Long Island.

- Caleb and Lydia Littlefield were inhabitants of Block Island. They were also the great-grandparents of Catherine Littlefield Greene, the wife of Revolutionary War General Nathanael Greene and a favorite dance partner of George Washington. Catherine was born on Block Island.

- The pirate Captain William Kidd frequented the areas around eastern Long Island and New York City.

- There was a slave rebellion in New York City in 1712.

- John Hughson (1700-1741) (Thomas) married Sarah Luckstead. They moved to New York City around 1736 and were proprietors of a tavern on the east side. They moved to a second tavern on the West Side about 1739. They let the slaves patronize their establishment. They also served as a fence for items stolen by the slaves. They were hanged in 1741.

- Caesar, Quack, Prince, Wan, Albany, Fortune, Cato, Othello, York, Will, Cambridge, and Venture were all slaves who frequented Hughson's tavern and were conspirators in the New York 1741 failed Slave Rebellion in which several buildings were burned. Caesar, the leader of the group, was good friends with John Hughson.

512

- Mary Burton (1725-) was an indentured servant working for the Hughsons, and she testified against them at trial.

- Peggy Kerry (-1741) was an Irish woman who became Caesar's mistress, lived in the Hughson tavern, and gave birth to Caesar's son.

- John and Sarah Hughson, Peggy Kerry, and a Catholic priest named Ury were all hanged as a result of the trials that followed the aborted slave rebellion.

- Before she was hanged, Peggy gave her son to John Hughson's daughter, Sarah (1725-). It is highly probable that he was raised by the Hughson clan, who moved from Westchester County to Dutchess County in 1742 to a location near Fishkill that became known as Hughsonville.

- John Hughson (1733-1794) (Thomas, William) was in the Dutchess County Militia during the Revolutionary War. He married Catherine Wells (1743-1802).

- Christopher Codwise, Jr. (1740-1785) was from New York City, part of a family of merchants and traders with plantations in the Caribbean Islands. He married Catherine Ditmars. They had three children: Christopher, Penelope, and Catherine.

- Christopher Codwise (1740-1785) moved his family to Fishkill after the British occupied New York City in August 1776.

- Christopher Codwise (1740-1785) was commissioned a 1st Lieutenant in the 2nd New York Infantry in November 1776. He was at the Battle of Trenton in 1776, Valley Forge, the Battle of Saratoga in 1777, and the Battle of Monmouth in 1778. He was a charter member of the New York Society of the Cincinnati.

- Christopher Codwise (1740-1785) was ordered to Fishkill ("on command") to recruit for the 2nd New York.

- His daughter, Penelope (1761-1816), married William Hughson (1762-1850) (Thomas, William, John).

- Fraunces Tavern in New York City was (is) a real place. It's where General Washington said good-bye to his officers after the war.

- At the second Battle of Saratoga, Bemis Heights, British General Simon Fraser was killed by an American sharpshooter from Col. Morgan's regiment. Three men aimed at him, and American General Gates (who had remained in his tent during the whole battle) in his report to Congress stated that Timothy Murphy was the soldier who struck the general. Gates' report is the only existing "evidence" that Murphy was the responsible marksman. Some historians question that assertion, however, and Murphy himself never said that he was the one who shot the general. Regardless, the bullet that struck Fraser led to his assault troops becoming disorganized. General

Benedict Arnold saw the opportunity, counter-attacked and won the battle. This victory led the French to join the war against England, which made possible the successful siege at Yorktown and the eventual American victory.

- President Washington took a trip through the northern states in the fall of 1789.

- Finally, Lieut. Christopher Codwise's horse, Lucky, was actually the name of Bill Dwyer's boyhood horse. They spent many happy hours together, riding the roads, trails, woodland paths, and beaches of Wading River. Lucky was, indeed, sure-footed in the snow...